FINAL BROADCAST

A Legal Thriller

Terry Huebner

Published by Thunder Road Publishing

ISBN 13: 978-0615976822
ISBN 10: 0615976824

Copyright © 2014 Terry W. Huebner

For more information on the author and his works visit
http://www.terryhuebner.com

For my children

1

The man smiled, raised his glass in salute to the television and downed the vodka in one long gulp. Raymond Burr as Perry Mason had just gotten the better of Hamilton Burger once again and the man appreciated the skill, virtuosity and style with which it had been accomplished. He had seen this episode before, of course, for he had seen them all before, many times. Perry Mason was sort of his hobby. He admired the great trial lawyer, for he had once been one himself, perhaps even the best and most famous trial lawyer of his generation. He was, after all, Daniel Patrick Lindsay, the boy wonder, the young lawyer who became famous when he got a rich doctor acquitted of killing his wife long before the advent of all-news channels on cable television. If CNN had been around back then, he would have been bigger than Perry Mason. He was a real-life Perry Mason, only better. It was the night before Christmas Eve and Lindsay poured himself another vodka and saluted the great trial lawyer once again as the signature theme music played.

If Lindsay *was* a great trial lawyer, he certainly wasn't one now. He hadn't seen the inside of a courtroom, at least as a lawyer, in years. His last big case had been when he cross-examined that lying cop in the actor's trial as part of the Dream Defense. That had been good. Everyone had seen on national television just how good he still was. He had gotten himself in shape for that one and it had paid off. But that had been more than a decade ago, and the time since had not been kind to Pat Lindsay. Too

1

much booze, too much spending and too few cases over the years had finally taken their toll. Friends from the old days tried to help him out by shoveling him a few scraps, cases he would never have looked at twice in his heyday, but he didn't even want to get out of bed for that shit. So he didn't. Most days, he just sat with his feet up in the sitting room off his bedroom watching TV and drinking vodka by the bottle. Some life. A friend had even gotten him the entire run of Perry Mason on DVD, but the box sat gathering dust on the floor in the corner of the room because Lindsay had never bothered to learn how to operate the DVD player.

Out in the yard, a figure clad all in black emerged from behind a dilapidated gazebo and leaned against the trunk of an orange tree. It was a cool evening and the man wore a jacket over a mock turtleneck and jeans. From this vantage point, he could see the entire rear portion of Lindsay's house, a plantation-style mansion, once lovely, but now showing its age and Lindsay's lack of upkeep. He could see Lindsay too, a dark shadow behind sheer drapes. The figure could see the lights from the television dancing on the walls of the room behind the drapes. He looked around the yard. A pair of rabbits played tag before disappearing into the far bushes. The man smelled something strong and fragrant coming from his right and turned in that direction. He thought it was jasmine, or maybe gardenias, he didn't know the difference. Something strong anyway.

Before Lindsay had let the place go to hell, it had been professionally landscaped, complete with an expensive lighting and watering system. Where once this was the scene of lavish parties, now the overgrown shrubs and bushes merely provided privacy from the prying neighbors in this North Palm Beach, Florida neighborhood. The water in the pool was a slimy green with algae and broken lawn chairs littered the flagstone deck, now cracked and crumbling. The outside lights were all off, victim of a court-mandated austerity campaign, and the only lights seen emanating from the house came from the kitchen on the first floor and the TV in Lindsay's bedroom on the second.

The figure picked his way through the debris in the backyard and came to a set of French doors, which led to an eating area off of the kitchen. He pulled on a pair of gloves as he peered inside. He turned the handle and the door opened, he had left it unlocked on a previous visit, and entered the house. He didn't have to worry about the alarm system either, for that was another victim of bill collectors and a civil judgment. He strolled into the kitchen, where he found six gallon jugs of Smirnov vodka sitting on a granite island next to a stack of unopened mail. Otherwise, the kitchen looked neat and clean, almost sterile, as though it hadn't been cooked in for months. The room smelled of orange-scented cleaning solvent.

Just for kicks, he opened the refrigerator. All it contained was a six-pack carton of Budweiser long necks with three full bottles left inside, a near empty jug of milk that looked lumpy, a couple of eggs in a dirty plastic bowl, a variety of salad dressings and barbecue sauces and a carton of baking soda. The man smiled. Lindsay must have wanted to make sure that he killed all of the odors. The freezer contained a box of Good Humor ice cream bars and a mostly full five-pound bag of ice. Couldn't run out of that.

The man moved through to the front hall in the manner of someone who knew exactly where he was going. He came to it from underneath a grand circular staircase that gently curved to the left as it rose to a large formal landing framed in ornate iron that seemed to come straight out of *Gone with the Wind*. From the discoloration down the center of the oak stairs, the man concluded that a carpet runner had recently been torn out. Across the way, between the stairs and the front entrance to the house, a door stood ajar. The man looked at his watch, still a little early, and considered his options. From the bottom of the stairs, he noted the smell of cigarettes wafting down from above. The only light came from the upstairs hallway and the man could faintly hear the sound of the television off in the distance.

Never taking his eyes off of the landing, the man crossed the front hall and pushed into the study. The room smelled musty with just a hint of lemon furniture polish. He silently closed the

3

door and flicked a light switch on the wall and a desk lamp went on. The room contained a beautiful, hand-carved desk in dark mahogany, inlaid in green leather, with a matching green leather desk chair and sofa, both worn slick and shiny with age. In the far corner, stood an empty TV stand. Built-in bookcases stained a dark brown covered the entire near wall and were crammed full of volumes in all shapes and sizes. More books, covered in a light patina of dust, were piled in stacks on the desk. The man walked over to the couch as though waiting for an appointment and took a seat. His eyes moved around the room and settled on the bookshelves. He closed his eyes, thought about his next move and waited.

Thirty minutes later, the man rose and moved to the door, cutting the lights before opening it. He peered out, seeing nothing, and moved out into the hallway and up the stairs, slowly and deliberately. He stayed to the right side, near the wall, where the stairs seemed to creek less. When he reached the landing twenty-two steps later, he glanced to the left and then back to the right, where light leaked out of a half-open door at the end of a long hallway.

When he reached the doorway, the man paused and stood just out of view, listening for sounds of movement. All he could hear was an infomercial for a chicken fryer. He stepped inside and looked around. The main part of the bedroom and master bath were to the right. The sitting area was straight ahead and around the corner to the left. The bedroom looked as though it hadn't been picked up in weeks. The bed was unmade, blankets pulled to the floor, clothes strewn everywhere. Two empty gallons of vodka sat on a nearby dresser. The room stank of cigarettes, mixed with spilled liquor and body odor.

The man took several steps into the room, far enough to see the back of the television in the sitting room, and put his right hand in the pocket of his jacket. He listened again. Still nothing but the television. He moved silently to the doorway and looked inside. Lindsay appeared to have fallen asleep on a small, worn loveseat, once blue and now a dirty grey plaid, with collapsed cushions and cigarette burns throughout. Three more empty jugs

4

of vodka and four dirty glasses sat on a nearby coffee table. He wore gray sweatpants, a pale blue golf shirt and no socks. His salt and pepper hair was wild and uncombed. He looked like he hadn't bathed in days.

The man took a deep breath and sighed, before reaching around and turning off the television with his left hand, his right hand remaining in his pocket. The silence seemed to startle Lindsay awake and he gradually began to come around. Through the haze of sleep and alcohol, a vague glimmer of recognition crossed his features. "Wha? Who's that?" he stammered trying to sit up. "What? Is that you? What are you doin' here?"

The man smiled. "How are you, Pat? It's been a while. It's good to see you." The man spoke calmly in a very quiet voice. "Don't you remember our appointment? I'm sorry I'm a little late. Traffic."

Lindsay smiled and blinked at his visitor, trying to will himself to remember, then seemed to grow confused. "I don't quite, well, you know, I guess I'd forgotten that you were coming." He looked at himself, growing a little embarrassed. "I would've gotten dressed or something. Sorry."

The man smiled a kind smile. "That's okay, Pat," he said standing very still. "You look comfortable. A man should look comfortable in his own home. There's nothing wrong with that. I know you've had a lot on your mind." The man was prepared for this. "You remember, I was coming by to meet with you about a new case." The man nodded.

This seemed to put Lindsay at ease somewhat. He nodded back, even though he didn't know what the man was talking about. "That's right," he said. "Tell me again. What's the case about?"

"It's a murder case. But we'll get around to all that." The man nodded in the direction of the empty bottles. "You look like you've got some dead soldiers there. I could go for a drink myself. Do you have a fresh bottle downstairs? A vodka on the rocks might hit the spot about now. What do you say?"

Lindsay brightened. "Sure. I think I've got a couple of bottles downstairs in the kitchen. I sent my girl out to get a couple of

5

bottles. I was thinking of having a party, you know. She usually leaves food and stuff on the counter in the kitchen."

The man smiled again, his right hand still in his pocket. "Then it's a plan," he said. "Why don't we head down to the kitchen? We'll talk downstairs over a drink." Even though he was still wearing gloves, the man was careful not to touch anything.

Lindsay struggled to his feet. He had probably gained at least fifty pounds since the man had last seen him and he hadn't looked all that good even then. Now he looked bloated and red-faced, a stroke waiting to happen. But the man couldn't wait. Lindsay grabbed a glass and looked outside, suddenly very aware of his surroundings. "Hey," he said following the man through the bedroom, "what time is it anyway? It's late, isn't it?"

The man smiled like a doctor trying to reassure a small child getting his tonsils checked for the first time. "Yes, it is late. Sorry about that. I just got in from Europe and my flight was delayed. Meeting with your new client. I was supposed to be here a couple of hours ago. You must've dozed off waiting for me. That's why you didn't hear the door. Not your fault."

Lindsay didn't remember any of this, but went along. Sometimes he forgot things, he knew, and he had to cover for it. Maybe he should cut back on his drinking. Maybe he'd be busier with this new case. That would be good. He took another look at the man as they made their way slowly down the hallway toward the stairs, craning to get a better look at him without being too obvious about it. It was tough because the man's face was largely in the shadows. The man noticed, but said nothing. "You look different," Lindsay said sounding a bit befuddled. "I can't place it."

The man laughed. "I've lost a little weight since you've seen me last. You know, clean living and exercise." He rubbed his chin with a gloved hand. "That, and I've got this beard now."

Both men laughed now. "That must be it," Lindsay said. "Maybe I'll try that exercise thing. I'm too old an Irishman to try clean living." They laughed again.

6

By now they had reached the landing, Lindsay trailing a little behind. The man waved his arm and made a big display out of looking down at the foyer. "You've got quite a house here, Pat," the man said. "You should be quite proud. The well-earned fruits of your labors."

Lindsay made a show of being modest. "Thanks, I appreciate that, but I've let the place go a little bit," he said understating the obvious. "I need to spruce things up. Maybe after we're done with this new case." He gestured toward the stairs. "Shall we?"

The man nodded. "After you," he said, placing his left hand on Lindsay's back in what seemed to be a friendly gesture. But just as Lindsay took the first step down the stairs, the man quickly moved closer, turned and placed his right leg in front of Lindsay's, while at the same time pushing Lindsay hard in the back.

Lindsay lost his balance, said, "Ugh," and tumbled over the man's leg and down the steps. He struggled to catch himself, but in his physical condition, really had no chance. He rolled down, picking up steam as he went. About a quarter of the way down, just as the stairs begin to curve to the right, Lindsay's head struck the wall hard on the left side, the force of which drove him back toward the iron rails on the right, where he scraped along while somersaulting around the curve, arms and legs flopping like a fish on the deck of a boat. Lindsay briefly disappeared from view and the man moved over to his right to look down over the rail and get a better vantage point. Lindsay appeared to be tumbling in slow-motion now, head over heels, as he headed for the bottom. The man heard the sound of glass breaking just as Lindsay reached the bottom of the stairs, his head bouncing off of the tile floor with a crack. Then all was silent.

The man looked down over the railing into the dark foyer. He could see Lindsay's body through the iron rails and he watched it for a moment waiting for signs of life. There were none. Lindsay didn't move. He took a deep breath, let it out and nodded, then slowly descended the stairs. He saw a smear of blood on the left wall where Lindsay's head had struck it and carefully navigated the rest of the stairs so as to make sure there would be no evidence of his presence in the house this evening. As he rounded the final curve of the stairs, Lindsay's body came into full view. He was more or less face down in a semi-fetal position, his head perched awkwardly at the bottom, his legs splayed out behind him pointing back up the stairs. He held the remnants of a broken tumbler in his left hand.

The man carefully stepped around the body, and hopped over the final two steps, which were littered with parts of the broken glass and an expanding puddle of blood. He could tell instantly from the angle of Lindsay's head that he had broken his neck in the fall and was now very much dead. Nevertheless, he removed the glove from his left hand and checked Lindsay's pulse with the knuckles of two fingers. Just as he thought. Lindsay was dead. He studied the body for several moments, then whispered, "Sorry, Pat, I didn't have a choice. It's probably better this way. You'll have one last moment in the sun. At least I gave you that. Merry Christmas." Then the man turned toward the kitchen and left the same way he had come.

2

The man adjusted the rearview mirror of the Camry and looked at his face. Did he look like a killer? He wasn't sure. What did a killer look like? Not like him, he thought, at least not yet. He called himself Rich and Rich is what his driver's license, insurance card and Social Security card said as well. Money can buy almost anything. He knew what at least one killer looked like, and that man had gotten away with it. Would he get away with it too? He had to. After all, he was a whole lot smarter than the actor. But the actor was walking around free, just like the rest of the innocent people, flaunting his guilt in the faces of his victims. At least everyone knew the actor was really guilty. On the other hand, if things went as planned, no one would ever know that Rich was guilty of anything. His task was a lot more complicated than just one night of rage. He looked at himself again for a long moment. Maybe if he didn't look like a killer, then killing would be just that much easier. No, better to look like a normal guy ... harmless ... safe.

He studied himself again, then readjusted the mirror and looked back out the rear window. "Dead," he said aloud before laughing at the irony. He shook his head back and forth several times trying to get his concentration back. "Got to focus!" he said stifling a yawn. He had been here so many times he was getting more than a little bored at the surveillance. Yet it had to be done. Preparation was the key to everything, he had known for years, from work, to sports to music, and, yes, to even killing

9

a man. You simply had to prepare, to commit yourself to doing the work necessary to make sure everything went the way it was supposed to. Due diligence, they called it. That's what Rich was doing every Tuesday and Thursday for more than a month now – planning and preparing. Due diligence.

Rich looked back at the house across the way, like so many previous nights as his plan began to germinate from the seeds of anger and resentment. The painful seeds of yesterday had finally grown into the harsh reality of today and the promise and satisfaction soon to come tomorrow. Rich grabbed a bottle of water off the front passenger seat and took a long drink. If he hadn't quit, he would have undoubtedly reached for a cigarette right now. After more than ten years, he still felt the unmistakable urge for a smoke when he got tense. He felt a small trickle of sweat begin to roll from his hair line down his neck and back. It tickled and he adjusted himself in the seat in order to scratch the itch and make it go away. He yawned again. The Camry was getting stuffy and the windows began to fog. Rich clicked on the engine and rolled down the front windows, letting the fresh air inside.

Rich looked at his watch – eleven forty-five. If everything held form, the mope would be out within a half hour, forty-five minutes tops, just like every other time. Although he could still feel the heat radiating up from the concrete below, a cool breeze flowed down the boulevard and felt refreshing against his skin. He leaned back in his seat and tried to get comfortable. Then he craned his neck out the window and looked back up the block in the general direction of the aroma of garlic, onions and curry carried along by the breeze. Damn, that smells good, Rich thought. Must be that Thai place up the street. Might have to get me some take-out. Haven't had Thai food in a long time. Can't get it there though. Might be seen. Might be recognized. Someplace closer to the condo. Maybe on the way back.

Rich's Camry was parked along Wilshire Boulevard, two parking spots west of where South Carmelita Avenue formed a T-intersection as it hit Wilshire, a few blocks southeast of the Brentwood Country Club. The house he was watching was the second one in on the east side of Carmelita, a two-story Spanish job, with white stucco and a red tile roof. A nice house on a nice, heavily-wooded street. Rich glanced over at the house once again.

Just then, a young couple strolled passed the house holding hands. Rich sunk down low in the Camry to avoid being noticed, although it appeared that the couple only had eyes for each other. The man wore khaki pants and a blue print sport shirt, while the woman, a tall blonde with long hair and longer legs, wore a lime green miniskirt with a sheer white blouse that was open at the waist revealing a flat, tan stomach. Rich let out a silent whistle in admiration. The man must have said something amusing, for the woman giggled and leaned into him. He pulled her closer and kissed her on the head.

When they reached the corner, they stopped under a streetlight, paused, and shared a long, passionate kiss, followed by another. Then Rich remembered that it was Valentine's Day and he suddenly felt jealous. After a moment, the couple turned left and headed east along Wilshire until they found their car about half a block up. Rich watched them until they were in the car, turned away as their car passed by him so that his face couldn't be seen and then looked back and saw them disappear as they headed west on Wilshire into the night and almost certain sex.

He looked back at the streetlight on the corner. It bathed the area in a warm yellow glow, which did not at all fit in with Rich's plans. The area along Wilshire was also fairly brightly lit. However, if he could do something about that streetlight, a strand of mature trees along Carmelita could provide him with just the level of darkness that he needed. The next streetlight stood pretty far down Carmelita and likely would have little effect on the front of the house. Surprised that he hadn't thought of this earlier, Rich made a mental note of the streetlight and wondered whether anything else had failed to occur to him. He didn't think so.

Rich spent the next half an hour fantasizing about Thai food and Thai women, not necessarily in that order. Finally, at twenty minutes past ten, he heard the click of a gate from across the way

11

and looked up. An instant later, a boyish-looking, middle-aged man with a mop of brown hair emerged from between two tall rows of hedges and strolled down the walk toward the street, a contented smile on his face. Rich looked at his watch again. "Just like clockwork," he said with a small smile of his own. The man held his keys in his right hand and his suit jacket slung over his shoulder with his left. As he approached a shiny, black BMW waiting at the curb, he pointed the keys at the car and the taillights flashed, popping the locks. The man paused as he opened the driver's door, looked back at the house and smiled again, then climbed in, started the engine and took off.

Rich waited a minute, checked his mirrors, then pulled slowly away from the curb. He knew from past experience that the man would take side streets up to the Country Club, wind his way over to San Vicente Boulevard, head east at San Vicente until it merged with Wilshire, then take Sepulveda Boulevard north past the UCLA campus and back toward his home in Bel Air, where the wife and kids waited for him. Some Valentine's Day. Rich cruised down Wilshire, not worrying about the lights. He grabbed a Dodgers cap off the seat next to him and pulled it on. The BMW caught up to him just west of Sepulveda and Rich glanced over at the man and grinned. The man ignored him, oblivious, the contented smile still on his face, and turned left on Sepulveda, while Rich turned right in search of all-night Thai food. "The fucking mope," Rich said as he watched the BMW's taillights disappear in the rearview mirror.

3

Two days later, Marty Kessler emerged from the parking garage for the block and a half walk to the studios of the local Fox affiliate just as the freak storm hit downtown Los Angeles. The sudden squall blew torrents of wind and rain sideways into the side door of the garage as Kessler opened it. "Jesus Christ," he said turning away from the rain and letting the door slam shut. He'd seen the black clouds as he pulled into the garage, but hadn't expected anything like this. After all, it hadn't rained in LA in weeks and downpours like this were virtually out of the question. Woefully unprepared for the sudden burst of weather, there'd been nothing about it in the forecast he had seen on the news while eating breakfast that morning, Kessler looked around and considered the possibilities. Dressed in a tan summer suit, all he had to protect himself from the elements was the brown satchel he carried over his shoulder. He stuck his head out the door to the main part of the garage and glanced across the way at the attendant's office. A rent-a-cop dressed in a light blue security guard uniform sat behind the glass talking to someone on a walkie-talkie.

Kessler ambled over and the guard looked up as he entered the small space. "Can I help you with something, sir?"

Kessler nodded. "I sure hope so. I've got to run over to the TV station down the street to do a show in a half hour or so and I was wondering if I could borrow an umbrella. It's really coming down out there and I don't have anything with me."

The guard had already begun shaking his head before Kessler was even finished. "Sorry, sir," he said. "We don't have any of them around anymore. We used to have a couple, but the people wandered off with them and never brought them back." He looked toward the entrance. "Wish I could help you. Sorry."

Kessler groaned. He waved his hand and said, "That's okay. I should keep one in the car just in case, but I don't bother. My fault, I guess. Have a good night."

Kessler looked at his watch. The broadcast started in thirty minutes. He wouldn't be on for at least fifteen minutes after that. He still had plenty of time. He retraced his steps, took a deep breath and pushed out into the wind and rain, his satchel over his head. Upon emerging from the doorway, he bumped into a woman similarly unprepared for the weather, said, "Excuse me" and started jogging toward the station, the rain pelting down upon him. He ran through the light at the corner, earning a screech, a horn and the finger from a young guy in a black Chevy Blazer and hurried to the front of the building.

Kessler made it through the revolving doors breathing hard and sweating, the storm making it look like he had just taken a shower in his suit. His shaggy, brown hair plastered against his skull, he couldn't have looked any less prepared for television. The guard at the security desk, a young guy named Bob, who manned the desk almost every time Kessler came through at this hour, laughed in spite of himself. Marty looked annoyed and tried shaking off the rain. "I'm sorry, Mr. Kessler," Bob said trying to contain himself, "but that's some look."

Kessler managed a smile. "I can imagine," he said. "Fortunately, I've got some time to clean myself up before show time."

"Well," Bob said, "you better get up there. You know where to go. Good luck."

Kessler stepped around the security desk and Bob clicked him through a small gate with a switch underneath a console. He hurried to a bank of elevators around the corner and hit the up button. "Geez," he said as he saw his reflection in the gold metal doors as they closed before him. He did indeed look like a sight.

His hair dripped rainwater into his shirt, now dark blue with perspiration and water. His pants were almost completely soaked up to the knees and he felt his feet sloshing in his loafers.

When the bell sounded and the doors opened on the fifth floor, a staffer Kessler recognized started onto the elevator and stopped in the middle of the doorway when he saw Marty. He was holding a clipboard and a cup of coffee. "Damn, Mr. Kessler," he said, "what hurricane did you step out of?" The staffer put the clipboard under one arm, took Kessler by the arm and pulled him out of the elevator. "Let's get you to make-up right away. They should be able to fix you up. Believe me, I've seen worse."

"From your mouth to God's ears," Kessler said as the staffer led him down a corridor to the left, around the corner and down another short hallway to the right and to the make-up room, where they found a nervous-looking woman holding another clipboard and wearing a wireless headset. Her jaw dropped when they approached. "Hey, Sher," Kessler said with a grin. "Pretty good look, don't you think?"

Sherrie Fielding was a senior producer and charged with making sure that everything on the show worked like a charm. She was tall and athletically lean, with long legs, a nice figure and a stylish brown, shoulder length hair framing high cheekbones and intense green eyes. When she smiled, she could be quite attractive, but no one at the station had ever seen her smile. Underlings avoided her and gossiped about her behind her back. Nevertheless, Sherrie Fielding's shows usually went off without a hitch. She dismissed the staffer with a nod and a glare, as though he had somehow been responsible for Marty Kessler's current condition, and pulled Kessler into the room.

"Kessler, you are going to give me a fucking heart attack. Sit down over there," she said directing him to a chair in the corner of the room. He half-expected her to come back with a dunce cap. She chewed on the end of a pen thinking about her options. Then she snapped her fingers and turned toward a young, attractive blonde, who watched from a few feet away, a towel in one hand, a comb in the other, and a bemused expression on her

15

face. "Barb," Fielding said sharply, "you get started on him. Clean him up the best you can, you know, try to make him look human. I'll find him a clean shirt and a sport coat. The tie is probably okay. You can't really see the water. I don't really care about the pants. No one will see those on camera because we'll stick him behind a desk." She looked back at Kessler in the corner. "What are you, about a 40, 42?" He nodded, afraid to speak. Then he frowned. "What?" she said.

"My socks are soaked."

"Suck it up." She looked back at Barb. "Let's get cracking. I'll be right back."

Fielding was back in less than five minutes with a Navy blue sportcoat and light blue oxford shirt. She found Kessler in front of a mirror, Barb blow-drying his hair. Fielding laid the clothes on the chair next to him and said, "Here, wear these. You'll look like a good Republican."

"Great," Kessler answered, looking at the clothes in the reflection in the mirror, "I'll lose all my clients."

Fielding watched Barb work Kessler's hair with a brush for a moment as though lost in thought. "Man, your hair is a bitch. It does whatever it wants to," Barb said while attacking an unruly clump of hair on the right side of Kessler's head. She worked at it with vigor as Kessler winced.

"You should have seen it when I was a kid."

Fielding seemed to emerge from her trance and briefly updated Kessler on what was to be expected of him this evening. "We've got you here to talk about the missing girl up in Tacoma. Stan Feldman will be on via remote. He will be taking the law and order position. Draw some good distinctions between the two of you. Be provocative. Provocative makes good TV." Fielding spent another minute or so giving him direction, then stalked off to kick ass elsewhere. Kessler looked at Barb in the mirror and shrugged. Barb just shook her head and continued working on his hair.

The show went well. They focused on the missing girl case with Feldman taking a tough stance on the forensic evidence, while Kessler upheld his liberal credentials and drew broad hypotheticals to make points that would have made the ACLU proud. During a commercial break, Feldman complemented Kessler on how well he made an extreme civil liberties position fit into seemingly unrelated facts. Kessler laughed. "I'm just trying to make good television," he answered.

"Keep it up," Fielding said in their earpieces. "Viewers love it when you argue about this stuff."

After the show, Kessler stopped by to return the sport coat to Barb. "Here, I think you'll need this back," he said removing the sport coat and laying it over a chair. "What do you want to do about the shirt?"

Barb grabbed his jacket and shirt off of a nearby rack. She had hung them up in hopes that they would dry. She touched the jacket on the sleeve and scrunched her nose to show that it hadn't worked. "They're still kind of wet. Just bring the shirt back when you can. God knows you're here often enough."

"Thanks."

Kessler had just hit the button for the elevator when Fielding caught up with him. "Nice job tonight. You and Feldman are a good combination. How did your clothes turn out?" The elevator door opened and they both stepped inside. "I've got to go down one floor. I'll ride down with you."

"They're still a little damp," he said.

Once the elevator doors closed behind them, Fielding pushed herself into him, wrapped her arms around his neck and kissed him deeply. "God, I've been thinking about you all day," she said coming up for air. "I can throw your things in the dryer while we're in bed. Meet me at my place. You've got the key, let yourself in. I'll be out of here in ten minutes. Make yourself comfortable, if you know what I mean." She giggled like a schoolgirl.

"Be glad to," he said and saluted. He gave her a quick squeeze on the rear end as the elevator doors opened.

As it turned out, he only beat her by five minutes and was just removing his tie in front of the open refrigerator when he heard footsteps and an instant later she burst through the kitchen door behind him. "You hungry?" he said rummaging through the top shelf without turning around.

She dropped her purse and keys on the counter and came up from behind him wrapping her arms around his chest. "I'm starving," she whispered in his ear. He turned and put both hands on her waist. They kissed deeply again and he moved his left hand up to her right breast. She groaned. Then he moved his right hand down to her ass and she groaned even more. Things are looking up, he thought. Literally. They kissed and groped their way out of the kitchen and through the front hall to the stairs. Eventually, after even more kissing and tugging at each other's clothes, they made it to her bedroom. When they were finished, he was out of breath and completely spent, while she seemed as though she was just getting started. She tried to coax another round out of him, to no avail. He rolled over and looked at the clock and the nightstand. "Geez," he said, "it's getting late. We've been at this a long time."

When he rolled back, he found her laying on her stomach pouting like a little girl. She reached under the covers and grabbed him. "You complaining?" she whispered.

He leaned down and gave her a long, slow, deep kiss. "No, not at all. But I still have to get going." He glanced out the window. "It's still raining like a bitch out there." Suddenly, a loud clap of thunder startled him and made him jump.

She glanced lazily at the window as though it mattered to her not at all. "I hadn't noticed." She rolled over on her back and pushed the covers down to give him a better view. She wouldn't give up easily. "We never really ate anything," she said. "Do you want me to go downstairs and make you something? I've got chicken downstairs in the refrigerator that would make a good sandwich."

Kessler had already gotten out of bed and was wandering around the room looking for his clothing, a sock here, a sock there, and then some underwear. He stopped to sniff the dozen red roses in a white ceramic vase sitting on a nearby dresser. "You have a boyfriend?" he asked. "Nice flowers."

"He's great in bed too."

18

"Lucky you," he said with a raise of the eyebrows.

He found his borrowed shirt out in the hallway. It was still damp from the race in from the street. He smiled. "Nice," he said eyeing her. "We forgot to throw the clothes in the dryer."

She sat up. "I'll do that for you now if you give me another thirty minutes."

He began putting his shirt on and started looking for his pants. "As much as I'd love to," he said looking under the bed, "I do have to get going, especially with the rain and everything. This stuff is dry enough, besides, it'll just get wet again when I go outside." He found the pants and put them on. Then he felt around for his keys. Didn't find them. He thought he remembered leaving them on the kitchen counter, but he was a bit distracted at the time. He came around the bed, leaned down and kissed her softly, his hand moving in for a quick squeeze of her left breast. He kissed her a second time and she tried to pull him down on top of her. He fought her off, kissed her on the forehead, and said, "You just lay here and dream about me." He looked down at her. "I'll call you tomorrow."

She pulled the covers up and watched him leave the room, then heard his footsteps on the stairs. Another loud clap of thunder echoed outside, followed by a streak of lightning and then more thunder. A couple of minutes later, she thought she heard the front door open and close, but wasn't sure, what with the sound of the rain and the thunder. Alone again. She got up, went to the door and closed it, then crawled back into bed and pulled the covers up.

19

4

Driving north toward LA from San Diego, Rich noticed the dark storm clouds rolling in off of the ocean up ahead. "Damn it," he said craning his neck to try and get a better look out of the side window as the road curved to the east. "It hasn't rained in fucking weeks." He pounded a fist on the dashboard. Wait a second, he thought, this could work out. He had hoped for rain, of course, but when you live in Los Angeles, you just never knew. You could go weeks, months even, with no rain at all and then the next thing you know, you've got more rain than you know what to do with – flash floods, mudslides, the whole ball of wax. He had even watched the weather forecast in the morning, not a fucking peep about rain. Yet here it was, right out in front of him, exactly what he wanted, and he wasn't sure he was ready for it. Frankly, he'd even given up hope.

He fumbled around on the car radio trying to find a weather forecast as he thought through the possibilities. Could he move up the timetable? Could he do it tonight if he had to? Sure he could. He was ready. Everything was assembled. All he had to do was make sure he had enough nerve and then follow through on the plan. He knew he had enough nerve. Lindsay proved that. He couldn't find a weather forecast so he settled on an all-news station out of LA and waited it out until they did the weather. Ten minutes later, he got his wish. A surprise *El Niño* storm had blown up out in the Pacific, west of LA, and was steaming ashore with severe storms and flash floods forecasted for the coast between the ocean and the mountains. *El Niño*, my ass, Rich thought. Whenever you screw up the forecast, blame it on *El Niño*.

He took the next exit, cutting off a guy in a blue pickup truck who responded with a horn and what appeared to be a string of expletives that Rich couldn't hear. A minute later, he was back on the 450 heading south for the condo going seventy-five. He felt the excitement building. He looked at his hands as he was driving. They were shaking. He felt goose bumps.

An hour later, he was back at the condo making final preparations. Things had been more or less ready for weeks now and all he really had to do was make sure that he hadn't forgotten anything. He pulled a black duffel bag out of a closet, which contained black scuba gear, gloves, nondescript black shoes with rubberized souls, a scuba mask and other related items. Underneath a black cotton towel he found a brown leather sheath about twelve inches long with a leather flap that closed with a snap. The sheath contained a small loop that allowed it to be attached to a belt.

Rich grabbed the sheath and examined it closely. He opened the flap and slowly removed a butcher knife, with a curved black handle and 7-inch ceramic blade. He knew from experience that it would cut through almost anything and was more than sharp enough to do the job. Six months earlier, Rich had found the knife in an upscale food store and purchased three of them with cash for just under $200. Untraceable. Expensive, sure, but untraceable. His ex-wife had bought a whole set of twelve ceramic knives a few years back, including a 5-inch model she used for boning chicken, which Rich wished he still had right now. The store didn't have the boning knives in stock so Rich had to settle for the 7-inch butcher knives. He took the knife into the kitchen and ran it under cold water, wiping it dry with a paper towel before returning it to the sheath and the sheath to the duffel bag.

When he was finished and had everything packed and ready to go, Rich took a bottle of water out of the refrigerator and walked into the dining room and sat down at the table to examine a

21

checklist that had been prepared, changed, reviewed and modified on numerous occasions over the past several months. He had separate checklists for each part of this plan.

Rich had bought the condo, a small farm in wine country outside of San Francisco and a tiny place in the LA hills when his marriage started to fall apart ten years ago. As his plans began to form and his need to change identities emerged, the properties changed hands several times, at least according to public records. By now, the current ownership of each was well-removed from Rich's old life. He felt confident that no one could trace easily the ownership back to him and find out who he really was, particularly now. Not that they would look. This place was tucked neatly into the back corner of a modest-sized development between the San Diego Freeway and the 805, just west of Balboa Park. The complex was quiet and pleasant enough and prices had appreciated decently over the years, at least for a condo, until the housing bubble burst anyway. It attracted mostly singles, young married couples or retirees looking to downsize.

Rich's building contained four units, each of which was entered from either a single front door or through a long hallway which led to each of the unit's one-car garages and funneled into the small lobby area. Rich tried to minimize his comings and goings to off-hours in order to lessen the possibility of being seen and noticed by the other residents. His unit was located on the first floor, underneath the stairway to the second floor, and across the hall from a young woman in her early-twenties. A spinster lived upstairs. She worked at a local library, taught piano on the side and had a piano in her unit. Rich occasionally heard her tinkling the ivories late in the evening. She played rather well and Rich enjoyed listening to her. Sometimes, when he heard her playing upstairs, he would sit quietly in the living room, lights out, and enjoy a glass or two of wine while she unwittingly serenaded him, mostly with classical music.

Rich's condo had several other key points which made it attractive to him. First, since it was located in the back corner of the development, it was more secluded than most of the other buildings in the complex. The back of his building faced out onto a rather scenic desert oasis that served as the habitat for a wide variety of birds and reptiles. This area was actually very pretty, but more importantly, people rarely ventured into it. Thus, Rich seldom had to worry about people wandering around behind his unit and looking into his windows. Rich could even sit out on his patio and enjoy the scenery without worrying about being seen. Finally, given its location outside of San Diego and its proximity to the expressways, the condo proved useful and convenient for quick trips to Mexico when circumstances allowed.

Inside, the unit was comfortable and reasonably spacious, with three bedrooms and two baths. Although it paled in comparison to the grand style in which Rich lived at the height of his career, he couldn't complain. The condo provided him exactly what he needed to live quietly, unobtrusively and make his many plans. Between the condo and the farm, he was more than satisfied.

Rich spent the next thirty minutes or so reviewing the checklist and packing his gear. Convinced that he hadn't forgotten anything, Rich loaded up the Camry before people started coming home from work and then returned to the condo to wait and think. The tension and excitement continued to grow. He once heard Sinatra say in an interview that he always felt nervous before a concert and realized that the feeling was necessary in order to ensure that he was ready and cared enough to give his best performance. Rich understood that and felt the same way.

He stood and looked out the French doors toward the oasis. Rich was eager to get out on the road, but he knew that it would be better if he waited, missed some of the rush hour traffic, and reached LA after dark. Still feeling the tingling in his fingertips and the butterflies in his stomach, Rich went into the home office and got on the computer. He found the radar for LA in an instant. Heavy storms still blew in off the coast pelting the city and the surrounding communities with huge amounts of rain. The National Weather Service had even issued several advisories warning of heavy rain, flash flooding and the like. To the west, more rain. Rich smiled. Perfect. A few minutes later, Rich stood at the door of the condo, his hand on the knob, wearing a black rain slicker. He took one last look around, nodded, and was out the door.

5

The traffic was heavier than usual, but manageable. Rich kept the Camry right in the flow of the other traffic, not wanting to do anything that could lead to a police stop. He didn't want to be noticed at all. Driving a Gold Camry in the midst of all that rain, he more or less blended in with the weather and his surroundings. He kept the radio off, preferring to lose himself in his thoughts, the plan and any possible deviations or unexpected developments. By the time he reached the 450, traffic had eased, even if the rain hadn't, and the Camry moved along in the right lane at close to the posted speed. The sun had begun to set now, a darker shade of gray on the western horizon. There would be no glimmering sunset or purple mountains majesty tonight.

He reached the city around eight, exiting the freeway south of downtown in order to grab a quick bite to eat and navigate along the surface streets until he reached his destination. He found a drive-through taco place, picked up three soft shell chicken tacos and a diet coke to go, then parked in the back of the lot to eat. He lost interest about half way through the second taco, too nervous to eat, and tossed his trash into a garbage bin as he pulled back onto Sepulveda Boulevard. Possibly a poor choice, the tacos were rumbling around in his stomach as he drove north through modest traffic, the rain still coming down in sheets. After a series of deep cleansing breaths, timed to the rhythmic slapping of the Camry's wipers, he felt better, almost calm and serene, for he knew that every block brought him closer and closer to achieving the next step in a goal that he'd planned for and dreamed about for so long.

Rich eased down Wilshire to the east, slowing slightly as he passed Carmelita, where he looked up the street and found no BMW yet. He glanced at his watch. It was still a little early, especially with the weather. Knowing that he had plenty of time, he decided to head east, then north so he could cruise the UCLA campus and get the lay of the land. Passing under the 450, he saw that the freeway appeared to be thinning somewhat. Good news. People didn't want to be out tonight. The scene on the UCLA campus was even more deserted. Although he saw a handful of people trying to stay dry under the awning of a bar down the block from the student union, that was about it.

He circled back toward Brentwood, picking up Carmelita just south of the Country Club and heading back toward Wilshire. He hit the last block and this time, could see the BMW facing him up ahead on the left. As he coasted by the car, Rich looked up toward the house and saw the glow from the porch light peeking through the hedges, although there was no direct view of the door from Carmelita. Perfect. He saw a light on upstairs, but that was no worry. He knew the main bedrooms were in the back of the house and out of view of the street.

The Camry paused for a long moment at the corner. Rich looked up and could see the pelting rain passing by the streetlight. He looked both ways down Wilshire. There were a couple of cars parked down the block to the west and one parked near the corner to the east. A pickup truck turned onto Wilshire a couple of blocks up to the east and headed away from him toward the freeway. Other than that, the Camry appeared to be the only moving vehicle in the area. He eased out into Wilshire, pulled a quick U-turn and parked the Camry about three car lengths ahead of the BMW under a large tree.

Rich cut the engine. Show time. No turning back now. His heart pounded with excitement. He took a couple of deep breaths and the calmness returned. Moving his seat all the way back, he struggled to remove a pair of black sweatpants, getting the openings caught on the rubber soles of his shoes. He pulled the scuba hood up over his head and grabbed gloves and a mask off of the seat next to him. One last look at his watch confirmed that it was time and he put on the gloves and the mask and got out of the car. He waited for the sound of lightning streaking across the sky before closing the door. He left the Camry unlocked, the keys in the ignition. He would be back soon enough.

Rich walked toward the corner, stopping under the shade of a small tree. He looked around in all directions checking for signs of life. Seeing none, he removed a small pellet gun from his waistband, aimed at the streetlight and waited for the sounds of thunder before firing two shots into the light. The light exploded, its pieces falling to the ground, the sound engulfed in the fury of the storm. One problem solved. Rich moved purposefully up the sidewalk to the second house from the corner. He paused when he reached the walkway heading to the front of the house and quickly surveyed his surroundings. Seeing no one, he turned up the walk, which curved between two rows of hedges as it neared the front door. The hedges formed a small corridor that turned to the right, then quickly back to the left, before opening up to form an alcove of green roughly twelve feet square and eight feet high surrounding the white stucco archway of the front door. A small iron gate crossed in front of the path at the opening of the alcove. The front door consisted of a series of heavy planks made of weathered wood, with wrought iron hardware and a small porthole window made of multi-colored stained glass. A black wrought iron light fixture hung to the left of the door casting yellow light into all corners of the private space.

Rich pushed through the gate, which had been left partially open. Although he'd been here before, Rich took in the area to make sure that nothing had changed. To his left, a woman's bike leaned up against the house. To his right, up against the row of hedge that ran perpendicular from the house, sat an iron bench large enough to seat two, next to a small wooden side table. Rain puddled on top of the table and ran in torrents off of the bench.

27

A small lake had formed and was growing in an uneven spot in the cement between the bench and where Rich was standing.

As another clap of thunder echoed in the air, Rich walked over to the door, unscrewed the light bulb in the iron fixture and plunged the area into almost total darkness, the only light emanating through the porthole window in the door from the kitchen in the back of the house. Rich strained to listen for sounds of life on the first floor over the pounding of the rain on the tile roof and the occasional clap of thunder and sizzle of lightning. Hearing no one, he inched toward the window as rain streamed down the front of his goggles and tried to peek inside.

Lightning streaked across the sky overhead and Rich jerked his head toward the walkway. He backed away and moved flat against the house, his heart pounding, his breathing increasingly shallow. The scuba gear was hot and he could feel itchy sweat trickling down his sides and lower spine. His mask had fogged so he removed it and held it up to the rain, rubbing the water around the inside to clear the lens. He put the mask back on and returned to the window as his hand subconsciously came up to the sheath in his waistband. He took a quick glance inside. Nothing. Then another, longer this time. Still nothing. From this angle, he could see the bottom four stairs heading up. Then he moved out in front of the window and looked down the center hallway toward the kitchen. Still no signs of life. He ducked down and crossed in front of the door, taking a position just around the corner and squeezing into a small area between the house and the hedge, where a garden hose lay in a tangled heap.

Rich shoved the hose over with his foot and made himself some more room. He pushed his glove back and looked at his watch. Right on schedule. Hidden from the street, rain pelting down around him, and thunder and lightning growing more frequent, Rich thought that he couldn't have planned this any better. As the minutes passed, Rich reviewed the details of his plan and reminded himself how and why he'd gotten to this place at this time on this night. As he did so, the old anger rose up inside and the adrenaline began to flow. He took the ceramic blade from its sheath and looked at it, now eager to use it.

He thought he heard footsteps. Footsteps on the stairs? Couldn't tell. Definitely footsteps. Definitely someone coming. Someone inside. The sounds died away. Thunder sounded in the distance. He studied the door for signs of movement – nothing. The way the door was positioned, Rich hoped to attack from behind. Rich had chosen this position for that very reason. Would he be alone? He had to be alone. Especially with the weather.

Rich moved slowly out from his hiding place, the knife held out in front of him, water dripping from the blade. Then he heard the steps. They were coming toward him now. A man's voice, "Goodbye!" Now more footsteps. They sounded like they were right inside the door. Rich moved closer, ready to strike. He heard the sound of a lock, then the door, hearing it before he saw it. The door slowly swung open, Rich closing in on it, nothing happening for several seconds until a figure emerged from inside, a man, a jacket of some kind over his head. He turned his back to Rich to pull the door shut, just as planned.

Rich pounced, grabbing the man around the front of his neck and trying to pull him in, while at the same time trying to find the front of the man's throat with the blade. But the jacket got in the way and Rich struggled to pull it aside. A clap of thunder roared overhead, both men lurching. The man's right arm came up in an instinctive defensive motion and knocked the knife off path and into the side of his own neck, a glancing blow just above the shoulder. The man flailed his arms, caught up in the jacket, and Rich lost his grip. Rich swung at him with the knife, catching him higher up on the neck this time, blood spraying the jacket as the rain continued to pelt them.

The man yelped and Rich grabbed him again, wielding the knife. The jacket had now fallen over the man's face and he scratched at it with his left hand so he could see his attacker. But Rich was on him now, catching him in the upper left chest with the knife, though not too deep. Rich fought to gain control of him with his left arm, but the man swung wildly with his right elbow, catching Rich above his right eye and dislodging the mask. Got to finish him, Rich thought. Got to finish him.

Rich lost his grip as he fumbled with the mask and the man tried to stumble away. Rich swung frantically again with the knife and slashed the man across the back of the left leg, causing him to stumble. Then Rich was on him again like a linebacker filling a hole and they crashed through the side table, off of the bench and landed in a heap in the standing water in the center of the alcove, Rich on top, slamming the man's face into the cement. They wrestled around on the ground, the man wrenching his face out of the water and spitting blood before Rich jammed the blade into the man's side under his right arm, the water quickly turning red. The man grunted, the air going out of him. Rich felt him weaken. He now had the upper hand.

Rich raised his arm over his head and came down hard with the butt of the knife slamming into the back of the man's head. Rich felt him sag and pulled the man's head up with his left hand and plunged the knife into an area just below the left ear, pulling hard and slicing across the man's throat all the way to his right ear. Rich felt the muscle and tissue give way and saw arterial blood spray the nearby hedges. He let go of the man and stumbled to his feet, spent. He bent over and put his hands on his knees gasping for air, his lungs burning from the exertion. He started to pull the mask off to better suck in more air, but then stopped. He turned and looked back at the door to make sure that help wasn't on the way. All he could hear was the rain pounding the tile roof.

Rich turned and looked back at his victim. He stood over him for a moment and watched the river of red flow from under the body, mixing in with the rainwater. Then he thought about DNA. He didn't want them to find any DNA. No DNA. Things were happening fast, too fast. Had to think. This wasn't what he planned. Was he wounded? He didn't know. He didn't think so, but he didn't know for sure. Had to think. Had to get back on track. Had he missed anything? Didn't think so. Had to get out of there. Had to move.

Rich tried to make his legs go. They felt like lead inside the scuba gear. A stitch pinched at his right side. He felt a stabbing there when he moved. Wounded? Broken ribs? Keep moving. Had to get out of there. He forced himself to step around the body, to avoid the pool of blood, and he turned and saw the body. He looked at the knife again. It was red with blood. He thought about dropping it, then decided to stick it back in the sheath. Stay calm! Don't hurry! No mistakes!

As he started to leave, Rich remembered something. He fumbled around with a zipper on the side of the scuba top. It was hard to work with the gloves on. Finally, he removed a small silver tube, holding it by the ends. Stepping around the body and the blood, Rich hurried over to his hiding place around the corner and dropped the tube next to the hose. He nodded, glad that he hadn't forgotten it, retraced his steps and headed out through the gate.

Rich made his way to the end of the hedge and looked first out toward Wilshire, then back up the block. Seeing no one, he walked briskly back to the Camry, the rain pounding him harder than ever. He thought about standing out in the open so that the pelting rain could rinse him off, but that would be reckless. He kept moving and got to the car, pulled the door open and climbed inside. He ripped the mask off as he started the engine and tossed it on the floor. He pulled the hood off and grabbed a towel off the front seat pushing it into his face. He took two more of the deep breaths, the pain in his side biting at him, and tried to compose himself. He'd done it. Yes, he'd done it, though it hadn't been easy. Certainly not as easy as Lindsay. Should've expected as much. He looked in the mirror. He did look like a killer now. He took another deep breath. Then he saw a flash out of the corner of his eye. What was that? He looked back in the mirror. Was it a car? Thunder clapped above him. Not a car. Just lightening.

Rich put the car in gear and eased away from the curb. Didn't want to stand out. Didn't want to get noticed. Nice and easy. Relax. You've done this before. Three minutes later, he took a right at San Vicente. Not a car in sight. He took two more deep breaths, but the pinch in his side was much worse when he breathed deeply. Still, he felt better, calmer now. His eyes darted back and forth, while he moved the Camry through the empty streets in the driving rain, fighting the urge to drive faster. As he turned left onto Wilshire, he saw a squad car pull out in front of him two blocks up and head in the direction of the freeway. Rich trailed the squad car and watched it drive right by the ramp to the 450. A minute later, Rich took the same ramp, punched it, hit the southbound 450 at fifty and was gone into the night.

6

The rain had largely stopped by the time Rich got back to the condo. As he got out of the car, he felt a stabbing pain in his ribs again. It had evolved into more of an ache during the ride back, and he wanted to get inside so he could look at it in the light. He took a black garbage bag out of a box on the shelf, and after removing all of the scuba gear, gloves and shoes, stuffed them into the bag, together with the knife, pistol and dark green bedspread that he'd used to cover the front seat of the Camry. As he pulled the black sweatpants on over his jockey shorts, he noticed a small cut and bruise just below his left knee. It hurt and would hurt worse in the morning. As he twisted the top of the garbage bag shut and picked it up, the ribs bit at him again and he said, "Shit," under his breath.

He looked at his watch – almost one o'clock. Surely no one would be awake now. Thirty seconds later, the door to the condo closed behind him. He dragged the garbage bag over to his utility room, opened it, and started stuffing everything he could into the washing machine, even the goggles and shoes. He then peeled off the remainder of his clothing and put it into the washing machine as well. He dropped the sheath containing the knife and the pellet gun into the laundry tub. After starting the washing machine and adding a cup of bleach, he poured liquid Tide straight out of the jug into the opening to the washer and closed the top.

Rich next turned his attention to the knife. Now standing naked in front of the laundry tub, he grabbed the sheath, which was stained in blood, and pulled the knife out by the handle. He noticed a crack in the handle, which must've happened when he hit Kessler on the head. The blade was covered with sticky, dark red blood. He examined the opening in the leather sheath, but couldn't see anything. He hated to do it, but didn't see any other choice, so he turned on the hot water, shrugged, and filled the sheath up with water. After a moment, bloody water began leaking out of the bottom and overflowed from the top. Rich kept at it for a minute, then shook his head, lifted the top to the washing machine and tossed the leather sheath into the soapy water. He should probably get rid of it anyway.

He rinsed the knife under the hot water, rubbing the sides of the blade softly with his fingers trying to get the blood off, before pulling a rag off of the shelf and using that. When he was satisfied that he'd gotten the obvious blood off of the knife, Rich went into the kitchen and returned with a large pot used when cooking pasta. He placed the pot under the still-running water and poured a couple of cups of bleach into it. The ribs bit into him again and he grimaced. He needed to get a look at those ribs. He tried twisting to see them, but the movement hurt so much it made his eyes water. He set the knife in the bleach water, waited for the water to rise up over the handle, and rinsed off his hands and turned off the water.

Rich walked into the kitchen and over to the window by the table, which looked out onto the oasis. The sky was clearing and he could see the faint light of the moon. He stood there for a moment reflecting upon what had happened, but harboring no feelings of regret. It was simply one more step on the path that had to be taken. Now that he was on it, really on it, there would be no turning back. He rubbed the area of his ribs, searching for a wound and finding none.

Rich took a large tumbler out of the cupboard, filled it with ice, and scooped a bottle of Jack Daniels up off of the counter as he shuffled out of the kitchen and back toward the bedroom. He needed something to cut the pain in his ribs and leg. The Jack

Daniels ought to help, or least make him forget about it. He entered the bedroom, hit the lights, set the bottle and glass on a dresser and pushed through into the bathroom.

Rich looked at himself in the mirror. He had always thought he was in pretty good shape, at least for a man his age, but now he wasn't so sure. He had hit Kessler like a ton of bricks, a man at least four inches and thirty-five pounds smaller than himself, under the best of all possible circumstances, with a weapon, and had still struggled to take him down. Sure Kessler was younger, but still. This was not what Rich had expected and certainly not good news. He might have to rethink things to avoid putting himself in situations like this, where brute strength, quickness or agility could make or break him. Maybe he needed to work out more. Yeah, he would definitely have to think about this.

Rich turned on the cold water and splashed some into his face. It felt good, almost refreshing. He turned his side toward the mirror and tried to examine his ribs. Already a red welt about three inches long and running straight down his side had blossomed into ugly purple bruises about the size of a dessert plate. He carefully poked and probed the area trying to figure out whether he had cracked ribs. Stabs of pain radiated up his side whenever he got near the area of the welt and took his breath away. "Shit," he said. He kept probing, testing the limits of the injury and the pain. This would be hurting for a while, but he didn't think anything was broken. Maybe just a small crack. He had broken his ribs in college playing intramural football and that had really hurt, worse than this anyway.

He took a quick inventory of his parts and didn't discover any overt wounds other than the ribs and the cut on his leg. He seemed to have a little bruise above his right eye, which must've happened when Kessler elbowed him, and his left wrist was a little sore when he flexed it, but that was about it. Not too bad really. The ribs did hurt though. Wonder when that happened, he thought. Probably when they crashed into the table. No, now he remembered falling into that iron bench.

He walked over and turned the water on in the shower before heading back into the bedroom for a dose of the Jack Daniels.

35

He poured the whiskey over the ice, filling the glass almost to the top, then draining it without ever letting go of the bottle. The heat of the liquid rushing down his throat felt good. Rich poured another glass and took it into the bathroom and set it on the counter while he showered.

He let the hot water cascade down his head, neck and back until it cooled. Then he got out and dried off, gently patting the ribs, and wandered back into the bedroom, found a T-shirt and a pair of athletic shorts in a drawer and pulled them on. The ribs barked when he raised his arms and pulled the shirt over his head. He went back into the bathroom, popped four ibuprofen, and finished the remainder of the glass, now mostly melted ice. Back in the bedroom, he refilled the glass, ignoring the ice, and took another long pull of the Jack Daniels. At this rate, he would be drunk in no time. He picked the TV remote up off the bed, clicked it on, and ran through the cable news channels to see if he'd made the news yet. Lindsay had worked perfectly. No suspicions that anyone talked about. Although he knew it was too soon, he felt too wired to sleep. When ten minutes of surfing proved fruitless, Rich tossed the remote on the bed, went back into the utility room and ran the washing machine again.

He looked at the knife in the pot, its black blade reflecting the overhead light in the bleach water, now a pale pink. Rich took the knife out of the pot, dumped the water and rinsed out the pot and the knife. He filled it with fresh water and added more bleach, placing the knife back inside. In the morning, he would run the knife through the dishwasher a couple of times and then maybe think about getting rid of it. He had others. Maybe he would take it up to the farm. Maybe not.

He shuffled back to the bedroom, the ribs hurting now more than ever, wondering when the ibuprofen would kick in. He stopped in the doorway as he finished another glass of Jack Daniels and thought about going back to the kitchen for more ice. "Fuck it," he said as he crossed into the room and shut the door behind him. He grabbed the bottle off the dresser and climbed gingerly onto the bed, propping up some pillows so he could watch television. He settled on an old Steve McQueen movie, which he watched as he finished the bottle of Jack Daniels. He wouldn't fall asleep until almost dawn.

7

Rich slept the fitful sleep of the intoxicated, and when he awoke, he felt the hangover of the inexperienced drunk who couldn't remember how and why he'd gotten his ass kicked at the local roadhouse the night before. *Was it something I said?* He wasn't sure exactly where he was at first and a wave of nausea hit him hard. He rolled into his pillow and then remembered something his mother used to say when he was still just a kid. "Never throw up in bed. Always get to the bathroom. If you throw up in bed, you'll regret it." Good advice, he knew. Once, while in college, he hadn't succeeded in following it and, he had to admit, his mother was right. He had regretted it.

Rich forced himself out of bed, the ribs snapping at him big time as he twisted to get his feet on the floor. He sucked in some air and growled. Sitting there for a second, he glanced over and saw the empty bottle of Jack Daniels on the nightstand. He regretted that too. The room smelled of Jack Daniels and Doritos, a half empty bag of which lay on the floor next to the bed. He didn't remember the Doritos, but suspected he would be regretting them soon enough. He growled again as though the bag of chips could hear him, then pushed to his feet and trudged off to the bathroom. He hit the light switch for the shower and surveyed himself in the mirror. He thought he looked ten years older than he had the night before. The Eye of the Tiger had vanished. No more drinking, he resolved. Too old for that shit.

38

Drinking is for young guys and losers. Besides, all it could do is screw up his plans. That's right. No more drinking.

He looked at his face, thought he saw something, and turned on the vanity light. He was right. He had a bruise and a bit of swelling above his eye where Kessler had clocked him. Great. He pulled up his and shirt looked at his ribs. The dessert plate was now a dinner plate and the purple was on the move. He poked at the welt, now more ugly and swollen if that was possible, knowing that it would hurt. It did. Unable to resist, he poked it some more trying to figure out how bad it really was. It hurt worse. Still not as bad as the broken ribs in college though. Probably just cracked. Not that it made a difference. You can't do much for ribs anyway. Still, it was good to know. He sucked in a deep breath and the pain radiated from the area of the welt like ripples in a pond, encircling his whole torso. "Damn," he said, disgusted with himself.

His mouth felt dry, like cracked leather. He filled a plastic cup with water and reached for the ibuprofen, wondering if he could keep it down. He figured he probably needed fluids and he needed the ibuprofen even more than that. He took four more caplets and washed them down. Deciding to skip the shower, he grabbed a pair of sweatpants out of the closet and stepped into a pair of old deck shoes and headed for the kitchen. Maybe some dry toast, he thought. He could smell the bleach all the way out in the living room so he took a detour to the utility room to empty the washing machine. The smell was even stronger in there and he dumped the water and rinsed everything off before popping the lid to the washing machine to hang up the scuba gear to drip dry.

He took things out of the washing machine one by one and hung them on a rack with a clothes pin, first a glove, then the scuba pants, then another glove, before getting to the scuba top. As he pinned the top to the rack, he noticed a slice about 2 inches long in the side of the top, underneath one of the arms. His hand instinctively went to his right ribs. Was he stabbed? How could that be? There wasn't any blood. He would have known if he'd gotten stabbed. He looked closer at the scuba top.

39

Turning it around as though he were about to put it on, Rich realized that the slice was not on the right side, but on the left, the opposite side of his rib injury. He let out a low whistle. Somehow during the struggle with Kessler this slice had occurred.

He put his finger through the hole and examined the cut in the rubberized material. The cut was clean and smooth with no jagged edges of any kind. It couldn't have come from the bench or the table or anything else. It had to have come from the knife. Rich whistled again. That was close. That could have been in his ribs, maybe in a lung or even his heart. That could have just as easily been him as Kessler lying dead in the rain last night. But it wasn't. Good fortune? Maybe. Or just plain dumb luck. Now he had to decide who was next. And how to make sure that this didn't happen again.

8

"Dammit," Benjamin Lohmeier grumbled as he examined the shirt. He was in his basement doing laundry, one of the chores for which he long thought he received much too little credit. "How does she do this all the time?" He looked at his wife's shirt more closely, one of several long-sleeved T-shirts in the same medium blue color she wore during colder weather. Under the fluorescent lights, he could clearly see a series of small spots dappled over the front of the shirt. They looked like grease or cooking splatter. He grumbled again and then rummaged through a series of small bottles of spot removers, each containing a different formulation depending upon the nature of the stain. Finding the right bottle, one designed for the removal of fat, grease and oil, he opened the top and dabbed a small amount of the solvent on each spot he could locate, rubbing the spots together to work the stain when he was finished. Hearing his wife's footsteps in the kitchen above him, Ben took the shirt and stomped off upstairs to give her some grief.

He found her at the stove sliding freshly cut vegetables off on a cutting board into a sizzling skillet. "Hey, Libby," he said drawing out her name so that she knew by the tone that he was annoyed about something.

"Yes," she said in the same manner, but pointedly not looking at him.

"How do you do this?" he said waving the shirt.

"Do what?" She stirred the vegetables with a wooden spatula. She still wasn't looking at him.

"You know what. Look at this shirt." He waved the shirt again. "How am I supposed to keep this stuff clean? It's got spots all over it. It's not easy to get these spots out all the time."

She finally glanced at him, but only for an instant. "Maybe it's fabric softener. I've told you about fabric softener. It leaves those little spots."

"You know I stopped using fabric softener a long..." He stopped when he noticed she was smirking into the vegetables. "Very funny," he continued, "but you're the first one to complain when I don't get the spots out."

"You know, dear, I cook. And when I cook, things sometimes get on my shirt. Now if you did all the cooking, maybe I could keep my shirts clean, but the last time I checked, you didn't want to do the cooking. I have boobs. When you have boobs, things fall on them. Would you rather I had smaller boobs? That way I could keep my shirts cleaner." She caught him taking a quick peek at her breasts. "Didn't think so."

"Maybe you should wear a bib, or an apron or something."

"And cover them up? You don't really want that, do you?" She posed. He peeked again. She laughed. "Didn't think so. Now I have confidence in you, dear. I know that with all your bottles and things, you can get those spots out. Now back to work so I can get dinner on the table or we won't be eating until midnight." Then she patted him on the arm and shooed him away. As she turned back to her vegetables, he took one final look, then trudged back downstairs.

Fifteen minutes later, as Ben sorted socks on the counter in the laundry room, Libby came downstairs. "Do you have the TV on?"

"No," he said without looking, "what's up?"

He turned and held one mismatched, white athletic sock as she clicked on a small television resting on a top shelf overlooking a table filled with folded laundry. The room was cold and smelled faintly of bleach. "Where's the remote?" she said fumbling through the laundry before finally coming up with

42

the remote control for the TV. She appeared somewhat frantic and Ben was puzzled wondering whether there'd been a terrorist attack or something which resulted in her apparent anxiety. "You know Martin Kessler, don't you?" she continued as she switched the TV from ESPN to Fox News. "You know, the attorney from California? The guy from the Owens trial?"

"Sure," Ben said still holding the sock. "He was the DNA guy from the Owens trial. Very, very good, probably the best in his field. He was on that symposium I did at the UCLA Law School in January, the one on high-profile defense work. We've also been on the same panels a few times on TV. Why, what did he do?"

More than a year before, Ben had been the lead counsel in what the media called, the Law School Murder. It had been the big media case of its moment and Ben had gotten a lot of publicity out of it. It had made him something of a media star. In addition to a lot of new business, some of which he took and much more of which he didn't, Ben had signed on with Fox News to provide legal analysis on its various programs two or three times a week. In addition to paying pretty well for not terribly much work, Fox had even agreed to shoot most of his appearances from the conference room at his office. In the process, he had learned a whole lot about television news. One thing he learned was that making TV was a lot like making sausages – you didn't want to know too much about either.

Ben stood there holding the sock while Libby found Fox News on the TV, but they were in commercial. She flipped to MSNBC. Another commercial. Then she flipped back and forth until she finally found Fox News back on in the midst of a news alert regarding a big storm about to hit the Northeast. Ben couldn't figure out what she was so frantic about. He grabbed her arm just above the elbow. "What is it?" he said. "What's the deal with Kessler?"

She turned and looked at him and he could tell by the look on her face she was about to tell him something unexpected. "He's dead. Someone killed him. They think it happened sometime after late Thursday night, Friday morning. They think he was

43

leaving a friend's house or something. They found him in the morning. Dead."

Ben stood there for a moment not believing her. "What?" was all he could muster. They both turned toward the TV when the report on the storm ended and the blonde talking head moved on to politics in the Middle East. After a long silence between them, Ben asked, "How? How was he killed?" His eyes remained on the TV.

She turned back to look at him, but he didn't turn toward her. He remained looking at the TV. He could feel her eyes on him. "He was stabbed," she said in a soft voice just loud enough to be heard. "They said his throat was cut."

"Where did it happen?"

"What do you mean?"

"I mean, where did it happen? You said a friend's house, right? Where did the friend live? Was it in LA?"

"I think they said it was Brentwood. Isn't that where ..."

Ben interrupted her. "Yeah, that's where Owens killed his wife and the other guy. Brentwood." He turned and they looked into each other's eyes for a long moment. Just then, the talking head said that she would have an update on the murder of a prominent lawyer Martin Kessler after the next break.

They stood there in silence wading through the endless stream of commercials – one for a diet pill, another for a mortgage lender, then a new drug for osteoporosis, followed by another diet pill. Eventually, the talking head returned. Following two stories and one brief film clip, she finally got to Kessler. After a brief setup, she threw it out to the correspondent in Los Angeles, a cutting-edge English guy named Jonathan Lang, who wore a slick suit, stylish glasses and possessed just enough attitude to make him interesting. Ben had met him once at a party he was invited to by some Fox News producers while he was in LA and liked him. He was a bulldog and a bit of a smart ass. He had really gone after the silk suits at the UN during a scandal about oil for food money in Iraq. And Ben learned that he liked his gin and tonics. Nothing wrong with that.

44

Lang said, "Kessler, who gained national prominence as a DNA expert as part of the "Dream Defense" assembled to defend actor Chase Owens a decade ago, was found dead early yesterday morning, his throat apparently slashed, outside the home of a friend in Brentwood. Ironically, Brentwood was the same community where Owens's wife, Michelle, was murdered, her throat too having been slashed. Sources close to the Los Angeles police department investigation tell Fox News that they are not aware of any connection between the two slayings, nor had they been able as of yet to identify any motive or suspects in Kessler's death. Owens, who was acquitted of his wife's murder in a highly charged and most controversial jury verdict, has said that he is still out searching for his wife's killer."

After another minute or two, it was back to the blonde talking head for more stories about politics in the Middle East. Ben looked down at his hands and realized he'd been twisting the sock into a knot. He dropped it on the table and reached up and turned the TV off. Libby slid her arm around his waist and he turned and put his arms around her. They stood there and hugged, not saying anything, and Ben suddenly became acutely aware of all the sounds in the basement, from the low rumble of the washing machine to the tumbling of the dryer to the faint sounds of the TV drifting in from the playroom at the other end of the basement.

"What do you think?" she said in the same small voice.

He hugged her tighter and kissed her softly on the head before answering. "I don't know," he said. He pulled back and looked at her. "He seemed like a good guy, the little I knew of him. I know he was a good lawyer. We thought about hiring him during Megan's case, but we really weren't questioning DNA per se so his talents would probably have been wasted. He was energetic, full of life." Ben's voice trailed off.

"Do you think they'll call you in?" Libby asked.

"Do you mean to go on air?" He shrugged. "I don't know. I would think there are better people out there than me to talk about him, people who knew him far better than I did, people who are way more prominent than I am, but they may get around to me eventually when they use up all the others."

After a couple of minutes, Libby turned and looked at him. Though he felt her gaze upon him, he continued to look straight ahead until the next commercial, then he turned and locked eyes with his wife. They stood that way for a moment, just looking at each other, until Ben broke away, shook his head and returned to the laundry. There wasn't anything to say. Libby tried to find the right words as she watched him go. Nothing came to her.

Libby went back upstairs and Ben busied himself with the mundane tasks of the laundry, his previous irritations gone as memories of Kessler swirled through his head. Ben had liked Kessler, liked him a lot, even though he didn't know him well. Kessler had one of those infectious, outgoing personalities that seem to draw people to him, that made him seem accessible even if you barely knew him. Ben mused that this was also one of the reasons behind his success. In a highly technical, often complicated and dry world of DNA testing and blood analysis, Marty Kessler's enthusiasm for the subject, boundless energy and skill in communicating it made him a star whether he was a lawyer in front of a jury, and expert on the witness stand or professor teaching students how to make the subject their own. He always seemed so alive, so full of life, Ben thought. And now he was gone. Another victim in Brentwood, just like the victims in the biggest case of his career and one where he helped get the actor acquitted of two murders he had undoubtedly committed.

Ben spent the next ten minutes folding and unfolding the same shirt until he heard the phone ring. He let Libby get it. He had been right. It hadn't taken long. Libby called down to him. "It's for you."

Ben glanced at the phone on the wall, sighed, and picked it up. "Hello?"

"Hey, it's me. You been watching the TV? We need to get you on the air." The words were spoken at warp speed in a single breath. Ben recognized the voice immediately. Me, was Marcia Roberts, one of the producers at Fox. He dealt with her a lot, liked her, but knew that she was as calm as a Shih Tzu on

46

caffeine. When he didn't respond immediately, she added, "hey, you there?"

"Yeah, I'm here. What's up?"

"Don't fuck with me, Lohmeier. I'm up to my ass in alligators trying to line people up on this Kessler thing and I need to know if you can do a couple of shows for me. First, I need you for two segments on *Sunday Live* tomorrow. You'll probably have to go downtown for that."

"Whoa," Ben said, "hold on a second." She still hadn't slowed down. "Take a breath. You're going to give yourself a stroke. Two segments on *Sunday Live*? Wow, you must be desperate."

"No, I just want to give you more good publicity. I assume you've been watching the TV."

"Sure. I've got MSNBC on right now."

"Funny. If you've been watching, we've had the best coverage between the cables and the networks, don't you think? Anyway, if you've been watching, you know that this story is big and getting bigger. Let's face it, it isn't every day when a lawyer gets killed, his throat slashed on his girlfriend's sidewalk."

"Girlfriend?" Ben said. "He was found at his girlfriend's house? I hadn't seen anything about that."

"Yeah, that's what we think. She was a Fox producer in LA. They had been fooling around for a while, from what we can tell. I don't think anyone's reported it yet, but Loretta is going to be on tonight and she may run with it. If not tonight, then probably tomorrow. Pretty juicy, don't you think? Could be a motive." Loretta Bergen hosted her own nightly show during the week on the Fox News Channel. The show was generally designed to focus on hot legal and political affairs issues, but Loretta took a backseat to no one when it came to a good scandal or a murder.

"It does put a different spin on things," Ben said. "No doubt about it. I sure wouldn't want to be the girlfriend, or the wife for that matter. You guys are going to eat them alive."

"No kidding," Marcia agreed. "Hopefully, though, we'll get a bit of an edge because she works for Fox, the girlfriend, I mean. Anyway, it isn't often when a lawyer gets murdered."

47

"And you have such high hopes, but they never get realized," Ben said.

"Really. Stuff like this rarely happens in real life. Usually, it's the celebrity doing the shooting, or stabbing or whatever. They don't usually wind up as the victims. But now that a lawyer has been attacked and even killed, who better to talk about it than another lawyer who got shot at and lived to tell about it? Why, Benjamin Lohmeier, that's who."

"Great," Ben groaned. "Glad to help. Better to be alive to talk about it, I guess." When Peter Renfroe, the real killer in the Law School Murder, confronted Ben in his office after he correctly ascertained that Ben had discovered his identity, he fired a shot at Ben, which narrowly missed, before being shot and killed by one of Ben's colleagues.

"Well," Marcia continued, "it's not the only thing you're known for, but you do have to admit it was your initial claim to fame. I mean, after all, you not only figured out who did it, but also escaped his attempts to kill you too. That's right out of TV and the movies. People want to hear about that stuff, especially now in light of the Kessler thing. Not only that, you knew Kessler, didn't you? I know we've had both of you on our shows at the same time anyway."

"I knew him a little," Ben conceded, "but not real well. I certainly didn't know him as well as a lot of other people did, like those guys on the Dream Defense. We were on a panel together at UCLA and I talked to him a couple of times about the Law School Murder case. I guess I could fake it."

"They'll probably also want to talk to you about what it's like to be stalked by a killer, you know, stuff like that, but I'll get you an outline of questions so you can look at it ahead of time."

Ben rolled his eyes, but didn't respond right away. After a couple of more minutes like that, he asked, "You said something about another show. Which one and when?"

"Oh, did I say? Loretta wants to have you on the show on Monday night, probably two segments as well. We're probably looking at the D-block and the E-block, you know, wrap you around the update at the bottom of the hour. A primo spot. It would be better if you could fly out though."

Ben shook his head and moaned. "You mean to LA? Naw, I don't want to do that. I've got several court appearances this week and a bunch of other stuff going on. That just wouldn't work. I can do it in the office or even go downtown to the studio if I absolutely have to. But I don't want to fly out to LA."

Ben lived in the western suburbs of Chicago, about twenty miles west of downtown. He worked in a small office about thirty minutes north of his home by car and about the same distance from downtown as his home. He definitely did not want to fly out to Los Angeles. She tried to convince him otherwise for a few minutes, insisting that, "it always looks much more impressive to be in the studio with the host. It's more of a personal interaction that really makes the guests look good. You almost look like the star of the show. I'm telling you, it's the way to go."

"Yeah, yeah, I know, you'll make me a star. Yada yada yada."

She tried one more time. "But more exposure means more clients and more cases."

"Maybe I should make you my agent."

"You could do worse."

"But remember, if you're out to get me new clients, make sure you get me the ones who can pay. Big bank accounts and big retainers are always better."

After a few more minutes of uncomfortable banter, Ben signed off claiming dinner was on the table and he had to go. He hung up the phone and sighed again. "The news never sleeps."

9

Unfortunately for Ben, he wound up driving downtown for the *Sunday Live* segments and flying to Los Angeles for the Loretta Bergen show. As Marcia Roberts promised, Ben did the first two segments of *Sunday Live* after the half-hour break. In the first segment, he was joined by Stan Feldman, a lawyer based in Los Angeles, who first became prominent nationally because of his ubiquitous analysis of the Owens trial on cable TV. The purpose of the segment generally was to reminisce about Kessler and his televised performance during the Owens trial. Since Feldman had followed the trial closely and had made a name for himself covering it, he took the lead. Ben had been a young prosecutor in Chicago at the time and had not met Kessler until years later. Consequently, he felt somewhat uncomfortable embellishing his relationship with Kessler for the sake of a television audience.

Soon, the first segment mercifully ended and they went into commercial. Feldman, who had been based in a Fox studio in Los Angeles during the interview, would not be involved with the next segment and prepare to leave. Although Ben could hear Feldman and various producers over his earpiece, he could no longer see Feldman on his monitor. "Hey Ben," Feldman said, "you still there?"

Lost in his thoughts over the upcoming segment, Ben was startled. The two lawyers had appeared on a few shows together

50

over the years, as well as the symposium where Ben had met Marty Kessler. "Yeah, right here," Ben said.

"Tough thing about Kessler. Hard to imagine, don't you think?"

"Sure is," Ben said. "Although I didn't know him well, obviously, he sure seemed like a good guy. And a great lawyer, of course."

Neither man seemed to know what else to say. After an uncomfortable pause, Feldman said, "Well, I've gotta run. See you soon. Take care of yourself."

"You too."

Ben thought the brief interaction was odd, but he understood it. The two lawyers, along with Kessler, shared something of a bond having practiced law, gotten involved in some way or another with high profile cases and appeared on television. It was a strange kind of celebrity bond, but a bond nonetheless. Ben thought that Feldman was trying to find a way to acknowledge it, to recognize the loss of another in that fellowship, however described, and to come to grips with the idea that they were all in it together.

Soon, producers chirping in his ear brought him away from such contemplation and back to the reality of the upcoming second segment. Since Marcia had given him a heads-up that they wanted to discuss the Law School Murder case and his experience being stalked by a killer, Ben had taken some time on the drive downtown composing his thoughts and considering how he wanted to handle the media onslaught that would surely be on its way. In deference to Fox, he had declined all interview requests until at least after the Loretta interview the following day, but wasn't sure how he would hold out thereafter. He could just say no, but that didn't exactly help the law practice and his boss back at the firm surely noticed the uptick in business after a Benjamin Lohmeier television appearance.

The second segment went better than the first as Ben was able to speak from personal experience about his involvement in the Law School Murder case. While the host tended to focus on the sensational aspects of the case, which culminated in a shoot out in the conference room at Ben's office, in an attempt to draw parallels between his case and the Owens murders, Ben kept trying to bring it back to Kessler's death and the obvious effect it had on his friends and colleagues. Eventually, the second segment ended with the host thanking him for his insight on the tragic events. Although Ben didn't feel particularly insightful, he thought it had gone about as well as could be expected. Just another few minutes of television that no one will ever remember.

Marcia Roberts caught up with him in the United terminal at O'Hare Airport the following afternoon. "I thought that all in all that went pretty well," she said. "You could have shown a bit more enthusiasm, but maybe somber was the right tone under the circumstances."

Ben, who hadn't thought he'd been particularly somber, didn't answer. Marcia filled the vacuum. "Anyway, I talked to the Loretta again today. I think she wants to lean more toward the personal with you tomorrow. You know, get inside your head. Try to figure out what it's like to be hunted down like you and Kessler."

"Whatever," Ben said, "although I don't really think I was hunted down exactly, and I know I don't want someone trying to get inside my head. I have enough stuff going on in there already without the television masses poking around in there too."

After a few more minutes of back and forth with Marcia trying to pump him up and Ben complaining about having to fly to Los Angeles, he managed to get off the phone by telling Marcia he had to go because it was time to board the plane, which wasn't true. He just didn't want to talk to her any longer.

Ben wandered back down the concourse and found a bookstore. He wanted to find something to read on the flight and picked through the magazines, coming up empty. He found a Robert Crais paperback that he hadn't read already and headed for the counter. While waiting in line, a gray-haired man in a sport coat and tan slacks tapped him on the shoulder and asked, "say, aren't you that lawyer who was on TV yesterday talking about that lawyer's murder Los Angeles?"

"Yeah, that's me."

"Nice job. I watch that show all the time. First time I've seen you on there. They should have you on again."

"Thanks."

By now, Ben had reached the front of the line. The man nodded and said, "well, it was nice meeting you. Good luck to you."

Ben thanked him, paid his money and made his way back to the gate. That was harmless enough. While he generally didn't get recognized all that often, he had to admit that most of the time, people treated him pretty well. They just wanted to say hello and congratulate him, like the man in the bookstore just now. Every once in a while, someone felt the urge to point out where he was wrong or debate capital punishment, but that didn't happen too often and when it did, more often than not he was able to get out of the situation relatively painlessly.

*****

Rich had been watching the program from the living room at the condo. He spent the first segment cursing at Feldman under his breath. Rich didn't think that Feldman knew his ass from a hole in the ground, an opinion born during the Owens trial. He didn't hold Ben in such high disregard. From the times he'd seen him on television, Rich thought that Ben seemed like a pretty good lawyer and he was more than a little impressed with the fact that Ben was able to crack the Law School Murder case and escape Renfroe's grasp in the process. Clearly, he was a hell of a lot smarter than Feldman. In a way, Rich was glad that he didn't have Lohmeier in his sights too. He might make a difficult adversary.

Since the murder, Rich had spent considerable time surfing the cable channels to check on the coverage of his handiwork. Most of it seemed fairly typical and routine, focusing on the sensational aspect of the crime with liberal doses of Kessler's impressive career and how great guy he was thrown in for good measure. This galled Rich to no end. Of course, he never expected to hear any respect or praise given to the man who planned the daring crime and carried it out so successfully. That would have to wait for the history books, for Rich's plans were extensive and if things went as intended, the focus of the world would shift away from the victims soon enough. He would get his credit in the end even if no one ever knew his identity. He would know. That was enough. The talking heads, they didn't know anything anyway.

10

Ben was thoroughly immersed in the adventures of Elvis Cole when the voice on the plane's intercom announced that the plane was starting its descent into LAX. The flight had been a relatively pleasant one, yet Ben's stomach still tightened until they were safely on the ground. A young woman rushed up to meet him at the gate, apparently one of Marcia's minions. Dressed in a dark blue business suit despite the LA heat, she was a tall thin blonde with the looks that television executives desired in their on-air talent. Ben thought she looked a little harried around the edges. Probably a long day. She would need to develop some more cool along with more experience. She introduced herself as Stephanie Gray and confirmed that Marcia had indeed sent her to escort Ben to his hotel and then on to the studio for his interview with Loretta Bergen.

Ben followed her to the baggage claim area to pick up his hanging bag and then outside to a waiting limo, the heat slapping him in the face as soon as the sliding doors opened. "A little hotter than Chicago?" Stephanie said as the driver took the hanging bag, a small overnighter and Ben's briefcase and put them in the trunk.

"Just a little. Especially this time of year. I think it was about twenty when I left."

A moment later, they were safely in back of the limo, whose air conditioning had been turned up high, replicating the artificial cool of the airport terminal. "That feels better," Ben said. "So, Stephanie, tell me, what's the plan?"

She tucked a strand of blonde hair behind her ear and folded her hands in her lap. Ben thought she had practiced this move before. "Well," she began, "as you probably know, Loretta typically broadcasts out of Washington DC." Ben nodded. "But she doesn't like to be stuck in the studio all the time so when there's a big story, like this one, she likes to travel out and see what it's like on the ground, so to speak. She came out yesterday and has already been reporting on location at various spots all day long. Last I heard, she'll be live in Brentwood for the show tonight."

"Does that mean I'm going to be doing my segments on location as well?" Ben asked.

Stephanie shook her head. "No. After we drop your stuff at the hotel, we're going to head right over to the studio so you can meet with Loretta and tape your segments. Oh, by the way," she said digging in her purse and pulling out a long envelope which he handed to him. "I've already checked you in. Here are your key cards and check-in information. Your room number is on the card envelope. I think it might be a suite."

Ben took the envelope and stuffed it into the pocket of his coat. "I'm sure it will be fine," he said.

She made a face. "We better hurry. We're behind schedule. Do you think maybe we could skip going to the hotel and head straight to the studio? I want to make sure we have enough time."

"No problem. As long as I have a place to change clothes, I'll be fine."

Ben had been to the Fox Studios in Los Angeles only one time previously, but these days, one television studio was pretty much like another. Stephanie had been right, they were running late and only got later when they got stuck in traffic since rush-hour in Los Angeles starts shortly after lunch. Ben found an empty conference room and changed into a dark gray suit and blue print tie, then he and Stephanie played hide-and-go-seek in their search for Loretta Bergen. They found her two flights up going over

56

some notes in a small set staged to look like a library, complete with legal treatises and reporters on the shelves, all designed to give just the right look for the viewers at home. Ben always laughed when he saw sets like this on TV because he knew as a lawyer that a full set of reporters, for example, would take up more than twenty times the shelf space available in the smallish room, maybe more. Nevertheless, it made for good visuals.

Loretta looked up when they entered and smiled. "Hey counselor," she said rising to her feet while juggling her notes, "nice to meet you finally." Although Ben had appeared on her show numerous times, he always did so from a remote location and had never met Loretta in person. They shook hands and she pointed to a chair opposite the one in which she had been sitting. "Have a seat and we'll chat. You can see we're giving you the den treatment," she said with a wave of her arm at the bookshelves.

"Yeah, I can see that. I feel like the secretary of state." Ben sat and they exchanged pleasantries for a few moments. Before going into TV, Loretta had been a trial lawyer and was still capable of conducting her interviews like cross examinations if circumstances warranted. Ben didn't expect that this time, however. Loretta was a small attractive woman with frosted blond hair in her early fifties, who laughed easily, both at herself and at the absurdities she saw in public life in America. She could be both disarming and a pit bull and had a particular knack for getting to the heart of the matter by asking just the question the viewer was thinking about at home. Ben liked her a lot and Libby was a huge fan. Among the talking heads in media today, Loretta Bergen was clearly one of the sharpest. "So," she said, "did they let you in on the plan?" Ben nodded. "Good. Since we're going to tape the segments in advance, we can have a more free-flowing conversation and edit out what we don't need or doesn't work afterward. Sound good?"

"Sounds good." Ben didn't mind taping a segment in advance, for he knew the producers would try to make it come off as well as possible. He wasn't the subject of a *60 Minutes*-style exposé so he didn't have to worry about them cutting the piece in order to make him look sinister or foolish. They spoke for a few more minutes before moving off to get makeup applied for the taping.

The interview itself went pretty well with a few fits and starts as a result of the fact that they were taping and not going live. It took Loretta about half an hour to get what she needed. They would cut that to about twelve minutes or so for the actual broadcast. When they were finished, Loretta looked at him and said, "that wasn't so bad, was it?"

"Better than a trip to the dentist," Ben said, "but only by a little."

Technicians crowded around them to remove their microphones and other equipment so they could leave. "Looking forward to getting out of this heat and back into the Chicago winter?" Loretta asked.

Ben shrugged. "I don't know about that. It is pretty damn hot out here though. Actually, I'm going to be in your neck of the woods this weekend. Since Presidents' Day is Monday and the kids have a three-day weekend, we're going up to northern Wisconsin for snowmobiling with my cousins."

Loretta put her hand on his arm and groaned. "Ohhhh, don't say that. Now I'm jealous." Loretta hailed from Wisconsin. "I haven't had a chance to get back all winter, not even for a Packers game. Whereabouts are you heading?"

"A place called Three Lakes. It's about a half hour east of Eagle River."

"I've heard of it. Lots of good snowmobiling up there. And I think they've had some good snow lately. I wish I were going along. You own a place up there?"

Ben shook his head. "No, I wish. My cousins do. It's been in their family for fifty years. It's perfect for the summer and the winter because it's on a string of small lakes. Just the right size for whatever you want to do."

"God, I really am jealous. Probably has a great bar up there too."

Ben laughed. "Of course."

"I knew it. Nothing like a good Wisconsin bar. You know, I used to love those court holidays when you could get away. Don't have those in this business. No such thing. You take a vacation and something always seems to happen. You're at the mercy of current events. I guess no one makes us do it so we shouldn't complain. Anyway, have a good time. Think of me slaving away under the hot lights while you're off having fun."

"Will do. You know what my wife says?" She shook her head. "She says the nicest people in America come from Wisconsin."

"Your wife is one smart woman. Tell her I said so. Maybe I'll get to meet her one of these days."

They shook hands and Loretta was off down the hall. Ben watched her go. About twenty feet away she turned and said, "Good job tonight. Thanks again." Then she waved and was gone.

Ben went to the steak house in the hotel for dinner. It was very good – a New York strip steak with all the trimmings. He took his second Heineken to go, put the meal on his room tab, or Fox's room tab, and wandered off in search of his room. Stephanie had been right, it was a suite, opening into a good-sized sitting area with a wet bar and the bedroom off to the left through a door in the back corner. The bellman had hung his bag in a small closet and his overnighter and briefcase lay on the bed. He slipped out of his shoes, jacket and tie, hit the bathroom and plopped down on the sitting room couch in front of the TV with the Heineken. He spent a moment trying to figure out the television, eventually getting the hang of it, and surfed the channels until he found Fox News just as Loretta Bergen went to her first commercial. Perfect timing.

Although he didn't care for watching himself on television as he found the experience surreal and uncomfortable, he figured he'd better watch this time. He wanted to see if Loretta had unearthed any new developments in Kessler's death and more importantly, he wanted to see how their editing job turned out.

Loretta did her best to put her spin on what was essentially the same news that had been running for about three days now.

59

Unlike some of her competitors, she tried to tamp down the sensationalism, not that she was opposed to being controversial. Still, she avoided jumping to too many conclusions without the facts upon which to base them. She teased her segments with noted trial attorney Benjamin Lohmeier as she went to commercial at the bottom of the hour. That nervous feeling in the pit of his stomach expanded as Ben watched even though he knew what had been said in the interview. Then Loretta was back and Ben was being introduced. The set did in fact look somewhat like an interview with the president, the books on the shelves forming a tasteful and intellectual backdrop. Loretta briefly walked him through the Law School Murder case just to remind those in the audience who may have forgotten or never known. She then fleshed out the details of the attack and its aftermath and then they went to commercial.

Ben suddenly felt exhausted just watching it. He took a few deep breaths and a long pull on the beer. He realized watching it how thoroughly lost in the moment he'd become during Loretta's questioning. Then they were back and she was asking whether or not he knew at the time that Renfroe had been stalking him.

"No, I had no idea. You have to remember, I was in the middle of a murder trial. My focus at that time was to make sure that my client was acquitted of those charges. It never occurred to me that he'd been in my office, going through my files and had been keeping tabs on me the whole time."

Loretta nodded. "Let me ask you this, do you think Marty Kessler knew he was being stalked? I mean, this doesn't strike you as a spur of the moment type crime does it?"

Ben began shaking his head before she even finished the question. "No," he said, "this doesn't strike me as a spur of the moment type thing at all. I can't imagine that it was. You don't just stumble across someone with a knife and cut their throat. I can't imagine that Kessler knew he was being stalked either. I may be wrong, but I don't think he knew anything until he was attacked."

"Tell me," Loretta continued, "what does your gut tell you? You're a trial lawyer. Will we ever really know what happened to Marty Kessler?"

Ben watched himself look off into the middle distance as he contemplated his answer. This really was the heart of it, wasn't it? Finally, he saw himself look back into Loretta's eyes. "Yeah, in the end, I think we'll find out what happened, more or less. With the kind of struggle we've heard about, there must be some evidence, maybe DNA, something we don't know about or maybe that hasn't been uncovered yet that will help the police get to the bottom of this. I think they'll crack it. It may take a while, but I think we'll find out who did it."

"I sure hope you're right," Loretta said.

About 120 miles south of where Ben was sitting in his lovely hotel suite, Rich clicked off his own television and tossed the remote on the couch. "Oh, but you're not right," he said aloud. "You're not right at all. I can promise you that."

11

Ben spotted his cousin, Jeff Wyatt, waving his arm overhead to get Ben's attention. Ben nodded his recognition. Ever the hale fellow well met, Jeff gave Ben an enthusiastic handshake and an exaggerated, "Missster Lohmeier, good to see you." Then, in a lower voice, "you ready for the big excursion?"

It was six o'clock on Friday night of Presidents' Day weekend. They were meeting at the food court at the O'Hare Oasis to get a quick bite to eat before hitting the road to northern Wisconsin for a weekend of snowmobiling. Ben laughed. "About as ready as I'm going to get. The thermometer in my car read 10°."

Jeff rubbed his hands together. "Yep, it's going to be a cold one up there. I hear minus twenty-five." Ben groaned. Jeff continued. "No big deal. If you're dressed for it, you won't even notice the cold. And we'll be dressed for it."

Ben shook his head and looked around. He and Jeff were the only two standing there. Everyone else was off in search of food. "I hope you're right."

Six and a half hours and two pit stops later, kids asleep in the back, they rounded the final curve in the woods and the small caravan slowed to a stop opposite a narrow gap in the trees to the right. A dented silver mailbox on a fence post shone in the headlights of Jeff's white van, the name "Wyatt" on its side in reflective stick-on letters. Ben knew from past experience that there was a driveway in there someplace, but tonight it was buried under a thick covering of recent snow. Jeff turned in front of the mailbox and rolled slowly down the long steep driveway toward the cottage, Ben following at a safe distance fearing that he would not be able to stop the SUV on the slippery slope and envisioning himself careening into the back of Jeff's van.

Well more than a foot of snow blanketed the driveway as the troop unpacked the cars and headed for the cottage and a good night's sleep. Ben looked up at the sky. Away from the lights of the city, millions of big bright stars floated above him like he could reach up and pluck them out of the sky. A few minutes later, Ben leaned over the kitchen sink and checked the temperature on a big round outdoor thermometer perched outside the kitchen window, the lights from the kitchen illuminating the dial – it read minus eighteen. Ben was surprised. He figured it was a hell of a lot colder than that.

He awoke to the smell of pancakes, bacon and sausages wafting in from the kitchen. Never a particularly early or graceful riser, he was among the last to make it up for breakfast. Given how late they arrived, however, no one was terribly eager to greet the morning. At least the kids got to sleep in the car on the way up. The cottage itself was a typical vacation home found throughout Wisconsin and Minnesota, two stories of redwood siding with an entrance off of the driveway. The attached two-car garage housed the Wyatt's collection of snowmobiles and jet skis, among other things. Down in the basement, there was a large, dorm-style room containing several bunk beds where the kids and their friends could hang out and sleep.

There was another bedroom on the first floor and a couple of more upstairs. The walls were paneled in smooth, heavily-varnished pine, wearing well despite its age. One large plank off of the kitchen was scarred with markings memorializing the respective heights of the various Wyatt parents, children, grandchildren, cousins and others over the decades. The focus here was not on the inside, but, rather, on the outdoors and the myriad of activities that could be enjoyed here throughout the year.

Ben found Jeff in the family room looking out toward the lake. "Good morning," he said as Ben approached and joined him.

"How did you sleep?"

Ben nodded. "Good."

"We have a veritable heat wave out there – minus eleven."

Ben looked out across the frozen landscape. Snow and ice as far as he could see, at least until the pine trees at the far shore almost a mile away. Even on the near side he couldn't tell where land ended and the lake began. "Doesn't look much like a heat wave. It looks like the moon, only with trees. Is there good snowmobiling in this weather?"

"Aw, it'll be great," Jeff said. "I went down to the lake a little while ago and there were already guys heading out in their trucks to do some ice fishing."

Ever the suburban boy, Ben asked, "how thick is the ice out there anyway?"

"Probably about two feet or more. More than thick enough."

After breakfast, everyone who planned to brave the elements met in the basement to get suited up. Over the years, the Wyatts had accumulated a wide variety of cold weather gear, and those in need picked through the extras in preparation for the worst. Ben grabbed a black helmet off a hook and headed out to the garage with Jeff and Steve Hoffman, a friend who came along on the trip with his wife and two boys.

It took the better part of an hour to get six snowmobiles of various sizes, horsepowers and descriptions up and running and out of the garage and down to the lake. It had all the makings of a beautiful day. There wasn't a cloud in the bright blue sky and the sun shimmered off of the snow and ice of the lake making sunglasses a necessity. Jeff conducted an impromptu refresher course in snowmobile operation for the kids, and the adults, while a couple of the older kids zoomed off on their own for brief excursions. The cottage was located on a chain of small interconnected lakes such that you could travel from one lake to another to another for miles without worrying about touching land. Since snowmobiling and related winter sports were such a

64

big part of the local economy, authorities worked hard to keep the high-traffic areas of the lakes and surrounding trails well-maintained and as safe as possible. Orange cones dotted the high-traffic areas in the central part of the lakes indicating a ice highway of sorts that people could follow from one place to another.

The group went at it full bore until lunchtime, people taking turns on the various machines and getting more and more comfortable with each passing time. Off to the right about a quarter of a mile, the land jutted out into the water and formed a corner of sorts separating one lake from another. Jeff took Ben and Bill off in that direction and stopped just short of the corner, opposite an area where the lake wasn't entirely frozen over for a patch of twenty yards or so, a small puddle of open water in the center. Jeff pulled up his visor and pointed it at. Ben remembered it from a previous trip. "See that?" Jeff said. The others nodded. "Stay well clear of that area. It's a discharge area for the town and the warm water keeps that little section from freezing over completely. You can either go well wide of it and around the corner, say twenty yards or so, or go through there," he said pointing to another area about ten yards back from the point itself in between two trees. Ben could see where a path had been worn through in the gap between the trunks. Jeff looked back at the open water. "Years ago, back when I was a kid, I went for a trail run up north of here near the UP with my dad and brothers. It was getting dark and we came across an accident near a patch of open water in a big lake. We were in the middle of nowhere with nobody around but us. This guy hadn't seen the open water and fell, crashed right into it. All you could see was part of the snowmobile and the top of the guy's helmet. It was still on his head. Don't know how long he'd been there, but it'd been long enough. Nothing you could do but call the patrols. Never want to see that again." Ben and Bill nodded. Point made.

They maneuvered single-file through the opening and Jeff led them through a second lake, around a similar corner and into a third. About a mile away, Ben could see a building in the distance. He immediately recognized the Pine Isle, a restaurant and bar Ben had been to with Jeff on a couple of occasions on previous trips. A small plume of white smoke drifted off into the blue sky from a chimney at the top roof line. Ben had traveled there by boat in the summer time and snowmobile in the winter, but never by car, and as they approached he realized that the place was set up more for snowmobile and boat traffic anyway, for the parking lot itself was rather small. They bumped up from the lake to land in the area where the dock was located in the summertime and Jeff coasted to a stop. Ten or fifteen snowmobiles were parked in various portions of the lot as people stopped in for lunch. "I thought maybe we could stop in for a cold one tonight after dinner," he said. "Unless we'd rather have a hot one."

"Sounds like a plan to me," Bill said.

Ben readily agreed and they continued through the parking lot to a path on the far side, which led to a series of trails through the woods and across a couple of more lakes before ultimately reaching the main road leading into town. Jeff took them down several side streets and a quiet little neighborhood before ending up at the local snowmobile dealer. He was always in the market for a new toy.

They browsed through the available used models since Jeff didn't want to spend really big money on a new machine. In addition to fast, he also liked flashy and gravitated toward two models at the end of the row, one fire engine red and the other electric blue. The dealer wandered over and Ben and Bill stomped their feet in the snow trying to stay warm while Jeff and the dealer went through the dance. They haggled for a few more minutes before Jeff finally settled on the red one and they went off to finalize the details. A few minutes later, Jeff was back, a big smile on his face.

"You all set?" Bill asked.

"Yep, but I can't pick it up until tomorrow."

They took a different route back, one Ben wasn't sure he could duplicate, and were back in time for lunch. They were soon back at it for the remainder of the afternoon. By the end of the day, everyone was tired and the kids headed back inside to watch a video. As the sun began to set, the three dads took turns trying to see how fast they could go out in the middle of the lake. The snow had been worn away from the traffic and the whole strip from one end of the lake to the other was icy smooth and fast. Ben thought it reminded him of a winter version of the Bonneville Salt Flats.

They each took five or six shots at it, with Bill not exceeding ninety or so. He just wasn't the daredevil. Ben had grown increasingly bold as the day progressed and ultimately got his machine up to 112 mph, careful at that speed not to encounter any traffic. He knew he was going fast because as he approached 100 mph, the plastic windscreen over the handlebars would flip inside out. He had to admit, the feeling was exhilarating. Driving his favorite silver machine, at least until he picked up the red one the following day, Jeff pushed past 115 mph, as fast as he could ever remember going. By then, it was getting too dark to drive that fast, so they parked the snowmobiles at the end of the lake and stomped up the snowy slope to the cottage.

They ate burgers, chips and salad for dinner, with people crowded around the dining room table, kitchen table and all the available seats in the family room while they ate. Ben, Jeff and Bill wound up alone at the dining room table recapping the events of the day. "I can't wait to pick up that snowmobile tomorrow," Jeff said. "I should call my brother and give him the business about it. That silver one I was driving today is really his. It's a nice machine, but I think I like the new one better. I sure hope it goes faster than his." He held his thumb and forefinger up about an inch apart. "At least a little bit faster anyway."

"Well," Ben said nodding, "I can now officially state that I have gone faster on a snowmobile that I ever have in a car."

Bill shook his head and laughed. "You guys are both nuts," he said. "I was scared to death going ninety."

They made fun of him and debated the virtues of speed for few minutes, not really coming to any firm conclusions, before Jeff said, "Pine Isle?"

Ben looked at Bill and they said in unison, "Pine Isle."

This time, the wives thought all three of them were nuts, but didn't stand in their way. Now that it was dark, the temperature had fallen back down below minus ten, so they had to adjourn to the basement once more to get bundled up for the short trip over to the bar. While Ben was putting on snow pants, Bill said, "you know, we could always just drive." The other two gave him a look. "All right, never mind. Forget I even said it."

Five minutes later, they were back down by the lake and the snowmobiles were rumbling to life. Five minutes after that, they pulled to a stop at the end of a long line of snowmobiles parked outside the Pine Isle. As he climbed down, Ben noticed that several of the machines were still running. He took off his helmet and pointed it out to Jeff, who said, "some guys do that if they're just coming in for a quick pop. That's Wisconsin for you. If you're from up here, I guess you'd never expect that someone would hop on your snowmobile and take off with it. Some guys just leave their keys in the ignition. Maybe those are the guys who are going to be inside for a while. But I'm not from up here. I'm from Illinois. I know better. I take my keys with me."

They went inside, dumped their helmets in wooden cubbyholes next to the bar, and found a table in the back by the juke box. While Bill wandered off to get the first round, Ben and Jeff checked out the selection of tunes. A couple of minutes later, Bill was back with three Leinenkugels. "Anything good on that thing?" he said handing Ben his beer.

"Mostly eighties stuff," Ben answered as they clinked bottles. "If you like Journey, you're in business."

"I like Journey," Bill said looking over Ben's shoulder. "If they have Journey, they must have Styx."

"We have a winner," Jeff said. He pointed to a song. "We have Styx right here."

"This isn't a Styx kind of crowd," Ben said looking around. "Unless it's *Renegade*, if we picked Styx, people would think we were gay lovers in for the weekend."

"Good point," Bill said. "Do they have *Wheel in the Sky*?"

"I think I saw that back here," Ben said running his finger down the glass. "Yeah, here it is." He took a dollar from his

68

wallet and slid it into the machine. "Okay, we get five selections. We'll start with *Wheel in the Sky*. What else do we like?"

They settled on *Bad to the Bone* by George Thorogood, *Eye of the Tiger*, *Little Red Corvette* and *Dancing in the Dark*, Springsteen's biggest hit even if it wasn't his best song, and returned to their table. It took a few minutes for their songs to come on. *Bad to the Bone* was first. "Good choice," Jeff said and they clinked bottles again.

"Don't think I know anything after the eighties anyway," Bill said.

"I don't think I do either," Ben agreed. "Nothing good anyway."

They talked a little and then Springsteen came on. "Should've picked *Pink Cadillac*," Ben said. "I think it's the B-side."

"Ooooo," Bill said, "that would've been good."

"My brother had a buddy who had a Caddy in high school. Wasn't pink though. Or a convertible for that matter," Jeff said.

Ben put his arms out. "What? Then want the fuck is the point?" he said razzing Jeff.

"Just saying."

They laughed, drank and talked about cars for a while. Ben got another round and brought it back to the table. "Pretty good crowd in here considering the weather." The bar was almost full.

"Hardy stock in these parts," Jeff said. "It's downright balmy out there."

"Say," Bill said tipping his bottle toward Ben, "you hear anything new on that lawyer's murder in California? I saw you on TV the other night talking about it."

Ben shook his head. "Nothing of substance."

"It seems like the cops don't have any idea what happened."

"Hard to say," Ben said. "They sure aren't talking about it. Although sometimes they don't talk. That doesn't mean they don't know anything. If he were having an affair, and I heard maybe he was, then maybe you would look at the wife. But I can't see a woman carving him up with a knife like that. He wasn't a big guy, but still..."

"You knew the guy, didn't you?" Jeff said. Ben nodded as he took another swig of his beer. "That must have hit kind of close to home."

"Yeah, especially another lawyer and all," Bill said.

"I suppose. I'm sure they'll figure it out sooner or later. They usually do."

They sat in silence for a minute and then moved on to sports and eventually to their wives. Ben was grateful for the change in subjects. He had been brooding about Kessler's death all week and the activities of the day had temporarily pushed it out of his mind. Now it was back. They joked about their wives, but Ben was more subdued than he had been earlier. Soon, they finished their beers and called it a night. Ben would still be thinking about Kessler when he finally drifted off to sleep, long after the rest of the cottage had gone silent.

12

Rich was eager to get back to the farm. Even though he knew the Presidents' Day traffic would be lighter than usual, he left the condo at six in the morning and hopped on the 5 heading in the general direction of LA. The Camry cruised at five mph above the posted speed all the way into the city, past Burbank and Santa Clarita. He stopped at a gas station outside of Paloma to get gas. As he got back in the car, he looked out toward the ocean. The morning was clear with very little smog and cooler than it had been in recent days. Going to be a nice day, he thought.

Soon, he was back on the road, exiting the 5 at Highway 152 and taking that west toward the ocean. He hit Highway 1 at Rio Del Mar. He drove along the coast for a few miles until he reached the Santa Cruz Highway and took that back inland toward San Jose. Most people would have stuck on Highway 1 and soaked in the spectacular views, but Rich had seen it all before and even though he liked the scenery as much as the next guy, he had work to do and was all about getting it done. Passing through Scotts Valley he knew he was close. Up ahead, he took a right, then a left, and then he was there. The dirt road poked out of the trees to the right. It looked like an access road to a forest preserve. Few people gave it much thought, which was just the way Rich liked it.

He steered the Camry through the trees, before reaching a chain-link fence that stretched all the way across the road. Dense foliage encroached on the road from both sides and the thick canopy of trees cast the whole area in dark shadows. The fence, looking a bit ragged and rusted, would be sufficient to keep out most unwanted visitors. If they reached this point, they would simply conclude they were in the wrong place, turn back around and head back to the main road. Rich took a small remote control that looked like the transmitter for a garage door opener out of the glove box, rolled down the window and aimed it at a thicket of bushes of to his left. Suddenly, he heard a click and the chain-link fence lurched off to the side allowing him to pass. He inched through the gate and moved off through the trees. Following the path around a series of gentle curves for about a quarter mile, he finally reached a clearing. The farm.

It wasn't really a farm. That's just what he called it. It was more of a sanctuary really, tucked back among the redwoods. The entire clearing itself encompassed about three-quarters of an acre, roughly circular in shape, and was completely surrounded by woods save for the dirt road itself. There were two structures in the clearing, the main house and the barn. The house stood in the back center facing toward him, a rambling raised ranch in chipped redwood stained a dirty brown. Rich thought it looked alternatively rustic and run down depending on his mood. Despite his lack of upkeep over the years, it was actually in pretty good shape. Richard's lone concession to home maintenance had been to repair the railing on the steps leading up to the front porch that stretched across the entire width of the house, and he only did that because he almost fell on his head when one of the rails gave way on him six months earlier. In case someone did happen along, he didn't want the place looking too good. Not abandoned, but not too lived-in either.

The barn, on the other hand, was actually a barn. Two stories of faded redwood, with swing-open doors wide enough to accommodate a horse and buggy, or an automobile, the barn was set nearer to the road, but off to the left near the edge of the clearing and facing perpendicular to the house toward the center of the open space. Rich pulled the Camry in front of the doors of the barn and parked, leaving the engine running. He walked to the doors, latched together with a padlock, and dialed the combination. He pulled on the lock with his right hand and it clicked open. He removed it, swung the doors open wide and pulled the car into the barn. On his way out of the barn, he placed the open lock back on the latch, leaving the doors open, and headed for the house.

Rich fumbled through a set of keys until he found the right one, unlocked the door and went inside. He stepped into a small entry way that led straight down a hallway toward the back of the house. The living room and family room were to the left, the kitchen occupied the center rear of the house, with the bedrooms down a hallway to the right.

The place smelled musty from having been closed up for several weeks. Rich decided to open some windows and get some fresh air inside. He opened a window in the living room then moved into the kitchen, placed the laptop that had been slung over his shoulder on the kitchen table and opened the slider. He walked over to the refrigerator and pulled open the door. There were a couple of bottles of beer, a 6-pack of bottled water and some assorted condiments, not much else. He thought of Lindsay's refrigerator back in Florida. Pretty similar actually. He yanked a bottle of water free from its plastic packaging and shut the door. He popped the top on the water and strolled over to the slider and felt a cool breeze blowing through the screen. It felt good.

Although Rich had lived most of his life in the Los Angeles area, he greatly preferred the area around San Francisco. The heat in LA, coupled with the smog and traffic, drove him nuts. While San Diego was better in almost every way, it was still a little too hot for Rich's taste. And monotonous. Every day was the same – sunny and beautiful. San Francisco, on the other hand, was just warm enough most of the time, its good days very good and its bad days, not that bad. You actually got to see clouds and weather in San Francisco. Rich kind of enjoyed the cooler blustery days when the rain and fog rolled in. The weather was alive around San Francisco. It had moods. Rich liked it even more because he knew that none of the geeks in the high-tech industry would ever give him a second thought. It was exactly the kind of anonymity he liked and needed.

Pulling the laptop from its case, he sat down at the kitchen table and fired it up. He took a flash drive out of his pocket and stuck it in the USB port on the side of the computer. He scrolled through some files and found one labeled, "Ohio". Rummaging through the laptop case, he located the two expandable file folders he was looking for, took them out and laid them on the table. Like the file on the computer, one was labeled, "Ohio". The other was labeled, "Wyoming". He couldn't decide what to do next, Ohio or Wyoming. Ohio probably required more preparation, not that Wyoming didn't have its own planning issues to worry about. He thought about it for a moment, then settled on Ohio. He would work on Ohio for the time being.

Back in the laptop case, he found his Internet dongle and slid it out of one of the pockets and connected it to the computer. After a moment, he clicked on his browser and hoped for the best. Sometimes the connection up here in the woods was a bit spotty. Then he got the connection. "Excellent," he said under his breath. He went to his favorites and clicked on a familiar site. A second later, it loaded and appeared on the screen. He'd been on this site countless times over the preceding year trying to figure out how to put things together. Certainly not beyond someone of his capabilities. He compared what he saw on the screen with a diagram he had removed from one of the folders. Not exactly the same, but the same basic idea. Good enough for government work.

Rich knew he couldn't rely exclusively on the diagrams and that once he started building it he might have to make changes on the fly, but that was okay. He had built things before and knew how to take things apart and put them back together again. Reverse engineering, they called it. In fact, he figured he might make improvements on the device once he started assembling it. He kind of relished the challenge. It would be the best part of the whole project, until the actual execution that is. Only he wouldn't be putting the finished product on the Internet.

Time drifted away as Rich studied the diagrams. He went to several more sites and did the same thing. He made comparisons, took detailed notes and thought through the various possibilities before eventually concluding that it was simply time to get on with it. Paralysis by analysis. He didn't want that. He needed to get going. If he had to go back later and make changes or start over, that was okay too. The only timeframe was the one in his head. And that pushed him forward.

He only acknowledged the passing of time when he finished the water bottle. Jesus, he'd been at this for more than two hours and he still hadn't unloaded the car. He minimized the browser and finally got around to doing it. From the outside, it appeared to be a typical barn you might find anywhere – about sixty feet wide by forty feet deep and two stories high. There was a window on the second story of each side, but none on the main level. Inside, the barn consisted of a wide open space with a pull down set of steps leading up to a hay loft. A separate room had been built in the front right corner of the structure, about twenty feet square. There were no windows.

Rich took three trips to move the groceries, various toiletries and a suitcase from the car into the house. The final two boxes would not be going in the house. He took the first from the trunk. It probably weighed fifty pounds or more. He walked over to the room and placed the box on the ground next to a steel core fire door. A small metal box containing a keypad was affixed to the wall next to the door, a red light shining at the top. Rich punched in a seven digit code and the red light went off and a green light next to it lit up as the door clicked open. He held the door with his foot and dragged the box over to prop it open. Then he went back to the car and removed the second box from the trunk, much lighter than the first, and carried it into the room.

As soon as he crossed the threshold overhead fixtures automatically clicked on bathing the room in bright fluorescent light. On one wall, tools of every description hung on peg boards above two large chests containing even more tools. Across the way, several saws and sanders sat in a neat row on a worktable. Against the third wall stood a worktable, four feet deep by ten feet long. Another worktable, eight feet long, stood in the center of the room. Each workstation contained additional pull-down lighting and there were multiple electrical outlets on every wall. A power transformer stood in one corner and an industrial cooler in another and the room had completely self-contained heating and cooling, as well as a large capacity portable generator in case of power outages. Fumes were vented to the outside. The entire space was neat, clean and organized and almost resembled an operating room, it was that pristine. It had cost Rich many thousands of dollars to assemble and it was his favorite place in the world.

Rich picked the large box up off the floor and the door clanged shut. He hoisted the box up onto the table in the middle of the room and began removing various items, a metal box about one foot square, several hoses, two circuit boards and various other metal components, wiring and electrical parts. He did the same thing with the lighter box, pulling a series of medical-looking supplies, such as tubes, clamps and other related equipment out and placing them on the table. He lined the various items up in a row as though he were arranging for a sale and when he finished, stopped to admire his work. Then he went back to the house and returned with the Ohio file and the laptop, which he placed on one of the tables and plugged into an outlet. He rubbed his hands together. "Now, let's get started."

13

Ben read the paragraph for the fourth or fifth time and yawned. He looked at the clock on his desk – still only two-thirty and he felt like he hadn't slept in a week. In truth, he hadn't slept much. Between his inability to get Kessler out of his head and the six-hour drive back from northern Wisconsin, he felt pretty used up. They hadn't been able to get the kids packed up soon enough, they had absolutely, positively needed to do just one more run on the snowmobiles, and before you know it, it was past ten o'clock before they had gotten home and almost eleven before they had gotten the kids into bed. Anyway, it was worth it. Everyone had a great time. Only now he was paying for it. He looked at the interrogatories he had been reviewing and sighed. He tossed them on the desk as he stood to stretch his back, then turned to look out the window as a freight train rumbled by.

Another gloomy day in Chicago, he thought. Too cold to snow and no sunshine either. Ben hated this time of year. The football season just over, baseball still a couple of months away, and hockey and basketball in the doldrums before March Madness and the playoffs. And the weather sucked to boot. He decided to go downstairs and get something to drink. On his way downstairs, he stopped in Nancy's office and watched over her shoulder for a moment as she typed a letter. "What?" she said as she sensed him, stopped typing and spun around in her chair.

"Nothing," he said with a shrug. "Just not in the mood today, I guess."

"Welcome to my world. If you are looking for motivation, you ain't going to find it here. I've felt like that every day since New Year's. Now get going so I can finish this letter." She turned back to her computer and resumed typing.

"You're no fun," he said leaving the room and heading downstairs.

In the kitchen, Ben found Casey Gardner drinking a glass of water and reading the sports section of the *Tribune*. "Hey," Casey said looking up, "when does football start again?"

"Labor Day. What's that, six and a half months? Sooner if you count the exhibition season. But The Masters is in April."

"That's better than nothing," Casey said as he folded up the newspaper and tossed it on a pile at the end of the kitchen table. "How was your weekend snowmobiling in the Great White North? You look sun burned, or maybe wind burned."

Ben rummaged around in the refrigerator and pulled out a can of Coke. He popped the top and took a drink. "Has to be wind burned. Although I had a helmet on just about all the time I was outside. It was so damned cold you had to have every part of your exposed flesh covered. Otherwise it would've been unbearable."

"It was cold enough here. It had to be brutal way up there." They talked about the weather and snowmobiling for a few minutes, then Casey asked, "I heard you got some TV gigs this week. Are you going to be doing them out in the garage?"

The garage was what the firm called its library and conference room. Ben took a sip of his drink and nodded. "I think so, or least I hope so. It's a lot easier doing them here than having to go downtown."

"How many have you got?"

"Two so far. I've got Flaherty tomorrow afternoon and then Geraldo maybe later in the week, although I think we may try to tape it after Flaherty."

Casey whistled. "Flaherty, huh? You got the big dog. Pretty impressive. Let's see how many times he interrupts you."

78

Ben laughed. Brian Flaherty hosted The Flaherty Focus, the highest rated show on cable news. You either loved him or you hated him. He was big, brash and full of himself. But he also had a knack for asking questions that his viewers wanted answered, as well as pushing his guests until they actually answered those questions. If that meant that he had to interrupt or occasionally bully his guests, so be it. Ben had only been on his show a couple of times and had thus far been able to dodge the full Flaherty treatment. He had been treated pretty well, probably because Flaherty agreed with what Ben had been saying at the time. "Maybe we'll have to run an office pool on how many times he cuts me off," Ben said.

"But why are you doing it in the afternoon? His show isn't on until seven o'clock?"

"Flaherty doesn't like to do stuff live unless he absolutely has to. He tapes most of his stuff the same day. I don't think he edits as much as some guys do though. Mostly he just records it live and then replays it for the show. I hear Ted Koppel was that way too, probably because his show was on much later in the evening and it would have been harder to get guests if everyone was live. But he edited more. Anyway, you feel a lot more pressure live. It's never really happened to me, but I hope if I really fucked something up, they would edit it out. Like if I sneezed on myself or something. I suspect if I just said something stupid they would leave it in and let the host rip me apart."

"I never really thought of that," Casey said. "I just figured they did everything live. I'm somehow less impressed now."

"It's not as easy as it looks," Ben said. "Think how easy it is to have the words come out wrong when you're standing in court up in front of a judge. We've all done that and that's not live in front of ten million people on television. By and large they're pretty good. Sure, if you know the subject matter you can catch them saying the wrong thing or faking it from time to time, but most of these guys don't want to look like idiots on national television."

"I don't want to look like an idiot when I'm all by myself."

"You and me both," Ben said.

79

They talked about the television business and their lack of enthusiasm for work for a few more minutes before finally dragging themselves back to their respective offices. Ben hung on until about five-thirty, when he simply couldn't take it anymore, packed up and headed home. There, he found everyone feeling about the same way he did, slogging their way through a long day after a fun weekend. The kids didn't even put up much of a struggle at bedtime, which was highly unusual these days. Ben and Libby watched a little television after the kids went down, mostly in an exhausted silence, but their hearts weren't in it either and they turned in early themselves.

Ben slept soundly and woke up feeling refreshed and rejuvenated. Libby took care of the kids and since traffic was light, he got to the office shortly after eight. The inspiration of senior partner Jim Schulte, the original part of the office was a white frame Victorian house built in the 1890's. To this building, Schulte had attached a storefront grocery store originally found around the corner in downtown Itasca. The grocery store served as the main entrance to the building. On the other side of the grocery store, Schulte had built a two-story addition, which housed additional offices for both the firm and for a handful of renters, primarily other lawyers. Facing the railroad tracks, Schulte built a structure that appeared to be a modest-sized garage, complete with an old gas pump on the east side and what appeared to be the entrance to a barbershop on the west. The garage served as the building's library and conference room.

Ben found a parking space out front, grabbed his briefcase, and entered the main entrance of the building under the Matt's Grocery sign. There was no identification for the law firm or any of its tenants anywhere. The front door opened into a lobby that could only be described as unique. Opposite the front door sat a church pew facing a large wooden reception desk and fax machine, and two rocking chairs flanking a small table. One corner held a credenza complete with book shelves, while the other contained an open icebox dating from the 1940's with artificial food inside adding to the rustic country feel of the room.

A chandelier hung from a white, ornate trey ceiling made of faux plaster.

Ben dumped his coat and briefcase on the church pew and stepped around it into the kitchen. He picked through the piles of today's newspapers, scanned a few headlines, nothing terribly interesting, then tossed the last one back on the table, gathered his coat and briefcase and headed upstairs. It would be a rather routine morning, mostly devoted to drafting discovery responses, taking a few phone calls, and updating a couple of the condemnation files he was handling for the local forest preserve district. Despite his recent notoriety and television appearances that kept him somewhat in the limelight, he didn't have anything particularly interesting going on at the moment. Even the smattering of criminal cases that had been coming in with increasing regularity in the wake of the Law School Murder were pretty routine and not overly exciting. He hated to admit it, but the television appearances were probably the most interesting and fulfilling part of his regular schedule these days.

Ben skipped lunch in order to prepare for the interviews later that afternoon and went downstairs to grab a bottle of water just as the other guys in the office were finishing eating. He walked into the kitchen and right into the middle of a debate about spring guns and their use and legality in protecting one's home and property. A spring gun was a gun, frequently a shotgun, which was pointed at the door or window of a person's home. It was set to go off automatically when triggered by someone engaging in a home invasion. Most states had outlawed or severely restricted their use to situations where the homeowner reasonably believed he or she was in danger of great bodily harm. A simple robbery wasn't typically enough. It was the kind of thing you studied in law school. As usual, Brad Funk took the hard-line NRA approach. The others, while hardly bleeding heart liberals, took a more moderate position in their continued efforts to paint Funk as some kind of right-wing nut. Some things never changed.

As Ben pulled a bottle of water out of the refrigerator, Brian Davenport asked him, "you had that same tort book I had in law school. Did you guys cover that spring gun case in torts? It involved that old couple, I think in Iowa, who rigged a shotgun to fire at a window in their farmhouse. Some guy came through the window to rob the place and the gun blew off the bottom of his leg."

"We did actually. Remember, they had pictures of the old folks in the book? They looked just like *American Gothic*. In fact, years ago, I was in the Cook County Law Library downtown and I read a law review article about the case. I can't remember why or how I stumbled across it, but it was written by one of the judges on the Seventh Circuit Court of Appeals and was pretty funny. I think the guy who broke into the house lost his foot and sued for negligence or some intentional tort. I don't think the old folks were charged criminally, but the guy who broke in actually won his case. The author theorized that he won because he was really, really good looking and there were a bunch of women on the jury. Eventually, I think the old couple was about to lose the farm and they wound up on the same side as the guy they shot and against the bank. I think they teamed up to stave off the foreclosure, save the house and pay off the judgment. Pretty entertaining article."

"Who did you bill for that research?" Casey asked.

"No idea," Ben said. "Hopefully one of your clients. I don't even know how or why I would've been reading it in the first place. Glad I did though."

"In my opinion," Funk said, "there's nothing wrong with a spring gun."

Nobody doubted that for a minute.

Ben headed out to the garage at about two-fifteen. About the size of a normal two-car garage, it had tall ceilings that reached a peak in the center. A beam ran across the room parallel to the peak on which sat various military helmets and headgear of the last century. On the far wall, underneath a set of small windows, sat two barber chairs, a potbelly stove and an old shoeshine stand. The wall on the left contained an entrance from the parking lot masquerading as an entrance to a barber shop, complete with a barber pole on the outside wall. The near wall

82

heading to the right contained built-in bookshelves where the firm housed much of its law library. In the corner stood a five-foot high cast iron antique bank safe, which didn't house much of anything these days. A large oak library table, approximately ten feet long, dominated the middle of the room, surrounded by wooden library chairs. A series of stuffed animal heads adorned the walls – deer, elk, a razorback and a stuffed horse's ass with the caption, *"Res Ipsa Loquitur"*, Latin for "The Thing Speaks for Itself".

Ben parked himself at the table and reviewed the notes he received from Flaherty's producer in an email earlier in the day. While Flaherty liked to be spontaneous and could deviate from the subject matter at almost any moment, no producer wanted the guest to look like a deer in the headlights. That didn't make for good TV. Unless the guest was a politician or movie star. Ben knew that they would be talking about a light sentence given a pedophile in a child rape case, but he suspected that Kessler's murder would also come up as well. He wasn't too worried about Geraldo. His shows were much looser and Ben was pretty sure that he wasn't going to be grilled in the same manner as he would on Flaherty's show.

The TV guys showed up about three. Although Ben once did a live spot from one of the barber chairs, and one of Geraldo's producers once had the camera pan around to get a better look at the unique interior of the garage, they typically set up so that Ben's back was up against the law books so it looked like Ben was broadcasting from a traditional law office.

The interview with Geraldo went first, focusing on the Kessler murder, but in kind of a touchy-feely way that made Ben uncomfortable. It was a relatively short segment and Ben didn't even get to say too much. Then they had to wait around for Flaherty's people to get ready. Since it wasn't live, there was no set time for the taping and Flaherty always seemed to value his schedule more than his guests. They just shot the breeze until Ben heard Flaherty's booming voice in his ear piece. "You there counsel?" Flaherty asked.

"Right here," Ben replied. "I'm ready whenever you are."

"Good. Let's get started. Give me fifteen seconds and we'll be ready to go."

Flaherty was even more brusque than usual. Ben got the impression that he wasn't very interested in the pedophile case, but since he typically made a big deal out of soft sentences for child abusers, he couldn't just let this one slide. Finally, he turned to the Kessler murder. "So, Mr. Lohmeier, while I've got you here, I've got to ask you about the Kessler murder out in L.A. I'm really starting to think that there's a karma thing going on out there. Those lawyers who got Owens off when everybody thinks he did it are starting to drop like flies out there. A couple of them die of natural causes, cancer or something, then you got Lindsay in Florida falling on a flight of stairs and now this. What do you think?"

Ben shrugged, caught a little off guard. "I never really looked at it that way," he said. "It certainly doesn't appear that anything like this could be related in any way. I mean, you have a couple of deaths by natural causes, then an accident, now a murder. We don't know why Mr. Kessler was murdered or who did it, so it's hard to speculate."

They batted it around for a couple of minutes, Flaherty insisting that his karma theory helped make the universe run better, before he finally said, "well, we'll be following this story closely and when something new comes out, counsel, we'll have you back on to follow-up." Then he ended the segment with a tease for the following segment and was gone.

Ben pulled his ear piece out thinking the segment had gone okay, then stood and helped the technicians pack up their equipment. Soon, they too were gone and Ben was left with Flaherty's odd karma theory rolling around in his head, his small contribution to cable news completed for the day. A couple of hours later, while on his way home, Ben thought about the lawyers in the Owens case, each celebrated in his own way, then more so by their unexpected victory. If they were dying off, there were still a few more to go.

84

14

Rich looked at the directions printed off the Internet while he waited for the light to turn green. It was a right at the next light, then about a mile down until another right onto a street that looped around to the left and came back out half a mile from where it started. The target looked to be a couple of hundred yards from the corner as the road started a gentle curve. He figured it might be a mall or some kind of an office park. Five minutes later, he turned at a McDonald's and discovered he was almost right. Hotels and restaurants. And one office building. There was a Marriott Courtyard on the corner opposite the McDonald's and a chain steakhouse. A Holiday Inn Express stood behind the Marriott, three stories of rooms in a long row facing the road, and more importantly, the beautiful two-story brick and stone office building across the way. Rich laughed. It was perfect.

Rich began to slow to double check the address on the building, but he needn't have bothered. Out front, a large ornate sign on a brick pedestal proclaimed that he was in the right place. He kept on driving down around the curve, where he pulled into yet another hotel, turned around, and headed back for the Holiday Inn Express. He parked the Camry under the overhang at the entrance to the lobby and went inside to check in. He had no trouble getting a room on the second floor facing the office building, at the end of the row of rooms near a side entrance, yet still directly across from his target. He paid with a visa card that had been established long ago just for this purpose, took his key card and Wi-Fi instructions and headed back outside to his car. Rather than bring his bags directly to his room, Rich drove back to the McDonald's, ordered a Big Mac meal, and dumped his driving directions in the trash can next to the fountain drinks.

Half an hour later, back at the hotel, Rich unpacked his suitcases and settled in. He looked at his watch – four-thirty. It was early March in Ohio and would be starting to get dark in another hour and a half or so. He pulled the binoculars from his suitcase and got comfortable in the desk chair, his feet up on the radiator, as he began to study the habits and rhythms of the building across the way. Although he expected to be in Ohio for at least two weeks, he would stay in this hotel for no more than a week. He wanted to find other lodgings before the operation actually commenced. There were plenty to choose from.

From his research, Rich had learned that the office employed about forty people. Half of them were gone by five-fifteen, another dozen or so by six, and four more by seven. Assuming his research was correct, there couldn't be more than four to six people left in the building, and only three windows remained lit on this side of the building. By eight o'clock, all of these lights were out and no cars remained in the parking lot. Of course, he couldn't see the other side of the building and wasn't sure whether there was a parking lot out back, though he didn't think so. Still, he hadn't yet seen his target.

What Rich didn't know was that his target had been gone by two o'clock, before Rich ever got to the hotel. By two-thirty, Spencer Laughlin was perched in the small examining room at his internist's office talking about things he never wanted to talk about with anyone, such as waiting in line at a ballgame to pee and then not being able to go when it was his turn; such as not being able to get things cranked up when his wife was finally in the mood. The indignity of it all. Spencer Laughlin, the big trial lawyer, didn't have such problems. Not him. No, he had shaggy brown hair and a boyish charm that made female jurors swoon. He had the looks and personality that had made him big on television. What he didn't have was emergency trips to the

86

bathroom at three in the morning that resulted in nothing. What he didn't have was plumbing problems, as his doctor called them. When he left his doctor's office at three-thirty, Laughlin had a headache and an appointment with a urologist in two days. What he didn't have was any desire to return to the office. Or to go home for that matter.

He wound up at the multiplex about halfway between his home and office, with a box of popcorn he didn't really want and a bucket-sized Diet Coke that would go right through a normal guy but would only remind him of his difficulties as he watched his first movie in over a year, a Denzel Washington thriller. He had hoped that an action movie would take his mind off things. It didn't, not really, but Denzel was interesting as always and he kind of liked the CIA stuff. Halfway through, he had to turn off his cell phone because the constant vibrations were driving him crazy. Maybe he wouldn't even bother to check the messages. Nothing could be that urgent. Besides, that's what he hired people for, to handle things when he wasn't available. And now he wasn't available.

It was already dark by the time the movie let out and Laughlin figured he should have gone home for dinner even though he wasn't the least bit hungry. He clicked the phone back on and half-heartedly checked his messages. If there wasn't anything interesting in the first five seconds, he simply stopped listening and deleted it. There wasn't anything that couldn't wait. Two from his wife, three more from his secretary, a couple from the chief kiss ass in the office, and a bunch more he didn't really care about. Typical day.

Laughlin took the long way home, circling through neighborhoods he hadn't visited in years, occasionally seeing glimpses of other people's lives through their open curtains as he thought about life, mortality and the simple things such as urinating when you wanted to. Eventually, with nothing better to do, he wound up at home, just in time to force down chicken he didn't want to eat, while putting on a happy face for his wife and the two of his children who decided to show up for dinner. He should tell them about his doctor visit, he knew, or least tell his wife first, but he decided not to, at least not yet. He wanted to come to terms with it himself first before having to come to terms with everyone else. They would be sympathetic, of course, and perhaps shocked, but he had no interest in their sympathy or their understanding or even their shoulders to cry on. No, he would wait until he knew more. Spring break was coming in a few days and his wife was taking the three kids to Hilton Head for the week, while he stayed to handle a hearing he allegedly couldn't get out of. Truth be told, he wanted the time to himself, at least part of it anyway. Now he had more reasons to stay home. Hopefully, he would come to grips with it while they were gone and then figure out to what to do.

*****

At nine o'clock, Rich decided to take some action. He was getting antsy. He scanned the exterior of the office building across the way with the binoculars. Finding no evidence of any cameras, which surprised him, he concluded that a tour of the exterior of the building was in order. He changed into a pair of black jeans, with a black fleece jacket covering a charcoal gray turtleneck and topped it off with a pair of black plastic glasses with clear lenses and a Detroit Tigers baseball cap.

Since the stairs were just around the corner from his room, Rich was out the door and in the Camry in less than a minute. He paused for just a moment at the entrance to the hotel and, rather than go directly across the street into the parking lot of the office building, turned right and circled all the way around the access road until he came back at the main drag, where he took another right in search of something to eat. Half an hour later, after chicken tenders and mashed potatoes at a KFC a mile or so away, he retraced his route, but this time turned directly into the parking lot and around the left side to the back of the office building. There, he confirmed that there indeed was no additional parking lot in the back, only a steel service door flanked on one side by a large green dumpster and on the other by five parking spaces. A driveway about twenty feet wide traversed the entire back of the building. Beyond the driveway was a wetlands area that probably served as water retention.

Rich paused opposite the steel door and noticed an electronic security keypad on the wall next to it, but no evidence of any cameras. He rolled down the windows of the Camry and could hear wildlife chirping from the wetlands. Off in the distance, more than a quarter of a mile away, he could see the lights of another small office building. He looked back up at the building in question. There were offices all across the back and a balcony in the upper corner. That office would provide a nice view of the wetlands. He knew who likely sat in that office. The parking spaces probably served as private parking for the target and his senior staff so they wouldn't have to park with the clients out front and could make a quick getaway when necessary. After a minute or so, Rich rolled up the windows and slowly cruised back around the front of the building to the main entrance of the lot, where he turned right and headed back up the block to the McDonald's for a cup of coffee before returning to the hotel. He now had the lay of the land, at least part of it. A good start.

Wearing the same outfit as the night before, Rich was out the door by eight in the morning and on his way to the county government complex for some additional research of the public records. With only a little bit of difficulty, he identified the owners of the office building, and eventually tracked down some possibilities for the target's home address. He returned to the office a couple of hours later and circled the building again, acting like a client visiting the place for the first time and searching for a parking space. More importantly, he found that four of the parking spaces in back were occupied – three of the spaces held Japanese imports, the fourth a Porsche SUV. He felt pretty sure he knew whose car that was. It was after all still March in Ohio. Bad weather could crop up any day. He probably saved the sports car for the summertime.

Back in his room, Rich grabbed the binoculars and waited for lunch time. At exactly twelve-thirty, the Porsche pulled out from behind the building, paused briefly to let traffic go by, then turned right and headed toward the corner, its driver in full view. When Rich saw the shaggy hair and boyish features, he knew he was in business. He made no effort to run down to his car and

89

follow his target. He would do that later, if necessary. Instead, he took the directions he found on the Internet and headed out to check out the addresses he found at the county offices. By the end of the afternoon, after some missteps and wrong turns, he had narrowed his possibilities list to two homes, one about ten minutes from the office and the other about twice that. Rich was betting on the closer one. After all, why would a guy build a beautiful new office if he couldn't put it close to his home and make it as convenient for himself as possible. The closer home was also a lot grander in scale, a French provincial number with a four-car garage in back. It seemed to fit the target better.

Rich found a grocery store parking lot and eased the Camry into a space in a crowded section. Then he called up the Internet on his smart phone and found the home on MapQuest. He scrolled over until he found the office location and tried to compute the likely route the target would take between home and work. Due to the relatively small screen on the cell phone, his work was relatively slow going. Since he didn't really know the streets that well it was mostly guesswork, but eventually he came up with the path and followed it back in the direction of the office. About a mile from the home, and shortly after entering the commercial district, he spotted a two-story medical building on the right side of the road with a parking lot that offered a good view of the street. If he was right, and the target did in fact take this route between home and work, then this spot would have a good view of him traveling from right to left as he passed by. There were also plenty of streetlights which would help after it got dark.

Now he would just have to test this theory. He looked at his watch – a few minutes past four. He didn't expect the target anytime soon, but then he didn't know what time to expect him. It could be five minutes or five hours. He thought he looked like just another guy waiting for someone visiting the doctor inside the building. Patients would come and go and no one would give him a second thought until the parking lot really starting to empty, which probably wouldn't be for several hours.

As rush-hour commenced, traffic began to build and the watch grew more challenging. Fortunately, there weren't many Porsche SUVs, even in this affluent area. Of course, if he had the wrong home and the wrong car, he could sit there all night and not see the person he was looking for. But that wasn't the case. Shortly after six, a Porsche cruised by that looked just like the one in the office parking lot. Rich hit the engine and moved quickly to the entrance of the lot. Because of the traffic, it took him a little bit of time to make the left turn, and he lost the Porsche in the flow of other cars. But that didn't bother him too much because he knew where he was heading. Since he was hoping to see the target at the home and confirm he had the right car and right place, he hustled through traffic before making another left into the residential part of town. He was about a half-mile out now and he took a right one block early so he wouldn't be seen coming up quickly from behind. He turned the corner just as the Porsche pulled into a driveway halfway down the block. Bingo. Now he just had to make sure he had the right guy. He eased the Camry down the block trying to time it just right. As he passed the driveway, he looked through the passenger side window and saw Spencer Laughlin emerging from his garage, his head down and his overcoat slung over his right arm.

15

The following day, Laughlin cleared his entire afternoon for his visit to the urologist and subsequent tests. The folks at the office thought it a bit strange that he would be gone for the second afternoon in three days without telling anybody where he was going or what he was doing, but they were used to his mercurial behavior enough to not ask any questions. Since his wife rarely visited him at the office or even called him on the phone during the day, she wasn't much of a problem either. He was done being probed and prodded by five o'clock. The doctor confirmed that he indeed had an enlarged prostate and possibly more than that. The results of a biopsy would confirm whether or not he also had prostate cancer. Either way, the doctor assured him, advances in treatment virtually guaranteed that he would live a long and normal life and would likely even be cured. Surgery such as the kind he needed was fairly routine these days, the doctor insisted. Laughlin took it with a grain of salt. He'd done enough medical malpractice work over the years to know full well that the only routine surgery was the surgery performed on the other guy. He took his stack of literature on side effects such as erectile dysfunction and headed for the door. He would read that when he finished *The Trial* in the original German. Now he needed a good stiff drink.

The real news occurred the following morning, when Laughlin learned that his most famous client was getting out of prison. Thomas Strustevich had been a rather undistinguished surgeon for most of his career. He was competent, but not spectacular, and certainly did not fit the profile of the rich, successful doctor. He had briefly had his own practice, but that didn't really work out, so mostly he worked in County hospitals and eventually VA hospitals. He actually liked working for the VA because he took comfort in the idea that he was helping veterans who had served their country get the treatment they deserved.

It was at the VA after the first Gulf War where Strustevich, already in his sixties, developed the theories that would make him famous, or rather infamous. While treating those returning from combat with grievous injuries suffered on the battlefield, he encountered numerous patients who didn't know if they could go on and many more who knew they didn't want to. He tried his best to understand them – their needs, their suffering, and their desire to end it all. At first, he found the notion abhorrent. He knew the Hippocratic oath. He knew that his duty was to inflict no harm. Yet, as he grew closer to several of these patients, he came to realize that forcing them to suffer for years and maybe decades may be inflicting the most harm of all.

He knew that this notion was really nothing new. Doctors had been helping terminally ill patients end their suffering for as long as there were doctors and patients. It happened in hospitals throughout America each and every day. Only no one talked about it. A little too much morphine here, not enough something else there and the patient could easily just slip away. Rarely did anyone look too closely at it since the patient was going to die anyway and everyone knew it and probably figured it was for the best. But those were the easy cases. The harder ones occurred when there wasn't a terminal illness, just long, pronounced suffering and an unflinching desire to end it. These were the cases that offended everyone's sensibilities.

Strustevich soon became obsessed with the cause of euthanasia. He began by writing articles and seeking out those with similar points of view, however, his efforts gained little traction. Eventually, he concluded that the only true way to bring this issue into the public consciousness was to take action, not just in the easy cases that no one knew about, but in the hard

93

ones that would make headlines. Although he knew eventually that he would cross the Rubicon, he began with the easier case of a Marine sergeant wounded in a mortar attack. Left paralyzed from the middle of his chest down, the man suffered immensely. He became a heavy smoker because it was the only thing he enjoyed in life. Smoking only further complicated his condition and eventually he developed a tumor in one of his lungs, which Strustevich was tasked with removing in a Detroit VA Hospital.

As he prepared for the surgery, Strustevich spent an unusual amount of time with this patient. They talked about life and death, suffering and relief, often late into the night. When the patient eventually said that he wanted to die and Strustevich was truly convinced that he really meant it, he replied that he understood and was ready to help. Having thought about this for some time, Strustevich had already devised a method for making it a reality. He designed and built a machine that would allow a patient to take his or her own life.

Called a *thanatron*, meaning "death machine", it was based upon the lethal injection system of execution used by many states. It contained three bottles attached to the patient via an intravenous line and connected by a series of tubes and hoses. The first bottle contained a simple saline solution, the second a solution of sodium thiopental designed to put the patient to sleep, and the third contained potassium chloride which stopped the heart. When ready, the patient would flip a lever or hit a button releasing the solutions in sequence. The whole process took only a few minutes and Strustevich would be present to pronounce death and ensure that the procedure was completed as intended.

That first Marine sergeant was the most difficult. He was scared that the thanatron wouldn't work and the man would be left worse off than he had started. But it had worked and the sergeant's life had floated away peacefully and easily. That first death attracted little attention. The authorities soon began to take notice, however, and when he did it again and again and started writing and speaking on the subject, everybody took notice and Strustevich became world famous as The Grim

94

Reaper. Investigations and charges followed, and when they did, Strustevich hired the flamboyant Spencer Laughlin, a local lawyer he had first seen on cable television, to defend him.

Laughlin and Strustevich had hit it off right away. Laughlin liked the older man's sense of humor, such as it was, and found him intelligent and highly principled. Most importantly, Laughlin, a liberal himself, believed in the cause. He viewed euthanasia as a civil rights issue of sorts and liked the image of defending a man of honor and principle. He also liked the publicity and knew that Strustevich would raise his lawyer's profile in the legal community nationally and put dollars in his pocket through higher fees and more and better cases. Laughlin realized that defending Strustevich would be expensive and time-consuming in the short run, but would undoubtedly pay off over time.

The first trial, on a second degree murder charge for assisting in the death of a retired auto worker stricken with stomach cancer, took six weeks to try and resulted in a not guilty verdict. Strustevich was now both a folk hero and a villain and Laughlin was even a bigger star. Feeling vindicated, The Grim Reaper pushed the envelope and stepped up his activities. He designed a newer and better thanatron, continued speaking out on the rights of the terminally ill and pushed his point of view wherever he could. The second trial, for assisting in the death of grandmother with emphysema, took place two years later and resulted in a hung jury, split evenly with six jurors voting to convict and six to acquit. By now, Strustevich had assisted in the deaths of more than forty people.

The public and the legal community in Ohio seemed equally split. There were suggestions that Strustevich had done more than simply provide the thanatron to some of his patients and had even pulled the lever for several patients unable to do it themselves. While the district attorney's office wanted no part of another trial, the district attorney himself figured that they couldn't just roll over and let The Grim Reaper continue to kill people. Strustevich had them in a real box. Eventually, they started talking about a plea agreement where Strustevich would agree to stop his activities in exchange for some form of probation. Privately, even Laughlin thought this was a good idea. He told Strustevich that his point had been made and that the public was moving in his direction. He had won twice. Why press his luck by rubbing their noses in it. Take the deal.

The Grim Reaper didn't see it that way. He viewed himself as the leader of a crusade and pushed on. When the prosecutors discovered evidence of more assisted deaths, some of them videotaped, they had little choice but to try again. The third time was the charm. Armed with the videotapes and a more favorable jury, the state finally secured a conviction for second degree murder and the judge sentenced the 74-year old physician to fifteen years in prison. Appeals were unsuccessful. Both Laughlin and Strustevich were devastated. Five years passed, with Laughlin visiting his client monthly, until the doctor suffered a heart attack and Laughlin began pushing for an early release on health grounds. After more than a year of working on it, including physical examinations and much haggling, the state finally agreed. Strustevich would be coming home in two weeks.

*****

Rich found out about the release from cable television in his hotel room as he peeled off his cold-weather gear at two in the morning. He had just returned from a fruitful surveillance mission at Laughlin's house. Dropping his car in a school parking lot three blocks away, he had walked over to the house that backed up to Laughlin's without seeing a single soul. After looking in all directions to make sure that he was clear, he simply strolled up the neighbor's side yard and cut behind the detached garage, which provided perfect cover. Picking through the dense landscaping, Rich easily found a dark spot at the corner of Laughlin's own garage that provided a perfect view of the back of the house. With the help of a small, portable telescope, Rich spied a security keypad on the wall opposite the French doors to the patio between the kitchen and family room.

At about eleven-thirty, Laughlin and his wife shut off the lights, set the alarm and headed upstairs. A moment later, lights went on in the master bedroom upstairs. They were off by midnight. About fifteen minutes after that, just as Rich was thinking about packing up and leaving for the night, one of Laughlin's sons, who looked to be about seventeen, appeared in the back hall. Without turning on any lights, he shut off the alarm and quietly snuck out the French doors to the patio, pausing for a moment to send a text message from his cell phone. Watching him, Rich tensed and prepare to flee in case the boy headed in his direction. Rich needn't have worried because the teenager turned up the driveway and hopped into a car which arrived just as he reached the street. Rich smiled. The kid reminded Rich of himself at that age. Up to no good.

Rich decided to stick around until the kid came home, figuring it was a school night and the kid probably needed to get at least some sleep. As it turned out, he was gone for little more than an hour, returning the same way he had left. He bounded down the driveway and up the steps to the patio with a satisfied smile on his face, causing Rich to wonder exactly what he'd been up to. Rich pulled out the telescope and watched him closely as he stopped at a planter on the patio and pulled a box containing a silver key out of an evergreen bush to unlock the back door. Leaving the door open, the boy returned the key to its hiding place and stepped back inside. Since he had turned the alarm off when he left, Rich would not be picking up the deactivation code this evening, for all Laughlin's son would do now would be to reset the alarm, but Rich would get the code soon enough. It was only a matter of time. A moment later, the teenager was back upstairs and Rich was half a block away heading back to his car.

16

Rich watched the house diligently for the next few nights. On the third night, he picked up the security code when the Laughlins returned after being gone for more than two hours. This allowed Rich to plant a small listening device under the breakfast bar in the kitchen the following evening when the family was out to dinner. He learned of the family's spring break plans the next night as Emily Laughlin and her daughter tried to convince Spencer to either move his hearing or come out to Hilton Head as soon as it was completed. Although Rich was thrilled to learn that he would have Laughlin all to himself, he nevertheless couldn't understand why he would rather be in dreary Ohio in the middle of March than lounging on a beach somewhere in South Carolina. Didn't make any sense. Maybe he had something going on the side or was just sick of the family and wanted some time to himself. Either way, it would turn out to be a big mistake.

Rich checked out of the Holiday Inn Express a day later and found a room in another chain hotel across town. He spent the next three or four days finalizing his plans and then it was simply a matter of waiting for spring break to arrive. He even had time to go see that Denzel Washington movie that Laughlin had seen days before. He wouldn't do anything that first night. He wanted to see for sure what Laughlin was up to, but after that it was go time. He had accumulated enough information since he had been in town that he felt comfortable and confident in his plan, and in his ability to pull it off.

Laughlin drove the family to the airport in the Porsche on Thursday evening. Everyone got a jump on spring break these days. Rich knew that the trip would take a while so he slipped in the back door while they were gone and took a look around. He particularly liked Laughlin's office on the first floor off of the living room, complete with cherry wood paneling and a leather inlaid mahogany desk. Rummaging through the briefcase left on a small leather couch in the office, Rich discovered the reading material that Laughlin had received from his urologist. He whistled as he paged through it. "Our man has pecker problems it seems," he said to the quiet room. "No matter." Within fifteen minutes, he was gone.

The following evening, with nothing really urgent going on at the office, the place cleared out early and with nothing to go home to, Laughlin was the last one out the door shortly after six. He stopped at the steakhouse next door for a leisurely dinner, then headed on home. After leaving the car in the driveway in front of the garage, he entered the house through the patio doors, turned off the alarm, and tossed his keys on the island in the kitchen. The sound of the forced air heat coming on broke the silence as he removed his cashmere overcoat and laid it across the back of the couch in the family room.

With everyone gone, the house had the feel of an empty stadium waiting for a game. Eventually, he wandered back through the butler's pantry and grabbed a wine glass out of the china cabinet on his way to the kitchen. On the island next to his keys stood a half-full bottle of merlot that he had cracked when he had gotten home from the airport the previous evening. Despite the wine cellar in the basement, which was more for show than anything, he wasn't much of a connoisseur. He popped the cork, sniffed the bottle and shrugged, then filled the glass and headed over to the family room and his favorite leather club chair.

He knew he didn't want to watch cable news and since he wasn't much of a basketball fan, he looked for either a Red Wings game or a movie. He soon discovered that the Red Wings were off tonight, so that left him with a movie. If he wasn't having issues, he might have considered porn or Cinemax, probably Cinemax since his wife paid the cable bill. That was out now. Why rub your own nose in it. He scrolled through the channels before settling on a thriller on HBO that had begun twenty minutes earlier. He nursed the wine as he watched the movie and tried to figure out what was going on in the plot. Within the hour, he felt himself starting to doze off, startled to look at his watch and discover that it was barely nine o'clock. He tried to stick it out until the end of the movie, but eventually gave up since he really wasn't into it. Figuring that maybe he would feel more refreshed after a shower, he drained the wine, left the glass by the sink and headed upstairs.

*****

Rich emerged from the work room in the basement precisely at ten. The house felt dead, empty, even though he knew it wasn't. Not yet. He crept to the bottom of the basement stairs and listened. Nothing. Just the click of the furnace. He made it up the stairs slowly, taking more than two minutes to navigate the side of each stair on the balls of his feet. No creaks on the carpeted steps. He paused again at the top and listened again. Still nothing. The basement stairs were placed near the end of the central hallway that bisected the middle of the home, near the kitchen and family room, which were now located to his right, and light from the kitchen spilled back down the hallway toward the foyer and front door. He stuck his head out and cleared both directions. Stepping into the kitchen, he saw the wine bottle and glass on the kitchen island and smiled, then glanced into the empty family room, now dark. Laughlin was upstairs.

He stuck his head in the office just to make sure it was empty, then crept upstairs, his silenced 9mm Beretta in his hand. A chandelier illuminated the upstairs landing and more light leaked out from the master bedroom, where Rich found Spencer Laughlin passed out on his bed, flat on face, arms at his side, still fully clothed but for his shoes. He was snoring softly.

100

Rich watched him for a minute. Then another. Finally, he cleared his throat and said, "Spencer?" There was no response. Just more snoring. He tried again, only louder this time. "Mr. Laughlin?" More snoring. Then Rich moved over to the other side of the bed where he could have a better look. Laughlin was out. Wearing gloves, Rich turned him over while he kept the gun pointed directly at Laughlin's head. Once Rich had Laughlin on his back, he slapped him briskly on the cheek, not enough to leave a mark, but enough to wake up a normal man, one who hadn't been drugged.

Rich nodded. The wine had done the trick. He had seen the open bottle on the counter in the kitchen and two more of the same vintage in the wine cellar. He drugged the open one and left it on the counter for Laughlin. Eventually he would drink it, probably tonight, but certainly within the next couple of days. He would replace it with one of the untainted bottles and take the first one with him on the way out. Confident that Laughlin would not be waking up any time soon, Rich headed back downstairs to get his things.

He returned with a backpack over one shoulder and carrying a box roughly two feet square. Rich laid the box on the bed and dropped the backpack to the floor. Then he looked around the room and took note of the windows. A couple of them had the blinds up and Rich quickly closed them so he couldn't be seen from the backyard. Then he took his thanatron out of the box and placed it gently on the bed.

It was truly a work of art, much better than the one Strustevich had used even though the design was similar. All of the parts were generic in nature, virtually untraceable and readily available here in Ohio. That was important. Now he came to the hard part. He had to get Laughlin's fingerprints on as many of the parts and mechanisms as possible, while hoping that whatever traces of the gloves he was using would not be too suspicious. After much thought, Rich concluded that the authorities would probably expect that Laughlin had sought help in building the machine, as he was a lawyer and not an engineer, but would not want the party who had helped him to be implicated in his death.

101

He struggled with Laughlin for almost a half hour before he was ready to proceed. Then he plugged the thanatron into the wall socket under the night stand and connected the vials of the three drugs that in combination would end Spencer Laughlin's life. He knew his machine would work, because he had tested it on a cat at the farm, but he checked and double-checked all of the connections. As he stood over Laughlin, something occurred to him that he had almost forgotten – the note.

Rich hustled back downstairs to the office, sat behind the desk and tapped the keyboard with a pencil. Already on, it fired right up. He opened up a blank Word document and using the eraser end of the pencil typed a simple note:

I can't face what's coming. I'm so sorry.
Please forgive my weakness and my mistakes.

Then he printed it and signed Laughlin's initials the way he had seen Laughlin had done in a letter in his briefcase. He studied the note. Vague enough to cover almost anything, yet specific enough to point to Strustevich and even the prostate problems. Perfect.

He hurried back upstairs with the note and the pencil, manipulated both with Laughlin's hands, and placed them on the nightstand. Then he inserted a needle into Laughlin's left arm. It was easier than he expected. After one last deep breath, he took the victim's right hand and flicked the red switch on the end of the machine letting Laughlin drop back down onto the bed. The machine whirred. The saline solution entered Laughlin's arm first, then the sodium thiopental followed a few moments later, putting Laughlin into an even deeper sleep. He made an exaggerated snoring sound at this point. The potassium chloride came last, stopping the heart just as intended. Laughlin made a final sound almost like a sigh. The death rattle? Rich didn't know for sure. He thought of the poem by T.S. Eliot – *This is the way the world ends. Not with a bang but a whimper.*

Rich stood silently at the end of the bed studying Spencer Laughlin as he died. He was mesmerized. No more television for him. He removed a stethoscope from his backpack and then put it back. There was no point. He checked the man's pulse. It was over. The thanatron continued to whirr. It would eventually shut itself off. Rich had thought of that too. He looked at the machine. He hated to leave it. Then he nodded, gathered up his things, and headed downstairs. He replaced the wine, putting the drugged wine in the box that had previously held the thanatron, took one last look around and was gone. Within an hour, he had cleared out of his hotel. Within four more, he was already crossing the border into Illinois.

17

Ben looked up as he heard Phil bounding up the stairs. A moment later, his out of breath boss stuck his head through the narrow French doors separating their offices and said, "Hey, come in here. You've got to see this." He turned on the television hanging from a bracket in the corner of his office and stepped back as Ben joined him.

"What is it?"

"I just heard in the car coming in that Spencer Laughlin, you know, Dr. Doom's lawyer, was found dead in his home. Looks like a suicide."

"Dr. Doom?"

"Yeah, you know, the suicide guy."

"Dr. Doom isn't the suicide guy. Dr. Doom is from Spiderman, or maybe the Fantastic Four, I forget which. It's been a while."

"Whatever."

"The suicide guy is The Grim Reaper, Strustevich."

"That's right. The Grim Reaper. I almost like Dr. Doom better. Anyway, they found Laughlin dead this morning. His wife and kids had apparently been out of town and no one had heard from him for a few days so they went in and checked on him and found him dead."

Ben stood there stunned as he processed the information. Another famous lawyer dead? Phil flipped the channels until he

104

found the story on CNN as Nancy came in and joined them. "What's going on?" she asked.

Phil told her, then turned to Ben and asked, "Did you know him at all or do any shows with him?"

Ben shook his head. "No, not that I can remember. He was on Geraldo a lot back in the day, especially during the Owens trial, but I hadn't seen him much lately."

"Wow," Nancy said, "this is real spooky. Especially with Dr. Doom getting out of jail in a few days."

Phil gave Ben a look and they both said, "The Grim Reaper."

"It's still spooky."

They watched the coverage for a few minutes. When the CNN reporter mentioned speculation that Laughlin had used the death machine, known as a thanatron, to kill himself, Phil groaned. "What? Did he just happen to have one laying around?"

"Maybe Dr. Doom had extras," Nancy said.

"How many do you need?" Phil asked.

"Some of them are probably in an evidence locker somewhere," Ben pointed out. "He had, what, two or three trials? They must've rounded them all up. Doubt the state returned them."

They went on like that for a few minutes until the coverage started repeating itself and eventually Ben and Nancy wandered back to their offices. A few minutes later, Nancy buzzed him. "I've got Marcia Roberts on the line for you. Should've figured that was coming."

Ben nodded. "Yeah, no doubt. Put her through." Ben waited until he heard the click of the call coming on the line, then said, "Hey, Marcia, what's up?"

"I'm so glad you're there. I'm really up against it here with this Laughlin thing hitting this morning and I need bodies."

"It's so nice to be wanted."

"You know how it is. The news never sleeps. Things happen and you have to move. You did hear about Laughlin offing himself, didn't you?"

105

"Yeah, a few minutes ago. My boss had CNN on in his office." She growled and Ben continued. "I'm not kidding. You guys were doing something on the budget and we flipped around until we found it on CNN. Apparently you aren't moving fast enough."

"Well, that's why I'm on the phone with Clarence Darrow."

"Okay, what do you need?"

"Can you get downtown to the studio like right now? I can put you on all afternoon, probably once an hour or two. Probably again in the evening."

Ben groaned. "I don't know. I'm in the middle of some stuff here." Truth was, he really wasn't all that busy. He could probably spare her the time. He just wanted to hear her beg a little.

"Come on, Ben, help a girl out, will you? Shit. Who made you a star anyway?"

"Hey," Ben said, "I resent that."

"You know what I mean. I keep you out there. I help put money in your pocket. Give me a break here and help me out. Bring your work with you. I'm sure they can find you an empty office to use between spots."

Ben had already thought of that. "You could always put more money in my pocket if you worked at it a little." He paused as though considering his options. He knew that competing producers on the same network often battled for the same guests, but when a big story hit, it was all hands on deck, and since Ben was already a "contributor" to the network, he was more available to everyone. "I suppose," he said finally, "I could spare you some time."

They hashed out the details for a few minutes before Ben signed off. He stuck his head into Phil's office and told him he was going downtown. "Should've figured as much," Phil said. "Any prime time?"

"Loretta probably."

Phil nodded. "That should be good pub. Don't throw up on yourself."

"That's typically one of my goals. I'll take some stuff with me to work on between spots."

Within five minutes, Ben was in the car and on his way downtown. When he entered the Fox studio downtown overlooking the Chicago River, an assistant handed him a stack of reading material on Spencer Laughlin and showed him to a closet-sized, windowless office on the second floor.

He did three spots in the afternoon and another during the dinner hour on the business network, then had to wait around for Loretta Bergen's show, which didn't come on until nine o'clock. Although he felt like he didn't have much to say and certainly nothing profound, the spots had generally gone pretty well. Usual cable news-type stuff. The briefing material had given him some additional knowledge of which he had previously been unaware, such as more details about Laughlin's other high-profile cases, information about Strustevich and his trials, and some stuff about his political aspirations.

By the time Loretta's show rolled around, Ben was tired and looking forward to getting it over with and going home. He was due on during the second block after the first commercial and was told that he could extend into the third block as well if things were going well, but not to count on it. What he hadn't counted on was making news. Perhaps because he was tired, he had inadvertently blurted out exactly what was on his mind. In response to a comment about Laughlin's alleged method of taking his own life, Ben had made a face, which Loretta had picked up on in the split screen view on her monitor. "Mr. Lohmeier, you seem bothered about something."

"Well," Ben said his mind suddenly going somewhat blank, "how do we really know at this point that he killed himself at all?" Then he really stepped in it, saying what he had been thinking for some time. "Really, when you get right down to it, the same goes for Pat Lindsay in Florida a couple of months ago. How do we know he really just fell down the stairs? There weren't any witnesses, were there?"

All the guests were talking at once and Loretta had to restore order. "With Lindsay," she said, "the coroner reported that he was legally drunk at the time. I think he had around a .2 blood alcohol level."

Ben was undeterred. "A lot of people drink. Lindsay drank. He drank a lot. That was no big secret from what we hear. Not a lot of people fall down the stairs and break their necks. It's worth considering given the circumstances."

Now they were off to the races. Soon, they were in the midst of a free-for-all, which didn't often happen on Loretta's program. Ben had put himself in the position of defending a theory he hadn't even really thought through. They argued about Lindsay, Kessler, and Laughlin and blew through three full segments. Toward the end of the final segment, one of the other guests, a former Los Angeles prosecutor with whom Ben had been on television previously, pointed out that Strustevich was soon to get out of prison and speculated how a new wave of publicity may have weighed on Laughlin.

"I don't buy it," Ben said. "By all accounts, Laughlin and Strustevich had always gotten along. Laughlin represented him in three trials and had visited him regularly in prison. Then he helped him get a medical release. Then, throw in the fact that representing him made Laughlin even more famous, especially when he basically won the first two trials. Being famous certainly didn't seem to bother Laughlin any. I'm just not seeing the distraught lawyer in all this."

"But we're also hearing stories about some possible health problems," Loretta said. "What do you make of those?"

Ben shrugged. "It's hard to say without more information. I'm just saying that perhaps we shouldn't take all this at face value."

When they went to commercial the last time, Loretta said, "good job, guys. That was pretty entertaining. Thanks."

"I didn't mean to start something," Ben said.

"But you certainly did," one of the other guests said.

"Yeah, well,"

"Don't worry about it," Loretta added. "You got me thinking."

Ben stewed about it all the way home. Although he realized that things often came off differently to an observer rather than a participant, especially on television, he grew increasingly concerned that he hadn't appeared to be some sort of a kook. He walked in the door, found Libby sitting on the couch with the television off, her hands folded in her lap, a smile on her face. She looked at him with eyes wide. He got the impression that she had just turned the television off, for he could see it glowing. Probably recorded the show, he thought.

"So," he said as he took his coat off and tossed it in a chair, "how bad was it?"

"Which show?"

He tilted his head and gave her a look. "Which show? I think you know which show."

"It wasn't bad at all. It was kind of like being in someone's living room with everyone talking at once. Very entertaining. I think some of the other people on the show took what you were saying to the extreme, but all in all, I think you only really said what a lot of people are already thinking."

Ben shook his head and plopped down on the couch. "Great. It was even worse than I thought. The lunatic spokesman for the idiot masses."

"Oh, it wasn't that bad at all. Besides, what if you turn out to be right? Then you'll have vision where the rest of the world wears bifocals."

He shot her another look. "Thanks Sundance."

Rather than live through it again on replay, Ben went up to bed. Since he had court the following morning, he didn't get into the office until ten-thirty. He poked his head into Dan Conlon's office on his way upstairs. When Dan saw him, he waved both hands over his head and yelled, "hey everybody! It's Oliver Stone! Who killed JFK?"

Ben just shook his head and went upstairs. Phil was sitting behind his desk and when he saw Ben he called, "hey, I thought I told you not to throw up on yourself."

Ben walked into Phil's office and stood in front of his desk. He shrugged and made a face. "I must've missed that part." Phil laughed. "That bad?" Ben said.

"No, I didn't think so, not really. It just sort of came out of nowhere. Loretta looked like she more or less lost control. My wife said she looked like she was herding cats."

Ben nodded. "Not a bad analogy really."

"You are going to have a hell of a time at lunch though. I think the guys have been working on their one-liners all morning."

"I gathered that."

"They're just jealous."

"Right."

Actually, most of the ribbing was out of the way by the time they had reached one of the local Mexican places they frequented for lunch. By the time they had returned to the office with their tacos and burritos, they were into a full-blown speculation as to who could have killed Lindsay and Laughlin, if they were indeed killed at all. They eventually agreed on virtually nothing other than the fact that Laughlin couldn't have been killed by a copycat since everyone thought Lindsay had died in an accident in the first place. Ultimately, it turned into a more vulgar and less sympathetic version of Loretta Bergen's show from the previous evening. A lot of heat, but not much light.

Ben's appearance on the show had done something else – it caused the telephones to ring non-stop. On his way out the door at three, Phil stuck his head in and whispered, "I'd leave early before you get lynched. That or offer to buy drinks for all the secretaries."

Ben looked up and pointed at him. "Now that's an idea."

They started filtering over to the bar across the way by quarter to six, the offer of drinks having satisfied those who chose not to come, the drinks themselves mollifying Nancy. Halfway through the second round, someone asked Ben, "when are you back on the air? I want to set my Tivo."

Ben took a drink of his beer and answered, "I told them I was busy and wasn't available until Monday." It was only Thursday. It would either die down completely or explode by then.

"Someone called from Flaherty's show," Nancy said. "Even the big dog noticed."

"Maybe by Monday they won't want me anymore."

Casey Gardner doubted it. "Laughlin won't be any less dead by Monday and I doubt seriously we'll know any more facts by then."

No one disagreed with that.

18

Ray Fisher tipped the cab driver, slung the folding bag over his shoulder, and grabbed the suitcase out of the trunk of the cab. As he walked up the driveway, he could feel the heat coming up off the asphalt. It was an unusually warm day for this time of year, with temperatures in the LA area reaching ninety. He couldn't wait to get inside and get the air conditioning cranked up. As he reached the front door of the three-bedroom ranch in Yorba Linda that he had called home for almost ten years, a bead of sweat was already rolling down his cheek. He set down the suitcase and fumbled through the overnight bag looking for his keys. He had been forced to leave his beloved Spanish villa in Westwood when his marriage fell apart due to their unusual circumstances.

But that didn't matter now. He knew now that a home is just a place where you lived and slept. He hadn't even been by the villa in Westwood in more than five years. There was a time when he didn't even like to take business trips because they would take him away from home. Now he might be gone for weeks at a time, just like this past trip which took him to the Midwest. He had owned his own technology company for more than twenty years, specializing in computer security and regulatory compliance systems. He ran the business out of his home, using one of his spare bedrooms as an office. Although some of the systems were fairly complex and quite expensive, he rarely kept any actual inventory on hand. Rather, as a wholesaler, he kept a virtual inventory, assembling the systems online from one of his myriad of vendors, who would put the physical products together and then ship directly to the customer under the name of Fisher's company.

The first thing he did after turning on the air was take a shower. He thought about picking up his mail from his post office box, but decided that could wait. After the shower, as he was getting dressed, he switched on the television and tuned to a cable news channel despite himself. He hated cable news. They were discussing the death of Spencer Laughlin, the famed lawyer from outside of Cleveland. Fisher sat on the bed in just his short-sleeved polo and his boxers, one of his shoes in his hand, his hair still damp. He remembered Laughlin from the coverage of the trial and had never liked him. He would not be missed, least of all by Ray Fisher. Laughlin was just another one of the leeches, and he deserved whatever he got. The way Fisher saw it, he had it coming. Maybe an ill wind does blow some good.

As he watched the coverage and the endless speculation, still holding the shoe, he considered the fickle nature of crime and punishment in America and wondered if it was better in a place like Turkey, or Saudi Arabia maybe. He probably wouldn't like it in any of those places either. He liked America. He liked capitalism. He had made a lot of money and had what most people would consider a good life here. Yet he knew in every fiber of his being, deep in his very soul, that there was no true justice in America. There was only justice for the few, for the privileged, for the connected and the chosen. The rest of us suffered through legal Darwinism. That had to change. He was trying to do his part to make it change. Part of it was all this shit on cable TV. All these idiots spouting all this bullshit when they really didn't know what the hell they were talking about. They had never been the victims of crime. They had never suffered loss. They didn't know. Someone would have to teach them. Someone would have to make them understand.

He watched for a few more minutes, thought about Spencer Laughlin hooked up to that machine, and all of these idiots trying to explain it, and capitalize on it, and get ratings, and make money off of a dead man. The whole thing disgusted him. Another dead lawyer. Another dead TV lawyer. What do they call that? A good start.

19

The phone calls didn't stop. Try as he might, Ben could not easily get out from under the comments he had made on Loretta Bergen's show the previous week. In addition to Fox's bevy of producers, Ben heard from local and national networks, bloggers, and a wide variety of newspapers, including the *New York Times*. He had literally opened the floodgates and now everyone with a voice and a forum was speculating about whether Laughlin and Lindsay had been murdered, and, if so, whether their deaths were linked to Kessler's. For his part, Ben did little to walk back his comments. In a reasoned and professional way, Ben calmly pointed out that there did not appear to be any definitive evidence conclusively establishing that Lindsay's death was an accident and Laughlin's a suicide. He had been concerned at the start that he would be labeled a conspiracy theorist – not necessarily an insult on cable TV – but that never really seemed to materialize other than the joking from the guys in the office. Expressing confidence in the police, he suggested that it would ultimately put an end to the speculation once and for all if they simply told the world what the evidence showed.

More than anything, the uproar put greater focus and attention on the police. In North Palm Beach, the police were forced to reopen a case they had already closed, while their counterparts outside of Cleveland were forced to conduct an investigation still in its infancy with a much greater degree of public scrutiny. Both departments felt compelled to reach out to one another and to the police in Los Angeles to determine whether there was any connection between the three deaths. Media personnel flooded the three cities in a feeding frenzy of activity with cable shows hop-scotching from one place to the other in search of the best visuals or the latest scoop.

Unfortunately, the police were not making much headway. In Florida, they couldn't prove that anyone had been in Lindsay's home other than his once-a-week housekeeper and no one really suspected a 55-year-old Polish immigrant of killing him. The only suspicious activity was a series of three telephone calls in the week preceding Lindsay's death, each from the same cell phone number, which turned out to be an untraceable prepaid burner phone. Despite digging, the police were unable to match the phone to anyone, nor did any of the neighbors see anyone coming or going from Lindsay's home in the days around his death other than the housekeeper, who had the great misfortune to discover the great trial lawyer's partially decomposed body at the bottom of the stairs.

Police in Ohio had similar levels of success. All signs seemed to point to a suicide, the public outcries notwithstanding. Initial toxicology results revealed that high concentrations of sodium thiopental and potassium chloride were found in Laughlin's system consistent with the use of the thanatron found at the scene. The medical examiner's office concluded that this was in fact the cause of death. Given their long and sordid history with Thomas Strustevich, however, they declined to state whether Laughlin acted alone or whether he had help, voluntary or not. They probably would have suspected the Grim Reaper's involvement but for the fact that he was still more than a week away from release at the time of Laughlin's death.

The machine itself was exhaustively deconstructed and tested for fingerprints and other trace evidence. Other than some smudges they were unable to identify, investigators only found Laughlin's fingerprints on the device. They also found evidence of latex, but did not draw any firm conclusions from this as to Laughlin's intentions. While none of his family members or coworkers told investigators that Laughlin had acted oddly or seemed depressed in the days leading up to his death, they were all unaware that Laughlin had recently seen either his doctor or a specialist. Even Laughlin himself had been unaware of the extent of his condition, for the biopsy results confirming that he did in fact have prostate cancer did not come in until after his death. Not surprisingly, most of this information eventually found its way into the public eye through rumors, leaks, and off-the-record confirmations.

*****

As all of this was going on, Rich took a trip to the northern plains. In late April, he stood at the tree line at the top of a ridge overlooking a valley below. Spread out before him like a bowl was the 110 acre ranch of Bobby Joe Gibbons, one of Jackson Hole, Wyoming's favorite sons and America's best trial lawyers. The sun was beginning to set behind the trees casting much of the valley into shadow. Rich could feel the temperature dropping along with the sun and he wanted to get moving before it got too cold. He looked at his watch and stamped his feet in an effort to stay warm.

Rich could not see the main road from where he was situated. The long ribbon of black top emerged from behind the trees to his left bisecting the valley as it gently curved to the right and then back to the left on its way to the main house and its handful of outbuildings. Although it was technically a ranch, it was mostly a ranch for show, even the smattering of livestock which dotted the landscape realized that little was expected of them. They were around to provide ambiance for the great lawyer.

As he looked at his watch again and was about to give up for the day, Rich heard a helicopter coming from behind him and ducked back into the trees where he wouldn't be seen. In the six days he had been scouting the ranch, he had seen the helicopter four times, always heading in the same direction from off behind Gibbons' spread to one of the neighboring properties. Since he hadn't been there early in the morning thus far, he suspected that the helicopter went out first thing in the morning only to return at the end of the day. He watched the helicopter grow smaller and eventually disappear into the distance and wondered who was on it and where they were heading.

Then he saw the truck. He pulled the binoculars from a backpack resting against a tree to get a closer look. It was the same late-model, blue Ford F-150 he had seen every day since he had arrived. The caretaker was here. Later than usual, but he was here. Rich only watched the first few minutes of his rounds because he wanted to make it back through the woods to his car before it got completely dark. He knew that the caretaker would take about forty minutes dropping off the mail, making other deliveries and generally checking the place out before hopping back in the truck and headed back the way he came.

Curious about the helicopter, he made up his mind to be back early the following morning. He also wanted to see if the caretaker, or anyone else for that matter, regularly stopped by the ranch early in the morning. Rich hadn't been there first thing on any of the days so far and even though he wasn't planning to make his move early in the day, it was always better to operate with full and complete information. He already knew, for example, that Gibbons split his time between the ranch and another place outside of LA and that he typically spent most of the winter in California except for occasional skiing trips. He didn't start spending significant amounts of time at the ranch until mid-May. Rich would be long gone by then. Gibbons would be gone soon after.

20

Ben pulled into the parking lot of DuPage County Forest Preserve District headquarters about fifteen minutes before the scheduled start of the monthly board meeting. Ben usually attended two meetings at the district every month, one a board meeting and the other a meeting of the land acquisition committee, which was responsible for condemnation matters. He parked and headed inside. Once buzzed through the doors into the main offices, he wandered back and found Karen Tilly, the land acquisition manager, on the phone in her office. He stopped at the door and she waved him in and pointed to one of the guest chairs. He sat down just as she hung up the phone.

"Hey, what's up?" she said with a smile. Karen was probably Ben's favorite client. Not only was she smart, she was a lot of fun and would never sell you out. They got along very well.

Ben pulled a file folder from his briefcase. It contained a summary of a large project complete with a color-coded map broken down by landowner. "So," he said as a perused his summary, "what do we have up again today?"

Karen looked at him and shrugged. "I don't know. It doesn't matter."

"Why not?"

"We have deer culling on the agenda."

Ben groaned. "What? I thought you only did that during the fall right around deer hunting season."

"We usually do, but someone decided to put it on the agenda today. I'm not quite sure what it's up for, that's not my area, but I saw it on the sheet and I heard people talking about it yesterday. I think maybe someone is trying to get something passed without a lot of public input, if you know what I mean."

"You mean they wanted to vote on it without a hundred screaming Bambi lovers showing up and calling them murderers."

"Something like that."

Ben knew from experience that the most contentious items on the forest preserve district's agenda year in and year out did not involve condemnation, the rights of the landowner, or even the value of open space in a mechanized world. No, the single item that caused the most public outcry and brought the most residents to a board meeting with passions ablaze was deer culling. Every year, the district commissioned extensive studies to determine whether deer and other wildlife had overpopulated various preserves and, if so, how many needed to be eliminated thru controlled hunts to bring the numbers in line.

There was typically screaming and yelling from the audience, and sometimes from the board as well. Some board members took the issue very seriously. Other members thought that the whole thing was a ludicrous waste of time.

Ben groaned again. "I'm going to be here until at least noon. Are you supplying lunch?"

"No, but I hear there are donuts in the caucus room."

"Let's go."

The caucus room was a small meeting room between the board room and the main district offices. It was not open to the public and board members and counsel frequently escaped to the caucus room for private meetings. Ben and Karen entered the caucus room from the back and found several board members milling about sampling the donuts. They each grabbed a donut and Karen asked, "so, Mr. TV Star, any good dirt on these murders?" She gave him a nudge. "You must have some secrets."

"You mean you're not giving me the Oliver Stone treatment like the guys at the office?" Ben asked in mock shock.

120

She laughed. "Funk told me about that on the phone. I was cutting you some slack." She made an exaggerated shake of her head. "I don't think you're a nut."

"Great. Now I can't even count on you."

"Sure you can. I'm just teasing. I really think you're probably right. What are the odds that all these guys are dying and it's a coincidence? Probably not that great. That would be some coincidence."

Ben stuffed the remainder of a chocolate frosted donut into his mouth. "True enough," he said while chewing. "Sure, the deaths seem to be suspicious, but they don't seem to have any proof. At least nothing I've heard about."

"You don't know any behind-the-scenes stuff that we regular people don't hear about?"

Ben shook his head. "No, not really. I'm not really connected on this one. It is something though. One dead lawyer in California, another in Florida, another in Ohio, all of them famous. Wonder what the connection is?"

"Maybe that they're famous. Maybe that they're on TV."

"Lindsay wasn't really on TV. Not that I know of."

"Okay, but he was famous." She thought about it for a moment. "Lindsay and Kessler defended Owens. Laughlin talked about the Owens trial a lot on TV. I remember seeing him. He reminded me of a surfer lawyer. Did you know him?"

"No, not at all. You're right, he had great hair. I knew Kessler a little. Didn't know Laughlin or Lindsay. Heard they were both kind of assholes, actually."

Karen made a face. "Really? Lindsay I can see. He looked full of himself. I kind of liked Laughlin though."

"Figures."

"He was kind of cute." Ben rolled his eyes. She nudged him again. "If I were you, I'd be worried," she said with a laugh. "You never know who's next."

"I'm not that famous," he replied as he followed her into the board room. Before he could make it through the door, she paused and turned, her eyes wide. "What?" he said.

"It didn't work."

121

She turned back and they entered the room. The gallery was completely jammed with spectators. Deer culling. Happens every time.

On his way back to the office, Ben drifted back to his conversation with Karen Tilly about the links between the three attorney deaths.

Could they really be linked? Could being famous be the link? Could he be in jeopardy? Assuming all three lawyers were murdered, there had to be a link somewhere.

Ben didn't get back to the office until almost one. The guys were just finishing up lunch. "Where have you been?" Funk asked.

Ben gave him a look. "They had deer culling on the agenda."

Knowing what that meant, they gave him a collective groan. "Any good stories?" someone asked.

Ben laughed. "Typical nut balls. Occasional insights overshadowed by raving lunacy."

"Who was the idiot this time?" Casey asked.

"Hard to pick just one. The best part was when Bill Mason got up and told a story about how he always sees dead deer at the side of the road in every other county, but almost never around here. He suggested that deer in DuPage County were smarter than deer in other counties. The people near me were grumbling about him. I'm not sure most of them realized he was making fun of them. By the way, Tilly thinks I'm right about Laughlin and Lindsay, not that I actually said for sure that I thought they were murdered, just said that it's possible. She doesn't think I'm crazy."

"She's just being nice," Casey said. "She even talks to Funk."

"She also said I should be looking over my shoulder. Hopefully she was just kidding about that."

"You're not famous enough to kill," Funk added.

"That's what I said. I hope we're right about that."

21

Ben was reading a condemnation case from the Illinois Supreme Court when Nancy came in and dropped his mail in the desk in front of him. "There you go," she said. "It looks like you might have an invitation in there."

"Thanks," he said as he continued reading. A moment later, Nancy cleared her throat and Ben looked up to find her still standing in front of his desk. "What?"

"I want to see what you were invited to."

Ben thumbed through the envelopes until he found the one that looked like an invitation. She reached down and grabbed a letter opener from his pen jar and handed it to him. He sliced through the thick stationary, removed an embossed card, and began reading silently to himself. "Hmmm," he said aloud and put the card back in the envelope.

"Well?"

"Oh," he said in surprise. "You want to know what it says?" She gave him the finger and he laughed. "You were right, it is invitation."

"And ..."

"And I was invited to a dinner and reception sponsored by the Chicago Bar Association at the Hilton downtown next month honoring Jimmy Moran for his long years of service to the profession, blah blah blah."

"Jimmy Moran? Why him? He doesn't practice in Illinois, does he?"

Jimmy Moran was the lead counsel in the Chase Owens case. He was the lawyer who put the Dream Defense team together. Although he was based primarily in Los Angeles, the Owens case had significantly raised his profile nationally.

"Some, but you're right, not too much." Ben said. "He is a big name though and with these recent deaths maybe they thought he would be a good draw."

"But you never worked with him. Why are they inviting you?"

Ben put his arms out palms up as though outraged. "Hey, I'm somebody. I appear on cable television."

She made a face. "Are you going to go?"

He thought about it for a second then said, "I don't know. If I can get Phil to fork out for the tickets I might. I suppose it wouldn't be bad publicity. We'll see."

"You should go," she said. "And take your wife."

"I could, but I was thinking maybe you wanted to go," he said with a laugh.

She turned on her heel and headed for the door. "Fat chance. You're not getting me into a dress for no chicken dinner. Just tell me how it went."

He took the invitation out of the envelope and looked at it again. Then he tapped it on his hand as he considered the fates of Kessler, Lindsay and Laughlin, even as Moran was being honored at the CBA. He wondered whether Moran had thought of that. He probably had given that he had worked closely with Kessler and Lindsay and might even know Laughlin as well.

"The Dream Defense," he said softly under his breath. He couldn't even remember all the lawyers who had worked on it. He googled them to refresh his recollection. More than half of them were now dead. John Goodrich had been Owens's original lawyer and had represented the actor for years, but he was really a corporate guy and not a criminal defense lawyer. He brought in William Delvecchio to handle the defense. For his part, Delvecchio had been around LA for years and had a solid reputation, but was not considered a high-profile criminal defense guy who could handle a case of that magnitude and his selection was a bit of a surprise to those in the LA defense bar.

Soon, there were rumblings in the media that Owens wanted a more prominent lead counsel for the defense team so Moran was brought on board. Before long, he had elbowed Delvecchio out of the way and was in complete control of the defense team. Delvecchio stayed around, and handled some of the less significant witnesses at trial, but did not in any way retain the prominence or the decision-making he had been granted when he was hired. It was Moran who had put the rest of the team together, bringing Kessler, Lindsay and others on board, and it was Moran who had handled the press and gotten the kudos when Owens had been found not guilty despite what appeared to be a mountain of evidence against him.

John Goodrich had died first, of brain cancer only a few years after the verdict. Shortly before his death, he had indicated publicly for the first time that he thought his former client was probably guilty. Ben remembered wondering at the time what had caused Goodrich's falling out with Owens since it should have been clear to him like it was to virtually every modestly intelligent person in the world that Owens had indeed been guilty of the double murder. Usually money had something to do with it, or perhaps Goodrich had a guilty conscience and wanted to make things right before he died. In any event, his pronouncement had little effect on what most people already knew.

The next to go had been William Delvecchio, having succumbed to cancer of the pancreas almost three years ago. Ben was surprised that it had been that long ago. He would have thought it had only been a year or so. Unlike Moran, Delvecchio's career had not really taken off after the Owens case. He would appear occasionally on various cable television shows, but not even too many of those, and was mostly known for being the lawyer replaced by Jimmy Moran and for a nasty divorce which briefly made the news not long before his death. He certainly never had a practice that extended beyond the LA area as far as Ben knew.

And then there were Lindsay and Kessler. Lindsay, of course, had been one of the most famous trial lawyers in the country and everyone who had ever paid any attention to the legal community and a good portion of those who hadn't recognized his name. Kessler, on the other hand, was largely unknown outside of his field of DNA evidence until the Owens trial and his videotaped hammering of the state's evidence had made him a star.

Now, along with Goodrich and Delvecchio, they were both dead, Kessler murdered and Lindsay maybe as well. Four lawyers from the most prominent case of their era dead, leaving only Moran and a few others who played very minor roles in the trial remaining. How strange indeed. Ben wondered about Goodrich and Delvecchio – could they had been murdered too? That notion seemed far-fetched. First, neither death was recent like the others. More importantly, how could you murder someone with cancer? Brain cancer and pancreatic cancer. Could you get much more of a natural cause then that? Perhaps in some rare circumstances each could have had environmental causes or at least contributions, yet that didn't seem to fit these facts. Maybe Flaherty was right. Maybe it was just bad karma, the cosmic result of a guilty man going free. And what of Laughlin? Assuming he was murdered too, which by no means seemed a sure thing, where does he fit in? He wasn't even a part of the Owens trial.

Ben surfed the web for a long while trying to learn more about Kessler, Lindsay and Laughlin before eventually coming to the realization that he was being ridiculous and doing little more than wasting time. Still, he didn't get much real work done the whole rest of the day. Every time he started to get involved in something, his mind would drift back to Florida, California, and Ohio and the three dead lawyers.

The same thing happened on his drive home. He attempted to take his mind off of it with a book on CD to no avail, then tried to drive it out of his head with loud rock music on the car stereo, only that didn't really work either. The hustle and bustle of dinner with the family, followed by homework and the bedtime rituals helped to a great degree until he came back downstairs after putting his daughter, Natalie, to bed to find

Libby watching Loretta Bergen and her panel's latest take on things.

Ben grabbed a bottle of water from the fridge and joined his wife on the couch. "Can't we watch something else?" he said.

"I think this is fascinating. And a bit spooky. I mean, what if this a strange sort of serial killing? I would think you of all people would be all over this."

Truth be told, Ben did not want to tell her that he was thinking about it more than she was. He didn't want to creep her out and get her stewing about it even more. He would just as soon change the subject. "I don't know," he finally said. "Maybe if there was something new, but this is the same old shit."

She turned to face him. "Oh, and I suppose it's something new when you're the talking head spouting off about God knows what?"

"Absolutely. Then it's the Sermon on the Mount. But I'm not on. So why don't we watch something on Tivo? Or we could go upstairs and play," he said with a big smile.

"But it's only nine-thirty." She tossed him the remote. "Find something to watch then."

22

Ben spent the next couple of weeks trying to keep his mind on his work without much success. More and more, he found himself drifting away to the events in Florida, California, and Ohio in a failed effort to try and make sense of it all. He appeared on a couple of shows and despite the frantic urging of producers to "make some news", he declined to crawl out any further on the limb than he had done with Loretta Bergen. The authorities in all three jurisdictions had pretty much circled the wagons, meaning there was very little new information to report. Even Ben felt like he'd been saying the same things over and over again and he had no doubt that the viewing public probably felt the same way despite the fact that the same producers who were hounding him were also insisting that ratings were up.

He started to feel himself becoming more inwardly focused and contemplative, rarely a good sign. He clearly wasn't as outgoing as usual, frequently skipping lunch with the guys and less willing to engage in the good-natured banter that typified the office even when he did go along. Libby began complaining that he was irritable, which he strongly denied in a stance that probably proved her point. Even the kids seemed a bit put off from time to time. When he finally got his April billing in, he discovered that his hours were down substantially and he suspected he would hear about it from Phil. But Phil said nothing, preferring apparently to cut Ben some slack given the circumstances and the impact they were having on his associate.

Ben appreciated the consideration, but fully expected it not to last if he didn't get back in the groove soon.

As the date of the Jimmy Moran reception grew near, Ben regretted telling Phil about it and wished he had just tossed the invitation in the garbage. Not surprisingly, Phil insisted that he go and suggested that he take Libby along with him. She had begged off, however, using the kids and her lack of desire to get all dressed up and go downtown in the middle of the week as an excuse, leaving Ben to make the excursion on his own. Although he often didn't mind so much when she decided to stay home from events like this, because he never liked to feel responsible for whether or not she was having a good time, he would have strongly preferred that she had chosen to attend this event. He wasn't sure who was going to be there, and at least if she went along, he knew he would have someone to talk to and perhaps even a ready excuse to leave early.

*****

In Yorba Linda, Ray Fisher learned about the Chicago Bar Association's reception honoring Jimmy Moran through one of his regular searches on the Internet and he dug around some more until he knew all of the particulars. He thought about it for a while, carefully weighing the pros and cons. With several good customers and even a vendor in the Chicago area, he could justify the trip for business reasons. Still on the fence, he called the CBA and discovered that there were tickets still available, although they were going fast, and if he wanted to attend this worthwhile event, he should probably order his tickets now.

Although he appreciated the hard sell, he figured he probably could have still gotten in on the day of the event, since charities are always willing to take your money. Nevertheless, he made a snap decision and put the tickets on one of his "special" credit cards. Then he hunted around for a good deal on airfare and booked a room in the same hotel as the reception. Now that he had decided to go, Fisher needed to put together a game plan for the trip. Time was short, and he wasn't the type to do anything without careful preparation. He buckled down and got to work.

*****

"You know, this place must've been really something back in the day, before it all went to hell," the tall man said.

The short man nodded and put his feet up on the coffee table, which contained remnants of fingerprint dust. "I agree," he said. "What this place needs now is a good power washing."

The two detectives with the North Palm Beach Police Department sat in Patrick Lindsay's study and discussed the day's events. Since Spencer Laughlin's body had been found in Ohio and the firestorm which had ensued following Benjamin Lohmeier's comments on Loretta Bergen's show, their bosses had been forced to step up the investigation into Lindsay's untimely death, for appearances sake, if nothing else. Crime scene techs had been redeployed, more testing conducted, and uniforms sent around to canvas the neighborhood again. The house had been thoroughly examined, but despite these efforts, little new had been learned.

Despite their lack of success, there was a growing sense between the two detectives that perhaps Lindsay had been helped down the stairs and didn't simply wind up there on his own. The calls from the burner cell seemed to particularly stick in their craws. There was no logical explanation for them other than someone setting up a meeting with Lindsay, someone who did not want to be identified. If there had been a series of calls from a variety of untraceable numbers over a period of months that would be one thing, but those three calls from that one cell phone, two of which lasted more than five minutes each, appeared to be an isolated incident that could not be explained.

"By the way," the short one said, "I talked to the woman from Los Angeles today while you were on the phone with the lab."

"Oh yeah? What did she say?"

"She said they finished going through the phone records for Kessler and his girlfriend – home, office, and cell."

"They come up with any matches?"

The short one grunted. "Nothing. Not a damn thing. They checked with Ohio and Ohio was going to look into it too. They are pretty backed up and aren't sure when they will get around to it, but it's a priority."

"We can't catch a break," the larger man said. "I think we're going to have to get something out of LA or Ohio in order to crack this thing."

"Unless," the shorter man said and paused. He waited for his partner to make eye contact, then added, "unless another body turns up someplace."

The larger man simply sighed.

*****

Shortly after dark, and more than a thousand miles to the north, a dark blue sedan pulled around the back of the building and parked. As Thomas Strustevich got out of the passenger side of the car, a man in a grey suit opened the back door to the building and greeted him with a nod. Given their previous history, they did not shake hands as Strustevich made his way past the man and into the building. Strustevich hobbled to the main corridor with the help of a cane, paused and turned to his escort. "Where are we going?" he said.

The escort looked at the old doctor and thought that his health truly had deteriorated in the past few years, but then again, he was far from a young man. "Conference room upstairs." The man stepped around Strustevich and added, "this way."

The doctor tapped his cane on the hardwood floor. "Let's do it down here. I think there's a room down this way." He pointed the cane to his left. "There's no elevator and I can't handle the stairs real well anymore."

The escort stopped and sighed. It's starting already, he thought, meaning the battle over control that had always marked the doctor's dealings with the authorities. He didn't want to start anything so he turned back and smiled. "Sure. I'll see what we can do. I'm sure they have something down here we can use. I'll be right back." Then he trudged off to the right where the stairs were located.

Strustevich had already parked himself in an empty conference room by the time the entourage arrived. He was seated at the head of a twelve-foot long mahogany table farthest away from the door. He faced sideways, both hands on the cane, which stood straight up and down between his feet. Seven people entered with a bit of a commotion. Strustevich recognized almost all of them. At least two worked for Laughlin's law firm – one had been Laughlin's number two man, the other an associate who worked on Strustevich's last trial. For all the doctor knew, he might be a partner now too. Two more were cops. He didn't like either of them. A couple more looked like prosecutors. He liked them even less than the cops. The final person to enter the room was a woman Strustevich did not recognize. She carried a thanatron and placed it in the center of the table without saying anything. Then she stepped backed into the corner.

The senior partner, a tall, reedy man named Schiller, whom Strustevich always thought would have been happy to get rid of him and his bad publicity, came over and shook the doctor's hand with a little too much enthusiasm. "Thomas, it's good see you. We're all so glad you were released. We only wish it could've been sooner."

Strustevich barked a joyless laugh. "You maybe, but certainly not them." He gestured with his cane in the direction of the prosecutors. None of them had taken a seat. They just stood there in a group around the other end of the table, glaring at him as though he was some sort of bug in a specimen jar. Although he knew he looked like hell, he wasn't about to give them the satisfaction of acting like it. Never a large man, he now appeared to be shrinking within himself and couldn't have held more than 140 pounds on his six foot frame. His clothes were too large and hung on him. He had lost most of his hair. The remainder was steel gray and cut very short, liver spots visible. He raised his chin in a proud gesture and returned their glares for a long, uncomfortable moment, before adding, "you haven't killed me yet." Then in a quieter voice, "not for lack of trying."

The senior lawyer took a spot at the table to Strustevich's right, while the junior one stood in the near corner. Finally, the senior detective walked around the other side of the table and sat down on Strustevich's left, opposite the lawyer. The doctor used the cane to swivel in his chair to face the man. "So, what do you want from me?" he grunted, although he already knew. He stared the detective down.

To his credit, the detective, a burly man named Pawlowski, held his gaze even though it was clear to everyone in the room that he would rather be almost anyplace else. He cleared his throat and said, "we would like you to take a look at the device on the table there and ask you a few questions about it, if that's okay."

Strustevich laughed for real this time. "What you mean is, you need my help."

The detective said nothing. He gave only the slightest of nods, the only concession he would make. No one would give in easily tonight.

The lawyer jumped in almost as if on cue. "Before we get started, I think we need to set a few ground rules …"

Strustevich cut him off with a quick pound of the cane. "Forget that bullshit," he said. "They aren't building a case against me, there's no case to build. So let's cut to the chase. What do you want me to do?"

Gesturing to the device in the center of the table, Pawlowski said, "I assume you know what that is."

Strustevich nodded. "A thanatron."

"Have you ever seen it before tonight?"

The doctor tilted his head and gave the detective the kind of look a parent would give a child who had misbehaved. "Now how could I have? I've been locked up for years, remember?"

"Right," Pawlowski answered. He looked at the device again. "What if you take a closer look at it? If you don't mind."

Strustevich nodded and used the cane to push himself to his feet. He shuffled around the lawyer, stopped opposite the device, pulled the chair and sat down. Resting the cane up against the table, he fumbled in the pocket of his flannel shirt for a pair of reading glasses. He placed both hands on the table in front of him and leaned forward to get a closer look at the thanatron. His right hand shook. Noticing, he placed it under the left to make the tremor stop. Everyone in the room seemed to be holding their breaths. No one said a word until Strustevich said to no one in particular, his eyes never leaving the machine, "Can I touch it?"

Pawlowski looked over the top of Strustevich's head to the senior prosecutor, who nodded. "Sure, go ahead."

The doctor struggled to his feet and reached out to pick up the device. He held it, assessing the weight and the solidity of it, then placed it down directly in front of his seat. He continued examining it for some time, occasionally uttering a "hmmm" or a "right" under his breath. No one spoke as he did so. Finally, he sat back in the chair with a look of admiration on his face and said, "mine were cheap pieces of shit compared to this."

"So this isn't one of yours?" Pawlowski asked.

"No, I told you that. This is the Cadillac version, or the Rolls Royce version. I made Chevettes. I just wanted to get the job done. This is different. This has nice workmanship. It looks engineered to a fare thee well. It's well put together."

A voice came from behind. The prosecutor, Roger Simpson, said, "what do you mean?" as he walked around the table and sat down opposite Strustevich. They eyed each other over the machine, each man fighting back their mutual hatred to concentrate on the issue at hand.

The doctor gestured toward it. "Look at the materials for starters – stainless steel, brushed aluminum, copper tubing, the IV line. This is good stuff, bought specifically for this purpose. He didn't scrounge for parts, that's for sure. It's heavy, substantial. Probably weighs more than twice what mine weighed, at least."

"Any idea where the parts came from?"

"No, not really. You could get this stuff a lot places around here, or at least you could at one time. I've not exactly been out and about, you know. It's fairly generic, but good generic, if that makes sense. Not cheap."

Now Pawlowski spoke. "That's what we've discovered. You could get this stuff around here."

"Or on the Internet."

"That too."

Strustevich looked at the machine again. He pointed to a switch on the side. "Take a look at this here." Both men stood to get a better look and those standing around the table also inched closer. "This looks to be some sort of kill switch or maybe an automatic shut-off."

"We think it was an automatic shut-off," Simpson said.

"Now why in the hell would you need that? That never occurred to me when I built them." He thought about it for a moment, then added, "maybe he didn't want to leave it running after it was done doing its job. Afraid it would short out or something. Family was out of town, right?" Simpson nodded. "Maybe he didn't want to burn the house down."

"Did you ever worry about that?"

The doctor smiled sadly. "No, can't say as I did. There was always someone there to turn it off when it was done."

"Maybe Mr. Laughlin was alone and knew there wouldn't be anyone there to turn it off."

"Or," Strustevich said before pausing. "Or the person who turned it on couldn't turn it off without revealing that he was there."

23

Bobby Joe Gibbons shook hands with his co-counsel outside the Boston restaurant and turned in the direction of his hotel. "Hey Bobby!" the senior partner asked, "we've got a car coming in a second. Want us to drop you at the hotel?"

"Nope," Gibbons replied with a half-turn, "I'm good." He patted his stomach with both hands. "Got to work off that fine meal. Much obliged for the offer. See you in the morning."

With a wave of his hand, he began the three block walk to the hotel. He did need the exercise and a walk in the crisp, cool evening air would do him some good. That part was true enough. But he was also tired of the company and needed a break. Not that they were bad people or bad lawyers. Not at all. They just weren't his people. He found himself in Boston to headline a medical malpractice case against a big drug company. The Boston lawyers – they called themselves a boutique plaintiff's firm – were a bit too East Coast stuffy for his tastes. Too much Harvard this and Yale that.

That wasn't Gibbons' style. He was just a good ol' country lawyer. A cowboy at heart. At least that was the image, and he'd been working on the image for so long he couldn't remember where the image started and the real man left off. He probably was the image by now, that's why the image worked so well. He was all country swagger and down home witticisms wrapped in snakeskin boots, fringed buckskin jackets and topped with a long, flowing mane of white hair.

Bobby Joe Gibbons billed himself as "The People's Lawyer" and he only represented individuals, frequently battling the odds against huge, multi-national corporations. He was on the side of David in his struggle against Goliath. This, of course, was a far cry from the Robert Gibbons who had spent almost a decade representing corporations after graduating first in his class from the University of Montana Law School. But he had seen the light, he would admit if pressed, and honed his persona to such a fine degree that it was now probably who he really was, more or less. Not that he couldn't crank it up and "put the cherry on the sundae" when necessary, as he liked to say with a laugh. That's what made him so great for cable television. His homespun commentaries made him a popular talking head for whatever trial was sucking up all of the oxygen at any given time. The only regret he ever had over his TV work was the fact that he wasn't the lawyer commanding all that attention in the courtroom. Alas, his true glory years in the courtroom had come too soon, a decade or two before televised trials and the instant analysis of same had truly become a cottage industry.

Above it all, Gibbons was a great trial lawyer, a man who had a gift for connecting with the everyday folks that frequently made up his juries. He won big cases, he won little cases. He made lots of money. Sometimes he worked for free. He often claimed to have never lost a jury trial, although a couple of strategic settlements and plea bargains over the years kept that well-publicized streak alive. Bigger than life, people were sucked in by his charm just like his juries. They simply wanted to be near him. He was a hoot. But he was more than that. A shrewd judge of people, he also knew which cases to take and which to pass on because he knew the law and preferred to stack the deck in his favor as much as possible.

These days, at a few years passed seventy, he had neither the energy, nor the attention span of his younger counterparts. That's what made TV so attractive. Now he confined himself mostly to cases where he didn't have to do all the detail work he used to love. He would let others work up the cases and he would serve as the figure head whose name brought in the clients. His was the face that everyone wanted to see. Gibbons called these "star turns" and it kept him out there and the money coming in. Now on his third wife, some of the millions he had earned over the years had made other lawyers rich and kept his ex-wives in the style to which they had become accustomed. But that was okay. It just came with the territory. He had lived a good life and wouldn't do much of anything differently.

As Gibbons strolled through the lobby of the high-end hotel, heads turned and necks craned to get a peek at the great trial lawyer and TV star in the flesh. While he occasionally tired of the attention, and when he did, he simply traveled to the ranch in Jackson Hole to get away, he mostly relished the adulation and acknowledged his well-wishers with a nod of his head as he passed by. Upstairs, he took off his jacket and tossed it in a chair. Then he kicked off his shoes and found a fresh glass on the mini bar into which he dropped one cube of ice and a healthy dose of bourbon. He had been staying at the hotel for more than a month, or shortly before the trial began, and except for a couple of short weekend visits back to Wyoming, had been there ever since.

His beloved soul mate, confidant and final wife, as he liked to say, Maria, usually accompanied him on all trips and had served as his chief assistant since before they became lovers almost thirty years ago. She had stayed for the first couple of weeks in Boston, but had returned to take care of some things back home and he missed her. If both of them were gone for too long, the inmates would be running the asylum back at the office. Although the hotel was about as nice as you could get on the client's dime, it still wasn't home. If Maria were here it would be close, but without her it was just another hotel. His nightly ritual since she had departed consisted of one bourbon over ice, sometimes two, as they discussed the day's events before he watched a little TV and went to bed. He didn't need to do much in the way of trial preparation since his primary responsibilities in this case consisted of conducting the direct examination of his client, the cross examination of the defendant's CEO, and the closing argument. The direct had gone well last week and the cross had been prepared months ago. The closing he could do in his sleep. Now it was just a matter of putting in the time.

He lounged on the bed and rummaged through the worn saddle bags that served as his briefcase in search of his cell phone. A moment later, his drink in one hand and his phone in the other, he called home.

"You're late," Maria said with no preamble. "I've already cleaned up dinner."

"Yeah, I know it. Dinner with the trial team. Command performance. You know how it goes."

They talked about their respective days for a while – his trial, her planting the garden at the ranch, with a few office odds and ends mixed in. Finally, she asked, "what are you drinking? I hear the ice tinkling in the glass."

"Just ice water," he answered.

"Uh huh, the kind that comes from Tennessee or Kentucky, I suppose."

He laughed. "Got me there. Without you here, I need something to unwind. Now, if you were here, well, then,"

"Don't be a dirty old man," she interrupted. "Someone may be listening."

"You wouldn't be saying that if you were here."

"Perhaps not."

They bantered for a few minutes until she said she'd better get going. "What? You got somebody there waiting for you?" he asked.

"You know better than that," she said and he did. "I'm just not feeling quite myself today."

"What's the matter?"

"Nothing to worry about. Just under the weather, that's all."

"Well, if you don't feel better tomorrow, then go to the doctor. I want you in top shape when I get home."

"Stop it," she said. "Neither of us have been in top shape for a long time."

"Nonsense. You're as beautiful as the day I married you." And he really believed it. While she knew better, she also knew

139

that he meant every word and that made all the difference in the world.

24

"Let me ask you about Laughlin," Simpson, the prosecutor, said. "More specifically, about your conversations with him."

"That would be privileged," Schiller the lawyer said.

"I don't want anything privileged exactly. I want to know if he ever gave you a hint that he was suicidal."

The Grim Reaper shook his head. This whole thing puzzled him. At first, he was suspicious of Simpson and Pawlowski and their friends. He assumed that they were out to get him like always. Now he didn't think so. He saw that they were puzzled too and were hoping he could actually help them. "No, never," he said. "Not once. I am ashamed to say that we hadn't talked about him at all in months, maybe more than a year. Once my health started to go down, it was all about getting me out. We used to talk about him and his family from time to time when he visited. Not in a long time though. I didn't even know he was sick. He never said anything. When was he diagnosed?"

"He went to his doctor, then to an urologist, shortly before his death," Simpson said. "Within days actually. He didn't even know the biopsy results."

"Prostate cancer? That's what I heard," Strustevich said.

"Yes, but very treatable from what we're told."

Strustevich folded his arms across his chest. "Especially these days. Very few men die from it, but a lot them have it when they die. But he didn't even know for sure?"

"No," Simpson said.

"Then why would he have been suicidal? And when would he have gotten the parts and built it?"

Simpson and Pawlowski both shrugged. "Good questions," Pawlowski said.

"Can you prove he bought the components?"

The two men across from Strustevich exchanged a look before the detective said, "we're still working on that."

They went through it for a while, eventually rehashing some of the same ground. The doctor seemed to be growing tired and the prosecutor noticed that the tremor in his hand seem to worsen. "Did he ever ask you how to build one of these things?" Simpson asked with a nod at the device. "I mean, he had to know from the trials how the thing worked."

"Sure, he knew how it worked," Strustevich said. "I have no doubt he could have built one. I just don't think he did. It wasn't his style. Honestly, he never liked the mechanics of it much. He may have believed in the cause, more or less, but the actual physical aspects of it ..." He struggled looking for the right words. "I think it kind of creeped him out, to tell you the truth."

"What do you mean by that?" Pawlowski said.

"I don't know," Strustevich said as he looked away in apparent search for what to say. "I don't want to say that he was squeamish, because that wasn't it exactly, but he never seemed to like the mechanics of it." He fingered one of the tubes before going on. "Like I said, he may have believed I was right, but he didn't understand, not fully, why I would do it, or even why a patient would do it. I don't he think understood coming to grips with ending it all. He wasn't at that point in his life, probably. Hard to say if that changed. Once he knew there was something with his prostate maybe he got a different perspective."

Pawlowski cut him off. "It doesn't sound like you believe it. That he killed himself, I mean."

Strustevich shrugged, then thought about it and shook his head. "It would be hard to believe he had reached that point. I'm pretty sensitive to that kind of thing and I never saw it from

Spencer." He looked at the lawyer. "What about you? You saw him every day."

The lawyer simply shook his head.

Strustevich looked back at Pawlowski. "Family? Wife? Kids?"

"No. They didn't see it coming either."

"Usually there are signs of some kind. Something. People saw him every day, talked to him every day and no one noticed a thing?"

Pawlowski shook his head.

The doctor pounded his cane once on the floor. "Then I don't buy it either. It's hard for me to see him letting someone hook him up to the machine."

"What about by himself?"

"Even harder to believe, I think. It's hard to stick an IV in your own arm. A lot of doctors couldn't do it, let alone lawyers. They could always do it to someone else, but not to themselves." The lawyers in the room ignored the dig. He looked closely at the thanatron again. "It's a nice piece of work. Someone went to a lot of trouble. Someone built it."

"Yes, they did," Simpson said after a long moment, "and we need to find out who."

25

Ben probably would have forgotten all about Mother's Day had Libby not reminded him several times in the days preceding the second Sunday in May, ostensibly to make sure he didn't forget his own mother. He managed to stumble through it without too much collective angst, mostly because his mind was focused elsewhere and he wasn't fit to engage in the typical partisan sparring over the celebration, and its comparison to Father's Day, which Ben insisted was considered a second-rate holiday. After dinner, he found himself alone at a table on his in-laws' patio sipping a beer and watching several of the kids kicking a soccer ball around the backyard. As the kids both worked themselves up and hopefully wore themselves out, his thoughts drifted to the dead lawyers and their families. Lindsay was divorced two or three times over and his kids were no doubt long since grown, but Laughlin and Kessler were still married and even young enough to have children who could be dramatically impacted by their fathers' untimely and violent deaths. Ben didn't know their particulars, but couldn't stop thinking about it.

Not one prone to such introspection, he was usually more intent on his own world and how to bend it to his will than he was on the feelings and needs of others whom he did not know and could not understand. His response to that was usually not to bother. He was something of an emotional capitalist in that regard. He figured if he acted in the best interests of himself, his family, and his close circle of friends, while doing the right thing, and everyone else more or less did too, then things should work out okay most of the time for everyone. Ben knew that his current mindset was out of character and the feeling troubled him. He wasn't exactly looking for growth. He felt fully evolved and marvelously well-adjusted. He knew who he was and was satisfied with himself. No cracks in the armor now, please.

Later that night, as they lay in the darkness, Libby asked, "did your mother have a good time tonight?"

"I think so. She said she did. Who knows? It beats sitting home alone ... she's fine."

"You could have been a little nicer."

Ben rolled over onto one elbow and faced his wife in the darkness. "What do you mean? I was perfectly nice to her."

"You weren't perfectly nice to anyone. I'm just used to it."

He glared at her for a moment then rolled back over and punched his pillow. "Bullshit," he said as he slammed his head into the pillow. Then, under his breath, he added, "if I wasn't nice to anyone she shouldn't feel slighted."

"Just think about it."

He didn't respond.

The following Tuesday, he appeared on Loretta Bergen's show with a lawyer and a former New York City cop, neither of whom he recognized. It didn't go well. The cop took after the investigators in LA and Florida, all but alleging mismanagement of the cases and general incompetence. Ben avoided that since he didn't really know what the investigators were doing and not doing. He figured the cop was probably a new guest who was trying to make a splash so he would be asked back again. Like Ben, Loretta seemed a bit skeptical and tried not to over-commit in her efforts to keep things moving. The other lawyer, on the other hand, a guy from California named Strauss, seemed intent on getting into with Ben, frequently throwing Ben's words back at him and trying to put words into Ben's mouth. Halfway through the segment, Loretta asked Ben flat out if he felt that the deaths of Lindsay, Kessler, and Laughlin were related.

Ben hesitated, not wanting to create more trouble for himself. Finally, he said, "you know, Loretta, that's hard to say without more facts, something unfortunately the investigators haven't been too open about sharing. While Marty Kessler was clearly murdered, the police haven't come to that definitive conclusion yet about the others."

Ben heard one of the other guests say something under his breath and then Strauss interrupted as Ben was about to continue. "Come on, Mr. Lohmeier, don't go soft on us now. You're the one who opened this can of worms, after all."

"I wouldn't go that far," Ben said before Strauss talked over him again.

"Of course you did. I think it's pretty clear that something pretty fishy is going on in these investigations and you know it. Now suddenly you try to back off and play nice with the cops."

Ben fought back. "I resent that frankly. I didn't start anything. I merely asked questions that needed asking."

"Come on," the cop joined in. "Why are you backing off now?"

As Ben began to respond, Loretta jumped in. "Whoa guys, let's get back on track. I think Mr. Lohmeier is a big boy who can speak for himself. Let him finish."

Ben could hear the other guests, but with the way the TV hook up was set up, he couldn't see them, which made things a bit more difficult. He knew instinctively, however, that he had to push back and not appear soft for a lot of reasons, personal and professional alike. "Thanks, Loretta, I would certainly prefer to speak for myself, if I could. I'm not backtracking at all. I believe there are questions here that need to be answered and that the investigators need to be more forthcoming about what they are doing and what they have uncovered. On the other hand, if these are three related murders, and they may very well be, they are conducting an investigation designed to apprehend the party or parties responsible for them and revealing too much information could get in the way of that effort."

"Couldn't these deaths just be a coincidence, Mr. Lohmeier?" Loretta responded.

"Sure they could, but none of us are trained to believe in coincidences and to take things at face value. It's always possible,

I suppose, but is it really likely? The more we find out, the less likely that seems."

"Of course there's no coincidence," the cop chimed in.

"Very well," Loretta said, "that's all the time we have. Thank you all." And she was gone.

"Okay, we're out to break," a producer said in their ears. "Thanks guys. Good segment."

Ben was fuming. "Are you guys still there? What in the hell is the matter with the two of you?"

The cop was already gone, but Strauss the lawyer responded. "What are you talking about?"

"What am I talking about? Where do you get off trying to put words in my mouth? If you've got something to say, go ahead and say it, but don't use me to make your point?"

"Come on," Strauss said, "get over yourself. Just trying to make good TV."

Ben followed up until he realized that he was ranting at dead air. Strauss was now gone too. "Asshole!" Ben said. He yanked off his earpiece and microphone and tossed them on the table. They were in the garage, and the camera guy and sound guy started to silently pack up their equipment. Both of them had been out there numerous times for various segments and Ben had gotten to know them a little bit. They were good guys. "Sorry about that," Ben finally said. "They were just really pissing me off."

The sound guy laughed. "No problem. Kind of spiced things up actually. They didn't come off too well, if it makes you feel any better. Can't see either of those guys becoming regulars. Not Loretta's types."

"No," Ben said, "I wouldn't think so. Not from what I know of her anyway. Have you seen either of them before?"

"The cop? A couple of times. The lawyer? No," the camera guy said. "They were trying to shake things up to make the producers happy. They just took it too far and got in your face."

Ben looked at the camera guy. "What do you mean?"

147

The man stopped what he was doing, a lens in one hand and the cap for it in the other. "I just think they got a little personal, that's all."

"No, not that. You said something about making the producers happy. What do you mean by that?"

"Oh that," he responded. "They both got on before you came in and they were talking to one of the producers who told them to mix things up a little and challenge you a bit to see if they could get some sparks flying. They like that kind of shit. You heard the lawyer. He said something about good TV. That's all it was. Giving them what they wanted. Normally you would be in on that kind of stuff, but I guess she thought it would look better if they blindsided you."

"So one of the producers told them to go after me?" Now Ben was really pissed.

"Yeah," the sound guy said.

"Which one?"

"I think it was Mandy," the camera guy said.

His counterpart nodded. "It was Mandy. The short blonde with the nice ass. She was in Chicago for a while. All the guys miss her. She wants to go network though. Stars in her eyes. Too bad." He looked wistful.

Ben couldn't remember if he had met Mandy before. "I'm not sure I know her."

"You'd remember her. She's like a toothpaste commercial. Wants to be on camera. Will probably get there too. Those kind usually do."

Ben helped the guys pack up and load their van before heading back inside to lock up the garage. Back in the main part of the office, he looked around for someone to bitch at, but everyone had already gone home. He really needed to vent. Rather than head home, he grabbed a beer from the kitchen and sprawled on the church pew in the lobby playing the interview over in his mind. It did nothing to cool him off.

He found Libby watching a home remodeling show and surfing the web on her laptop when he finally got home an hour and a half later. She looked up when he came in and shook her head. "I had a feeling you wouldn't be too happy," she said. "I thought about going to bed and pretending to be asleep, but figured that would be cowardly. Besides, I wanted to hear your reaction while your head was still burning. Who were those two dufusses anyhow?"

Ben tossed his briefcase on a chair and sat beside her on the couch. "Just two guys trying to get more face time."

"That's what I was thinking too."

"You know the worst part? One of the producers put them up to it without me knowing."

"You're kidding? That kind of sucks. How do you know?"

"The guys who come out to the office to do the taping told me. They heard it before I came in. I was running kind of late."

"Who did it? Not Loretta, I hope."

"No. One of the twinks who works for her. Wants to make a name for herself."

"What are you going to do?" She had stopped what she was doing and was looking at him now.

He shrugged. "Probably nothing. Not sure what I can do. I'll say something if I ever run into her, but other than that, all I can do is be ready for it next time." They sat in silence for a minute or two, Libby having paused the TV. "How bad was it?"

"Not bad at all. Your son came in after brushing his teeth and caught the end of it. He thought you should have punched the other lawyer. I don't think he realized you were probably a thousand miles apart."

"Good boy. I probably would have punched him if my arms had been long enough."

"The other two looked worse than you did. I wouldn't feel bad at all. You almost looked like the soul of reason."

"Almost?"

She patted his arm. "You forget, I know you."

26

"So, do you have any ideas?"

Thomas Strustevich studied the prosecutor and the detective. "About who built it?" They nodded. "I haven't the foggiest notion." He looked down at the thanatron and fingered one of the tubes. "It's a nice piece of work and all, but anyone could have done it, really. It's not rocket science. It took some effort, of course, though I guess if you're planning to kill someone, then effort isn't out of the question."

Pawlowski wagged a finger at the doctor acknowledging the point. "We've talked about that too. This isn't something you would slap together in an hour or two, right?"

"Right."

"So it follows that this was in the works for a while."

"I would think so."

"I mean, he had to have figured out a plan, designed the device, bought the parts, received them, and assembled it. That takes time. Then figured out when to use it."

"Yeah, true enough. And tested it, of course. I wouldn't think you'd go to all that trouble just to hook him up and have it not work."

"Right. That too. How would you go about testing it?"

Strustevich leaned back and clasped his hands behind his head. He sort of liked the idea of lecturing them. They needed him. Some concept that was. "A couple of ways," he continued. "You could always test it on yourself, just use something harmless like a saline solution in each tube. Or if you really wanted to make sure, you could do a practice run on an animal and see if it worked."

"There's no way to tell if either was done here?"

"No, not unless some trace evidence of some kind was found on the device or in the tubes. Did you find anything like that?"

"No, nothing."

"Then your guy was careful. Not surprising given the effort involved."

"Given the amount of work involved," Pawlowski said as he leaned forward to make his point, "this probably wasn't a crime of passion."

"Well, I wouldn't say that exactly. There are different kinds of passion. But if you're saying crime of passion in the way you guys talk about it, you know, I saw my wife in bed with another guy and grabbed my shot gun and took care of them kind of passion, then no there was too much time for that. This probably took weeks. Again, assuming he didn't really commit suicide in some form or another."

"Which you don't believe he did," Simpson said.

"No, I don't."

"Then that brings us back to who," Simpson said. "You don't have any ideas?"

"No, and I'd probably tell you if I did."

"Probably?"

"Yeah, I think I'd tell you. I'd even tell you if I thought he did it himself. I'm too old to fuck around with you guys now. What would be the point? No, something bad happened here to a guy I liked and respected. He did a lot for me, stood by when my 'so called' friends were jumping ship with all the rats. He could have done one case and moved on, but he didn't do that. He told me early on that he was my lawyer through thick and thin or until I didn't want him anymore. He came to see me in prison when he didn't have to. Not a lot of lawyers do that. And then he got me out. No, he stuck by me. And I wasn't always the easiest guy to deal with either. I did my own thing. Didn't always listen."

151

Simpson grabbed a pitcher and poured himself a glass of water and took a long drink. Then he held the pitcher up to the doctor, who shook his head. "All right. Have you heard from anyone with any threats or suspicious comments?"

"You mean like hate mail? No, not really. Nothing stands out. Sure, I got mail over the years, some supportive, a lot not so much, especially in the beginning. It tapered off a lot over time. I wasn't getting much anymore. I'm sure the prison made copies of the whole lot of it." He crossed his arms across his chest and barked out a laugh. "I'm sure a lot of folks thought I was dead a long time ago."

"Anything pick up when you started your attempts to get released for health reasons?"

The Grim Reaper looked up at the ceiling and considered the question. "No, I wouldn't say so. Look at me," he said slapping himself on the chest. "I'm an old man with not much time left. I'm yesterday's news, and when I do go, I'll be a footnote. People don't bother much with that and why should they?"

"What about Laughlin, did he get mail?"

Strustevich looked at the lawyer and they both nodded. "Sure, in the beginning. He used to tell me at first that I was making him real popular. He used to joke about it. You know, any publicity is good publicity. He hadn't mentioned anything about that in years. I doubt he got much lately."

They both looked at the lawyer, who nodded his head in agreement. "Not too much and nothing threatening that I ever heard of, not lately anyway."

"Did he ever save any of it?"

"Only the funny ones." The prosecutor gave him a look. "Some of them were quite clever. In the beginning, Spencer would occasionally bring one or two to staff meetings and read them aloud for a few laughs. They were funny. Spencer always figured that someone who was out to get you probably wouldn't have warned you ahead of time."

"Perhaps not," Simpson agreed. "Still, do you have copies of any of these letters?"

"No, I don't. I can ask his assistant and see if they saved anything."

"Please," Simpson said and turned back to Strustevich. "What about you? Did you save any of your fan letters?"

"No," the doctor scoffed, "why would I bother? What would I do with them? Like I said, the prison might have copies. Ask them." He scratched his chin. "Have you ever thought that this might have nothing to do with me? He had other cases."

"Yeah, we've thought of that," Pawlowski said. "We've spoken to his office and they are putting some of that together for us, but, frankly, they don't see anything in any of his cases that could point to something like this."

They batted it around for a while, then decided to call it a night. On his way out the door, Strustevich paused and turned to face Simpson. "I'll help if I can," he said and offered his hand. Simpson nodded and took it. Then Pawlowski did the same. They each handed Strustevich a business card. The drive home took fifteen minutes with a retired intern from the VA behind the wheel and Strustevich riding shotgun. No one spoke until they were in the driveway of the doctor's three-bedroom rambler, which had certainly seen better days. "Thanks for the ride," Strustevich said as he dragged himself out of the car. The driver waited until Strustevich had shuffled up to the door, fumbled his keys out of his pocket, unlocked the door and pushed it open. He turned and waived in response to a tap of the horn and watched the car back out of the driveway and pull away.

He thought about Laughlin and his death as he struggled to stoop down and pick up the mail that was jammed through the slot in the front door. He took the handful of envelopes through the living room to the kitchen and dumped them on the counter. "I need a drink," he muttered under his breath before rummaging through a cabinet looking for liquor. He didn't even know if he had any in the house and he didn't have a car of his own to go out and buy some more. Whatever was there would have been there from before he had gone to prison. Earlier in the week, he had enjoyed a celebratory single malt scotch at a friend's place upon his release, but that had been it.

The kitchen was dark because the only light that worked was the one over the sink. The overhead light was burned out. He pulled out two long, thin bottles; one was cooking sherry and the other vermouth. What in the fuck was he ever doing with sherry? He put the bottle on the counter. It would be poured down the drain. The vermouth, on the other hand, had potential depending on what else was in the cabinet. Next, he found an unopened bottle of red wine. He could live with that if necessary. He leaned over and saw two more bottles in the back and struggled to get them out. One was gin, which wasn't much good by itself, but the second, ah, the second was the mother lode – an unopened bottle of Jack Daniels. Excellent.

He found a glass in the top cabinet, peered at it, and discovered a light coating of dust. Prison could modify your habits and lower your standards, but he wasn't this desperate. He squirted a dab of Ivory liquid into the glass and cleaned it with some hot water and a sponge, then dried it with a towel before hobbling over to the freezer for some ice. He stuck his head in and discovered an empty bin and ice trays with tiny old cubes shrunken to the size of marbles. Nope, that wouldn't do. He tossed the bucket and two ice trays in the sink for cleaning and refilling, grabbed a paring knife out of the silverware drawer and sat down at the kitchen table.

Sighing, he popped the top on the whiskey and poured himself half a glass. He took a long pull on the drink. It burned on its way down, but felt good. Strustevich liked the burn, the taste, and the effects of the booze. He had been going at it pretty good before he had gone inside and it was beginning to become a problem back then. Prison took care of that and he hadn't had a single drink while inside, not even the swill that gets passed around from time to time. It wouldn't be a problem now and so what if it was? At his age, what the hell difference would it make?

He finished the drink and poured himself another and thoughts of Laughlin hooked up to the thanatron bit at him along with the whiskey. Could he really have built the thing and killed himself? Strustevich doubted it. He didn't have it in him.

154

Maybe he had help. A sip of the whiskey. Less burn. Who would have helped him? Don't know. Another sip. Why do it before he knew the results of the biopsy? Makes no sense. Laughlin was a smart guy, a great trial lawyer. Wouldn't he want all the facts? I think so. Another sip. Then another bigger one to finish the glass. Starting to get a buzz on now. Better slow down. Thought about it. Poured some more, all the way to the top this time. This would be the last drink. Absolutely the last one. Took another sip.

Laughlin came back to him and the whiskey started to back up in his throat. He forced it down and thought about patients from the distant past, guys at the VA, old soldiers with no hope and no families, just fading away. Those guys needed help. They had pain and suffering from serving their country and their country turned their backs on them. Rotting away just like he was rotting away now. That wasn't Laughlin though. He was in the prime of life. It didn't make sense. The prostate thing was nothing, easily taken care of. Sure, some guys reacted differently to being sick, he'd seen that many times, but not Laughlin. His makeup was different than that. No, this just wasn't right. Everything about it was fucked up.

Another sip of the whiskey. Damn it was good. He'd missed it all right. Another sip. Good. Very good. Outstanding. Another sip. Could have really used the ice though. He looked over and saw the mail sitting in a pile and pulled it over. He separated the letters from the catalogs and set the catalogs aside. They would be going straight into the garbage. The rest didn't look like much either – a couple of bills, a credit card invitation, and a white, business size envelope with his name and address printed on the front in all capital letters with blue pen. He picked up the envelope and turned it over. There was no return address. What the hell is this? He grabbed the paring knife and sliced through the top of the envelope. Inside was a single piece of paper folded into thirds. He squinted through his growing stupor at the single line written in the same block print and quickly dropped the paper back on the table, the bile rising again in his throat. He pulled himself to his feet, staggered over to the sink and vomited. Ten minutes later and now totally sober, he fumbled through his pockets for the business cards. Then he made the call.

27

Pawlowski arrived first, disheveled and out of breath, his tie undone. Simpson came a couple of minutes later looking much the same. Before long, there were cops all over the place. The neighbors didn't miss this, Strustevich thought. Simpson and Pawlowski kept everyone outside at first. Pawlowski found gloves in his overcoat pocket and pulled them on. Simpson told the other two to wait in the front hall while he stuck his head out the door and got gloves of his own and a pair for Strustevich. A moment later all gloved up, he turned to Strustevich and said, "Alright, where is it?"

"Kitchen table. This way." He turned, gestured to follow him and led them down the hall, the gloves still in his hand. They reached the kitchen and he stepped aside to give the other two a good look. The piece of paper sat in the middle of the table, the knife next to it on one side and the bottle of whiskey and empty glass on the other. The rest of the mail was pushed across the table. The return envelope lay on the floor by one leg of the chair upon which the doctor had been sitting.

Pawlowski eyed the bottle and asked, "was that before or after you opened the letter?"

"Before. It had been a while."

"Are you going to put those on or what?" Simpson asked as he gestured toward the gloves in Strustevich's hand.

"What for? I'm not going to touch the goddamned thing again."

The prosecutor nodded. "Tell us what happened."

The Grim Reaper relayed coming home, gathering up his mail, and taking it to the kitchen, where he had had a drink or two. Maybe more. "After a couple of pops, I started to go through my mail. Wasn't expecting anything much, maybe a few hate letters. Didn't expect this." He gestured toward the piece of paper on the table.

"Did the fellow who drove you ever come into the house?" Pawlowski asked.

"No, not when he picked me up or when he dropped me off."

"Was the letter there when you left to meet with us?"

"I assume so. The mail was already through the slot and on the floor, but I hadn't gone through it yet."

"So someone could have slid it into the mail slot while you were gone?"

Strustevich scratched his ear. "Yeah, I guess so. Or even when I was here for that matter. Not that it makes much difference."

"Well, if someone dropped it off in person, then maybe one of your neighbors saw him do it," Pawlowski said. "We'll canvas the neighborhood. You get hate letters a lot?"

"Some. Back in the day. Actually a lot, some pro and some con, at first. Then less over time. None since I've been out. Yesterday's news, I guess."

"What about while you were in prison?" Simpson asked.

Strustevich gave him a bark. "On and off. Not so much in recent years. Lately, mostly reporters. Or maybe do-gooders."

They stood around and looked at each other for a minute. Strustevich had the odd thought that he wished he had kept the place up better. Finally, Simpson looked back at the table and said, "well, I suppose we'd better look at it." He and Pawlowski inched closer to the table. Simpson pointed to the envelope on the floor. "Is this the envelope it came in?" Strustevich nodded. Simpson and Pawlowski both crouched down and looked at the envelope. "No return address," Simpson noted.

"Cleveland postmark," Pawlowski said. "Must have been mailed." He looked up at Strustevich. "Did you touch the note or the envelope after you called me?"

The doctor shook his head. "No."

"Okay then." Pawlowski got to his feet. Simpson did the same and pulled the chair away from the table so they could get closer. The sheet of paper was folded into thirds and the bottom third had folded over the middle, obscuring the writing. Pawlowski placed both his gloved hands on the table and leaned over within inches of the paper. "Looks like ordinary copy paper," he said. "No signs of a watermark anywhere. Might be able identify it or the envelope, but I doubt it will do any good. Probably run of the mill stuff."

Simpson nodded silently and then took the gloved forefinger of his left hand and pulled down the bottom third of the paper to reveal it's writing. It contained just three words.

YOU INSPIRED ME

"Jesus Christ," Simpson said. Pawlowski just sighed.

They looked at each other before both looked up at The Grim Reaper, who stared at the page without saying a word. He slowly looked up and met their eyes. Then he shook his head. "No idea," he said.

"No idea what?" Pawlowski replied.

"No idea who, what or where. Or why. Just no fucking idea." He turned, walked over to the sink, took a glass from the cabinet above and filled it at the tap. He appeared to lean against the sink for support as he sipped the water, his back to the others.

"Okay," Simpson said, "I think we can accept that. But this has to mean something, don't you think?"

"It means the killer is a fucking lunatic, that's what," Strustevich countered, his back still turned. "He's fucking with you, Mr. Prosecutor. He's fucking with the cops. He's fucking with me."

Simpson stood. "Perhaps, but he sent this note to you."

Strustevich turned back to face them, anger on his face. "So what?" he said his voice rising. "This isn't about me. I'm an old man. Nobody cares about me. He's just using me."

"Or she."

"Or she." The doctor waived his hand across face as if to dismiss the notion of a woman being the killer. "But this isn't a woman thing, you know that. Women don't do this."

"I don't think so either, to tell you the truth," Pawlowski said. "But still,"

"But I don't know. This is just someone being, I don't know, smart. Or trying to be. Someone impressed with himself. Not that I'm a psychiatrist. If this same asshole killed all those other lawyers and now Laughlin too, this can't be just about them and it sure as hell isn't about me."

"Who said anything about any other victims?" Simpson said.

Strustevich gave him a withering glare. "What? Lawyers, famous lawyers at that, getting killed all over the place and they aren't connected? Don't bet on it. Murder isn't like the flu. It isn't contagious."

"Sometimes it is," Pawlowski said. "Copycats happen."

The doctor scoffed. "Like this? I doubt it. This guy is being smart, clever. I don't know why or who, but it isn't about the lawyers. Can't be. Something else is going on here. You just have to figure out what." He stared down at the note and shook his head. "I don't like being used. Not like this."

"Nor do we," Simpson said. "But it's not my job to solve the other killings, whether they are connected or not. If they even are murders at all." Strustevich gave him another look. "My job is to solve this one. If they are connected, and I don't know that they are, if we solve this one, we solve the others."

The three men stood there in silence for a moment, the cop and the prosecutor looking a bit silly in their gloves. Finally, Pawlowski broke the spell. "We need to get the forensics guys in here to examine the note and the envelope to see if there is any usable evidence."

"Right," Simpson said. "At least we know now that it wasn't a suicide. Unless it's just the work of someone trying to screw up the investigation." Pawlowski left to get the crime scene techs. Simpson looked at the doctor. "Why do you think the killer would tell us it's not a suicide?"

"Just fucking with you." The comment hung there in the air. "Or maybe he didn't think I'd tell you about the note." Pawlowski came back with two people carrying equipment cases and wearing gloves. He stood next to the doctor, who said in a low voice, "they aren't going to find anything."

Pawlowski nodded. "I know."

28

"God dammit, Lohmeier, cut me some slack here." The speaker was Marcia Roberts and Ben didn't much feel like cutting anyone some slack. "It wasn't my fault you got your ass handed to you."

"I didn't get my ass handed to me. I was set up. There's a difference."

"Maybe, but I didn't do it. I didn't even see it. I did hear about it though. Nice work."

Ben was stilled pissed off about the Loretta appearance and he was extracting his pound of flesh from Marcia. "It doesn't matter who did it. You're all the same. Just vultures." He didn't really believe that, of course, but he knew Marcia could take it and dish it out. "And why didn't you see it, not that fewer viewers isn't better?"

"I think I was in bed with my husband."

"Right. I'm supposed to believe that?"

"It happens."

Stopped in his tracks and not wishing to pursue this angle, he moved into the information gathering phase of the operation. "So, do you know a producer named Mandy, works for Loretta?"

Marcia laughed, more of a cough. "Yeah, I know her. Everybody knows her. And she doesn't work for Loretta. She must have been filling in. She's a riser." Marcia laughed again. "In more ways than one."

"So all the women hate her because she's hot?"

"Not just the women and not just because she's hot, although it pains me to admit that she is hot. No, people don't like the way she uses her looks to her advantage. But that's not really it either. There's just something about her. I shouldn't really say since I don't really know her that well, but everybody pretty much says the same thing. She's just, kind of, I don't know, sneaky, duplicitous, two-faced. People think she's one way to the higher ups and another to the rest of us grunts."

"That wouldn't exactly make her unique, would it?"

Marcia paused. "Probably not, but you throw in the looks and the way she sashays around and there you have it – dislike. Like I said, it isn't just the women. The men don't think much of her either. Sure, they stare at her ass, but that doesn't mean they want to work with her or trust her. But don't get all sanctimonious on me. You've probably gone all googly-eyes over her yourself."

Ben shook his head even though they were talking on the telephone. "I don't think so. I don't think I've ever met her."

"She used to be in Chicago."

"That's what I hear, but it sounds like I would remember meeting her or even seeing her."

"Oh, you would have remembered. She's blonde, a size 4 with big boobs, probably fake by the way, and a great ass. Not that I hold any of that against her. Just pointing out the obvious."

Now Ben laughed. "I didn't know you cared about such things."

"Funny. Still, you've got the give the girl her due. She's quite a little package. She's going places. Not sure how sharp she is, but she's going places."

"Sharp enough it seems," Ben said.

"So true. She belongs on TV. I could see her doing hair commercials."

"The techs said toothpaste."

"Yeah, I could see that too. She's got that Vanna head."

"Huh? What do you mean?"

"Good old Merv Griffin had a theory that people with big heads looked better on TV. As the story goes, he hired Vanna

White for the Wheel not because she was so gorgeous, he could find a lot of gorgeous girls to turn letters, but because she had a great big pumpkin head that would photograph well on TV."

"Hmmm, my wife has a pumpkin head."

"Then maybe we've got the wrong Lohmeier on TV."

"You probably do, but she's too smart to stick her foot in her mouth in front of a million people on cable a couple of times a week."

"We get more viewers than that. Geez Lohmeier, what do think this is, MSNBC? By the way, how do you know she set you up?"

"The techs told me. They heard her while they were setting up their equipment."

"Then they were probably right. What are you going to do about it? Better to get along with someone like her than start something that may not turn out well."

That was the question, Ben knew. What could he do about her? Probably nothing. It felt good to vent though. "I know. Just trying to get the lay of the land, that's all. Now, what was it you needed again?"

"I need a couple, three segments this week and the same next week. And maybe Memorial Day weekend."

Ben groaned. "I don't want to do Memorial Day weekend."

"Do you have plans? Going anywhere?"

"No, not really. Why me?"

"We hear something is about to give on Laughlin. It may be bullshit, but that's what we hear."

"Hear from whom?"

"Sources in the PD, I think. Or maybe the prosecutors. Someone."

"Probably the prosecutors. The police don't give a shit about the press, absent pressure."

"You could provide that pressure. I'm offering you the platform. Help move the process along."

Ben sighed. "You mean stick my neck out in the name of good ratings."

"Good journalism."

"I'm no journalist. Just a talking head on cable TV."

"Don't sell yourself short."

29

Ray Fisher arrived at O'Hare International Airport shortly after Noon local time and rented a car, a non-descript domestic sedan with plenty of room and a large trunk. After making a couple of necessary stops, he checked in at a budget hotel three blocks from the Hilton at two-thirty. Tired from the early flight from the West Coast, he forced himself to take a nap. He slept fitfully and woke about four, went into the bathroom and washed up. Then it was over to the Hilton to get the lay of the land. Although he had thought about his plan almost endlessly, he nonetheless knew it was better to get on site and make sure that things would go down as intended.

Fisher had been to the hotel once before, but that had been years ago and he knew that there had been changes since and that trusting his dim memory of the place could prove disastrous. Sure enough, he discovered upon his arrival that the hotel had undergone extensive renovations in recent years and wasn't at all how he remembered it. He toured the lobby area, examined the schedule of events, then covered the first three floors of the hotel, checking out the various ballrooms. From there, he found all the exits and wandered into the service areas looking for freight elevators and various back of the hotel departments. Satisfied, he returned to his hotel to complete preparations for the evening's events.

*****

Rich pushed through the double swinging doors and walked purposefully down several hallways until he found the place he wanted. He had learned long ago that if you acted like you belonged, people just assumed that you did even if they didn't recognize you. That was particularly true in a place of this size, where no one could know everyone. He was now in bowels of the Hilton hotel, picking through rows of uniforms on standing racks. He picked a couple of possibilities and followed an Hispanic employee to the men's locker room. It was a dark, dingy space, with three rows of lockers surrounding rickety benches for seating. The lavish renovations had obviously not extended to this part of the hotel. There were four other workers in the room and Rich stepped through to the back, his head down to avoid eye contact and discourage conversation. He found an empty locker. Some lockers had locks on them, most did not. He had the row all to himself and could hear a couple of employees speaking Spanish in the next row over.

Already wearing black polyester pants with a white shirt and black tie, he really only needed to worry about the jacket. He took the first jacket from the plastic laundry wrapping and looked at it. It looked like a cheap black sport coat and he tried it on – a little snug through the shoulders, but passable. From what he had already seen, this would be what the bellman or drivers wore, maybe the security people too. He could also probably pass as a musician playing in one of the ballrooms. The second jacket was also black, but a shorter, tighter fitting Eisenhower-style jacket. This would be what the restaurant people and room service waiters wore. It would get him greater access with less attention on the guest floors and perhaps the service areas, but he went with the sport coat he already had on and hung the rejected jacket on a hook in an empty locker. He pulled a small black handheld device from his pocket. If he held it to his mouth it could pass for a walky-talky. In reality, it was a portable stun gun. Although he hoped he wouldn't be needing it, he had it ready if he did.

Rich turned his back to the aisle as another employee came, changed and departed, then waited for the locker room to clear out before heading out himself. Having thoroughly studied a schematic of the hotel, he knew exactly where he wanted to go. He checked his watch and found he was a bit ahead of schedule, then followed a couple of housemen moving some tables to a distant ballroom. He let them go ahead and paused in a long, tunnel-like basement corridor that connected one part of the hotel to the other. It was in this corridor that the hotel stored its stock of banquet tables and chairs, literally hundreds and hundreds of each. They sat on rolling carts for easy transport and were pushed up against the side of the wide corridor in rows of two or three. The tunnel was dark, only lit by single bare caged bulbs every fifty feet or so of the entire length of more than three hundred feet. It smelled of cigarettes.

Rich covered the entire length of the tunnel to get a better handle on the inventory in storage and doubled back and found a spot about halfway down the tunnel, making a small space for himself on a chair behind three carts of tables. The spot was dark and secure. Rich could not be seen from this location unless the carts hiding him were moved. Any tables needed for the evening's events had likely already been retrieved and the banquet rooms set, but if more were needed, those would come from the ends and not the middle where Rich was hiding. The coat of dust on the racks confirmed as much. He checked his watch, put his feet up on the rail of one of the adjacent carts and made himself comfortable. He had some time to kill. The calm before the storm.

30

The dinner and reception for Jimmy Moran was to begin at seven o'clock at the Hilton downtown on Michigan Avenue and Ben left the office about half past five. He got caught up in traffic for the Blackhawks playoff game on the Eisenhower Expressway and didn't hit the parking garage around the corner from the hotel until ten minutes before it was supposed to start. Wearing his best charcoal grey suit and with the fresh haircut Libby had insisted upon, he walked into the opulent lobby and searched for the board with the day's events so he could figure out where to go. He found it on the near side of the lobby and headed in that direction. About halfway there, a voice from behind him called, "hey Ben."

He turned and saw Stan Feldman striding toward him. He threw up both arms in a gesture to show how surprised he was to see Feldman and then the two lawyers shook hands. "Good to see you, Stan," Ben said. "I didn't know you'd be here."

"They asked me to come out and say a few words. I've gotten to know Jimmy pretty well since the Owens trial and since I cut my teeth on TV doing commentary during the trial, they thought I had a decent perspective and could say something intelligent. Not sure they're right though."

Ben laughed. "Don't worry. You're probably dealing with weak competition."

"That always helps. Say, do you know where we're supposed to go?"

"I was just checking that on the board over there. I think it's the Grand Ballroom, not that I know where that is."

They walked over and scanned the board. Although both men were lean, Feldman stood four or five inches taller than Ben Lohmeier's five foot nine and was fairly dark, while Ben was blonde with striking green eyes that occasionally drew stares. Ben was right, it was the Grand Ballroom, which a concierge told them was on the second floor, just beyond the landing at the top of a spectacular set of circular stairs at the back of the lobby. The two men wandered off in that direction.

"To tell you the truth, I'm really glad to see you," Ben said. "I wasn't really all that enthusiastic about coming tonight and I was afraid that I wouldn't have anyone I knew to talk to."

"I know what you mean, but I think more people know you than you think. I'll bet people come up to you all evening asking about Lindsay and Laughlin and Kessler. Hell, I've been meaning to call you myself. I was watching you on Loretta that night and I was wondering if you knew something the rest of us didn't."

"No, not really," Ben said shaking his head. "Just spouting off without any information like most of the guys on TV do. You think I'm nuts too? The guys at the office are comparing me to Oliver Stone."

"I believe it, but, no, I don't think you're nuts at all. In fact, I think that you are almost certainly right. We've both been around too long to believe in coincidences. You just said what most people here tonight are probably already thinking."

They reached the top of the stairs and saw a short line forming in front of them to check in at a series of banquet tables. As they slowly made their way to the front of the line, Ben asked, "since you're speaking, do you have to sit up front with all the celebrities?"

"I doubt it. Usually save those spots for the bar association people who are trying to bask in the reflected glow of the honoree."

They checked in, received a small packet with a name tag, and were directed to the doors behind the check-in tables. As they entered the room, they paused, and Ben whistled. "This is a big room,"

Feldman agreed. "I'll bet they could put more than a thousand people in here."

"At least. There have to be more than five hundred in here already." The room was enormous, with five huge crystal chandeliers overhead and countless round banquet tables for guests. Ben pointed to a line of guests snaking down the middle aisle, then followed it up to the front of the room. He saw Jimmy Moran in the distance standing in front of the head table greeting those who had come to honor him. "I think we're supposed to get in line and shake hands with the great man."

"Looks that way. May as well do our part," Feldman said.

The two men got in line and slowly made their way toward the front of the room. After a while, Ben got near enough to get a good look at Jimmy Moran, whom he'd never met. "He's not a very big guy, is he?" he whispered into Feldman's ear.

"No, he's not, but he's been ill too. He looks thinner than usual. Cancer, I think. Not sure what kind. Leukemia maybe? I hear he's doing better though."

When they reached the front of the line and he saw Feldman, Moran seemed to light up. "Stan, it's great to see you. I was so happy to hear you were coming and were willing to say a few words on behalf of an old warhorse like me."

They went back and forth for a couple of minutes as those in line probably grew impatient, then Feldman turned and gestured to Ben. "Jimmy, this is a friend of mine, Ben Lohmeier. We've done a few shows together and you've probably seen Ben on the cable shows as well."

Ben shook hands with Moran and was again struck by how small and frail the other man appeared. "Of course I recognize Mr. Lohmeier," Moran said. "I really admired your work on that law school case. I know how hard it is to be in the spotlight like that. That was good work." He slapped Ben on the shoulder then leaned in closer and said in a softer voice, "I also saw your conjecture the other night on Loretta's show. I wouldn't mind a

171

few minutes of your time later this evening to talk about it, if you don't mind. I think you were on the money."

"I'd be happy to talk about it," Ben said, "but we better get moving or the other people waiting are going to mutiny. I'll look you up after the speeches."

Ben and Stan Feldman wandered off to the bar in the near corner in search of a libation. Three different lawyers came up to Ben to say hello while he was waiting for his gin and tonic and two more stopped by the table within the first five minutes after they had sat down. Ben hadn't really known any of them and didn't say much more than hello.

"I told you that you were more popular than you realized," Feldman joked as he held up his scotch and soda for Ben to clink glasses. "A lot of these guys wish they were in your shoes. Don't ever underestimate the power of television."

"No, I guess you're right. And to think, all it took was getting shot at by some nut."

"That, and you won the case and solved the mystery."

"Well, I solved the mystery. I didn't actually win the case. They had to drop the charges. Who knows what the jury would have done."

"Bullshit," Feldman said. "You did better than a not guilty. You made them give up. And people remember that. I'll tell you, you'll have to lose an awful lot of cases before it comes close to overshadowing that big win." With that, Feldman drained his drink. Ben had barely started his own. "I need another drink," Feldman said.

"Easy Stan, we just got here."

"Don't worry about me. I've got a room upstairs. As long as I can make it to the elevators, I'm good. I learned that lesson a long time ago."

"Ah," Ben said, "that explains it. I'm not so lucky." He held up his glass. "This is my one and only drink of the evening. One and done. After that, it's Coke or ginger ale or 7 Up. I do not want to be the poster boy for drinking and driving."

They talked for a few more minutes as the guests found tables. Ben saw very few open seats. He recognized some of the people at his table, but didn't really see anyone he knew well in the entire room. Thank God for Feldman, he thought.

While everyone started to look for a place to sit and the reception line shrank, Ray Fisher stood in the back of the room in his best dark blue suit and watched. When the line was down to six people, he hurried to the front of the room. Moran was so engrossed in accepting the congratulations of his many well-wishers, he didn't even notice who was waiting at the end of the line. As Fisher stepped forward, Moran reached out his hand and froze, a look of shock briefly crossing his face. He quickly looked around and scanned the audience. "What in the hell are you doing here?" he hissed as his smooth, practiced façade momentarily evaporated.

Fisher gave an exaggerated laugh to show anyone who might be watching that everything was alright. "You aren't happy to see me, counselor?" he said. "I'm disappointed. And after I've come all this way and gone to all this trouble. I paid for my ticket. Isn't my money good enough for you? You've taken everything else."

Moran seemed to regain his composure and his spirit. He stepped close to Fisher and said in a low voice, "You don't belong here. I'll call security if I have to."

Just then, someone stepped to the microphone at the head table and announced that they were ready to commence with the festivities. Fisher looked delighted. Moran forced a smile on to his face. "Oh, I'm sorry, Jimmy," Fisher said. "I better grab a seat. We'll catch up later. You can count on it." Fisher reached out his hand this time, which was ignored, turned on his heel and walked away. Moran watched him go before coming to the somewhat uncomfortable realization that everyone was watching him and waiting for him to take his seat at the head table. Then he smiled and waved to the crowd. Everything was fine. The show was about to start.

31

Bobby Joe Gibbons' trial in Boston ended earlier than expected. Midway through their case, the defendant corporation realized that things were headed south in a hurry and approached the plaintiff's team about renewing settlement discussions. Soon, the offer was in the ballpark they had been hoping for all along and Gibbons' co-counsel wanted a payday badly enough to push for an acceptance. Back in the good old days, Gibbons would never have gone along with it. He would have counseled and cajoled and convinced everyone to see it through to a jury verdict in their favor, for in his world, there was nothing better than that moment when the jury came back, looked you in the eye and handed you a big victory. He lived for that moment, his very life was predicated on it. There was a time when he would have died for it. Not anymore. That was years ago. Now, he would argue fire and brimstone in order to get the settlement he wanted. Given his track record, he wasn't wrong then. Given the realities of life, he wasn't wrong now either.

He had been itching for a settlement for a while. His nightly conversations with Maria had taken on a markedly different flavor in recent days. Rather than buoy his spirits, he now found them very disquieting. Despite her protestations to the contrary, Maria did not sound right and she wasn't simply tired and he wasn't imagining things, as she insisted when he brought it up. Almost a decade earlier, she had been diagnosed with breast cancer after a routine mammogram. Fortunately, the cancer had

174

been caught in its earliest stages and the treatment had been quick, effective, and not particularly debilitating, at least for her. Bobby Joe, on the other hand, had taken it like a sledgehammer to the chest. He realized, perhaps for the first time, that she was really his whole life, his everything, more important than all the cases he had won and could ever win. That was just stuff—stuff you could buy, stuff you could have, stuff you could be. She was what made all that stuff worth having and he couldn't imagine living without her.

Gibbons had long believed that he would die first, a brilliant star that would simply flame out for good one day and that Maria would go on forever as the shining light for all those who knew her. He hoped that would be the case anyway. Her illness had convinced him that he would fall into a deep, dark hole without her, unable to function and not wanting to go on living. Having just gotten off the phone with Maria, Gibbons couldn't get his worst fears out of his head. But for the perfunctory settlement stuff and celebratory dinner with the client and his fellow counsel of record, he would have rushed back home as soon as the parties shook hands on the deal.

As a result of delays at the airport and bad weather over Wyoming, Gibbons didn't reach home until almost noon the following day. He found Maria in the kitchen, still in her robe and making coffee. She turned at the sink and stuffed a Kleenex into her pocket before he could see. Though she looked like hell, the sight of her was still the most beautiful thing he could imagine. He wrapped his arms around her and kissed her on the head. She tried to shoo him away without success. "Alright, alright," she said in a raspy voice, "you're going to suffocate me if you're not careful." He finally loosened his grip, stepped back, and examined her, one hand gripping each of her shoulder. What he saw worried him. She looked pale and disheveled, not at all the vibrant woman at the center of his world. She reluctantly made eye contact and offered a weak smile. "I know I must look a fright," she said as she tried to smooth her hair.

He didn't let go. "You're the most beautiful thing I've ever seen," he whispered into the top of her head as he pulled her to his chest. "Always have been, always will be. But you've got to tell me the truth. What is it? Is it the cancer? Is the cancer back? Have you been to the doctors? What do they say? You've got to tell me. I can see you're sick. I could tell on the phone. I wanted to come home. I should have ..."

She finally pushed away from. "The cancer? Oh my God, no. Is that what you think? Robert Gibbons, you old fool, you wonderful old fool." Now she hugged her husband. "No, the cancer isn't back. I don't look that bad, do I?" She tried to laugh. "I've just had this nagging cold or flu for a few days or so that I can't seem to shake. It's nothing. And it certainly isn't cancer, that's for sure. I would know if it was, believe you me. This is nothing like that."

Gibbons wanted to believe her, needed to believe, but didn't, not fully. "Have you been to the doctor?" he asked again.

"No, I haven't felt the need to. I'm just a little rundown fighting this virus, or whatever it is. But if it will make you feel better, I'll make an appointment if I don't feel better in couple of days. How's that?"

He wanted to object, to shake her and talk sense into her, but that would only cause her to dig in her heels and wait even longer, so he acquiesced. "Okay, but you have to promise."

She kissed his cheek. "I promise." She broke free from his grasp and backed away. Sizing him up and down, she said, "you don't look so hot yourself. You must be worn out from the trial and the flight and all. Why don't you go lay down on the couch and I'll fix you some lunch."

Although he recognized her diversion for what it was, he had to admit that she was right. He was beat. What with worrying about her, he hadn't been sleeping well and the travel always wore him out these days. Shrugging off his buckskin jacket, he shuffled over to the big leather sofa, sat down, and pulled off his boots. He piled a couple of pillows at one end and stretched out, his right arm folded over his eyes, his legs straight out. Within a minute or two, he had drifted off, just as Maria sat down at the kitchen table to catch her breath.

He followed her around for the next two days while trying to appear not to and she seemed to be getting better. Or maybe he was getting used to her. Dinners were the standard meat and potatoes affairs that he had long insisted upon and since she was never a particularly big eater anyway nothing seemed too much out of the ordinary when she merely picked at her food. His worries receded a bit. On the morning of the third day, he found her in the bathroom with her head between her knees and toilet paper stuffed up her nose trying to staunch a nosebleed. Following a series of rapid-fire questions that displayed as much cross-examination skill as concern, she confessed it was the second, or maybe the third, such event in recent days, but that it could get dry at the ranch, as everyone knew, and that there was nothing to be alarmed about.

Gibbons wasn't buying it. He was more than alarmed. Frantic, he demanded that they immediately go to the hospital. She insisted that it was nothing and that she was feeling better. They went back and forth about it, and as was their custom, she eventually prevailed. He practically watched her sleep—every toss and turn, cough, or wheeze heightening his anxiety. The following afternoon, after realizing he had neither seen nor heard from her for almost two hours while he reluctantly conducted some much-neglected work from his wood-paneled home office, he searched the house and found her lying unconscious on the floor of the basement in front of an open plastic storage box filled with scrapbooks, ice cold, and a trickle of blood coming from both nostrils. He called 911.

Things went rapidly downhill from there. She regained consciousness later that evening at the hospital and as he did his best to keep her spirits up, he sensed that she was more concerned about him than herself. Her doctors were flummoxed. They took blood, did an MRI and a CAT scan and didn't seem at all confident in any diagnosis. She seemed to be sliding away and they didn't know what to do about it. He burned through his Rolodex calling on every contact and specialist he knew trying to get help, and soon, they began assembling at the ICU as Gibbons stalked the halls and railed against anyone and everyone within earshot. By the following afternoon, she seemed to realize that she was sliding downhill with little chance of recovery and tried to say good-bye as her faculties started to desert her. He was having none of it. The great trial lawyer was not going to lose this verdict.

In the midst of all this, Gibbons learned that cattle at the ranch had also been getting sick and that several had already died. The ranch suddenly became the focus of attention for those trying to determine the cause of Maria's illness. Before the investigators in the hazmat suits from the State Department of Health had managed to identify a tainted water supply, Maria Gibbons had already lapsed into a coma. The doctors told her husband that there was little more they could do. Less than a week after he had returned from Boston, Gibbons' beloved wife was gone. Lost in his shock, anger, and grief, was the fact that he too had already started to feel ill.

32

Dinner was above-average, especially for this kind of event. The speeches were pretty good too. Feldman went for humor and the crowd seemed to like it. Even the mayor, sitting next to the guest of honor, appeared to be having a good time. Like most everyone else, Ben watched Moran's reaction to the speeches. At first, he seemed a bit out of sorts, perhaps uncomfortable with all the attention, but eventually he warmed up, and by the end, actually seemed to be enjoying himself. Ben could sympathize. He wasn't sure he could sit there and be the center of the attention, yet unable to actually influence the result. It was like watching your own life story on TV and not knowing the outcome. He thought of those old Dean Martin roasts and shivered. Better him than me.

Moran himself spoke last, after the praise and the jokes and the attempts to somehow link him to the bar association Ben doubted he would ever join. The nerves seem to have returned – Moran appeared jittery and ill at ease once again. His remarks appeared to be almost entirely ad libbed as though he was making it up as he went along. The delivery wasn't very good either, shocking for such a gifted and successful trial lawyer. Most significantly, was the utter absence of any reference to the trial that made him famous, for Moran never mentioned the Owens trial once or even hinted that he ever even knew about it.

As the speech unfolded and grew more curious by the minute, Ben glanced around the room and confirmed that he wasn't imagining things, as he saw confused looks on the faces of many of the onlookers. Feldman just looked concerned. Ben nudged him under the table. Feldman just shook his head as though making eye contact with Ben would acknowledge the unspeakable disaster that they were witnessing. When Moran ended his remarks, it felt like all of the air had been sucked from the room and it had to come rushing back in before anyone could begin to applaud.

Moran himself looked relieved, embarrassed, and scared all at the time. He was sweating profusely, the sheen on his forehead visible even from the back tables. He scanned the crowd nervously looking for something or someone. Back and forth he went as the mayor and various bar association officials tried to shake hands and congratulate him. Soon the applause started to die down and people began to take their seats once again. Ben watched him continue to search the room until he stopped and stared directly at their table. He appeared to make eye contact with Feldman, who waved his hand in congratulations. Moran nodded, seeming to pull himself together, and finally sat down.

People crowded around the honoree congratulating him, shaking his hand, and slapping him on the back. Feldman watched him carefully from his seat. Ben watched Feldman and his concern was plain to see. "Well, that was weird," Ben said.

"Agreed," Feldman responded, his eyes still on the head table.

"What do you make of it? I don't really know him, but he seemed spooked or something. You know him, what did you think?"

Feldman finally pulled his eyes away from Moran and met Ben's gaze. "You're right," he said. "Spooked is a good word for it. I can't explain it. Maybe I was wrong. Maybe he isn't well."

Ben leaned in close. "What gets me is he didn't even mention the Owens trial or the Dream Defense at all. Sure, maybe he gets tired of talking about it, but people here were dying to hear about that stuff, a big, high-profile trial like that."

Feldman vigorously shook his head. "No, that's not it. I've never known him to grow tired of talking about the Owens trial. It was his biggest glory. Who doesn't want to talk about that?

180

Especially at something like this." He gestured around the large room. "It's like the Rolling Stones not doing *Satisfaction*. Makes no sense."

"You're right, and on top of that, he looked fidgety almost. He was fine when we talked with him, then he gets stage fright or something? A guy with his experience? Something weird ..."

Just then Moran himself appeared at their table, a forced smile on his face, still sweating. Up close, he looked even worse. "Hey, Jimmy," Feldman said trying to cover up their conversation, "great speech."

Moran looked around and pulled a chair from a neighboring table and dragged it close between the chairs occupied by Ben and Feldman. They slid back to give him more room, exchanging glances that confirmed their thoughts of a moment ago. Moran looked at Feldman, then around behind himself as though to ensure he wasn't being overheard, before focusing on Ben. "Mr. Lohmeier, Ben," he said in a low voice. He moved even closer. Ben fought the urge to back away. "Remember earlier, when I said we needed to talk?"

Ben nodded. He could see Feldman watching intently over Moran's shoulder. "Sure. Of course."

"We really need to talk."

"Okay, go ahead. What's up?"

Moran shook his head. "No, not now, not here. Later," he said. Ben's confusion must have been obvious. Moran put his hand on Ben's forearm in an imploring gesture. He looked around again. "There are too many people around now. Too many ears. We need some privacy."

"Okay," Ben said slowly. Now he was really puzzled. "Sure. Whatever you say. Just tell me when and where."

"Good. Thanks." Moran seemed relieved. "I'm staying in the hotel. I have a room upstairs. We can talk there after this is over. I have to make the rounds, you know. I can't just disappear upstairs with everyone still here."

"Of course not."

Moran took a deep breath and let it out. He looked to be figuring something out in his head. He glanced at his watch.

"Tell you what, can you meet me in my room in forty minutes or so? That should give me enough time to shake some hands and get back upstairs."

Ben looked at his watch too. "Sure, I can do that."

Moran got to his feet. He suddenly appeared more at ease. He reached out his hand and Ben shook it. "Okay then," Moran said. "I'm in room 1810." He repeated himself. "That's 1810. I'll see you in forty minutes or so."

"Sounds good. See you then."

With that, Moran was off, leaving Ben and Feldman to stare at each other in disbelief. "What in the hell was that all about?" Ben asked.

"No clue."

"Did you notice how he was looking around when he was done with his remarks?"

"Yeah."

"Well, I thought he was looking for you because he stopped searching once he saw our table."

"So did I," Feldman said, "But I think he was looking for you, not me. That's pretty obvious, isn't it?"

"Yeah, but what does he want with me. I just met him."

"It's got to be these deaths, these murders, if they really are murders. What else could it be?"

Ben knew he was right. "Nothing probably." He got up and said, "let's go get another drink."

Feldman rose as well. "I thought you were one and done."

"I was, but that was then and this is now. I thought I'd be out of here by now."

"Never a bad idea to have another drink," Feldman said.

The two men headed over to the bar, got a drink, and wandered around the room for a while. Feldman introduced Ben to a couple of lawyers Ben didn't know and Ben did the same with a few of the locals. It turned out that Ben was more interesting and popular than he realized because countless lawyers came up to him to introduce themselves, renew acquaintances, and ask him about the deaths of Lindsay, Kessler and Laughlin, which seemed to be what everyone was talking about. Even a couple of reporters tried to get a comment or two. Ben did his best not to make any news, but when a Fox camera crew found him in the corner caucusing with Feldman, he felt like he had to give them a couple of minutes as Feldman took his drink and disappeared.

The reporter, a Ken doll named Rob Franklin, who looked like he should be modeling underwear in the Sears catalog, set up the shot and then the lights came on and they were ready to go. Franklin looked into the camera, flashed his white teeth, and said, "let's test the sound." After a moment, he pointed to the gin and tonic in Ben's hand and said, "you might want to dump that."

Ben didn't get it at first, then looked down and said, "oh, right, not a good look." He stashed the drink on a nearby table and returned to his spot. "Thanks."

"No problem."

Then they began and spent a minute or so waltzing through the preliminaries and what a great evening it was, and so on and so forth. The lights were hot and Ben felt himself starting to perspire. Maybe that second drink wasn't such a great idea after all. They continued for a couple of more minutes without anything significant coming up until Franklin dropped the bomb. "I've got to ask you," he said with a flash of the TV smile, "about your recent comments on Fox News that the deaths of three prominent lawyers – Patrick Lindsay, Martin Kessler, and Spencer Laughlin may all have been murders and may even be related. I saw you huddling with the guest of honor, Jimmy Moran, earlier and wonder if that was what you were discussing."

Ben felt like he had just been conked on the head with a brick. He practically winced. All intelligent thought vanished from his head. Fortunately, Ben had been on television enough to know that he had to keep smiling and hope something came to him. It didn't, not really. He started to make a joke about it before recalling in the nick of time that you couldn't joke about possible murders. Then he weakly dodged the question and a couple of follow-ups. He finally babbled something about congratulating Moran on his long career and great accomplishments and the interview mercifully ended. It probably lasted no more than three minutes and felt like three hours.

Franklin flashed a real grin this time and offered his hand. "Thanks counselor," he said. He knew he had caught Ben off-guard and scored and was clearly pleased with himself.

Ben knew it too. He immediately thought about how bad this could look once edited and felt like taking the camera. "My pleasure," he said as he took Franklin's hand. Both of them knew he didn't mean it. The camera lights shut down and Ben blinked as his vision slowly returned to normal. He looked up to see Feldman standing two tables over and pointing to his watch. Ben looked down at his own watch. More than forty-five minutes had already passed since his conversation with Moran. "Damn," he said.

Feldman walked up and said, "you're late."

Ben grabbed his drink from the nearby table and took a swallow. "I know it. I notice that you ran away when the TV guys showed up."

Feldman shrugged. "You're the local hero, not me. How'd it go?"

"Train wreck."

"What happened? You had kind of a deer in the headlights thing going at the end."

"That bad?"

"Probably not, but I'm kind of sensitive to it since I've had my own deer in the headlights moments on national TV. Not your best work, doubt it's your worst either. What did he say that got you going?"

"Huh, well, he asked whether I was huddling with Moran about the murders, er, deaths, whatever they are. He must have been watching. Completely threw me."

"Jeez, you only spent about two minutes with Jimmy." He looked around. "You just never know. They could be anywhere. Did you deny it? What you were talking about, I mean."

"Of course I denied it. Then I mumbled something incoherent, talked about the wonderful honor for a great lawyer or some bullshit like that."

184

"You didn't say anything about meeting him in his room?" Feldman was shaking his head.

"No, nothing about that. I was blindsided, not in a coma."

"Good, then it wasn't that bad. I would just make sure the reporter isn't watching when you go upstairs. I'd get going, by the way. Jimmy didn't look like a guy who would handle waiting real well about now."

Ben looked around the room at the thinning crowd. "No, probably not. I don't see him anywhere, do you?"

"No, I don't either. I was looking for him when you were doing the interview, but I couldn't find him. He must have already escaped upstairs. You'd better go."

"What about you? Where are you going to be?"

"I'll take the elevator with you. I'm on 10, 1004 I think." He pulled a key card out of his pocket in a small envelope and checked the number. "Yeah, I'm in 1004."

The two men slipped from the room and headed for the stairs. They could hear an orchestra playing somewhere in the vicinity. "Listen to that," Feldman said. "Live music."

"At least someone's having fun. Probably dancing too. Women in low cut dresses."

"Beats looking like a dufus on TV."

Ben growled. "Thanks." He stopped and looked around. "Wait," Ben said, "there has to be an elevator around here somewhere." They turned and went back in the other direction. Down at the end of a long hall, they spotted a small group forming. "That must be it up there." It was. They slowed and let the group filter on to one car and then hit the up button after the door had closed. Feldman turned to see if anyone was watching. "Anything?" Ben asked.

"No, we're good."

One minute passed, then another, before the bell signaling the next car sounded. The doors opened. Empty. They stepped inside and Ben quickly hit 10 and 18 and the doors closed. "I feel like James Bond," Feldman said. "Maybe we need a secret handshake."

185

"Great idea, but I don't think Bond has a secret handshake. Besides, you don't look like James Bond. More like Q."

Feldman made a face. "Is Q the one in charge?"

"No, that's M. Q is the techno-geek."

"Thanks a lot. No, we're just two dumb lawyers thinking they're on a spy mission. What's more pathetic than that?"

"Don't know. Depends on what he says."

The car stopped at the 10th floor and Feldman started to get out. He rested his hand on one of the doors to keep them from closing and turned to face Ben. "Stop down when you're done."

"I'll call you on my shoe phone." Ben paused. "Maybe we're nuts."

"Maybe we are."

"Do you think so?"

"No. You?"

Ben shook his head. "Afraid not. I wish we were."

33

Ben rode the elevator to the 18th floor. As the bell rang and the elevator slowed, he felt butterflies in his stomach and wished he hadn't had the gin and tonic. Or eaten the food. He wasn't sure why he was nervous, but knew without any shadow of a doubt that he was. He exited the elevator and turned to his left coming to a long hallway that went in both directions. A gold sign on the wall in front of him indicated that room 1810 was to his right so he went in that direction. Like the ballroom, the guest areas seemed to be from another era, with elaborate floral wallpaper and wainscoting in gold and rose. The carpet was a royal blue. Brass light fixtures looking like candles dotted the walls. Ben remembered that the hotel had fairly recently been renovated, but he wouldn't have expected this. Perhaps the goal of the renovation had been to make the place look more like its heyday. He reached the end of the hallway and another sign pointed him to the left. The doors were further apart here, no doubt due to the fact that the rooms in this part of the floor were larger, maybe suites. The doors were staggered so that no two doors were directly across from each other and each door occupied its own little alcove. Halfway down the hallway on the right, he found Moran's room.

Ben stopped in front of the alcove and hesitated, not sure why. He looked in both directions and saw no one. Then he listened carefully. Nothing. He stepped into the alcove and listened again. Still nothing. Finally, out of excuses, he stepped forward and knocked on the door. Moran opened it almost instantly, a drink in his hand, a relieved look crossing his face. Ben almost jumped. He hadn't expected Moran to be waiting by the door. "Good, you're here," Moran said. "I thought maybe you weren't coming." He held the door open and stepped aside, waving Ben inside with the hand holding the drink.

Ben walked past him and down a short hallway that opened up into the sitting room for Moran's suite, then turned to see Moran closing and latching the door behind him. The older man quickly closed the distance between them and held out his hand, which Ben took. It was clammy and wet, not necessarily from the drink Moran had been holding. He had removed his suit coat and loosened his tie and Ben could see that he was still sweating profusely despite the fact that the room was relatively cool. He looked all wrung out. Ben figured he was about to find out why.

Moran motioned him to a chair. The room had more of the look of faded elegance, this time in cream and mauve. There was a small wet bar and fridge framing the front of the room, with a small sofa flanked by two chairs forming the seating area. A Williamsburg-style desk was in the far corner with a not-so-comfortable looking chair. Ben took one of the chairs in the sitting area. "I'm glad we could talk privately without people watching us." Moran said and forced a laugh. "As a lawyer, I'm of course used to being the center of attention, but this awards stuff is for the birds. He took a drink and Ben noticed that his hand was shaking. "That's why I don't do much television. I'd rather just try my cases."

Ben watched him intently, then said, "no, I understand completely. I didn't want to do TV either at first, but now I kind of enjoy it. When I don't have anything interesting going on in my cases, it gives me something to keep the blood pumping."

"And you're good at it. I watch you a lot." He took another drink and then remembered his manners. "Look at me. Enjoying a cocktail and I haven't offered you anything."

Ben smiled. "No problem. I'm good. I'm driving so I'm at my limit. Don't want to get pulled over on the way home."

"You sure?" He stepped over to the fridge. "This thing is fully stocked and it's their dime. Might as well enjoy it." He laughed. "If you get pulled over, I'll get you off." He placed his drink on the bar, steadied himself with one hand and leaned over to open the fridge and rummage through its contents. Ben noticed three empty mini-bottles of vodka on the counter. "Let's see, we've got all sorts of booze in here – soda, juice, water …"

Ben relented. "Okay, I'll have a bottled water. Can't get into too much trouble with that."

Moran grabbed a bottle out of the fridge, handed it to Ben and sat down on the sofa. They made small talk for a few minutes as Ben studied his counterpart. He really didn't look well, Ben thought. Whether he was suffering through some illness or it was something altogether different, Ben could not tell. In any event, Jimmy Moran was clearly agitated and something was eating at him, literally or figuratively.

Moran drained his drink and slowly got to his feet. "I should probably quit for the night myself, but one more ain't gonna kill me." He found another vodka in the fridge and poured the contents into his glass. Then he seemed to make up his mind about something, nodded and finally got to the point. "I suppose you want to know why I asked you to come up here." He gestured around the room. "To my humble abode as it were."

Ben took a pull on his water. "I must confess that I am kind of wondering."

"Well, I'll tell you." Moran's voice took on a sense of urgency. He leaned forward. He was no longer the smooth, confident advocate that Ben had witnessed throughout the Owens trial and in the years since. "I was watching that night on the television, watching Loretta Bergen when you said that we may have a string of murders on our hands. Famous lawyers. Dead lawyers. All murdered. You know what? I think you're right on the money. Right on the goddamned money." He pointed at Ben with the hand holding the drink. "All of them. Pat Lindsay, Marty Kessler and Laughlin over in Ohio. I think they were all murdered."

189

Ben laughed a nervous laugh. "I appreciate the endorsement, but a lot of people think I sort of stepped in it, so to speak, on that one."

"But you don't think so, do you?"

Ben took another drink. He held his arms out palms up. "No, not exactly, but I don't know anything. I don't have any inside information. No one is talking to me outside of other talking heads on cable TV. What do I know? I haven't seen any evidence. As you know, it's all about evidence."

Moran got up and started pacing, all nervous energy and ideas spilling out as though he would explode if he didn't get them out. "It has to be murder. All of them. Has to be."

"Okay, some of that is obvious. Kessler for sure. There's no proof that I know of about Lindsay. Word is he was a drunk."

"Sure he was a drunk," Moran agreed. "So what? He could clean himself up. He did that during our trial. Never had a problem then."

"That was a long time ago. He's had a lot of problems since then, hasn't he?"

Moran continued pacing. "Yes, I suppose so, but that doesn't mean he wasn't pushed down the stairs. Come on, fell down the stairs? How often does that really happen?"

"Who knows? We could probably get statistics on that if we wanted to. Still, there's no proof that I know of."

"True. Let's assume he was killed."

"Big assumption."

"Nevertheless, let's assume it. Then you have Laughlin. Do you really buy a suicide there?"

Ben shrugged and took another swig from the water bottle. "Don't know. Never met him. Don't know him. Am I suspicious? Sitting here in your hotel room, sure I am. But again, that's without any evidence. Would it surprise me if it wasn't suicide? No, not at all. But this isn't my case. I had the facts, most of them anyway, in the law school case, and access to the evidence. I don't have that here and neither do you. Are you saying the deaths are connected?"

190

Moran paused his pacing and stopped in front of Ben. "They have to be."

Ben was skeptical. "What's the connection?"

"I don't know, but you can find one."

"Me? Why me? I'm not a cop or an investigator. Like I told you, I don't have access to anyone or anything. How am I going to find out? Why don't you do it?"

Moran sighed and considered Ben for a moment as if trying to decide whether to confide in him even more. When he spoke, his voice was soft and pleading. "Look, I'm not well. I look like hell and I feel worse. I've had cancer, got cancer. Melanoma. I don't have the energy for this and I may not have the time for it either."

Ben didn't know what to say. Finally, he simply said, "I'm sorry. How bad is it?"

"Bad enough, I guess. I'm not dead yet. I'll be kicking for a while. But that's not the point."

"I'm just not sure what you want me to do. And I'm not sure why me."

"Because you can do it. You've done it before. I can hire you or at least pay your expenses."

Ben was shocked. He hadn't seen this coming. "I've got to ask you, why are you doing this? Why are you so upset about this? I understand you knew Kessler and Lindsay ..."

"It's more than that," Moran interrupted. "I just know it. Something is going on here. Too many people are dying and it doesn't make any sense."

"What's the common denominator? I don't see it."

Moran sat down in the chair and took another pull on his drink. "It's got to be the trial. Got to be the Owens trial somehow."

"How does that drag Laughlin into it? He wasn't part of the trial. He was just another talking head, like I am today."

"I don't know."

Ben thought of something. "What about you? Have you been threatened? Is that it? Has someone threatened you?"

Moran nodded, then shook his head. "No, not really, not unless you count tonight."

Ben leaned forward. "What happened tonight?"

"Fisher was here. Ray Fisher."

"The father?" Moran nodded. "Here at the hotel?"

"At the reception."

"I didn't see him. Where was he?"

Moran took another drink. "He was in the reception line. At the end. A few people after you."

"What did he say? Did he threaten you?"

Moran waved it off. "Nothing like that. He's too smart for that. Just said he was watching me, that sort of stuff. It only took a minute, then he was gone."

"Has this happened before?"

Moran thought for a moment. "Sure. Over the years, he has shown up places and said shit like that before. He's watching or he hasn't forgotten. Or how do I live with myself. That kind of thing. No real threats. I just figured he was sort of a crackpot."

"A crackpot with a dead son whom he is convinced was killed by a man you helped set free."

"Right. I know that, which is why I always cut him some slack. I understand where he's coming from. But tonight was different. There was more menace in it somehow. Maybe I'm just jumpy, although I don't think so. Tonight seemed more threatening. Besides, he's never come halfway across the country to pull my chain before."

Ben considered this information. "You should probably tell someone about this. Report it. Make a record of it. Just in case."

"What good would that do?" Moran with a cynical laugh. "You know as well as I do that that's a waste of time. I could go get an order of protection if I wanted to and it wouldn't be worth the paper it's written on." Ben knew this to be true. Battered women did this all the time and still wound up the victims of their abusive spouses, often fatally. "It's just pissing in the wind," Moran continued. "Maybe it isn't Fisher at all. To tell you the

192

truth, I was always more worried about someone like him when I didn't hear from them, not when I did."

Now Ben got up and started pacing. "Alright. Maybe it's worth thinking about. Okay, tell me about Fisher."

Moran proceeded to tell Ben about a decade's worth of harassment on the part of Ray Fisher – showing up places when Moran was speaking, sitting in the back of courtrooms during Moran's trials, making disparaging comments in the media, confronting the lawyer on the street. There were no real overt threats, just the unmistakable notion that Fisher was out there watching, never forgetting, and always seeking justice for his son.

Moran was right. It didn't seem to amount to much and Ben wasn't sure that a man bent on murder would announce his intentions in this way. Then it occurred to Ben that maybe Fisher realized that the object of his scorn and hatred was seriously ill and might not be around forever and that perhaps vengeance had better come soon or it wouldn't come at all. He didn't articulate this thought to Moran, though he had little doubt that Moran had already thought of it himself.

They started going in circles. Ben moved the conversation to the other members of the Dream Defense. They talked about Lindsay and Kessler, exchanging stories about the enthusiastic DNA expert, before Ben asked, "What about Goodrich and Delvecchio? I understand they died of cancer."

Moran got up, walked over to the sink, rinsed out his empty glass and filled it with water. Apparently the bar was closed, or at least out of vodka. Moran took a long drink, filled the glass again and then walked over to the window and looked out at the lights of the city. "Yeah, they both had cancer. Goodrich had a brain tumor – surgery, chemo, radiation, the whole bit." He paused, his back to Ben. After a long silence, he said, in nearly a whisper, "he thought he had beaten it, but it came back. Worse than ever. Cancer is like that."

Ben let the thought linger for a moment. "I read somewhere that he and Owens had a falling out?"

Moran turned. "Yeah, they did. I think he wanted to make peace with his actions in representing a quote, guilty man, end quote." He made the quotation signs in the air. "I don't blame him, I guess. Everyone has to deal with his own demons."

Ben nodded. He got that. "What about Delvecchio?"

Moran considered the question. "As you might imagine," he began, "Bill Delvecchio and I were never close. The Owens case was his case to start with. This was his big chance. His moment in the sun. Then the client decided he wanted someone with a little higher profile." He laughed at the memory. "So I came in to take over the case and Bill never really got over it. He was a good soldier, he said the right things. He mostly did the right things. He could have just quit, but he didn't. He worked hard, helped out, and stuck it out. He did a good job."

"Would he have won the case had you not come in?"

Moran gave him a look. "You know the answer to that. Not his fault though. The stars were aligned for me."

"How was he behind the scenes?"

"He didn't always agree with trial strategy," Moran said.

"But you had the final word."

Moran nodded. "I did. Anyway, Bill didn't always approve. He raised his objections, decisions were made, and we moved on. He was a good soldier. When the verdict came in, he celebrated like all of us and he was entitled. He won too. After the trial, we went our separate ways. I would run into him at the courthouse, or at functions in LA, but that was pretty much it. The divorce raised a few eyebrows, but that was pretty much it."

"He had cancer too?"

"Yes. I don't know the details though. He sort of fell off the grid when he got sick. The divorce, I think, came first, or started first, then he got sick. He was gone not long after that. Too bad. He was still fairly young."

"If you guys are being targeted, then obviously neither Goodrich nor Delvecchio could have been murdered," Ben said.

"No, you wouldn't think so," Moran agreed. "That was a while ago too."

Moran looked suddenly very weary, like his energy was waning. Ben decided to cut to the chase. "Okay, I guess I see where you're coming from. I'm not sure how I can help, but what do you want me to do?"

34

Ben left Moran's room in something of a daze, his head spinning. The elevator bell sounded and the door opened just as Ben walked up and he started to enter the elevator without thinking and ran straight into a hotel employee coming off pushing a large case. "Sorry," Ben said as he backed up and let the man maneuver the cart off the elevator, before getting on himself and hitting the button for the 10th floor. A couple of minutes later, Ben was knocking on Feldman's door. Feldman opened it wearing his dress shirt and slacks and carrying a drink, without his jacket, tie, shoes or socks. "Come on in," Feldman said. "That took a while."

"Nice feet," Ben said as he stepped past the other lawyer.

Feldman laughed as he closed the door and looked down at his feet. "As a matter of fact, I happen to think that my feet are quite handsome."

"And I suppose you think you look like George Clooney too?"

"No, I'm not that drunk." He stepped over to the mini-bar and opened it. "What's your pleasure? Vodka martini, shaken not stirred? Then perhaps we can play baccarat."

Ben took a seat on a small couch and scratched his cheek. "Funny. Just a bottle of water if you've got one."

Feldman rummaged around and pulled a small bottle of water from the fridge and tossed it over to his colleague. "Here you go." He sat on the bed and stretched his legs. Then he took a pull from his drink and said, "So, what did the great man want?"

196

Ben shook his head and spent the next fifteen minutes relaying his conversation with Moran. Feldman listened intently in spite of the buzz he was carrying and asked a few serious questions in response to Ben's story. "So where do you start?"

Ben shrugged. "No idea. Don't have a lot to go on, do I?"

"You really going to bill him? He probably expects you to. And he can certainly afford it."

"I don't know. Expenses maybe. Depends how much time I spend on it, I guess. I'm not really sure what to do, how to get started."

They sat in silence for a moment, then Feldman said, "I suppose you can treat it like a lawyer defending his client. Assume your client has been charged with the murders and take it from there."

"Yeah, I guess, but if that were the case I'd be allowed discovery and police reports and autopsies and financial records and everything else the cops have, or at least would be willing to turn over."

Feldman gave him a mirthless laugh. He knew what that meant. The state often failed to turn over everything. Occasionally, they even got caught. "But you won't be getting any of that. Not without connections."

"And I've got none of those."

"I might be able to help you a little with Kessler. That took place in LA and I know some people. I could at least give you a couple of names to talk to. But I've got nothing in Ohio or Florida." He thought for a moment. "Maybe Jimmy does. He's got those little satellite offices all over the place. He probably knows people."

"He does," Ben agreed. "He told me he can get me people to talk to in Florida and obviously LA, but he doesn't have anything in Ohio either. He said he'd poke around to see if he could come up with someone in the Cleveland area."

"That's something anyway."

Ben held his arms out palms up as if to say, "not much" and Feldman nodded and took another drink. They batted things back and forth for a few minutes until Ben finally said, "what if

197

I'm wrong? Just totally nuts and Moran is too and you are too? What if this isn't one guy out there doing this? What if there is no connection to these deaths? What if Kessler was a random thing, maybe a robbery or a lover's thing? What if Lindsay got drunk and just fell down the stairs?"

"What if he was pushed?"

"What if Laughlin up and killed himself? What if there's nothing to any of this and we're just plain nuts?"

"Then I guess you won't come up with anything." Feldman laughed. "I'd like to see you say that on Loretta's show and see what happens. 'You know, Loretta, I guess I'm just nuts.'"

Ben shook his head. "You know what I mean. If I turn out to be wrong, everyone else will be saying it for me."

"Maybe, maybe not. They'll probably move on to something else by then. But I doubt we're wrong." He paused. "Do you think we're wrong?"

Ben and Feldman looked at each other in silence for a long moment before Feldman raised his eyebrows to reaffirm the question. Ben looked away first. "No," he finally said, "probably not. Not unless it's a copycat thing. Other than that, it would be too big a coincidence."

"Defense lawyers don't believe in coincidences."

"None that I know of anyway."

A few minutes later, Ben picked up his car and made his way to the Eisenhower Expressway. He thought about the mess he had gotten himself into. Traffic was light and driving on autopilot, he reached his exit in no time and pulled into his driveway shortly before eleven o'clock. He could tell right away that the house was still and that Libby had likely followed the kids up to bed. Deciding not to wake her up with the sound of the garage door opening, Ben parked his car in the driveway and decided to go for a stroll to clear his head, if that was even possible. The night was clear and cool, approaching freezing, and the moon shone brightly through the trees overhead. Ben stuffed his gloved hands into the pockets of his wool overcoat and looked in each direction at the end of his driveway, before crossing the street to the elementary school and meandering over to the playground in back until he eventually found a seat on the merry-go-round.

Ben sat there for the better part of an hour, occasionally pushing the ride in a slow circle with his foot as thoughts of Moran and the others circled his head at about the same rate of speed. He watched as the lights in the neighboring homes began to go dark. Several raccoons ambled across the park to parts unknown in search of food and havoc to raise. They gave Ben a fairly wide berth. Finally, having accomplished nothing, he rose and headed home.

Although the back door was unlocked, Libby had indeed gone to bed, so Ben made his way upstairs to join her. He stumbled around in the dark getting undressed and ready for bed trying to be as quiet as possible so as not to wake her. After brushing his teeth, he tiptoed across the room and inched into bed. Just as he was settling under the covers, she said, "you smell like you've been out drinking."

Ben sighed. "You could have said something so I didn't wander around here in the dark like an idiot trying not to wake you."

She giggled. "But you were trying so hard. I didn't want to ruin it for you."

"Thanks loads."

"How was it?"

Ben didn't really want to get into it. "It was okay. Stan Feldman was there. I got interviewed by some TV guy."

She rolled over. "Really? I missed that. What channel?"

"I don't know," he said as he fluffed his pillow. "Just as well. Feldman said I looked like a deer in the headlights."

"Now I really am sorry I missed it."

"Thanks for the support." He rolled over to face away from her.

She patted him on the butt. "Don't want you to get too full of yourself." She rolled back over and looked at the clock. "Geez, it is late. You must have been having fun despite what you say. Better get to sleep."

"Right." Within a couple of minutes, Libby began to snore softly. For Ben, sleep did not come easily. And when it finally came, it was neither satisfying nor restful.

35

Rich held his breath when the first two of the housemen passed by, but needn't have worried. Engaged in a conversation in rapid-fire Spanish, they never noticed him. Neither did several more workers over the next forty-five minutes. Then it was time. He slid out of his hiding space and looked around the tables in both directions. Seeing and hearing nothing, he moved back in the direction from which he had come. As he exited the corridor, he found a cart empty of tables and grabbed it to take with him so he would look like someone in the middle of a task. Sliding the cart along in front of him, he made his way to the service elevator and then up to the ballroom level.

He found the Grand Ballroom and went around back to the service area before sticking his head in a back door. The party was winding down. He scanned the room and couldn't see anyone he knew. Good. He ducked back into the hallway and listened to the music coming from the ballroom next door and headed in that direction. Outside that room, the party still apparently going strong judging by the sounds of music and revelry, he found a series of musical instrument cases pushed up against the wall, including a large, black case he had positioned with the others earlier in the evening. Large enough to hold a tuba, among other things, the case had four large latches and moved easily on wheels.

Rich pulled the case away from the group and headed down the hall and around the corner and back in the direction of the service elevator. In the distance, in front of the open elevator shaft blocked only by a pull-down cage door that looked like a prison cell, stood a man talking on a portable radio. Dressed in black, like Rich, and facing away from him, the man appeared to be engaged in an animated conversation. With the music and activity in the back of the house, Rich could not hear what was being said. Security, Rich thought. He paused and considered his options. The man would certainly not take Rich for a member of the security team since they had never met. About twenty feet to the man's right stood a set of swinging doors that led out to the guest elevators. Rich went in that direction. Just as he reached the doors, the man ended his conversation, turned, and said, "here, let me get those doors for you." He came over and held one door open with his foot while pushing the other open so Rich could maneuver the case through the opening.

"Uh, thanks," Rich said looking down so the man couldn't get a good look at this face. He pushed the case through the opening and turned toward the guest elevators. The man followed.

"Busy night?"

"Yeah, but it's always busy around here, huh?" Rich said.

"You got that right. Say, what do ..." but he was cut off by a call on his radio. He pulled it from his belt and said, "duty calls."

Rich took this opportunity to move on to the elevators. "See you around," he said over his shoulder.

"Have a good evening," the man said as he turned away to answer the call. In a moment, Rich was gone.

He found no one waiting at the guest elevators and picked up a house phone and dialed "0".

"Hotel operator," the voice on the other end said.

In a slight Hispanic accent, Rich said, "this is Ricardo in room service. I've got an order here for Jimmy Moran, but I can't read the handwriting on the ticket. Could you give me his room number please?"

She gave it to him without a second thought and he thanked her, hung up, and hit the "Up" button. He rode the elevator up to Moran's floor alone, his head down, taking deep breaths to calm himself. The moment he had been waiting and planning for

202

was now upon him. A bell sounded and the elevator slowed to a stop. As the doors parted, Rich took one more deep breath and pushed the case out and directly into Benjamin Lohmeier.

Lohmeier, smaller in person than Rich would have expected, appeared lost in thought and walked right into the case coming toward him without waiting to see if anyone was getting off the elevator. He mumbled, "sorry" and backed away, allowing Rich to pass before getting on. The two men never even made eye contact. As far as Lohmeier was concerned, Rich had been just another faceless hotel employee to whom he gave not a second thought.

Rich paused to make sure that Lohmeier was indeed gone, then pushed the case toward Moran's room. He reached the door a minute later and gave it a firm knock before stepping aside, out of the view of the peephole. He pulled the taser from his pocket.

Moran opened the door and said, "I'm glad you came back. There's one more thing …" stopping in mid-sentence when Rich stepped into the doorway. "What?" was all he could get out.

"Hello, Jimmy."

36

Ben had a routine status call in downtown Chicago the following morning and another after lunch so he didn't get back to the office until almost three. Since it was Friday afternoon, he thought about heading straight home. With the status of his files all-too-fresh in his mind, he decided to get a few more hours of work in so he didn't have to come in over the weekend. He trudged up the stairs and found Phil and Nancy standing in front of Phil's TV. "This can't be good," he said as he dropped his briefcase on Phil's couch. "I'm surprised you're not golfing."

"It isn't," Phil said. "And I should be. I was just about to call you. Jimmy Moran's gone missing."

Ben stepped over to the TV. The report was just finishing. He had missed the gist of it. "What's going on? What do you mean he's gone missing? I just saw him two nights ago. I was in his hotel room for crying out loud."

Phil and Nancy both turned his way. "Do tell," Nancy said.

Ben felt himself flush. "Not much to tell. He was worried about all these lawyers dying and thought I could do something about it. I think he was venting. He was upset that Ray Fisher was at the reception."

Phil whistled. "Fisher was there? I hadn't heard that. Well, apparently Moran had reason to be concerned. They say he missed his flight back to LA and no one has seen or heard from him since the other night."

"You mean since the reception?"

"Looks like. The Chicago cops are looking into it. Nobody's saying too much about it here, but his office is sounding the alarm. They're worried he's next. Or maybe was already next."

"He was worried about it too," Ben said. "I thought maybe it was just Fisher being around. Although Stan Feldman knows him and thought he genuinely seemed worried."

"What did he want you to do about it?" Nancy said.

Ben shook his head. "I'm not sure. He thought I had some gift or something since I had helped catch one murderer. I tried to tell him that I wasn't a cop or investigator, but he wasn't buying it. He wanted to hire me to look into it. We never got around to firming that up. We were supposed to touch base next week."

"He's got some pretty serious scratch," Phil said. "What were you going to charge him?"

"No idea. Didn't get that far. I frankly thought he might cool on the idea once he got back to LA. I figured running into Fisher had freaked him out, what with the other guys dying."

"Well, duh," Nancy said. "Can you blame him?"

They ran through it until Phil said, "maybe you should call someone. Tell them what you and Feldman know. It seems relevant now."

"Yeah, I guess," Ben said rubbing his hand through his hair. "His office? The cops?"

"Probably the cops," Phil said. "Don't want them to call you first. Better to get out in front of it just in case."

"Yeah, okay. I'll call Nelson. I have his phone number in my office somewhere. He'll know what to do or who to put me in touch with." Scott Nelson was a Chicago police detective with whom Ben had worked as a prosecutor and again as the lead detective in the Law School Murder case.

"By the way," Nancy said, "your TV friends have been calling and blowing up your phone non-stop all afternoon. You can guess what that's about. I think you owe us all drinks again."

Ben groaned and went into his office to check his messages. Nancy was right. They had been blowing up his phone. He had ignored his cell phone while downtown. He had other calls that he had to return too and he did those first. Since it was late enough on Friday afternoon, he was lucky to just leave messages in most cases.

As he rummaged through his desk looking for Nelson's phone number, Phil stuck his head in on his way out the door. "Did you get a hold of Nelson yet?"

"Just looking for his number now."

"Well, keep me posted. I want to be kept in the loop on this one. One, I'm curious. And, two, well, I just want to be kept in the loop. Don't be afraid to call me on my cell over the weekend. No bottles in the ocean this time. Got it?"

Ben felt Phil's eyes on him so he looked up and met Phil's gaze. "Got it," he said.

"Good."

Ben caught Nelson in his car. "To what do I owe the pleasure, counselor? Or should I say, national TV star?"

"Jimmy Moran."

"What about Jimmy Moran? Not my case. Not unless he turns up dead somewhere within the city limits."

"Okay. Who's working his disappearance?"

"Don't know and not sure I want to find out," Nelson said. "This promises to be a real heater, especially if he does show up dead, God forbid. Not sure I want my fingerprints or name attached to it. Let someone else get the tan."

Ben knew that a heater was a case that brought lots of attention, or heat, be it political or media or otherwise. Most guys who knew what's what didn't want to be anywhere near a heater. "You know Moran was in town to get an award from the CBA the other night?"

"I heard something about that. Trying to get some good scoop for the TV people? You're quite the star these days. Even my wife watches."

"No, nothing like that. I may have actual information."

Nelson sighed. "Am I really going to want to know what you're about to tell me?"

"You mean you personally, or you, the Chicago Police Department?"

"I mean me personally. On a lovely Friday afternoon I could give a fuck about the department."

"Probably not."

They sat in silence, each waiting for the other to break it. Finally, Nelson sighed again and said, "go ahead, ruin my weekend."

"Well, it's like this," Ben said. "I was invited to this thing the other night at the CBA, probably because I'm local and I'm on TV a lot. I had never met Moran before, but I had met Kessler a few times. Stan Feldman was there. I know him from TV. You know who I mean."

"I've seen him. Go on."

"Anyway, Stan introduces me to Moran and he's really freaked."

Ben spent the next ten minutes filling Nelson in on the reception, Feldman and Moran. When he had finished, Nelson said, "so you were in his hotel room?"

"Yeah, for twenty minutes or so, maybe a half hour. Then I went down to Feldman's room and talked to him for about the same amount of time, maybe a little less. I wanted to see what he thought since he knows Moran and I don't."

"You do now apparently."

"I suppose I do now. Not really though."

"And he was really upset about seeing Ray Fisher?"

"Yeah he was. Apparently Fisher really keeps tabs on him, shows up at things all the time; goes out of his way to make sure Moran knows that he's watching him, hasn't forgotten and never will forget. Not sure why he doesn't follow the jurors around. I mean, really, he must know who they were by now. After all, they're responsible for the acquittal, not Moran."

"Spoken like a true lawyer," Nelson said. "You want all of the credit and none of the blame. And maybe he does follow them around too, for all you know." Nelson thought for a moment. "If Moran is so bothered by Fisher, why doesn't he just go in and get a restraining order?"

"Come on, Scott, Moran's no fool. He knows that a restraining order won't do him any good. If Fisher wants to do something, a piece of paper signed by a judge isn't going to stop him. Every lawyer knows that. We just don't tell our clients that when we get one."

"True."

"So, what do you think?"

"Not sure what to think," Nelson said. "Sounds like he had reason to be a little spooked, but you and I both know that two days does not a disappearance make. There's lots of explanations for this, you know that. Maybe he's off on a toot somewhere. Maybe he's got a woman on the side that he's seeing. Is he married?"

"Divorced, I think."

"Then maybe he's cheating on his girlfriend with a married woman. Or maybe he wants to get away for a few days. Or maybe you and Feldman are right and he's scared to death, has reason to be, and wants to go underground for a while until someone catches whoever is killing all these lawyers, assuming, of course, that one guy is in fact doing it. So, to answer your question, I don't know what to think. I don't really know anything yet. And I'm pretty sure I don't want to know."

"Then what have you heard?" Ben said.

"Not much. Nobody else knows anything either. I heard the people upstairs are pretty pissed at Moran's people pointing fingers when we don't even know yet if anything's happened to the man. I heard they sent someone over to the hotel to look at his room, but the maids had already cleaned it. It looked like a clean hotel room. Other than that? Nothing. Probably nothing to know. What were you hoping I'd do with this little conversation?"

"Not sure. That's entirely up to you. I just thought I should let someone know and since I know you, you got the call."

"Duly noted. And for which I am eternally grateful, you can be sure. Well, I'll let someone know what you said. You may get a call from someone if it comes to anything. Hopefully he shows up tomorrow and we can forget about this conversation. As for the other lawyers, you really think someone is killing all of them? That's what you seem to be saying on TV."

"I don't know," Ben said, "I really don't. Someone killed Kessler and no one knows why exactly. Laughlin sure doesn't seem like a suicide candidate."

"They said he had cancer."

"Treatable prostate cancer. A lot of guys get that. And then there's Lindsay. Maybe he's a drunk who fell down the stairs and maybe he's not. Just too many coincidences for my taste."

"I hear you. I don't believe in them either. I just don't want one to pop up in my town on my watch. If he shows up dead, I want it to be in LA and not here."

As they were about to hang up, Nelson said, "it would probably be a good idea to keep that stuff in Moran's hotel room under your hat for a while. I don't think I would bring it up the next time you were on TV. First, you don't want Fisher suing you for hinting he's a murderer. And second, I just wouldn't bring it up for now. Let's see how things play out. I don't think you want to become the story."

"You're right, I don't."

Against his better judgment, Ben returned Marcia Roberts' call after he hung up the phone with Scott Nelson. As expected, she was frantic. "Where have you been? I've been trying to get a hold of you for hours."

"I know. I know. I was downtown in court all day and didn't get back here until a little while ago."

"You have a cell phone, don't you?"

"I do, but I didn't know anything was going on. I didn't hear about Jimmy Moran until after I got back to the office. Now, what is it you want from me?"

"What do I want from you? What I wanted at first, hours ago, was for you to go on Flaherty tonight. For whatever reason, he seems to like you, and as you know and have probably heard, he doesn't like everybody. But unfortunately, most of his show is already in the can so it's too late to get you on there. Now I'm looking for a couple of segments on the Loretta's show. She's going to go live, like always, so if you're not too busy, I can get the guys on the phone and get them down there."

Ben groaned. "I was afraid you were going to say something like that."

"The word is you were at that shindig the other night with Moran. What happened? You may have been one of the last people to see him before he vanished."

"I wouldn't exactly say he vanished. It's only been a couple of days. He could be anywhere trying to avoid the likes of you."

"Not to mention the nut ball running around killing all these lawyers. You and I both know that guys like him are never really off the grid. Somebody's always trying to get in touch with them. From what I hear, they don't do a thing in that office without him signing off on it."

Ben knew she was probably right. Guys like Moran don't just wander off. He had to walk a fine line here though. Enough people saw him talking to Moran in the ballroom that he couldn't deny having had the conversation. He didn't want to tell her about the hotel room though. As much as he didn't want to lie to her, he also knew that he would become the story once his meeting with Moran in his hotel room got out and he didn't want that to happen. By telling Nelson, he had informed the authorities, which was good enough for the time being.

They worked out the logistics and then signed off. The other good part of sticking around for the show is that it made him work late and continue trying to catch up on things. Ben called home to let Libby know that he would be late. "Whatever," she said and quickly hung up with the excuse that she had something on the stove. Ben couldn't tell whether she was irritated or really busy. Probably a little bit of both, he assumed. He concluded that he had better tread carefully when he got home.

As much as he knew that he still had plenty of work to do, his heart wasn't really in it and he couldn't get his mind off of Jimmy Moran. He was almost relieved when the phone rang and Stan Feldman was on the other end of the line.

"I hope to hell you sent him into hiding," Feldman said without preamble. "I don't want to even consider the other possibilities. This is getting too fucked up."

"I agree. And now I get to go on TV tonight and talk about it."

"Bad decision," Feldman said. "I just turned off my phone and stopped returning messages."

"You're probably right. But you realize that people already know that we saw Moran the other night at that reception, don't you?"

"Sure I know. All the more reason not to return my messages."

"That's okay, Stan, I will make sure to drop your name in there the first chance I get.

"Seriously, though," Feldman said, "did he say anything about disappearing for a while?"

"I wish, but no, nothing like that. He was upset, sure, but he didn't say anything about hiding out anywhere, if that's what you mean."

"Shit. I figured you would have mentioned it the other night if he had. So what do we do now?"

"I called Scott Nelson. He's the detective that handled the Law School Murder case. I know him and I think I can trust him."

"Did you tell him about the meeting in Moran's hotel room?"

"Yeah, I did. He wasn't too sure what to make of it. He did tell me that it probably wouldn't be a good idea to talk about it on TV."

"I agree with that. I wouldn't want to open up that can of worms. Not yet anyhow."

They agreed to keep in touch, and before long, the TV crew arrived. The show was surprisingly low-key and devoid of too much needless speculation. It was almost as though everyone was expecting the worst, but didn't want to say anything about it for fear of making it come true. Ben felt like he was at a wake. During the commercial break between his two segments, Loretta spoke into his ear, "Ben, was he freaked out or what? You saw him, what do you think?"

"Loretta, I just don't know. Like I said, I never met him before the other night so I don't really have anything to base it on. Stan Feldman was there. I think you know Stan."

"I know him. Go on."

"Well, Stan was there and he's known Moran for years. He didn't seem to think Moran was acting too strangely, but honestly, it wasn't the time and place for that stuff. He was receiving an award."

Soon, they were back on air, and when his segment was over, he hadn't made any news. A success.

*****

In a Motel 6 outside of Omaha, Rich was washing down a hostess apple pie he had purchased from a vending machine with a glass of orange soda and watching the show with interest. When it ended, he turned off the TV and smiled. No real news. A success.

37

Bobby Joe Gibbons died of cardiac arrest brought on by radiation poisoning at 7:52 the following morning, four days after his wife. By nine o'clock, the hospital had issued a statement announcing his passing. By nine-thirty, a media feeding frenzy had already erupted and the phone had started ringing. Ben had learned of Gibbons' death from the Drudge Report, which posted a photograph of Gibbons under its flashing red light with the caption, "Another". Ben was staring at Gibbons' face on his computer screen when Marcia Roberts called.

"It's the she-wolf," Nancy said over the intercom. "Someone else die?"

"Bobby Joe Gibbons. Just came over the Internet."

"Damn," Nancy said after a pause. "I was just kidding. Sorry, that wasn't funny."

"You didn't know."

"Do you want her?"

Ben stared at the phone. "No, but put her through anyway." A few seconds later, his phone rang and he picked it up. "Hey Marcia," he said.

"Have you heard?"

"Yeah, I happened to be checking out Drudge and there it was. What are they saying?"

"We're hearing heart attack, but that's not the real cause. We're hearing there's radiation poisoning. Killed a bunch of animals at his ranch first, then his wife and now Gibbons himself."

"Then there's no chance of natural causes."

"Doesn't sound like it. You add this to the others, maybe Moran too if he doesn't turn up, and you're up to five. Five fucking dead lawyers. You know what this means? There's no dicking around now. We've got a serial killer out there targeting lawyers. Nobody can deny it now. Even if one of the others turns out to be natural causes, which you and I both know won't happen now, that still leaves us with at least three or four murders, and probably five."

"I can't argue with any of that," Ben said. "Must be a zoo there."

"It's crazy nuts. Things are going to get out of control if Moran shows up dead."

"What do you need from me?"

"Anything you can give me and then some. You're our go-to guy on this. We could get you on the phone for starters,"

"I don't want to do the telephone. I don't know why, I just don't."

"Okay, I'll get the guys out there."

They worked out the logistics with Ben extracting a guarantee that he wouldn't be on air for hours at a time, not that it did him a lot of good. Once they signed off, Ben sighed. His day had just gone to shit. He picked up the phone again and called Libby to tell her that he would probably be late again. She said that she understood, she had already heard about Gibbons and was expecting it, but Ben wasn't sure he believed her. On one level, she undoubtedly understood and would even acknowledge that all the television work was undoubtedly good for business. On the other hand, she had a visceral dislike of Ben putting it ahead of their family regardless of the reason or the benefits.

Since he hadn't gone to court this morning, Ben had worn a golf shirt and khaki pants to the office, which wouldn't do for television. Fortunately, he kept a sport coat, blue oxford shirt and striped tie on a hook behind the door, so he shut the door and changed. As he was tying his tie, Phil stuck his head in. He had gotten to the office a couple of minutes earlier. "Big TV day?"

"Yeah unfortunately," Ben said.

"They said on the radio that Gibbons may have gotten nuked."

"That's what I hear too."

"Fuck. That sucks." He eyed Ben closely. "You need me to pull Funk or Conlon in to help you out? This could get worse before it gets better, especially if Moran's next."

Ben thought about it as he adjusted his tie. The help would be welcome, but being the guy who needs help wouldn't be. He didn't want to get that reputation. More than that, he liked to run his files as he saw fit. He didn't want one of the other guys undercutting him, intentionally or not. "Let's see how it plays out the next few days. Maybe things will settle down. Hopefully Moran will show up none the worse for wear."

Phil gave him a look that said he wasn't counting on that last bit coming true. "Okay, that's fine. Keep me posted." He turned back into his office and closed the French doors as he said, "and don't step on your dick. I'll be watching."

"Sometimes it just gets in the way."

Once he finished with the tie, Ben grabbed his sport coat and a stack of forest preserve files and headed downstairs to the garage. He hadn't gotten very far into organizing things when he saw the television van pull into a parking space across the way. "Already?" he said under his breath. Marcia Roberts must have mobilized them even before they had spoken on the phone. Ben got up from the library table and unlocked the barber shop doors to let in the two techs. It was the same two who usually came. Sometimes they just sent one tech, but not too often.

"Gonna be a busy one," the cameraman said as approached. His name was Jeff and he was tall and thin and in his mid-thirties. Ben liked him.

Ben stepped aside and Jeff maneuvered his way into the room with his equipment. "So I hear," Ben said. The second tech, a shorter guy about the same age, but with a beard, followed

215

behind. His name was Rob. He was also a good guy. Ben watched as they set up. "When is the first spot?"

"I'll have to call down," Rob said. "From what we heard on the drive out, sometime between ten-thirty and eleven."

Ben looked at his watch – it was already twenty past ten. "Alrighty then."

The first spot went off at a quarter to eleven and covered the rest of the show, the second took three full segments between eleven and Noon and the third two segments between one and two. Then they had a break to go out and grab something to eat.

They got back to the office shortly after three and Ben called Marcia Roberts. "Anything?" he said.

"Nothing on Moran. We had someone speak to his assistant and she's so wacked out she won't come on camera. She thinks he's dead."

"You think he's dead too."

"So do you, don't you?"

Ben frowned. "I hope not. It's starting to feel like it though."

"It started to feel like it yesterday. Today, I would be shocked if he showed up alive, know what I mean?"

"Unfortunately."

"Too bad too. About the assistant, I mean. Would have been great TV."

"You're all heart. Anything new on Gibbons?"

"Just what we thought before. Somebody poisoned the water hole, as Woody from *Toy Story* used to say."

"How did they do it?"

"Not sure," she said, "although they've known about it for a while since Gibbons' wife went first."

"That might establish some sort of timeline. Like, when did the animals get sick, the wife get sick and so on. Not that I know anything about any of that obviously."

"No, but that's a good thing to throw out there maybe," she said.

"Yeah, but I don't want to start pontificating about science or something when everyone knows I don't know a damn thing about science. I feel like I've been saying the same thing over and over with nothing new. I can almost hear the channels changing and the TV's shutting off all over America."

"It hasn't been that bad. People don't usually watch for hours at a time, much as we'd like them to. That's what cable news is all about. People get their fix then move on to something else."

"I know. Still, if something new comes in, you've got to let me know so I don't look like an idiot."

"I will. Just remember, there's nothing wrong with being provocative. Conflict stirs the pot and makes good television."

"So, start an argument with Flaherty, that's your advice?"

She laughed. "No, he doesn't need any help there. If he needs an argument, he'll start one himself. You can disagree with another guest though. You know, play devil's advocate."

"Ah, that's what you call it. Just don't set me up."

"Me? Never crossed my mind."

The four o'clock segment was a pretty routine rehash of some of the others from earlier in the day, so much so that Ben felt it had been a bit dull. Flaherty's show was another matter entirely. Although the host typically brought a unique intensity to his program, Ben sensed that he was especially juiced today. Toward the end of their segment, Flaherty said, "so, counselor, what do you think? Are they going to catch this guy? And if so, how soon?"

Ben squirmed a little. "Well, that's the million-dollar question, isn't it?"

Flaherty pounced. "I sense doubt on your part. What? You think this guy is too smart for all the cops and feds that are going to be hunting him now?"

"You are certainly right that the ante has clearly been upped now and there will undoubtedly be a new focus and intensity to the investigation. On the other hand, you have to admit, assuming that we are indeed looking at at least four murders and perhaps more, committed in varying locales in decidedly different manners, that the person responsible has brought uncommon planning and dexterity to the equation."

"So you agree that he's a smart guy?" Flaherty said.

"You'd be a fool not to think so."

217

Once the segment had ended, Flaherty complemented Ben on his performance. "I'm sure we'll be seeing you again soon, counselor. You've got to wonder, though, how many he's going to kill before they catch him. This doesn't look like it's going to end soon."

"No, unfortunately it doesn't."

As it was just past five-thirty when they finished taping the Flaherty segment, Ben decided to go back upstairs to his office and catch up on what he'd missed during the day. He ran into Nancy outside the copy room on her way out the door. "Anything exciting?" she said.

"Not really. I think I spent the whole day repeating myself without saying much. Anybody left upstairs?"

"Nope. Just you. You got about a million phone calls today too. I think your mailbox may be full."

"Great. Just what I need."

They said their goodbyes and Ben headed upstairs. Although his mailbox wasn't full, it was close. He had thirty-four new messages, twenty-nine of which were from members of the media, a handful of those from reporters he had actually heard of, plus one message from Feldman, another from Nelson and one more from a golfing buddy. That left only two on any of his files and one of those was from Karen Tilly at the forest preserve, who would never bust his ass about anything. Could have been worse.

He called Feldman first and then Nelson. The reporters he ignored. While he knew that it was often good politics to return the reporters' phone calls too, today was not the day for that. He had started keeping a file with a list of the dates, times and phone numbers of all the messages he received from media people just in case he needed them later. Frequent flyers got better treatment, as did those who said or wrote nice things about him. He wrote the names and numbers on a yellow legal pad and set it aside.

Ben surfed the Internet as he talked to Feldman, who didn't have any news to report. He was just a little freaked out and had to commiserate with someone. Unlike Ben, Feldman had actually

218

met Gibbons a few times and had done a lot of cable television with him back in the Dream Defense days. "He was a fucking character," Feldman said talking about Gibbons. "I've heard that in some of these smaller injury cases he had in recent years, he would walk out in front of a jury with absolutely no preparation whatsoever and give an opening statement or a closing argument and make it look like Shakespeare. All he would get from his associate would be a short outline of who the parties were, what the injuries were and how much they were asking for and that would be it. I'd be shitting bricks if I tried to do that. I can't believe he's gone."

"Makes you wonder who's next," Ben said.

"Yeah."

Although Ben had a feeling of dread when he called Nelson, it turned out that the detective called trying to find out if Ben had heard anything, not to report bad news. "This is getting to be a habit," Ben said when Nelson answered.

"And not a good habit, unfortunately. Well, is this another brick in the wall or just another coincidence?"

"You know how I feel about coincidences."

"And you know I'm right there with you," Nelson said. "I really am starting to get a bad feeling about all this. I just hope my bad feeling pops up in another jurisdiction."

"That's altruistic of you."

"You know what I mean. Another heater is not what I'm looking for."

"I get that. Can't blame you."

Nelson confirmed that he hadn't heard anything regarding Moran and that there was really nothing to be done until they either heard from the man or uncovered some evidence that led them to believe that he was the victim of foul play. He did, however, confirm one piece of news that would undoubtedly change the landscape – the feds were now on their way.

Ben hung up and surfed the web a little more. Then he looked at his desk and the list he had compiled of things that he needed to get done. Once again, as had been the case in recent weeks, his heart wasn't in it. He could see the sun peaking through the blinds to the west. It was starting to get a little low in the sky. This would be another beautiful summer night when he wouldn't be home in time to play with the kids or probably even help put them to bed. He knew Libby was growing frustrated over his absences and figured it was bound to reach the boiling point sooner rather than later and he didn't blame her. He felt the same way. He recognized that things were spiraling in a direction he didn't like. While he obviously felt an obligation to the firm and enjoyed the television work because it was interesting, mostly enjoyable and frankly something different that broke up the monotony of practicing law, his family had to come first. He knew that. He believed that. He wanted that. Still, he couldn't always control that.

He couldn't get the dead lawyers out of his head. Kessler, Lindsay, Laughlin, Gibbons and maybe even Moran. Had they really all been killed, and if so, by the same person? He knew that deep down the feeling of dread he had been experiencing was telling him that one person was likely responsible for these deaths and perhaps more to come. He sat silently, looking out his window across the railroad tracks toward the golf course beyond and seeing none of it. Never noticing when darkness had come, Ben was only jarred back to the present by the sound of a door slamming downstairs. The clock on the corner of his desk read eight forty-five. He rubbed his eyes, got up, grabbed the sport coat off the back of a chair and headed downstairs. One more show to do.

38

The news of Gibbons' death overshadowed all competing media stories such that all everyone was talking about was the four dead lawyers and asking the same question – where was Jimmy Moran? Reporters showed up at his house in the hills, outside his condo on Wilshire Boulevard and flooded his office in Century City. So inundated were they at the office that Moran's office manager had to close the place by eleven, not that any work was getting done anyhow. They were halfway between mourning and sending out a search party of their own. The ripple effect, felt at every police department charged with investigating the death of any of the lawyers and even some that weren't, caused proactive measures to be taken. Tip lines were established and then overrun with calls. Overtime was authorized and additional officers assigned to each investigation. Press conferences were scheduled and friendly reporters received off-the-record briefings. The brass consulted their PR specialists. One City Hall after another held meetings to plot strategy and consider damage control. To the anger of all, summer vacations were postponed. Most of all, fingers were pointed and some ducked for cover as the eager sought out the red lights of the cameras.

As chaos ensued, the unseen ringmaster of this circus carefully drove his tan Camry from the Motel 6 in Omaha through Nebraska to a Holiday Inn Express in Boulder, Colorado to the Firecracker Inn, a few blocks off of the strip in Las Vegas, before finally returning to the condo in San Diego, never once driving the Camry faster than the posted speed or doing anything that could possibly call attention to himself, not that he could have easily done that in either a college town or Sin City. The rooms were clean, with fast food nearby and most importantly, the cable television worked. The radio coverage was a bit spotty out on the road, but God the talking heads at night more than made up for it. Rich almost felt like a kid on Christmas Eve driving all day to Grandma's house in anticipation of the big day. In his case, he was driving all day in order to get to a room with a television so he could watch the talking heads pontificating about his exploits without ever having a clue as to who he was. Best of all, they didn't know their asses from a hole in the ground because they had no idea what Rich was up to and why. The only one who seemed to have something of a clue was Benjamin Lohmeier. Of all the talking heads, Rich probably respected Lohmeier the most. His analysis seemed reasonable and well thought-out and Lohmeier didn't even seem too impressed with the sound of his own voice. Most importantly, Lohmeier had credibility based on real-life experiences. He had managed to solve a high-profile murder, clear his client and save his own skin in the process. He had been the hunter and the hunted and had still prevailed.

Night after night, guest after guest pontificated on the motives and psychology of the vicious killer of these great lawyers. Speculation varied wildly and Rich was most amused by the repeated efforts at amateur psychoanalysis, although to be fair, a show or two even included a real psychologist willing enough to put his professionalism aside long enough to babble on regarding something about which he knew nothing. Although bone tired from all the driving, with a stiff back and a headache, Rich nonetheless was eager to settle in for a quiet evening at the condo watching people he didn't respect misread his motivations while wrapping themselves up in the glory of actions they allegedly abhorred. Having grabbed a take-out burger and fries from a place in a strip mall on the other side of the highway, he found a cold beer in the fridge and ate sitting on the couch in front of the television.

222

Rich flipped back and forth between CNN, MSNBC and Fox News as he finished his dinner. Even Flaherty covered the story on Fox. Normally, he only went for the sensational stories when he didn't think he had much of a choice. He clearly preferred to stick to politics and the attempts by the so-called progressives in the media and government to wage their war against the traditional values of his folks. He wouldn't cover it every day. Such an omission was far less likely to happen at CNN and would never happen at MSNBC. Rich would not be disappointed. Those channels were all over the story too, with much of their focus on the whereabouts of Jimmy Moran. Despite his recent death, Gibbons received relatively sparse coverage. Apparently, since he was already dead, the media couldn't do anything about that, but Moran may still be out there somewhere, and if dead, someone had to find him. Where would that be? And when? One talking head gushed more than the next. Most galling to Rich was watching the lawyers whom he knew had only a tangential relationship with Moran talking as though they had been close friends and colleagues for their entire careers. He found himself talking back at the television, giving his own commentary to the commentary on the screen. He was better than they were, this much he knew for sure.

Bergen devoted her entire show to the deaths of the four lawyers, really five once Moran's body was discovered. Rich found himself focusing on her show and flipping channels less, particularly when Lohmeier came on. Lohmeier looked worn out and less energetic than his usual self, as if the events of the past few days had taken something out of him. Thinking that he had been one of the last people to see Moran alive, and maybe the last person to do so, must have taken a toll on him, Rich thought. Still, he had acquitted himself decently on the program, never engaging in outlandish speculation and unsupported theories. He mostly stuck to what he knew, though Rich knew that he was likely leaving some details out of his narrative. Rich wondered about this. Perhaps he had been advised to do so by the police. On the other hand, Lohmeier was appearing on shows like he typically would and wasn't off somewhere hiding behind closed doors.

Rich watched the rest of the show in relative silence, his commentary to a minimum. Bergen did a pretty good job of keeping things moving while sticking mostly to the facts. Rich didn't always agree with her, but he recognized that Bergen was a fairly skilled interviewer, probably from her years as a trial attorney. She had a knack for actually listening to the answers her guests gave and asking relatively thoughtful follow-up questions, something rarely seen from many of the other cable TV hosts, who seemed too intent on simply rattling off their prepared series of questions without bothering to consider the answers they received in return.

Rich felt comfortable that there was no evidence out there that could link him to the murders of any of the five lawyers. He had been too careful and too smart for that. The chance of blowback was minimal. Nevertheless, he understood that once Moran's body was found, the heat would ratchet up considerably. The authorities would have little choice but to conclude that all five lawyers had been murdered, and likely by the same person, even though they couldn't really link any of them together. With each passing murder, and there would be more murders, the odds that all these deaths were merely a coincidence would become miniscule. Not even the dimmest of investigators would conclude otherwise. Rich clicked the pause button on the remote and stood stretching his back. He thought about that in silence for a moment. Perhaps he needed to mix things up and tossed them a deflection or two. If he did it the right way, he could stir things up even more and put them further and further behind. That would be a kick. He tossed the remote onto the couch and headed off to the bathroom. He would think about that in the shower.

*****

Ben climbed up into the barber chair and watched as the two techs packed up their equipment. There was little small talk. The subject matter of the broadcasts had drained the event of its enthusiasm and infused it with a solemnity that didn't promote the trivial back and forth in which they usually engaged. Ben was beat. Now that the adrenaline rush of live television had dissipated, his sagging energy level really got a hold of him. Having skipped lunch again, there was literally no fuel left in the tank and he felt completely sapped. Both his throat and his eyes were dry and he fumbled in his pocket for some drops, which he put into each eye as the techs finished up. Soon, he was locking the door behind them and turning off the lights to the garage so he could go back upstairs to his office and get ready to finally head home.

He found a stack of messages and some draft correspondence on his chair, glanced at them and tossed them on his desk. He considered picking up the phone to call Libby and tell her that he would be leaving soon. He didn't do it. She'd been growing increasingly frustrated with the late hours and his darkening moods. Rather than try to explain the many things occupying his thoughts, he chose instead to let the wound fester and put off the confrontation and the angry words which would inevitably ensue and be difficult to forget.

This was somewhat unusual for him. He was typically more than willing to engage in verbal skirmishes with his wife. That's just how they expressed themselves and one friend of theirs had even joked that the banter in which they were often engaged was some sort of perverse form of verbal foreplay. Ben wasn't sure about that, but he did recognize that this was usually a regular method of communicating for the two of them. Years ago, back when he was a prosecutor, Ben was more susceptible to dark moods and the lonely trips inside his own head were far from uncommon. In recent years, with the responsibilities for putting bad guys away long gone, these bouts of self-examination occurred less and less and the moods that went with them rarely materialized.

With each passing death and the responsibility for discussing it on national TV ever increasing, Ben could feel the darkness lurking around him. Of course, being aware of the situation helped, but only a little. Libby had suggested that he take some time off and/or skip the television work for a while. While that seemed to be a good idea on the surface, he couldn't bring himself to do it. Neither could he purge from his consciousness the desire to figure out why these men had been killed and who was responsible. And he knew if he could hold out for just a couple of weeks, the Fourth of July weekend was approaching with his family's annual trip to Libby's aunt's place in Michigan for fireworks and related festivities. He looked forward to it every year and really looked forward to it now. He just needed to buckle down and get through the next two weeks.

Ben shuffled around on his desk looking through stacks of paper for his diary. He couldn't remember whether he had court in the morning. He didn't think so. Then the phone rang. After hours, once the last of the secretaries had gone, the office phones would ring on every line in every office. Thus, Ben did not know whether the call was for him and on his direct line or for some other person in the office. If the call had been for him and had come in on his private line, then it would go directly to his voicemail. If not, the call would go to the firm mailbox. He let it ring. He found his diary and satisfied himself that he didn't have court either of the next two days. Relieved, he began to pack up his briefcase to head home. Then he stopped. He wouldn't be doing any work at home this evening. It was already too late. Instead, he would just grab his suit coat, lock up and head out. As he shut out the lights in his office, the phone rang again. He looked over at it on his desk. Maybe it was something important. He didn't want to answer it. He knew he didn't have to answer it. He sighed. Then he flipped the lights back on and stepped back over to his desk, picked up the phone and said "Benjamin Lohmeier."

"Mr. Lohmeier," the voice said. It was a metallic, computer-generated voice.

"What?"

"Mr. Benjamin Lohmeier, please," the voice said.

"What? Who is this?" Ben was confused.

"I want to speak to you, Mr. Lohmeier," the voice said. "I have been watching you on television. I am a friend. I am very impressed."

"Okay," Ben said, "but who are you? And why are you hiding your voice? Do I know you?"

"No, you do not know me. We have never met."

"Then why do you want to talk to me? And who are you? I don't understand."

The voice laughed.

It was strange hearing a computer-generated voice laugh, Ben thought.

"Clearly, I am the one everyone is talking about," the voice said.

Ben sat down on the bench, the cord to the phone stretching all the way across his desk and pulling the receiver toward him. He didn't know what to make of this. His heart was racing. "Are you telling me that you are the person who killed Gibbons and the others?"

The voice laughed again, the sound sending chills up Ben's spine. "You might say that I am responsible for their deaths, yes."

"What are you saying? Are you saying that you killed Lindsay, Kessler, Laughlin and Gibbons? And what about Moran? Is he dead too? Did you kill him too?"

The voice betrayed an eerie lack of emotion. Being computer-generated, of course, it could do nothing else. "I said what I said. As for Moran, he should turn up shortly."

Ben was frantic now. "Does that mean he's dead? Is he dead too?"

"I said he will be turning up shortly. That's all you need to know. But that's not why I called."

Ben wished that he had a tracer on his telephone, but he knew that probably wouldn't help. If whoever this was was willing to call him on the phone, he probably had also already taken steps to ensure that his phone call could not be traced. "What do you mean, he's going to turn up?"

"You will see soon enough," the voice said. "I just called to compliment you on your television performances. I have always been impressed with you. Your analysis is reasonable and thoughtful, unlike most of the other fools on cable television. I

227

was also very impressed with how you solved the law school murder. We'll have to talk about that sometime."

"Well, okay," Ben said. Things were happening too fast. He'd been caught off-guard. He wanted to keep him on the line though, assuming it was a he. The more the voice talked, the more Ben could learn. "What do you want with me?"

"I want you to keep up the good work," the voice said.

"What? What does that supposed to mean?"

"I meant just what I said. Keep up the good work. That is all for now. Goodbye."

Ben heard the click of the call disconnecting and then nothing but dead air. He stared at the phone, then slowly reached over and hung it back up on the cradle.

39

As media coverage of the murders continued to increase and intensify, you couldn't swing a dead cat without hitting a reporter at any of the law enforcement headquarters investigating the deaths of the attorneys. In Palm Beach, Florida, reporters were pushed out onto the sidewalk in the sweltering heat and confined to an area entirely devoid of shade in the hopes that they would either melt or find a better place to go. All the while, the chief of police sat in his air-conditioned office with the door shut and locked. His chief of detectives, on the other hand, fearing the worst, found it necessary to work out in the field pursuing new "leads". Meanwhile, a junior detective on the Lindsay case poured over the telephone records of the once great trial lawyer looking for something, anything unusual that might lead to a workable avenue of investigation. What he discovered was mostly a lot of nothing, although three calls from untraceable burner phones piqued his curiosity.

The first call, made ten days before Lindsay's body was found, lasted just seconds, the next about three minutes. Attempts at triangulation revealed that the calls were likely made locally, within a radius of five miles from Lindsay's home. The third call, made four days later but from a different number, seemed to originate from the same general location. Of course, none of that told the young detective named Javier Martinez if the same party made both calls or what was discussed in either conversation.

Two other interesting tidbits were revealed by Detective Martinez's investigation. The first was that Lindsay didn't receive all that many phone calls in the first place. In fact, on three separate occasions in the preceding year, Lindsay's phone service had been disconnected due to non-payment of his bill. Furthermore, he no longer maintained a separate office location, preferring when he did work, to do so out of his home, and his phone number and office number were one in the same.

The second interesting tidbit occurred when Martinez discovered a telephone call between Lindsay's home and a number based in North Miami. The call took place on the evening before Lindsay's death and lasted approximately six minutes. Martinez eventually traced the call to a construction trailer for a townhome complex currently under development north of the city. The call took place at about eight-thirty in the evening, long after all the employees on the project had gone home.

Martinez spoke to the construction manager at the site, who was very cooperative. Although the man acknowledged that he had heard of Lindsay, he was unaware of any dealings between anyone at his company and the famed attorney. The man denied making the call himself and a canvas of his employees confirmed that either they didn't know who Lindsay was, or denied making the call or both. Further investigation revealed no dealings of any kind with Lindsay in a professional manner, nor was Martinez able to identify any personal connection between Lindsay and anyone associated with the company.

In the end, Martinez was forced to conclude that the call and its location was one of convenience, an available spot found by the potential killer to make a phone call that could not be traced. Or else it was nothing. While no signs of break-in were found at the trailer, the construction manager confided that occasionally the door to the trailer was inadvertently left unlocked at the end of the day. He rationalized that there was little in the way of valuables located inside other than construction plans and the like, and as the man pointed out, those were hardly state secrets. Martinez found no reason to disbelieve him or any of his employees and his frustration over reaching yet another dead end was tempered somewhat by the fact that it did point in the direction that Lindsay may have indeed been the victim of foul play. As Martinez leaned back in his squeaky desk chair and propped his feet up on the corner of his battered metal desk, he wondered when he was going to catch a break.

*****

Detective Adam Phillips of Los Angeles's elite Robbery Homicide Division pulled the murder book off the shelf and slapped it down on his desk. It was past eight in the evening and the squad room was deserted save for Phillips and a junior detective looking to score points with the brass. The murder book contained everything relating to the investigation into the death of Martin Kessler more than four months earlier. Phillips and his partner had caught the case in the regular rotation and knew the spotlight was on them from the get go. Kessler had been a prominent attorney in Los Angeles, and even Phillips knew him from the Owens case. The local celebrity-driven press was all over them.

Unfortunately, their best efforts had been stymied almost from the start. The killing had taken place in a rare LA monsoon, meaning that any real physical evidence relating to the killer had been compromised, if not washed away entirely. Phillips suspected, but did not know for sure, that the killer may have also been wounded in the brutal attack given the amount of knife play that took place in the small area outside the front door of Kessler's girlfriend's home. The weather had rendered any traffic cameras in the area almost useless, not that there had been cameras in the immediate area in the first place. Of course, the storm also kept witnesses to a minimum because LA is hardly the capital of foul weather adventurers.

Phillips and his fellow investigators didn't have much success in identifying the motive for Kessler's killing either. While he appeared to have been having an affair at the time of his death, there was no evidence to suggest that his wife had been aware of it, for she vehemently denied it and the investigators on the team generally believed her. Phillips had interviewed her himself on

231

two occasions and she first denied that it was even possible that her husband had been cheating. Later, having apparently reconciled herself to the fact that it may have been going on, she nevertheless continued to insist that she had never had an inkling of it. Likewise, Kessler's colleagues at the office denied any knowledge of the affair and also expressed surprise when learning of it.

All things considered, Phillips tended to believe that neither Kessler's wife nor his colleagues knew about Kessler's infidelity, which would rule out that as a motive for the murder. That left Phillips with two alternatives, one of which was seen as highly implausible and the other difficult to prove. As with all criminal defense lawyers, Kessler took some heat from those skeptical of the use of DNA and other scientific analysis of blood and other evidence on behalf of criminal defendants. While television shows such as *CSI* exposed the general public to the scientific analysis of evidence and in some ways even heightened the bar for the prosecution to prove things in the same way they did on television, many still viewed the use of such technologies as voodoo science and helping defendants get off on a technicality.

These detractors, particularly those associated with the alleged victims of criminal defendants represented by Kessler, provided Phillips with a fertile pool of possible suspects. However, without something more, it was like finding a needle in a haystack. Phillips wouldn't know whom to suspect absent some previous manifestation of aggression toward Kessler, rendering virtually every member of a victim's family or close friends of the victim as possible suspects. Combing through them was somewhat of a daunting challenge and one which Phillips undertook with the help of a couple of other of the unit's junior detectives and uniformed officers.

Despite their best efforts, the team hadn't really turned up anything promising, as Phillips was reminded of on almost a daily basis. But Phillips didn't feel alone since his lieutenant received similar reminders from his captain, who received similar reminders from the chief of police, who received similar reminders from the mayor, who received even more outraged

232

reminders from the City Council, the press and most importantly, from his constituents.

The one name that did stick out for them all was Ray Fisher. Ever since the death of his son, Fisher had been a bitter and outspoken critic of the Los Angeles defense bar, with a particular focus of his anger and resentment firmly centered on the members of the Owens defense, of which Kessler was one. He raged, quite correctly in Phillips's view, that Moran, Kessler and the others had helped Owens literally get away with murder. Fisher had appeared countless times on television, mobilized victims' rights groups and sponsored protests against the hijacking of the criminal justice system by unscrupulous defense attorneys. Over the years, he'd become something of a caricature, doggedly pursuing Owens and his assets to such an extreme degree that some even viewed his motives as lying in his own selfish, pecuniary gain. Phillips, for his part, didn't necessarily believe that, nor did he believe that Fisher was a crackpot, as others had occasionally concluded. Losing a child to a violent death entitled a parent to some slack, Phillips felt. On the other hand, having seen Fisher up close and personal on a couple of occasions, not to mention his numerous television appearances, Phillips had to conclude that Fisher was not at all an unlikely suspect, nor an undeserved one.

Neither Phillips nor any of the other investigators had spoken to Fisher yet, and they tried to keep their tracking of his movements during the dates in question as surreptitious as possible. Since Fisher lived in the LA area and Kessler was murdered in Brentwood, proximity was not an issue. Fisher could've easily gotten to Brentwood, committed the murder, and returned to his home without anyone being the wiser. The fact that he lived alone and had few close friends made it that much easier. His daughter, Brenda, with whom he had made frequent television appearances, particularly in the early years after the Owens case, lived not far from her father and by all appearances the two were still quite close. However, it appeared that most of their visits took place at her home so that Fisher could spend time with his grandchildren.

233

Fisher's motive for killing Kessler, and also Moran should he prove dead, was obvious. His motive for killing the other lawyers, something that had to be considered now with any suspect, was less clear. None of the others had any real connection to the Owens case other than as occasional commentators on cable television while the saga unfolded night after night. Phillips realized that linking the victims would eventually become a necessity. Nevertheless, the only killing in his jurisdiction and therefore on his plate at the moment was the Kessler killing, so that remained his focus. He was content to leave the other potential murders to those poor saps working those cases and dealing with the pressure brought on by their bosses, their boss's bosses and the media in their respective cities.

Although they hadn't made a lot of outward progress, Phillips and his colleagues were diligent in working the case and keeping up with appearances. The brass understood that they didn't have a lot to work with and were somewhat sympathetic, at least until the next dead lawyer showed up and the media glare intensified once again. Phillips thought about Moran. He sincerely hoped that the lawyer would turn up any day now, alive and well and surprised at all the commotion, even if deep down he did not expect that to occur. What he secretly hoped for most was that if Moran did indeed turn up dead, he did so in a faraway jurisdiction like Chicago, where he was last seen alive.

Phillips paged through the murder book and settled on the catalog of evidence retrieved thus far. He scanned the list and found what he was looking for near the bottom of the second page – one silver vial containing cocaine. It had been found lying in the mud in the bushes next to the front door of Kessler's girlfriend's home, just a few steps from where Kessler's body had been found. Phillips scrolled through the book until he found two photographs of the vial lying there amidst the trampled footprints of the likely killer. The footprints were basically useless, having been rendered free of any workable detail by the heavy rains. The vial of cocaine wasn't of much use either. It contained no DNA and no fingerprints. The small quantity of cocaine found inside, less than an ounce, was nothing unusual and similar stuff could be found in more than a thousand locations in LA on any given night. Still, the cocaine had gnawed at Phillips and the other investigators almost from the beginning. Toxicology tests revealed that Kessler did not have any of the drug in his system, nor were they able to conclude that he was a user through analysis of his hair. Conversations with his known associates, including his wife and girlfriend, elicited a uniform denial whenever the subject was even broached. The witnesses were unanimous in saying that the idea of Kessler using cocaine was absolutely laughable. Faced with this unanimity of opinion, Phillips concluded that they were probably telling the truth.

If that was so, then to whom did the cocaine belong? Kessler's wife seemed to be an unlikely candidate and his girlfriend appeared wired without using the drug. LA detectives considered the possibility that the drug indicated that Kessler's death may have in some way involved a drug case on which he had been working or had worked in the past. Analysis of the lawyer's files, which took place only after a dispute over confidentiality with Kessler's law partners had been resolved by a judge, had proven inconclusive. While Kessler had worked some drug cases in the past and had a couple of others pending at the time of his death, nothing jumped out at Phillips or the others. Kessler was usually involved more with blood analysis than drugs, yet investigators kept digging hoping for a break.

That left the killer. Could the killer's rage, established by the mayhem at the crime scene and the damage to Kessler's body, have been fueled at least in part by the drug? Phillips had seen it before. Cocaine binges resulting in violent deaths were not uncommon in LA or any other major city. But this murder scene did not seem at all spontaneous. The killer had lain in wait for Kessler to emerge from the home, presumably tracking his whereabouts sufficiently to know that the lawyer was inside on this night. Moreover, the killer had picked the perfect night to strike, one where the torrential rains would keep witnesses to a minimum and limited the visibility of anyone who may have stumbled across the scene, not to mention the fact that the sounds of the storm, complete with thunder and lightning, likely covered any sounds of struggle or even screams that Kessler may have made before his throat was cut. In addition, the area in front of the home where the killing took place was entirely hidden from the street. Under those circumstances, the only person who could have reasonably witnessed the attack on Kessler was his girlfriend. And she stated that she had been upstairs in bed and had not seen him to the door that last time.

The evidence suggested that this was a premeditated act of violence committed against Marty Kessler at the perfect time in the perfect place for reasons which remained unclear. Phillips could imagine the killer, perhaps wounded himself, leaving the scene, the rain washing away the evidence, escaping down the front walk to the street, covered up against the elements and hiding any injuries he may have sustained himself, virtually invisible even if he had been seen. Then Phillips thought of the streetlight at the corner, apparently blown out by a shot from a pellet gun. No, Phillips concluded not for the first time, this was surely not a spontaneous act of rage fueled by drugs. Phillips thought about the killer as he absently thumbed through the pages of the murder book without really looking at any of them. It was quite a plan, he thought. This killer would not be easy to catch.

40

Ben sat on the bench in his office for a long time staring at the telephone, his heart pounding, hearing nothing but the words of the computer-generated voice ringing in his ears. After a while, he got to his feet and went over and looked out the window behind his desk. Then he began pacing. He thought that maybe he was being pimped, that the guys in the office would storm in laughing any minute now. But they didn't. Deep down, he knew this wasn't a joke. He knew that he just spoken with the killer. He grabbed a legal pad and pen off of his desk, tore off the first page and started writing notes about his conversation with the voice. He wanted to get as much of it down on paper as he could while it was still fresh in his mind. As he scribbled his notes, he wasn't sure if he was remembering things correctly even though it had only been a few minutes. When he was finished, he had more than a page of notes scrawled in a shaky hand.

Ben looked at his watch – it was already eleven-thirty. Libby would be in bed already and she would be furious that he hadn't even bothered to call. He thought about what to do. He decided to call Scott Nelson. He found the detective's card on his desk and turned it over for the cell phone number written on the back.

Nelson picked up on the third ring. "Lohmeier? Why in the hell are you calling me this late? I'm standing here in my shorts getting ready to go to bed. This had better be good."

"He just called me," Ben said.

"What? Who just called you?"

"I think it was the killer. At least he said he was the killer. Maybe not in so many words, but that was the upshot of it."

Nelson paused before responding. "How do you know it was the killer? Did he come right out and say that he had done it? And who did he kill?" Nelson's voice was low and serious. He knew that Ben was not joking around.

Ben sat down in his chair and composed himself. Then he continued. "He must've been watching me on Loretta's show tonight. After we were done and the technicians had left, I came up here to my office to pack up. Then the phone rang. I didn't answer it. It rang again. And like an idiot, I picked it up and there he was. He had a mechanical, computer voice."

"What you mean by that?" Nelson said. "A computer voice?"

"He sounded like a robot. It was like what you see in the movies. He was talking, but it wasn't his voice. The voice was a metallic, computer voice. Like he was speaking into something and another voice was coming out. I think they call them modulators, voice modulators."

"So it was computer-generated?"

"Yeah, that's right. Computer-generated."

"And how do you know it was a he?" Nelson said.

"I guess I don't." Ben paused. "But did you ever really consider that these murders were committed by a woman?"

"No, but that doesn't mean that they weren't. "

"Still,"

"Still," Nelson said, "it was probably a man, but could have been a woman."

"Right. It could've been a woman. It wasn't though, at least I don't think it was. I wrote down some notes. I should've done it as he was talking, but you never think of that at the time."

"That's okay, shit like this happens all the time with witnesses. Just tell me what he said the best you can remember."

Ben spent the next several minutes relating the conversation to Nelson, who mostly just listened. When he was finished, Ben said, "that's about it. I don't think I missed anything."

"Okay," Nelson said, "that's not a lot. It's more than we had before, but it's not a lot, assuming that it was really him. The killer, I mean."

"You don't think it was really him?"

"It's not that, but it's always possible that someone was fucking with you."

"Do you think it was a prank? It didn't sound like a prank to me. I thought that maybe it was at first. I was kind of hoping it was more than thinking it was, if you know what I mean. I don't really think it was a prank, do you?"

"No, I don't, not really. I guess it could have been some asshole trying to be a wise guy, but we have to assume that it was legit, at least unless we can prove otherwise."

"Okay."

"Now, I'm going to have to make a few phone calls right away," Nelson said.

"Calls to whom?"

"I'm going to have to call the feds, for starters."

"The feds?"

"Yeah, we suspect that we have a series of murders across state lines. When that happens, the feds are all over it. You know that."

"Yeah, okay, I get that."

"Where are you going to be?"

"When? Right now?"

"Yeah," Nelson said, "for about the next half hour or so?"

"I was just about to drive home. It should take about half an hour."

"Give me your cell phone number. I'll call you in the car when I know more."

Within five minutes, Ben was out the door and heading for his car. He was especially vigilant as he walked through the parking lot. The evening was quiet and still, the heat of the day radiating up off of the blacktop. As he reached his car, he looked around and didn't see a soul. He could hear the muted sounds of the bar across the way on the other side of the building.

Nelson called him back twenty minutes later. "Okay, here's the deal," Nelson said. "I made a couple of calls and the feds want to meet with you in the morning, say eleven or so. Do you have court or anything?"

"No, I'm good."

"Then we'll see you then."

"Scott?"

"Yeah?"

"What's going on? Is there anything I don't know about?"

Nelson laughed. "Probably. But that doesn't mean that I'm not in the dark too. Remember, these are feds we're talking about. I'm just a lowly Chicago police detective. I don't mean shit in their eyes."

"Got it. See you tomorrow."

Ben made it home ten minutes later. The house was dark and still, the only light being one left on over the stove. He rummaged around looking for evidence of dinner and found nothing. Ben went downstairs to get a beer out of the basement fridge and then came back up and sat in the dark in the family room for more than an hour hoping to get tired enough to sleep. As he nursed his beer, Ben ruminated over the day's events. He thought about Moran, how frail he had looked just the other night compared with how large and full of life he had seemed on the television footage of the Owens trial, a man fully in charge of his life and his world. He figured now that Moran's body would show up in a day or so, maybe a week on the outside, causing more furor in death than even the Owens verdict had elicited in life a decade ago. How many more famous men, he thought, would be remembered more for their deaths than for anything they did in life? He took a sip of his beer and remembered Moran in that hotel room just a few days ago, sweating and afraid. Ben wondered what, if anything, he could've done in the past few days that could have prevented this outcome. He knew the answer was nothing. Now he just had to make himself believe it.

240

41

It was almost two before Ben climbed the stairs and went to bed. He had changed in the bathroom and had even skipped brushing his teeth so as to not wake Libby up. He crept across the room and slipped into bed to the sounds of her soft snoring. He tossed and turned for most of the next four hours, occasionally drifting off for a while. He finally gave up the ghost shortly after six and headed off to the shower. She was brushing her teeth when he finished. "You're up early," she said after she had rinsed and spat.

Ben was not known to be an early riser. "I have court in Waukegan this morning," he said with his face buried in his towel. He didn't want to start the day talking about the phone call or anything else relating to dead lawyers strewn about the countryside. She nodded and he wasn't sure whether she had bought it. She probably had and was simply waiting for an explanation of his late evening. He didn't give her one.

Before Libby was even out of the shower, Ben was dressed in his finest "meet the FBI" suit and was downstairs pulling a Coke out of the refrigerator. Since he didn't drink coffee and certainly needed the caffeine, Coke was pretty much the lone alternative. He was out the door and on the road before seven. It was cool and clear and promised to be a glorious day, exactly the opposite of everything going on inside his head at that very moment. He stopped at Dunkin' Donuts to pick up two donuts on the way in and got to the office by a quarter to eight feeling as though he'd

241

never left. He was the first one in so he dutifully fulfilled his obligation of turning on all the lights as he made his way out to the garage with the second of his donuts. He wasn't ready to go back up to his office. Half an hour later, Nancy's voice came over the intercom. "You're in early."

"Yep."

"Not very talkative today?"

"Nope."

"Okay then."

The drumbeat of arrivals for the day had begun. No one came out to the garage to visit him. Ben saw Scott Nelson pull his Ford Taurus around the back of the garage and park at about ten forty-five. Ben had done nothing since his arrival but sit and wait. And think. He got up from one of the barber chairs and went over to the door leading from the garage to the parking lot, unlocking it. He opened it as Nelson walked up.

"How's it going?" Nelson said and the two men shook hands. Ben shrugged. He stepped aside to let Nelson in. "That's what I thought. I figured I'd get here a little early so we could talk."

Nelson took a seat at the conference table as Ben resumed his perch in one of the barber chairs.

Ben forced a smile. "I see you're wearing your best Sunday suit for the occasion."

Nelson puffed out his chest and brushed off his sleeves. "My fed suit." He studied Ben for a moment. "You look like shit."

Ben shrugged again. "Didn't sleep much. You don't exactly look like Brad Pitt yourself."

"No, I suppose not."

Nelson gave Ben a brief update into his activities over the previous twelve hours. They didn't amount to much other than generally reaching out to those involved in the investigation and letting them know what had transpired.

The two agents from the Chicago field office of the FBI arrived promptly at eleven o'clock. Ben figured they'd been waiting around the corner to arrive precisely at the specified time. One was a man and the other a woman. They both wore blue suits and drove a dark blue Crown Victoria. Ben stepped down from the barber chair and repeated his actions with Nelson by opening the door from the garage to the parking lot. He didn't necessarily need the FBI agents interacting with any of the office staff. As he stepped aside to let them in, he looked up at the balcony and saw Nancy smoking a cigarette. So much for secrecy. He stepped back inside and closed the door behind him.

The man introduced himself as Assistant Special Agent in Charge Daniel Lonergan. He looked a bit more rumpled than the typical fed, with thinning brown hair that was neither short nor long nor apparently combed. He immediately struck Ben with his wry smile as someone who could have a wicked sense of humor. The woman was another matter. Tall and lean with straight blonde hair cropped at the shoulders, she looked as though she had just been carved from a glacier. Lonergan introduced her as Martie Swenson and she and Ben shook hands. Her hand was cool and her grip strong.

"Find us okay?" Ben said. "Some people have trouble."

"No problem. GPS worked fine," Lonergan said.

The group exchanged pleasantries for a moment, if small talk with the feds can be described as such, and then everyone sat down at the conference table.

Lonergan looked around the room at the unusual decor, from the barber chairs to the antique bank safe to the animal trophies on the wall and smiled.

"You a hunter?" Ben said.

Lonergan tilted his head and glanced around again. "I suppose you could say that, but not that kind of hunter. No trophies on the wall."

Ben glanced over at Swenson, who stared back expressionless. "So," he said, "about the telephone call."

Lonergan put up his hand. "Hold on for a minute. We'll get back to that. Let's start with the dinner for Jimmy Moran."

"Okay."

"Detective Nelson told us that you called him a few days ago to tell him about the dinner and your subsequent conversation with Moran in his hotel room, is that right?"

"That's right." Ben relayed the story pretty much in chronological order. The agents listened intently, asking few questions. When Ben got to the part about the interview with local television, Lonergan cut him off. "I actually saw that interview on TV that night," Lonergan said.

"Deer in the headlights?" Ben said.

Lonergan smiled. "Maybe a little bit. Not too bad though. I've seen worse."

"You know, you should probably talk to Stan Feldman as well. He was there that night. He was there when I first spoke to Moran. In fact, he introduced me to Moran because I had never met him before."

"He's on my list," Lonergan said. "Now, he didn't go upstairs with you to meet with Moran, did he?"

Ben shook his head. "No. He went upstairs to his room, but he didn't go with me to Moran's room. I stopped by his room after I talked to Moran, but he didn't see Moran or talk to him after the reception broke up. He would've told me."

Lonergan was taking notes. Swenson continued to stare at him. "Tell me what happened when you went upstairs," Lonergan said.

Ben went through the story slowly and deliberately. He had told it enough times now and it probably sounded very polished and rehearsed. He couldn't do anything about that. It was what it was. Again, Lonergan let him pretty much work his way through the narrative without irruption. When that was finished, they turned the conversation over to a discussion about Ray Fisher. "Why do you think he was so focused on Fisher?" Lonergan said.

Ben scratched his chin and glanced over at Nelson, who nodded. "The obvious reasons, I think. Moran and Fisher had something of a history dating back to the trial. Fisher would show up places unexpectedly to try and shake Moran up or something. He would show up in courtrooms and at social functions where Moran was present and make sure Moran knew he was there."

"He was at the reception as well?"

"That's what Moran said. I didn't see him myself."

"Okay. Did Moran ever say that Fisher threatened him in any way?"

"Not directly, no," Ben said. "My impression is that Fisher was trying to intimidate him. You know, even I had seen him on TV from time to time over the years making comments about Moran and the others. I think Owens was probably the most proven guilty man in the history of American jurisprudence. But that's not Moran's fault. The jury could have and should have found him guilty. We have to accept the judgment of juries if the system is going to come close to working, you know that."

"True enough."

They moved on to the phone call from the night before. Ben went through it slowly, in a less practiced manner since he'd told it only once before. Lonergan listened closely. Swenson continued to stare. When Ben finished, Lonergan said, "have you told us everything you can remember?"

"I think so. I have some notes upstairs that I took after I hung up. The conversation didn't last that long. I think I've covered everything."

"Can you get me a copy of those notes?"

"Of course. As soon as we're done I'll go get them and make a copy for you."

"Would you say that you are convinced that this was a legitimate call? By that, I mean do you believe that this was from someone involved in one or more of these murders?"

"Convinced? I wouldn't say convinced," Ben said. "Having reflected on it for half a day or so, I would say more likely than not, but I'm not convinced, no. Not yet."

Lonergan smiled. "Spoken like a true attorney," he said. "But I see what you're saying."

"I'm just trying to tell you what I think," Ben said.

"I get that. What about it makes you more likely than not to believe that this may have been the killer?"

"I'm not sure. It just felt real to me, genuine in some way."

"There are a lot of kooks out there," Lonergan said. "You must know that. There are a lot of people that try to insinuate

245

themselves into high-profile investigations. This could be one of those. Just some nut looking to get his fifteen minutes of fame, so to speak."

"Maybe. Doesn't the computerized voice modulator, or whatever it's called, indicate that this was more than that?" Lonergan shrugged. "It seems like an awful lot of trouble to go to for just a prank."

"True," Lonergan said. "Those voice modulators are not that difficult to find these days, unfortunately. There are a lot of techno-geeks out there with them. You'd be surprised how many guys call up their girlfriends and try to scare the hell out of them using one of those things."

"Are you telling me that you don't believe this was the killer?"

"No, I didn't say that. I try not to take a firm position without sufficient evidence. After listening to you, I would tend to think it was a legit call. Did the caller offer any details regarding these deaths?"

"No, he didn't."

Lonergan stopped him. "What makes you think it's a he? With the computerized voice, how could you tell?"

Ben made a thoughtful face. "I suppose I can't know for sure. Something about the voice seemed male though, probably because in the back of my mind I was already thinking about how all these people were killed. Somehow it seems like more of a male crime."

Lonergan glanced in the direction of Swenson. "You're probably right, but it's usually wise to leave that kind of thing up to the profilers." Ben thought he saw Swenson's mouth twitch. Maybe that explained all the staring. Maybe she was a profiler and he was being profiled. Lonergan continued. "Let's go through it again. Maybe something will jog your memory by telling it again."

So Ben went through it again. When he was finished, he looked at Lonergan said, "So, what's next?"

Lonergan nodded thoughtfully, then wrote something on his pad before looking up. "I think we should probably put a trace on your phone lines. The office, I mean. There's no reason to believe that the person behind the call would know either your cell phone or your home number, is there?"

"No, I wouldn't think so. But I'm not sure how comfortable I am with tracing phone calls. We're a law firm here. We can't let you just record conversations between lawyers in the office and our clients."

Lonergan waved off the concerns. "No, I wasn't talking about that. I was talking about tracing where the calls originated from. Tell me how your phone system here works. Does everyone have an individual line or do the calls come into a central hub of some kind?"

Ben went through the phone system as best as he could given that he wasn't a tech guy either. There was a firm number and each person had an individual line as well.

"Okay, we'll do this," Lonergan said after Ben had gone through it. "We'll put a tracer on all the calls coming in from the outside, meaning that we can identify where they originated. Now that doesn't mean that we are recording any phone calls. I would suggest we do that too." When Ben started to protest, Lonergan held up his hand. "Now hear me out. We can put a device on the phone that would allow you to hit a button and record the telephone call. We could put one on the phone in your office and maybe put one on the phone out here if you spend a lot of time out here in the conference room. No calls are recorded unless you hit the button to start the recording. How's that sound?"

Ben nodded in agreement. "That would probably work."

"Look, let's be honest. This may be a one and done thing. This guy may not call again. Or he may be some nutcase that has nothing to do with the deaths of anybody. But I don't want to take that chance. I want to be prepared in case he does call again. He may be looking to establish some sort of dialogue with you about this. Maybe he wants to brag. Maybe he wants to see how much we know, not that you would necessarily know that. In any event, we should be prepared in case he does call again."

Ben went upstairs to get his notes. When he got back with a copy, it looked as though no one had spoken since he had left the

247

room.   After exchanging business cards and promising full cooperation on the part of everyone, the agents were gone. Nelson remained. The two men watched the agents get in the Crown Vic, back out of their parking spot and drive away. Ben looked at Nelson. "You didn't have much to say."

Nelson stuffed his hands into his pockets. "Fed-itis." Ben looked puzzled. "Fed-induced laryngitis. I've discovered over the years, that where the feds are concerned, better not to say too much."

"We're on the same side there."

"Hopefully," Nelson said with a knowing glance.

42

The Calumet-Saganashkee Channel, or Cal-Sag Channel for short, is a navigational canal in southern Cook County, Illinois. It serves as a channel between the Little Calumet River and the Chicago Sanitary and Ship Canal. Over sixteen miles long, running from east to west, it was dug over an eleven year period and completed almost one hundred years ago. The Channel services barge traffic in what was an active zone of heavy industry in the far southern neighborhoods of the City of Chicago and adjacent suburbs. These days, it is used more as a conduit for wastewater from southern Cook County, including the Chicago Area Tunnel and Waste Reservoir, which flows into the Illinois Waterway. In the summertime, pleasure crafts dot the Channel. The western four and one-half miles of the Channel flows through the Palos Hills Forest Preserves, a large area of parkland operated by the Forest Preserve District of Cook County.

Like many teenagers before him, Bobby Breedlove had a favorite spot in the forest preserve that extended down to the banks of the Channel. He had learned about it from his older brother, Steve, who used to go there and get high with his friends a decade earlier. Bobby, a senior at Carl Sandburg High School, kept up the family tradition and had been going to a particular spot with his friends ever since they had gotten their drivers licenses. Today, Bobby and his friend, Jason Spitlock, parked their dented Honda Civic off of a dirt path at the west end of the forest preserve and picked through the trees to their spot overlooking the Channel. The area was in a small thicket of bushes nestled at the edge of a grove of trees, just shy of the clearing that led down to the water. From their typical position, they could see out over the Channel to the other side, but people in the water could not easily see them back amidst the brush.

They weren't particularly worried about either the car or themselves being discovered because this was western Cook County, far from Chicago's city limits. This far out, the forest preserve and County Sheriff's deputies were not terribly interested with what was going on. They had bigger problems inside the city itself. Bobby had an ounce and a half of pot and some rolling papers in a plastic bag stuffed in the pocket of his jeans, while Jason carried a six-pack of Rolling Rock long neck bottles in a paper sack. They got to their spot a few minutes later and settled in to have a good time.

It was about six-fifteen in the evening and it wouldn't start to get dark for another couple of hours, this being late June and the midst of the longest days of the year. Bobby had taken a few friends to the spot over the years and Jason was one of his regulars. Occasionally, a few more joined them, including a girl or two for make-out sessions, but tonight, it was just the two of them. Bobby took the pot and rolled a joint as Jason popped a beer for each of them. They sat around and bullshitted about girls as they drank and got high. No one bothered them and aside from one boat heading east, a small 10-footer with an outboard engine and two guys in it, probably fishing, they didn't see a soul for the first hour.

Eventually, about halfway through his second beer, Jason Spitlock had to take a piss. "Nature calls," he said as he stood and stretched. He held the joint between his teeth. He took one last pull and handed it back to Bobby. "Be right back," he said. He entered the clearing, where a small slope led down to the water and unzipped his fly. He apparently intended to piss off the bank toward the water. As he started to relieve himself, he glanced down to watch the steady stream of urine arcing toward the water's edge and saw the body of Jimmy Moran wedged up against a large rock four feet from the water. "Shit," he said and jumped back. He turned back toward Bobby, the stream of urine leading the way. Then he caught himself. "Bobby, you got to see this. Come here, quick."

Bobby was looking skyward and blowing smoke up into the air. He looked down in the direction of his friend only to see Jason facing sideways and still pissing. "That's okay, you don't got nothing there that I'm looking forward to seeing."

By now, Jason had finished and was zipping up. "No, it's not that. I'm not shitting you. Get your ass over here now! There's a dead guy down there."

Bobby stopped laughing. He could tell by the look on Jason's face that the other boy wasn't kidding around. He got to his feet and hurried over to where Jason was standing. They took a couple of steps forward and peered over the side. There he was, Jimmy Moran. Of course, Bobby didn't know it was Jimmy Moran because he didn't know who Jimmy Moran was. The two of them just stared for a minute saying nothing. Then Bobby said, "look at his fucked-up neck."

"Yeah," Jason said, "it looks like somebody tried to cut his head off."

"We've got to get the fuck out of here," Bobby said. "We should call the cops or something."

"And tell them what? We were standing here getting drunk and high and we found a dead guy?"

"No, not that," Bobby said. He considered it for a minute. "Okay, we'll do this. We'll get out of here, then call the cops and tell them where to find the body."

"That won't work. How are we going to describe where we found him. Besides, we're stoned, at least I am. I don't want to get busted just because I'm trying to call in that we found a dead guy," Jason said.

They debated what to do, occasionally glancing down at the body. Faced with the possibility of getting caught smoking dope in close proximity to a dead body, they eventually decided that discretion was the better part of valor and that they would hold off telling anyone about it until the following day, which was Friday. They would come back after school to hang out, "find"

251

the body, then call the cops. Only this time, they wouldn't have any dope or any beer. If someone else found the body between now and then, so much the better. If anybody figured out that they had been there, which they agreed seemed unlikely even in their mildly-altered state, they would explain that they had never looked over the side. "What if they do a *CSI* thing and discover it's my piss down there?" Jason said.

Bobby looked at him for a minute, thinking that sounded stupid, but then said, "we'll tell them that it was dark when we got here and you never saw the guy." They agreed that might work, forgetting that they weren't going to tell anyone about it tonight, took one last look at Moran laying there in the dirt, and went back to clean up their spot. That was the plan. When they got back to their car, Jason paused. "Wait a sec," he said. "Might as well finish my brewski. No sense wasting it." They both chugged what was left of their beers and got in the car.

Bobby backed out to the dirt road. "Let's stop at the 7-Eleven on the way back and get some altoids."

"Good idea."

They decided on the way back that they would neither call, nor text each other about the evening's events just in case somebody decided to look into such things later. Bobby was proud of himself for even thinking of this. Jason was fairly impressed with him as well. They batted around the idea of bringing another friend or two the following afternoon, eventually concluding that it wasn't worth the risk and since they had discovered the body in the first place, no one else deserve the credit.

As it turned out, when they returned at three-thirty the following afternoon, Jimmy Moran was still where they had left him. No one had found the body. Twenty-four hours and the brighter light of the afternoon made the site even more gruesome than it had been the previous evening. The two boys stared at Moran for a couple of moments, before Bobby pulled his cell phone from his pocket. "Better get to this," he said. "To be honest with you, I didn't sleep well last night thinking about how we left him here without telling anyone."

252

"Me neither."

Bobby finally made the 911 call at three thirty-five in the afternoon. The first squad car arrived in the parking lot of the forest preserve twenty minutes later. Bobby and Jason had been waiting for them there. They hopped in the squad car and directed the two officers back to where Bobby and Jason typically parked their car, then led them on foot to their regular spot. "This is where we come and hang out sometimes," Bobby said gesturing to the small clearing in the thicket of bushes.

Not wanting to let Bobby have all the glory, Jason jumped in. "Right after we got here, I had to take a, I mean, I had to go to the bathroom so I walked over to the edge." He shrugged. "I was going to go over the side then I saw him laying down there."

Jason had gestured over the side toward the water. The four of them walked over to the edge and looked down. Moran's body lay in a crumpled heap exactly where it had been the evening before. The first cop, actually a sheriff's deputy of about thirty, said "jeez." Bobby looked at him and wondered if this had been his first dead body.

The second deputy, a decade or so older, recognized Moran. "Shit. That's Jimmy Moran," he said. "We better call this in right away. This is going to be a shitstorm." He looked at the two boys, then back at the body, then back at the two boys. "Did either of you ever go down there?"

Bobby and Jason said "no" simultaneously. Jason added, "I started pissing over the side before I actually saw him."

"But you didn't go down there?"

"No, neither of us did. Just my piss."

Bobby looked at the older officer. "Who is Jimmy Moran?"

By four o'clock, three more squad cars and an evidence van had arrived at the forest preserve. By four-thirty, Lonergan and an FBI team were on the scene. The news hit the wire services by six, at which time Ben was already on his way home, having promised Libby he would be there for dinner with the family. He had no TV appearances scheduled for the evening and looked forward to a peaceful night at home with the family. He might

253

even catch the Cubs game, but would definitely not be watching any news programs.

The phone call came fifteen minutes later. He was heading south down Route 83 coming up to the Oakbrook Center Mall less than ten minutes from home when Marcia Roberts called him on his cell phone. Ben saw the number on the caller ID and groaned. "Not tonight, Marcia," he said after he clicked the receive button. "I've got plans tonight."

"They found Jimmy Moran's body."

"Shit," Ben said, "where did they find him?"

"Near the banks of a place called the Cal-Sag Channel in a forest preserve. Two teenagers out for a good time found him. Apparently, his head had been practically cut off."

"Just like the Owens case."

"Yeah, just like the Owens case. They are saying he'd been there for a couple of days or so."

"What do you want?"

"Can you get to the studio downtown or do you want people to come to your office?"

Ben maneuvered into the right lane. "I'll go downtown. I'm right near the ramp for the expressway." Once the light turned green, Ben went through the intersection and was on the ramp in less than a minute. "I'm on my way."

He called home as soon as he had merged onto the expressway. Libby said "okay" when he told her and hung up the phone without further comment. He knew she was pissed, but figured she would probably get over it given the magnitude of the story. Then again, maybe she wouldn't.

The inbound traffic wasn't too bad, with a few slow pockets here and there, and Ben made it to the parking lot near the Fox News studios a couple of minutes before seven. Within half an hour, he had been given the once over by the makeup crew and was on the air on and off for most of the next three hours. Each of the three major cable news channels preempted their regular programming and covered Moran's death exclusively. While Ben and many of the other talking heads sought to keep things in perspective, others were not so circumspect. With so much time

254

to fill, networks resorted to supplementing their usual commentary with "on the scene" interviews, which ranged from thoughtful to ridiculous.

Meanwhile, the media descended on the forest preserve and were met with a phalanx of Cook County Sheriff's deputies blocking their way. The FBI had formally taken charge of the scene and that left plenty of deputies to keep the media and related onlookers at bay. Never had the Cal-Sag Channel received so much attention and several camera crews went either upstream or downstream to get better views of the waterway and provide some perspective for their viewers. One particularly enterprising local television outlet sent someone down the Channel on a boat to get a better look from the water. They were met by a County amphibious unit, but not before they provided their viewers with a good shot of the searchlights upstream illuminating the area in and around where Moran's body had been found.

With the discovery of Moran's body, media presence in the jurisdictions where the other bodies were found also intensified. Investigators in those locations, however, believed privately that Moran's death might spread the coverage around a bit, while increasing the federal involvement in the case, thereby eventually easing the intensity somewhat and lessening their respective degrees of culpability over their failures to locate the killer. There was no question now that the deaths of these five lawyers were now the number one story in the country.

No one was talking about the president's healthcare law, nor the country's budgetary problems. Peace in the Middle East, and foreign affairs generally, were virtually ignored. All everyone wanted to talk about was who did it and why. Chase Owens even broke his media silence and issued a statement, prepared by his public relations people no doubt, saying he was saddened to hear of his former lawyer's death and cautioned people from speculating as to its motive. He was forced to hire outside security people to surround his Brentwood home, before quickly arranging a golf vacation in Florida.

255

Social media served to fan the flames even higher and bring the case to a whole new level. Lawyer jokes abounded, both on Facebook and Twitter, and some of them were even in good taste. Conspiracy theories, always a successful by-product of prominent deaths, exploded all over the Internet. Truth be told, investigators combed the Internet looking at both reliable sources of information and even those somewhat less respectable than supermarket tabloids for information, ideas and potential leads.

Ben was forced to admit that he was doing a bit of the same, when his wife caught him firing up his laptop after finally getting home that evening. Since it was a Friday, there was no need to turn in early because no one would be going to work in the morning. The kids had just gone to bed when Ben got home and he was expecting the worst from his wife. After stopping upstairs to kiss the kids good night, he was pleasantly surprised to find her in the family room flipping channels checking out the coverage of Moran's death.

While she was at least talking to him and seemed to understand why he had to go and be part of the coverage, she still wasn't exactly warm and fuzzy where he was concerned. It was more or less a détente at this point, not much more. Ben sensed that part of her attitude reflected a growing concern on her part over the fact that Ben was now a fairly prominent attorney who appeared on TV, not unlike some of the men who had already turned up dead. He had already thought the same thing.

*****

Rich learned about Moran's body turning up when he overheard two women talking about it as he was checking out at the grocery store. He rushed back to the condo and flipped on the television and admired his handiwork in between grilling and devouring a steak for dinner. He flipped back and forth between the three main cable channels and spent a little more time watching Lohmeier on Fox. The lawyer made no reference to his telephone conversation with Rich and Rich wondered whether Lohmeier believed he was actually speaking to the real killer, or just a crank caller.

Either way, Rich had gotten a kick out of the conversation. He hadn't revealed anything of substance and took great pleasure in the fact that Lohmeier was clearly stunned and shaken up to hear from him. Although Rich was confident that Lohmeier would be talking to the authorities and probably even the FBI, that didn't concern him very much. He had taken great steps to ensure that his communications from both the condo and the farm were untraceable by even the best tools of the FBI. This protection had caused him to spend a lot of time and even more money, but he felt it was worth it. Besides, he'd been itching to use the voice modulator for some time and had even considered using it to shake up his previous victims, before ultimately deciding against it.

He hadn't made up his mind if and when he was going to contact Lohmeier again. Now that Moran's body had finally shown up, maybe it was a good time to get in touch with a lawyer again. If he had indeed talked to the feds already, they probably were trying to put additional security measures in place that would help them trace his calls and find out who Rich was and where he was calling from. Rich felt confident that such measures would be useless and he didn't give them a second thought now that his own countermeasures were already in place. Moreover, the feds' involvement could also prove quite useful. He had planned all along to drop a few red herrings into the basket and was eager to see how successful he could be at getting the investigators to chase their own tails. That was just another part of the fun.

43

The weekend was relatively quiet and Ben occupied himself by getting some stuff done around the house. He cut the grass on Saturday and then took the kids to watch their cousin's Little League baseball game across town, while Libby went out shopping to prepare for the Fourth of July weekend. The Fourth was a week from Tuesday, so they had the weekend plus Monday in addition to the holiday itself. That meant that Ben really just needed to get through this week until he had a break. He had already told Marcia Roberts that he planned to be gone for the Fourth of July weekend and the producer wasn't terribly upset about it, since most programming was altered over the holiday anyway when the hosts and anchors of the various programs also took some time off. Unless something huge happened between now and then, Ben wouldn't necessarily be needed over the long weekend.

The weekend ended much too quickly and soon Ben was back in the office on Monday morning. He had two calls from Agent Lonergan waiting for him and another from Detective Nelson. He returned Nelson's first. "Do you know what Lonergan wants?" he said to Nelson.

"I think he just wants to make arrangements to set up his equipment and touch base with you now that Moran's body has been found. He's been pretty busy over the weekend."

"I can imagine. How about you? Are you still on the case?"

"Technically yes, but obviously we're taking a backseat to Lonergan and his boys. Which means that we get to do all the grunt work and they get all the glory if we wind up catching whoever's responsible for this."

"Makes sense."

"I trust you haven't received any more phone calls from your friend with the mechanical voice?"

"No, nothing. I was wondering though whether we should have the place swept for listening devices. "

"I can see that. Talk to Lonergan about it. The feds have a lot of toys they like showing off. When you call him back, mention that and maybe he'll bring something with that can put your mind at ease a bit."

Ben called Lonergan and left a message. The agent called back twenty minutes later. Ben could hear that he was outside. "Where are you? Are you at the crime scene?"

"The beautiful Cal-Sag Channel," Lonergan said. "We need to make arrangements to put our equipment in. I'm assuming you haven't received any additional missives from our friend?"

"No, nothing." Ben mentioned the possibility of a sweep for listening devices.

"We could probably do that. Let me get someone on that," Lonergan said. "I'm pretty backed up here, but I don't want to wait too long in case the voice gets in touch with you again. Now that Moran's body has been found, he may be eager to brag about it."

"I thought about that too."

"How about tomorrow morning? I should have everything ready to go by then. If I'm not out there myself, I'll send someone else. Are you going to be around in the morning?"

"Yeah, I'll be here."

Ben got through the rest of the day relatively unscathed. Marcia Roberts called him about three, lining him up for the evening's broadcast. Ben had begged off the other shows and had arranged to only do the Bergen show at nine. The techs would be meeting him at a local cable outlet in Oak Brook, not far from Ben's house, so he could go home and have dinner with

259

his family before the short trip for the show. Marcia complained and tried to push him for more availability, hinting that she had been having trouble lining up guests, ostensibly due to the fact that the Fourth of July holiday was approaching and people were going on vacation. Ben wondered if there was more to it than that, but kept silent.

An agent working for Lonergan called not long after and arranged for a meeting at Ben's office in Itasca at ten the following morning. They would bring all the necessary equipment and would even conduct a sweep of the premises for any listening devices. Lonergan had come through. Ben had talked to Phil on the telephone and he too was pleased that the FBI was going to do the security sweep. He was pleased about that, but little else. He felt the need to point out that Ben's billable hours were down and several outstanding projects were behind schedule. The suggestion stung, but deep down Ben knew that Phil was telling the truth. Despite what he thought were his best efforts, he hadn't gotten much done in the last couple of weeks and was indeed falling further and further behind on his work. Normally, the light holiday week both before and after the Fourth of July would give him an opportunity to catch up. Ben knew that with the Moran case and everything else exploding, that might turn out not to be true.

Ben watched a little cable TV while he waited for Libby to get dinner on the table. The hysteria over Moran's death was escalating, which Ben could tell from the coverage in the *Chicago Tribune* on Sunday and again this morning. He even saw a brief snippet of Ray Fisher on one of the competing networks. A reporter had caught up to Fisher outside of his office and the man did not look at all displeased over Moran's death. "All I can say," Fisher said with a sneer, "is that what goes around, comes around."

Loretta's show went off largely without a hitch. Although the intensity level among the other guests had amped up a little bit, Ben tried very hard not to make any news himself. He was on for two segments, the second of which also included Stan

Feldman, who was there to give personal remembrances of Jimmy Moran.

In the commercial break before Stan came on, one of the producers urged them to contradict each other to spice up the show. "Not my job, sister," Feldman said. "You have to get someone else for that. Mr. Lohmeier and I are pretty much on the same page here."

At the next commercial break, Feldman asked Ben, "how's it going? Anything new? We haven't talked since Jimmy's body showed up."

"No, not much. You know, I was hoping ..."

"Yeah, me too."

The following morning at ten, Ben was already in the garage when Lonergan and his crew pulled around from the front and parked at the end of the parking lot. Nelson joined a moment later and Ben met the group at the barbershop doors as they paraded in from the parking lot. They spent some time showing the techs where to put their equipment and a young agent began a security sweep of the premises looking for listening devices. Ben, Lonergan and Nelson adjourned to the kitchen while they left the techs to their work. Swenson had not come along. She apparently had other work to do, other people to stare at. Ben took a seat on the far side of the kitchen table and stacked the day's newspapers in a pile off to one side. Nelson took a seat opposite him. Lonergan stood in the doorway. "Can I shut this?" He said gesturing to the door.

"Sure, go ahead," Ben said.

Lonergan sat down next to Nelson and appeared to compose his thoughts. Lonergan told them that the site at the Cal-Sag Channel was basically a body dump. Moran had not been killed at that location. The wounds to his neck, which were substantial, would have generated a lot of blood, little of which was present at the scene. There had been no rain in the area for the previous several days, which meant that it was overwhelmingly likely that Moran had been killed at another location. He had few if any defensive wounds and only a couple of modest bruises on his face and forehead, neither of which amount to much. Toxicology results were pending.

According to Lonergan, Ben had likely been the last person to see Moran alive, other than the killer. The investigation uncovered that no one had visited Moran after Ben had left the room. Early the following morning, a maid found a "Do Not Disturb" sign on the door and had moved on to the next room rather than clean Moran's room. Since Moran was only scheduled to stay there one night, the front office made a routine inquiry as to whether Moran's plans had changed. When Moran hadn't answered a telephone call, the front desk sent the bellman up with the pass card. He returned saying that neither Moran, nor any luggage had been left in his room.

"So what are you saying? That Moran was abducted at the hotel?"

"Unfortunately, there are limited security cameras at the hotel. We don't have any evidence of him leaving, certainly he did not check out, which doesn't mean he didn't manage to leave unnoticed. None of the front office, bell staff or doormen recall having seen him after the dinner. Of course, few guests actually check out of hotels anymore. The staff slips the bill under the door sometime overnight and then merely charges the credit card and the guests either leave the key cards on a table in the room, or just toss them. New cards are issued every time someone checks in any way."

"Sounds right," Ben said.

"That brings us back to your meeting with Moran." Ben started to speak and Lonergan held up his hand. "Hold on, give me a minute here. I know you told us all about your conversation with Moran. What I want to know now is, did you see anything or anyone that looked out of the ordinary as you were going to and from his room that night? Try to remember. Maybe you saw something or someone that didn't seem significant at the time, but now, may turn out to be."

Ben leaned forward, his elbows on the table, and thought back to the meeting with Moran. He talked them through his recollections. "Like I said, I went up in the elevator with Stan

262

Feldman. We went up there alone, just the two of us, no one else on board. Stan got off first and went to his room, the door shut and I continued up to Moran's floor. I got off and walked down the hallway, around the corner and down again until I found Moran's room."

"Did you see anybody in the hallway or waiting by the elevator?"

"No, there was no one. Once I got upstairs, the hotel was pretty quiet. It was getting pretty late. It was probably after nine-thirty already."

"So, you spend your time in Moran's room and talked about the things that you've already told us. How long were you in his room?"

"I would say about half an hour or so."

"Okay, now you're done talking with him and getting ready to leave. What happened?"

"I got up and he walked me to the door. We shook hands and I told him that I would be in touch in a few days."

"Did anyone come to the door while you were inside with him?"

"No, no one."

"You open the door to leave. Was there anyone in the hallway when you left his room?"

Ben thought about it for a minute. "No, there was no one there. I had to walk down one corridor, then turn and go down another to get to the elevators. There was nobody there in either hallway. I didn't see anyone."

"Okay, so you get to the elevator. Was anyone waiting for the elevator when you got there?"

"No, there was no one. I pressed the button for down, I was going down to Stan Feldman's room to tell him about my meeting with Moran, then I waited for the elevator."

"How long did it take for the elevator to arrive? Was it there already when you pushed the button?"

"No, I had to wait for it." Ben thought back to that night at the hotel. "I waited probably a minute or so for the elevator to arrive. No, that's not right. When you're waiting for an elevator,

263

a minute is kind of a long time. I probably waited between thirty seconds to a minute for the elevator to get there."

"Okay. What happened when the elevator arrived?"

"First, the bell rang, then the elevator got there and the doors opened."

"Was anyone on the elevator when the doors opened?"

"Yes, I started to get on right away and almost ran into someone getting off."

Lonergan looked intense, but Ben didn't even notice. He was looking back in his mind's eye at that night at the hotel. He was seeing the doors to the elevator open. "Good," Lonergan said. "Describe the person on the elevator. Was there more than one person?"

"No, there was just one. It was a man."

"A man? Describe him."

Ben closed his eyes trying to remember. All he could remember was the cart. "The man was pushing a cart. More than waist height. It probably came up to my chest, maybe a little lower. Probably somewhere between my waist and my chest. Not much lower than my waist, if at all. It was pretty wide, say three to four feet."

"Describe it. What color was it?"

"It was black. Solid black with silver handles, corners, that kind of thing."

"So it was a case rather than a cart? It was solid all the way through?"

"Yes, it was solid from top to bottom. It was black and solid. Kind of like a large luggage case or maybe a musician's case. A trunk, maybe. You know, the kind you can put a musical instrument into. Or even room service. I've seen room service carts like that. A big cart on wheels with multiple levels you could put trays of food onto. It was like that."

"So it was a large black case or cart or trunk that you could either put luggage, room service orders or maybe a musical instrument into?"

Ben realized how that all sounded, then shrugged. "Yeah, something like that. I've seen a cart like that used for all three of those things. Probably not so much luggage though since your average traveler wouldn't use a cart quite like that. It would be more for someone working at the hotel, maybe audiovisual equipment or a musician or food service, something like that."

Nelson was also leaning forward intently now.

"Good," Lonergan said, "we're making progress. We've got the cart, now who was pushing it?"

"He was a man, definitely a man."

"Describe him."

Ben tried to remember the man pushing the cart, but his focus at the time had been on the cart. "I remember the cart mostly because my focus was on the cart when I almost ran into it. It came out of the elevator first and when I ran into it my eyes went down and I stepped back out of the way."

"But you said it was a man pushing the cart. Is that right? What do you remember about him?"

"I remember seeing the cart, stopping, then stepping back. The cart stopped too for a second until I was out of the way, then continued out of the elevator. The man who was pushing it, it was definitely a man, was tall, or least he seemed taller than me, several inches taller."

"How tall are you?" Lonergan asked.

"About five-foot nine or so," Ben said. "He was taller than that."

"Was he six-foot? Was he taller than six-foot?"

"I would say he was at least six-foot and maybe an inch or two taller than that. He was wearing dark clothes, black or navy blue. At the time, I guess I thought he may have been an employee or a musician or something."

"Why employee?"

"Because that's how all the employees dressed, at least the men. They wore either navy blue or black sport coats or jackets and dark pants."

"He looked like an employee? You also mentioned musician. Why did he look like a musician?"

"Partly because of the cart, but also we stuck our heads into a party that was going on down the hall and there was a band playing. The musicians were wearing similar looking dark jackets and pants. I also remember seeing some big carts like that that I assumed were for the musicians and their instruments. I don't remember seeing any room service waiters, but I wouldn't be surprised if they wore something similar as well."

"Okay," Lonergan said, "we'll check on that. What about his face? What did he look like? What color hair did he have?"

"I remember him being dark – dark suit, probably dark hair, maybe a beard. His hair was short, maybe a buzz cut or something close to that. But it was dark. His beard was dark too. Yes, he definitely had a beard. A goatee or full beard, I can't number which, but some sort of beard."

"How old was he?"

"I don't know exactly, but I would say he wasn't really young. He wasn't a teenager or someone in his twenties. He was probably at least forty. I only glanced at his face. I don't remember him being a young guy at all."

"Did he say anything?"

"No, nothing."

They went back and forth like that for little while longer, and Ben unable to flesh out any more details on the man with the cart. Then a knock came at the door and Lonergan stood and opened it to find one of his techs on the other side. "We're done setting everything up. If you want to come out to that room with the heads, I can explain how everything works."

"Good idea," Lonergan said. "Let's go out to the conference room."

44

Ben led the others back out to the garage. He welcomed the break. The technician led them through the process of recording the call, which was little more than pressing one button to start the recording and a second to stop it. The recordings were digital and would be stored in the small device itself, as well as off-site on an FBI computer somewhere. A second tech joined them a few minutes later and revealed that the sweep of the firm's offices revealed no listening devices of any kind.

Within minutes, the techs were gone and Ben was left in the garage with just Lonergan and Nelson. "I feel kind of stupid for not having remembered some of this stuff earlier," Ben said.

"No need," Lonergan said with a wave of his hand. "None of us were focused on that until now. We didn't know Moran was dead." Lonergan took out a pad and wrote the date the top and underlined it as though to move the conversation into a new area. "There is something else I was hoping to discuss with you. In light of the fact that the voice, the killer, has contacted you, and operating under the assumption that he's the real thing, we have something we would like to propose." He paused. "We would like you to establish some sort of dialogue with him."

Ben was somewhat taken aback. "Dialogue? What do you mean by that?"

"We're operating under the assumption that the person who called you is in fact the killer, and that he will likely talk to you again. Just to help ensure that this takes place, we would like you to utilize your television appearances to engage in a dialogue with him."

Ben was stunned. He looked at Nelson, who also looked surprised. "What are you proposing I do?"

Lonergan paused again. "For lack of a better word, we would like you to … provoke him a little."

"Provoke him? You want me to provoke someone who has already killed as many as five lawyers? What are you, nuts?" He looked back at Nelson, who was shaking his head.

Lonergan proceeded to outline his plan. Ben would use his television appearances to increasingly question the capability of the suspect to escape capture. Ben was to start out with a few innocuous comments to see whether they triggered a response, then move to ever-increasingly inflammatory language in order to help ensure a response. Ben was dumbfounded. "This guy has killed five people already."

Lonergan remained calm. "We're very much aware of that and we will take every step possible to protect you and your family from any possible repercussions."

"Repercussions? That's some word for it. You're asking me to put a target on my back. I've got a wife and two small children. Why would I do such a thing? Why would anyone do such a thing? It's nuts."

Lonergan was shaking his head even before Ben finished speaking. "No, it's nothing like that. We would never ask you to put a target on your back."

Nelson decided to speak up for the first time. "With all due respect, Agent Lonergan, that's kind of what it sounds like to me."

"Rest assured," Lonergan said, "that is not our intention at all."

"Then what is your intention?" Ben said.

Lonergan sought to calm things down a bit. "It's like I said before, it seems as though the voice, whoever it is, is willing to engage in a dialogue with you. From what we know, he hasn't contacted anyone else, just you. Obviously, the more information we can get from him or about him, the better chance we have of finding out who he is and catching him, hopefully before anyone else dies."

"I can understand all that, but what specifically do you want me to do?" Ben said. "Do you want me to acknowledge on national television that he called me?"

Lonergan made a face. "No, nothing like that, not yet anyway. We were just hoping that you could find a way to open up more of a dialogue with him. Perhaps you could say something that would encourage him to contact you again so you can talk further."

"Like what?"

Lonergan fumbled looking for the right words. He was looking all around hoping to find the right phrase floating somewhere in midair, his arms gesturing in a searching motion. Finally, he said, "maybe you could say something like, 'if I were talking to the killer, then I would tell him this or that.' You know, something like that."

Ben leaned back in his chair and sighed. He glanced over at Nelson, who shrugged. "Well, that was sure a lot of help," Ben said after a moment.

"Do you have anything scheduled for the rest of the week?" Lonergan said.

"Probably tomorrow and maybe Thursday."

"Okay then, see how you feel about it during the next broadcast or two. At least give me that."

Ben shook his head and frowned. "The best I'll give you is that I'll think about it. I'll be on probably tomorrow, that's Wednesday, and maybe Thursday. I'm not going to be on Friday or at any time through the Fourth, unless something catastrophic happens, which will probably be my wife hitting me over the head. I guess that means that I'm probably not going to do anything along these lines until at least the middle of next week, assuming I'm back on the air sometime after the holiday."

"Do I take that to mean that you have plans for the Fourth of July?"

"Yes, we always go to visit relatives in Michigan. I'm not telling you where. We'll be gone from late Friday or early

269

Saturday until at least late in the evening of the Fourth, maybe even the fifth."

"Okay, that's fine. Good," Lonergan said. "We can work with that. All I ask is that you think about it. As for the recordings, if he calls, you know what to do to record the phone calls. Obviously, if he calls, get in touch with me right away as soon as you hang up. You have my numbers. Call me anytime." Lonergan paused. "There's one other thing you should know."

"What's that?"

"There's going to be a reward offered."

Ben and Nelson both groaned. Lonergan held up his hand. "I know what you mean. It wasn't my idea."

"How much?" Nelson said.

"I think 50k, for starters."

"That'll bring out all the phonies looking for a quick score," Nelson said.

"He's right," Ben said.

"I know," Lonergan said. "Like I said, not my idea. The folks in charge think it's worth the hassle. Time will tell."

Within five minutes, Lonergan was gone. Nelson stayed behind. "What did you make of that? As if I couldn't tell already?" Ben said.

Nelson was standing at the door leading to the parking lot having just watched Lonergan leave. He turned and faced Ben. Nelson looked at him for a long moment his hands on his hips. Then he scratched his head and frowned. "At first, I thought he was out of his mind, just like you did. He did manage to temper that notion a bit. I really don't think he wants you to do anything that's going to make you and your family a target. If that blew up in his face, his career would be over. What he's really hoping is that you manage to get some back and forth going with this guy so he can get some information that will lead to an arrest, or at least push the investigation in a positive direction. I don't think they're making any real progress at the moment. I know we're not, and he's looking at what he could do to move this thing forward. An investigation like this is a bit like a shark, it has to constantly be moving forward. Once it stalls, it's dead in the water. No one wants that. Right now, there isn't much progress. The only new thing we've got is that Moran's body showed up. It's never a good thing that new evidence only arises when another dead body shows up."

"Then I guess I have something to think about," Ben said. Nelson nodded.

*****

The office was relatively quiet for the rest of the week in advance of the holiday, which was good because Ben didn't get much of anything accomplished the entire time. Fortunately, Phil was out of the office and a couple of the lawyers and staff members were also away on vacation. Every time the phone rang, Ben practically jumped out of his skin. He was particularly nervous after his lone television appearance Wednesday evening. Reluctantly, he even hung around the office by himself for almost an hour afterward to give the voice a chance to call back. It didn't.

The broadcast itself did not elicit the same fireworks as other episodes, but Moran's murder was still all everybody was talking about on television and off. The wild speculations that ran rampant immediately following the discovery of Moran's body had been transformed into more of an unspecified tension among the hosts and guests alike. Since many of those involved were lawyers themselves, they either empathized with the victims or were starting to get concerned about becoming a potential victim themselves.

Ben did not say anything particularly provocative on the telecast and did not focus any specific statements at the man behind the voice. He decided to take a few days to think about the whole affair before he did anything or made any decisions. He figured that the long weekend in Michigan would give him ample opportunity to weigh the pros and cons prior to coming to any sort of conclusion. He did not discuss the situation with his wife, nor did he hear from either Lonergan or Nelson for the rest of the week. On Thursday afternoon, he phoned Stan Feldman in Los Angeles and discussed the matter with him. He did so

271

while working out in the garage so no one in the office could overhear him and be the wiser.

"I don't know, Ben," Feldman said. "You more than anybody knows what happens and what it's like to be in the crosshairs. I wouldn't think you'd want to go too far in that direction."

"I hear you. I'm certainly not planning to turn this into the Gunfight at the OK Corral, if that's what anyone thinks. I got the impression from talking to him the last time that he likes watching shows about himself and he has been watching shows that I've been on."

"And you're sure he's the real thing?"

"Seems to be," Ben said. "The investigators seem to think so too. It certainly seems like a lot of trouble to go to if you're not really the guy."

"That's true. I'm just not sure what information he would give you that would tend to implicate himself or anyone else. I would think he would more likely provide you with information or evidence that would point in someone else's direction, rather than his own."

"I thought of that too, but I'm not sure I can get around it."

Ben felt better after talking with Stan Feldman, despite the fact that they hadn't really accomplished anything. It felt good to talk about it with someone who shared his perspective. He thought about his old friend and former colleague, Mark Schaefer, with whom he had worked so closely on the Law School Murder case. He hadn't talked to Mark in a while and Mark would probably be a good sounding board over stuff like this.

Ben tried Mark's cell phone and got his voicemail. He wasn't sure that Mark ever checked his voicemail so he didn't bother leaving a message. Mark would see that he had called and would likely call him back within the next day or two.

Mark called Ben back right before Ben was getting ready to go home. The secretaries had already gone and there was no chance of being overheard. "What's up buddy? I see you called." Mark said.

"Same old shit, different day."

After a bit of small talk, the conversation turned to the hapless Chicago baseball teams, with Mark opining that despite many promises, the prospects of the Cubs looked hopeless at best. While he didn't quite agree, it was hard for Ben to argue with much conviction. Sure, anyone can have a bad century, but at some point, you have to recognize the reality of the situation. After baseball, the topic turned to golf and the recent U.S. Open, which featured Tiger Woods fading in the final round, something that disappointed neither of the two lawyers. "My view is, if he was going to break Nicklaus' record, he would've done it already," Mark said with some degree of certainty. Mark was known for such pronouncements. He wasn't prone to waffling or equivocating.

"I'm not so sure. He's still awfully good."

Eventually, Mark got them back on track when he said, "been catching you on the tube quite a lot lately. That Moran thing is quite a kick in the head." Mark was unaware that Ben had been likely the last person to see Moran live. They hadn't spoken in more than two weeks. Ben gave him the crib notes version. "Holy shit!" Mark said. "I wish you'd told me about that sooner. I had no idea. What'd the cops think? Have you heard anything?"

Like Ben, Mark practiced criminal defense law. Unlike Ben, he did so almost exclusively and was a ready encyclopedia of knowledge about the Supreme Court, famous cases and the rules of evidence. A history major in college, Mark spent much of his free time doing something few lawyers do – reading up on the law. He never ceased to amaze Ben with some new tidbit of information or insight that he had never considered. During the Law School Murder case, they'd proven to be a good team in that respect. They got along well and enjoyed bouncing ideas off of each other. While Ben could be more flashy in the courtroom, Mark typically employed an "aw shucks" demeanor that juries and judges alike seemed to respond to.

Ben filled Mark in on the events of the last week or so, beginning with the dinner at the Hilton downtown, through his conversation with Moran, and culminating with the phone call from the voice and his conversations with Nelson and Lonergan. "Sounds like you got a lot on your plate right now," Mark said. "I don't envy you."

"What do you think I should do?" Ben said.

Mark laughed his familiar big laugh. "I have no fucking idea. Having given you that remarkable degree of insight, I would suggest that you take everything this man tells you with a grain of salt. You don't know him. I would sooner trust Nelson, if I were you. From our experiences last time, he seems to be a good guy and a straight shooter, plus you had a relationship with him in the past. I would consider what he says very seriously. As for the fed, you know how I feel about these things. I'm very jaded when it comes to prosecutors and cops. They have a very narrow view of things. Mostly it starts with their best interests and ends with their best interests. I would think about what you want to do for yourself and your family, not what they think you should do. Don't let him convince you of anything. Remember, you don't owe them a thing. You owe your family everything."

"I can't disagree with any of that. The problem is, this case has gotten under my skin. I haven't been able to think of much of anything else for weeks now."

"I can understand what you're saying," Mark said. "You're more of an outside the box thinker than I am. You're better at solving puzzles, working through the clues, that sort of thing. I'm more of a straight ahead guy, a linear thinker. I see what's in front of me and then I take it from there. I'm not an outside-the-box kind of guy, unfortunately. But you'd better be careful."

"I know that. Don't give me the country bumpkin routine though. I have known you too long for that."

"I just don't get the whole Ray Fisher thing," Mark said after a time.

"I don't know much about him, to tell you the truth," Ben said. "All I can tell you is Moran was really afraid of him. Sure he comes off as something of a crackpot, but who can blame him?"

"No doubt about that. Are there stalking laws in California? Do you know? You can't just follow people around and show up places. Especially in California, with all those celebrities, you'd think they'd have some sort of protection."

"Maybe it's the other way around. Because of all the celebrities in California, being followed around is more or less accepted. They've got the paparazzi and everything out there. Personally, I think DiCaprio ought to be able to go out to dinner with someone without being hounded by reporters and photographers. I think Jennifer Aniston ought to be able to go to the grocery store, or go jogging on the beach, whatever."

"I agree with you. She certainly should be able to jog on the beach," Mark said with a laugh. "If you notice, most of the trouble with the paparazzi happens when they do something stupid and go over the line and either harass or endanger the celebrities. I don't have any sympathy for that. I remember I saw video of Brittany Spears leaving the courthouse in LA a few years ago when she was in court for doing some dumb thing or another. Well, these morons surrounded her car when she was trying to drive away and she accidently ran over some guy's foot and they tried to say it was her fault. She's driving a car for crying out loud. Get out of the fucking way."

"I agree completely. I wonder with regard to Ray Fisher, whether he always skirted the line but was careful never to cross it."

"Could be," Mark said. "He seems smart enough to know how to do that."

"Besides, what's in it for Jimmy Moran if he complained? How would that look if the world-famous lawyer in the trial of the century came out and said he was afraid of the father of one of his clients' alleged victims? That wouldn't look very good, now would it?"

"No, it wouldn't. What sort of shit would he do?"

"He would show up places where Moran was speaking, or in courtrooms when Moran had a case up, stuff like that. Moran didn't say anything about Fisher going over to his house or office or anything like that."

"I suppose he could have gotten an order of protection."

"They aren't worth the paper they're printed on, you know that," Ben said.

"Yeah, that's true. But why focus on Moran or Kessler? I can see Fisher being mad at Moran and wanting to off Owens. That I can understand. But why would he take it out on Moran and other lawyers rather than go after Owens himself? You would think that ultimately, Owens would be the target, not the lawyers. After all, he thinks that Owens killed his son, not his lawyers."

Ben thought about that for a second. "True enough. Obviously, I've never met Ray Fisher. I've only seen him on television. He was at the hotel that night according to Moran, but I never saw him. From TV, he looks like a guy that could do something crazy though, don't you think?"

"He does give off that vibe, no doubt about that. Of course, I've noticed over the years that the media tries playing him up as being a little nuts. That seems to be their spin on things. Like the guy is supposed to just forget that his son was murdered or something."

"I don't think we need to worry about that," Ben said. "I don't think Ray Fisher is ever going to forget about that, or forgive either."

45

Phil did his usual last day before the holiday thing. Nancy started calling him about eleven asking when the office would be closed for the weekend. Of course, Phil himself didn't come in. He was probably out golfing somewhere. By Noon or so, he called back to tell everyone to leave at three. Same thing happened almost every holiday. He probably knew that everyone was going to leave by three anyway whether he said so or not.

Ben didn't wait for three; he'd already left half an hour earlier. Libby was surprised to see Ben turn into the driveway as early as he did. She'd been out watering her plants with their daughter, Natalie. Natalie was especially excited to see her father. She rushed down the driveway barefoot, all wet and muddy, and gave her daddy a big hug.

Once Ben had arrived home, the kids started hounding their parents about leaving for the beach. Libby's Aunt's place was right on Lake Michigan and had its own beach. The kids loved the place. The adults did too. While they had knocked around the idea of leaving on Friday evening, Ben and Libby had known all along that it was probably not in the cards. They just wouldn't be ready to go in time and the Friday traffic from the Chicago area through Indiana into Michigan was awful, especially on holiday weekends like this. Still, they used the possibility of leaving early as motivation to get the kids to finish up their chores and get their stuff together for the trip. Having convinced the kids that three hours in the car Friday night wouldn't be the

277

most fun, everyone agreed that they would try their best to be out of the house and on the road by nine the following morning.

Ben went upstairs after dinner to surf the web for a while and catch up on anything he may have missed during the previous few days. At least that's what he told Libby. He really went upstairs to think about the voice some more, along with Jimmy Moran, Ray Fisher, Marty Kessler and the rest. He came down about an hour later hoping to watch some mindless television. He found Libby and Natalie in the family room watching an episode of *Say Yes to the Dress*, an insipid show about spoiled brats picking out their wedding dresses on television from a chic Atlanta bridal shop. Natalie in particular loved the show. Ben stood in the doorway and groaned loudly. "Silence, out there!" Libby said. "She's just about to pick the dress she wants." Libby and Natalie then made predictions about which dress she would choose.

Ben groaned again and looked over his shoulder at his son, who was playing a video game on a handheld console. His son looked up, opened his mouth and put his finger inside in a gagging motion. Ben nodded. "You know what I'm going to do?" he said loudly enough to be heard in the family room, "I may get some guys in the office and we're gonna start our own show. We're gonna call it, *Say No to the Ho*." His son laughed and gave him a thumbs-up.

"Shush," Libby said, "it's almost over. Keep your pants on." Ben groaned again. "Besides, Mr. Smart Guy, they already have that show. It's called, *The Bachelor*." Ben smiled. She was probably right, although he still thought he could make money with his own show. Maybe get Howard Stern to host. He spent the next several minutes thinking about variations on the theme while waiting for the bridal show to end.

Try as they might, they were not on the road by nine o'clock as they had hoped. A flurry of last-minute activity, including the obligatory picking up and bed-making that Libby insisted upon before they left for anyplace, delayed their departure by more than an hour. They didn't exactly dodge the holiday traffic either. A trip that took them about seventy-five minutes in good traffic took almost two hours and they arrived in Michigan at one-fifteen local time, just in time for lunch. Libby's Aunt always had plenty of food around and had undoubtedly spent the previous week or two preparing her menus for the holiday.

The estate was located a few miles past the Indiana border. It was owned by Libby's Aunt Mary, and her husband, Albert Sandford. There were two houses on the property – the "big house" and the coach house. It was the kind of setting you might find in an issue of *Architectural Digest*. All in all, it was a magnificent setting and one which never ceased to brighten Ben's mood and refresh his batteries. He rarely brought any work along with him on the trips, and even if he did, managed to figure out a way not to get around to doing any of it.

The entire property was surrounded by an iron fence partially hidden by extensive landscaping. Although Ben knew the code to the gate, it was unnecessary because the gate was open when they arrived. In and amongst the flowers and shrubbery outside the main entrance to the property, Mary Sandford had planted hundreds of small American flags for the holiday. Ben drove slowly through the gate and down the gravel drive which led around the side and to the back of the coach house. They found a minivan parked outside the garage in back. Libby's sister and her family had already arrived. Ben unpacked the car while Libby and the kids ran over to the big house to say hello to the Sandfords.

Later, as he strolled down the stone walk that separated the two houses, Ben took a deep breath and checked out the property. It was a beautiful day, with clear blue skies and temperatures in the low-eighties. He walked around the back of the big house and looked out toward the lake. The back yard of the estate was beautifully landscaped with mature trees and beds of flowers in full bloom. Ben wandered over to the edge of the yard, where a bench sat on the edge of a bluff with sailboats, speedboats and jet skis dotting the water in the distance.

He sat there for a while just enjoying the sights until he heard a commotion coming from the big house back behind him. He turned and looked over his shoulder to see the kids running back toward the coach house with their mother trailing behind them. No doubt getting their suits on to go down to the beach. Soon, he heard the kids bound out of the coach house and he rose and met them in the middle of the back yard. Libby once again was following behind, having changed into her swimsuit and wrap and carrying a tote bag. "They were eager to get down to the beach. It's a beautiful day. You should get your suit on and come down," she said as she hurried off to join the children at the tram that led down to the beach.

"I'll think about it," Ben said as he watched them go.

Ben caught up with Albert and Mary Sandford in the kitchen of the big house, Mary skittering around preparing one thing or another for dinner the following day. Albert watched her work, occasionally stealing nibbles of this or that while trying not to get yelled at for doing so. It was a little game they played. Albert and Ben shook hands. "Good to see you," Albert said.

"Likewise. How's it going?"

"Great, just trying to get everything squared away for the weekend."

The three of them chatted for a while, which meant that Mary did most of the talking and Ben and Albert did most of the listening. Eventually, Ben and Albert adjourned to the family room, where they talked for a long time about this and that, but nothing too serious. Albert had a gift for knowing when to push and when not to. Having lived with Mary for so long, he was an incredibly good listener and could literally talk about anything. Finally, Ben looked at Albert and said, "duty calls. I think I better at least wander down to the beach to see what everyone's up to down there."

"Sounds good," Albert said.

Ben took a dip in the hot tub after dinner. On a clear afternoon, you could sit in the hot tub and look out across the yard, through the trees and past the bluff to see the lake and the skyscrapers of downtown Chicago on the distant horizon. You couldn't see the buildings from the beach due to the distance and the curvature of the earth, but they were framed perfectly between the trees from the hot tub. Tonight, Ben made it in just before sunset, a spectacular combination of reds, oranges and yellows melting into purples and blues before finally going grey and then black. He sat back and let the combination of jets and 104° water soothe his muscles and relax his mind. He stayed in for a long time, during which various combinations of children and adults came and went, some sitting on the side, like Libby, and others venturing into the tub itself, like Albert.

After the sun had gone down in such spectacular fashion, the kids all adjourned to change and watch a movie. A couple of the adults went along for the ride, while Ben and Albert stayed and relaxed in the hot waters. Now that they were alone, Albert felt comfortable in broaching the subject. "We've been watching you a lot on TV lately," he said.

Ben laughed. "You have to have better things to watch than that," he said. "After a while, it all gets a bit monotonous, even for me."

"But you're the only person I know who's on television," Albert said.

"At the moment, but there are probably members of the family somewhere who could still shoot up a liquor store and wind up on *America's Most Wanted*," Ben said.

"Until then, you're it." Albert paused before continuing. "Mary doesn't say much, but I think she's a little worried, you know, with all the lawyers getting killed. You're the one lawyer in the family so she frets about it."

Ben leaned all the way back and raised his legs so his toes were sticking out of the water. He looked at them for a moment before answering. "No one's gonna get me out here. I can always hang out here until they catch the guy."

"Sounds like a plan."

"Seriously, I think Libby feels the same way, although she doesn't really talk about it either."

They sat in silence for a while, soaking up the warmth of the waters. Ben took a deep breath, held it, then let it out long and slow. He tilted his head back and closed his eyes. The breeze off the shore. The faint sound of the waves through the trees. It was hard for Ben to imagine a more peaceful and relaxing moment. He savored it for a while, then dropped his head back down and opened his eyes. Albert was looking at him thoughtfully, a kindness and gentleness in his eyes and manner that was always there and never ceased to make Ben feel comfortable and welcome. "Don't you ever wonder," Albert said in a quiet voice, "what's at the heart of it?"

Ben nodded slowly. "Every day," he said in a voice that was barely above a whisper. "It can really only be a few things. Revenge, I suppose, for one thing or another. Whether directed at an individual, or lawyers as a group, we may never know. Or maybe he's using all the murders just to cover up one or two specific victims. I thought of that too. The answer to that question seems to me the key to figuring out who it is and perhaps catching him. Short of some glaring error, which he hasn't made yet, that would have to be it."

Albert gave a weak smile and spread his hands. "Or maybe he's crazy. Some people just are."

"That too."

46

Ben slept late on Sunday morning. When he finally awoke, it was almost ten o'clock Michigan time. A few minutes later, having changed into a swimsuit, T-shirt and a pair of sandals, he wandered downstairs still feeling somewhat bleary-eyed. A group of kids were watching a movie in the family room and he rounded the corner into the kitchen to find Libby making breakfast. Albert was sitting in a chair drinking a cup of coffee as he watched her finish up the eggs, sausages and pancakes that would serve as breakfast for the group. "Good morning," Albert said as Ben entered the kitchen. "Sleep okay?"

Ben groaned. Never much of a morning person, Ben found early-morning displays of good cheer to be a chore at best. Not that this was early-morning exactly, which Libby rightly reminded him upon hearing his response. "It's early somewhere," he said under his breath.

Ben took a glass from the cupboard and poured himself some orange juice. He joined Albert in watching Libby cook. After a few minutes, slowly warming to the occasion, he said, "Mary up yet?"

Albert smiled. "Still asleep." Mary Sandford was even less of a morning person than Ben and couldn't reliably be counted on to make an appearance much before lunchtime.

"Looks like a nice beach day," Albert said. Ben glanced out the window to see another sunny day.

After breakfast, he opened up his laptop and checked his email. Finding nothing of significance, he surfed the web for a while trying to catch up on the latest news and sports. Often, a few days at the beach made him lose touch with what was going on in the world. Normally, this wasn't a bad thing and he enjoyed the idea of being more or less completely out of touch and unconcerned with current events. Now, however, was not one of those times.

After a while, he closed his computer and headed back upstairs to check for messages on his cell phone. Somewhat surprised, he found none. Feeling somewhat relieved, he left the phone on the charger, went back downstairs, grabbed some sunglasses and headed outside. He started toward the big house, then veered off across the yard toward the bench at the end of the bluff. He sat there for a while, closed his eyes and let his mind drift away. Slowly, it came back to Jimmy Moran, Marty Kessler, Spencer Laughlin and the others. Although the trip to the beach had begun to rejuvenate him, it wasn't having completely the desired effect. The sound of the computer-generated voice drifted back into his head.

Having decided that he needed a diversion, he rose and strolled over to the tram to make his obligatory trip to the beach. Once consisting of plastic lawn chairs attached to a wooden base and carried up and back via a cable and winch system, the tram was now significantly upgraded to include elaborate wooden bench seats and an accompanying storage compartment for transporting food and other items. Where once the rickety tram made everyone a little nervous, now it was safe and secure and people didn't give it a second thought, particularly since a set of stairs now ran next to the tram all the way down to the bottom. If there was any problem with the tram, all they needed to do was stop and step over the gate to the steps.

There were ninety steps or so from the top of the tram to the bottom, at which there was a small platform for loading and unloading and a hose and shower for washing the sand off before you headed back up to the house. About fifteen more steps led to a large shed for storing beach gear, such as chairs, inflatables and even a kayak. A deck stretched out behind the shed that overlooked the beach. The deck was surrounded on the beach side by a bench and a pair of oversized covered beach chairs faced out toward the lake. A chiminea stood in the corner for the occasional campfire. During the heat of the day, the deck was largely in shade due to the trees and related foliage on the seventy-five foot bluff rising directly behind it. Benjamin always found the deck to be a particularly peaceful spot and he stopped there often to read a book or just relax for awhile when he wasn't in the mood to go all the way down to the beach itself.

Today, however, Ben decided to bite the bullet and take the final ten wooden steps down to the sand. He picked his way along a narrow path through the dune grass, ultimately emerging at the top of a small sandy slope which looked down on the rest of the beach to the water's edge. Libby and the others had set up some beach chairs and a couple of umbrellas. Libby had gotten up just as Ben had started to come down the slope and he watched her head down to the water to begin her habit of looking along the shoreline for shells and small fossilized rocks called crinoids. Further up the beach, Ben noticed Libby's sister and her husband doing much the same thing, a hobby which had never interested Ben in the least. Ben took Libby's seat and adjusted the umbrella to provide the maximum shade and he watched her at work. Out in the water, the kids frolicked in the waves.

Ben closed his eyes and tried to drift off without much success. He paid sporadic attention to the kids flopping around on a blue raft. They were wearing life jackets and they weren't out too far, so Ben wasn't terribly concerned with his own lack of diligence. He thought about the lake and the Cal-Sag Channel and the usefulness of a large body of water for dumping a body. He considered Moran and his death. From what he had learned, the killing had been particularly brutal, with the killer cutting Moran's throat and virtually severing his head from his body. There was no evidence that the killing had taken place in Moran's hotel room in Chicago and Ben wondered how the killer managed to subdue Moran and transport him from the hotel without anyone being the wiser. He thought about the large trunk or musician's case, whatever it was that he had seen coming off the elevator that night. Could that have really been the killer?

Ben racked his brain trying to come up with additional details of that brief encounter at the elevator. He was so focused on the case, unfortunately, that he simply could not remember much about the man who was pushing it. Tall and dark clothing, Ben thought. Just like you told Nelson and Lonergan. He was closing his eyes trying hard to remember when Libby came back.

She stopped off at a small cooler and took a fresh Coke Zero from the icy water inside. He had watched her bend over the cooler and had been admiring her cleavage. She stood, the dripping can in her hand. "Did you want anything?" she said. She leaned over to get something out of the cooler for him. He admired her again.

"No, I'm good."

She stood up and grabbed another chair before he stopped her. "You know, on second thought, I guess I would like something to drink."

She bent over the cooler again. She stood when he didn't say what he wanted right away. "Well,"

"What have you got in there?"

She bent over the cooler again. He continued watching her. She fished around inside and Ben could hear the rattling of cans and bottles. "There's Coke, water, and lemonade. And, of course, Tab, but I don't think you want that." She stood bent over and looked at him. He made a show of pausing while trying to decide. Then she caught on. She looked down at herself, then stood and faced him. "Are you just yanking my chain?"

Ben laughed. "I don't know what you mean."

She had both hands on her hips now. "Like hell you don't."

"I'll have a bottle of water," he said.

"You sure? Or do you want me to look around some more?"

He put his hand on his chin and looked skyward. "Hmmm," he said, "no, I think the water is fine."

286

She bent over and pulled the water from the cooler and tossed the bottle at him, cold water splashing him as he caught it. "Hey," he said, "that's cold."

"Better than you deserve," she said as she sat down in the beach chair next to his.

He laughed again. "What's a guy supposed to do? His wife bends over, he's not supposed to look? If I look, I'm in trouble. If I don't look, I'm in more trouble."

"Uh huh. You'll pay for that."

Ben stayed down at the beach for a little while, even getting up at one point and going in as far as his knees. Occasionally, he went all the way in and wandered out and splashed around a bit with the kids. Not today though. The water was cold, but after a few minutes, he got used to it and it cooled him off considerably. Still, Ben wasn't much of a water person outside of the shower and the hot tub. Going in up to his knees was plenty good enough.

Ben went back upstairs a little while later, heading back to the coach house to take a nap. The coach house was empty and Ben went upstairs and laid down on the king-sized bed in his room, kicking his sandals to the floor. He almost immediately drifted off into a restless sleep, never feeling completely asleep nor completely awake either. After a time, he fell into a series of apparently unrelated dreams, unidentifiable images and fragments of events and conversations. The final one, which ultimately jarred him awake, involved him running through dark woods at night, unclear whether he was chasing someone or being chased. He awoke feeling groggy and unsettled, exactly the opposite of what he had hoped for when he came up from the beach. He glanced over at the clock – he'd been out for almost two hours. It seemed like minutes. After a quick trip to the bathroom, he pulled on his sandals and dragged himself back downstairs. He had intended to go over to the big house to see what was going on, but outside ran into a small contingent heading in his direction. Led by Mary Sandford, the group included Libby, her sister and a couple of the kids. "What's up?" Ben said when they reached him halfway between the two houses.

"We're heading over next door," Mary said.

"To the coach house?" Ben said.

"No," Libby said, "Aunt Mary is taking us next door to look at the Finney property. Apparently they are never out here and we've never had a chance to look at it before."

Ben thought about it for a second and decided to tag along. Mary led the group past the back of the coach house to a gate and pressed the button on a keypad at the end of the gravel drive. The gate slowly slid open. The south end of the Sandford property was bordered by a private road. The road dead-ended right outside this gate. A car reaching the end of the private road would be faced with three distinct properties. The Sandfords' was through the gate to the right. The Finney property was straight ahead. A third property curved off down to the left and was not visible from the road. Ben had always been somewhat intrigued by this third property, although Mary Sandford had told him on a previous occasion that it didn't amount to much. She said that the parcel itself was nice, but the house on it was a modern glass job that she didn't care for. Owned by an elderly couple, she wasn't sure if that property would be inherited or put on the market after the couple passed away.

They walked through the gate and around the corner and onto the Finney property. While considerably smaller than the Sandfords', it was still more than an acre in size. The main house was an old frame number, painted white with black shutters, and was situated near the back of the lot, relatively close to the bluff. It needed a fresh coat of paint and some sprucing up. Off to the right near the front of the lot were two structures. The first was a modest garage. The second was a large, two-story rectangular structure made largely out of glass. This was originally built as an art studio for the previous owner, Mary informed them.

According to Mary Sandford, the Finney's overpaid for the property several years earlier and had been trying to unload it almost ever since. A successful commodities trader with family on the East Coast, Brian Finney didn't want to accept any less than what he had paid for it. A trader never wants to lose a trade, after all, and the property largely sat vacant once he had decided

288

to buy a grander place on Nantucket Island that was closer to his relatives. "Occasionally, you'll see somebody out here," Mary said. "The Finneys probably come out for a couple of weeks over the summer and you may see friends of theirs out here using the place every once in a while, but for the most part, it just sits here empty. Originally, Finney planned to knock all the buildings down and put up a big new house, but I don't think he's going to do that now since he's trying to unload the place. Once the market tanked though, he won't ever get back what he paid for it."

Ben followed the others around saying little and mostly listening to their conversation about the property, which largely consisted of a running dialogue by Mary Sandford. Soon, the group wandered back over to the Sandfords' place. On his way out, Ben paused and looked back at the house sitting at the bluff and overlooking the lake. He thought it was quite a nice parcel indeed.

The fireworks were held on Monday evening, the 3rd of July. The Sandfords belonged to a country club just up the road. Every year, one of the members sponsored the annual fireworks display. The club also hosted a barbecue for its members and guests. Since Albert Sandford did not play golf, the best way for the Sandfords to use up their spending allotment at the club was to buy tickets for the Fourth of July barbecue. The barbecue consisted of a wide assortment of food items, from crab leg appetizers to barbecued ribs to a sundae bar, not to mention games and balloons for the kids.

Tables and chairs were set up under two large tents and everyone ate and drank to their heart's content, from dinnertime until dusk, when the fireworks were held two holes over on the golf course. People assembled on lawn chairs along an adjoining fairway until it got dark enough for the display. Meanwhile, kids would be running up and down the fairway, throwing footballs and frisbees, and waving glow sticks connected like rings to form little neon hula hoops.

The fireworks display itself was spectacular as usual. Accompanied by patriotic music, the display was as good or better than any Ben had ever seen, the rockets rising over the trees and exploding directly overhead. Somewhere between John Philip Sousa and Ray Charles singing his version of *America the Beautiful*, Ben finally decided that he was in. He had made up his mind to do whatever he could to help the authorities catch the killer of his fellow lawyers. Whether he did it exactly the way the FBI wanted him to was another question, but he would do his part to see that the killer would be brought to justice. He could do nothing else.

He glanced over at Libby, her smiling face reflected in the red and blue light of a particularly large blast. He knew that he couldn't tell her everything, that it was not a decision she would likely support, but he knew he would do everything he could to protect his family while still doing the right thing and catching the man responsible for at least five deaths and maybe more already.

47

Wearing a worn captain's hat over a floppy dark wig and sunglasses to go with a T-shirt, shorts and deck shoes, Rich wandered up and down the boardwalk at the Santa Monica Pier. He looked like just another boat owner enjoying the long holiday weekend. He found the boat he was looking for near the end of a long line of similar vessels. It was a 39-foot cabin cruiser, christened *Scales of Justice*, and painted a slick red and white with gold trim.

Years before, Rich had owned a similar boat himself, which he had housed in a slip at the other end of the marina. He missed his boat, one of the things he had given up when he embarked on this mission, and it felt good to be back at the pier. Very little had changed over the years and he knew his way around quite well. He navigated the pier with the ease and nonchalance of a long-time man of the sea.

Once, more than a decade earlier, he'd actually been to a party on the *Scales of Justice*. In the years since that first party, the boat's owner, a lawyer named Nicholas Karras, had seen his profile greatly increase in the LA legal community and beyond. He had parlayed a growing legal career and his television appearances as a commentator for the Owens trial into a series of celebrity clients leading to more fame, more money and more clients. Unfortunately, his increased celebrity status had taken a toll on his marriage, and for the past year or so, he'd been living primarily on his boat. That was okay though, because he enjoyed the bachelor life at the pier. A steady stream of younger women, the occasional divorcee mixed in with women looking to land a high-profile husband, kept him quite happy. Karras liked variety. Rarely did the same woman make more than three or four trips to the boat. After a 25-year marriage, he wasn't looking to settle down anytime soon. He just wanted to have a little fun. And fun he was having. Since the details of his divorce were still playing out in the court system, he also needed to keep an eye on his money, hiding some of it from the ex-wife, while still making sure he had enough to keep up his lifestyle.

Rich had learned from previous research that Karras had planned on taking one of his new conquests out on the boat for the Fourth of July fireworks, but that he had nothing planned for this, the evening of the third. Holiday weekends brought out all the boat owners, whether the experienced ones who knew how to handle their craft out in the water, or those who merely stayed at the dock, mixing margaritas for their friends and occasionally washing the boat off with a garden hose.

The pier was crawling with people for the holiday weekend and Rich blended in perfectly. No one gave him a second glance. Rich waited for the boat next to the *Scales of Justice* to slowly back out of its slip before making his move. Now there were three open slips on either side of this target. That wouldn't last past sundown. He carried a large wicker basket and looked like someone bringing refreshments to a party. Which is exactly what he was, although not exactly the kind of party Karras would be hoping for.

Rich climbed aboard the *Scales of Justice* like an experienced sailor. Since he had learned that Karras would not be back for some time, he wandered around the deck as if he owned the place. That was part of the plan. He was acting like just another boat owner, or in this case, a close friend of another boat owner. After spending a few minutes tidying up the deck, just like a good friend would, Rich found the spare key in Karras' hiding place, unlocked the door, entered the cabin and went down below. Wearing latex gloves, he was careful not to leave any fingerprints.

292

The boat had a generous salon at the bottom of the steps and two bedrooms, one large and one small, together with a small kitchenette and the head. He remembered that Karras had spent a great deal of money fixing the boat up, he'd bought it used as most boat owners do, and had even upgraded it again since Rich had been on board years before. The appointments were relatively plush, a lot of leather and dark wood, and the bedroom even had what appeared to be a queen-sized bed. "I'll bet the chicks love that," Rich said with a laugh as he peeked inside, which looked just like the bachelor pad every wealthy lawyer on the make should have.

Rich walked back into the salon, where he had left his basket. He spent the next few minutes going through the cabin, examining, not for the first time, the details of Nick Karras' life on the water. After a while, he walked over to the base of the stairs and looked outside to find the sun starting to get low in the sky. He realized it wouldn't be long now, so he began to get ready, taking various items out of his basket in preparation for the party to come. Once he had finished, all he had to do was wait.

About ninety minutes later, Nick Karras picked up takeout Chinese from his favorite spot down the street from the pier and was soon pulling his black Mercedes S Class sedan into a parking spot at the base of the pier. He strolled down the boardwalk carrying his Chinese food. The sun was setting out to the west and he paused at a T-intersection, where the boardwalk met a row of boat slips and admired the colors of the sunset. Although many of the other boats were starting to come in and dock for the evening, Karras found that the boats on either side of the *Scales of Justice* were still out to sea. The boat on the near side, a 60-footer that Karras lusted after, probably wouldn't be back. Its owner, a retired orthopedic surgeon, frequently took the boat over to Catalina Island during the holidays.

As he climbed aboard, Karras did not sense that anything was amiss. He was looking forward to his Chinese food, and more importantly, to a rendezvous the following evening on the Fourth of July with a particularly lovely model in her late-twenties, with whom he hoped to share the fireworks, both in the sky and later down below in his cabin. He had not a care in the world. He took out his keys, unlocked the doors to the salon, slid them open and headed downstairs.

Karras was whistling the Beatles' *Good Day Sunshine* when he bounced down the stairs carrying the Chinese food. He stopped whistling at the bottom of the stairs when he saw Rich sitting on the couch opposite him, a 9 mm Beretta pointing directly at his chest. Karras stood on the bottom step and stared at the gun and the man holding it. "Who are you?" he said. "What do you want?"

Rich removed the white captain's hat and sunglasses and smiled. "Is this any better? Do you recognize me now?"

Karras studied him for a moment trying to make a connection.

"What if I did this?" Rich said as he removed the dark wig that covered his thinning buzz cut. "Of course, you may not remember the beard," he said as he rubbed his goatee.

As soon as Rich removed the wig, Karras' face shown in instant recognition. "What?"

"We'll have time to get to all that," Rich said. "Now, close the door to the salon. If you make any attempt to get away, or say a word, I'll put a hole in you." He waved the gun and Karras did as he was told. "Good, I was getting hungry waiting for you." He sniffed the air. "Smells like Szechuan. My favorite. Now, please put the Chinese food on the table." He gestured toward the table with the Beretta. Karras stared at him for a moment, the wheels turning in his head trying to decide what options he had. "Don't even think about it," Rich said. Karras hesitated, but placed the bag down on the table as instructed. Rich reached into his basket, which was now right next to him on the couch, and pulled out a taser, aimed it at Karras' chest and fired. The two electronic prongs jetted out of the end of the device and struck Karras on the right side of his chest with a crackling sound. A moment later, he dropped to his knees like a stone and rolled over on his side. He gasped in pain. "Now, remember what I said," Rich said. "No talking." He pointed the Beretta at Karras, now writhing on the floor, and leaned in closer to the man, who

294

had stopped groaning. An instant later, sufficient voltage having coursed through his body, Karras was out like a light.

Once Karras was out, Rich reached into his basket once again, pulled out a few items and got down to business. He grabbed two sets of plastic flex cuffs and bound Karras' hands behind his back and his ankles together. He took a roll of duct tape and wrapped it several times around Karras' head covering his mouth. After finding a chair on deck and bringing it down below, he sat Karras up on the chair and duct-taped him around his chest, arms and thighs, effectively fastening him to the chair and rendering him unable to move. Then, after rummaging around and finding some silverware, he proceeded to start in on Karras' Chinese food.

Halfway through his second helping of Szechuan chicken, Karras started to come around. Rich zapped him again and out he went. Rich wasn't ready to deal with him just yet. When he finished his dinner, he washed it down with a Heineken he pulled out of a small fridge. He dropped the silverware into the basket and placed the Chinese food next to it on the floor. He would be taking all of that with him and would dispose of it later.

He sat sipping the Heineken when Karras came around for the second time. Rich maneuvered the chair so it faced him on the couch. It was now full dark, but Rich still had some time. Karras came around slowly, blinking at first before becoming wild-eyed as his brain scrambled to make sense of his current circumstances. After a few seconds, his eyes locked on Rich and Rich saw the look of recognition in them.

"Ah, you're back," Rich said. "Yes, it's me. I suppose you're wondering what I'm doing here, literally. Well, we'll get to that eventually, but the answer your next question is yes, I do plan to kill you. Just like I killed the others. So, one way or another, I will make you even more famous than you already are. That should make you happy. After all, being rich and famous has been your goal for a long time, hasn't it?" Karras tried to talk under the duct tape. Rich waved him off. "Don't bother trying to talk. I already know the answer. You should also know that although you will be the next lawyer in line, you won't necessarily be the last one. Still, you are in some pretty good company and you should draw some solace from that."

Karras struggled with his binding as Rich walked over to the stairs and went up to the salon door. Peering out, he saw that there was still some activity out and about on the pier. They would have to wait a little while longer. He went back downstairs and slapped Karras on the back. "Don't bother struggling. There's no point. I have you wrapped up too well for that. There's no way you're going to get away." He pulled three items from the basket. The first, the ceramic butcher knife he had used on Kessler. He held it up. "This is the knife I used to dispatch one Martin Kessler. It was a bit more difficult than I anticipated, but was still ultimately satisfying." He placed the knife on the coffee table. Karras' eyes followed. Then he displayed a long coil of nylon cord. "You should recognize this," he said. "One of your more famous clients used something pretty much like this to kill his wife. Of course, you weren't able to get him off, now were you? Tough luck there. Good publicity though." He placed the cord on the coffee table next to the knife. Then he held up the Beretta. "This, of course, you've already seen." Rich stood five feet in front of Karras and looked carefully at the gun. "It's a beautiful, almost elegant piece of equipment," he said. "I haven't used it on anyone as of yet. Perhaps you could be the first. Perhaps not. I haven't really decided how I'm going to finish you off. You can rest assured, however, that you will be, as they say, swimming with the fishes pretty soon."

Karras' eyes widened and he continued to struggle to get out of the chair. Eventually, with all the force he could muster, he managed to topple the chair over on one side. Rich sat down on the couch and watched the other man struggle, getting great amusement out of Karras' attempts to free himself. After a couple of minutes, exhausted by the effort, he paused to regain his strength. With his mouth fully covered by the duct tape, he struggled to breathe through his nose and his face turned a bright cherry red.

Rich laughed and got up off the couch and squatted right in front of Karras. "You know, as much as I admire your unwillingness to give up, your efforts really are futile. All you're doing is wearing yourself out. You're still going to be breathing in carpet fuzz. You may also have a stroke or heart attack and we can't have that." He looked at the duct tape on Karras' mouth. He pointed to it and said, "now, if you promise not to scream, I'll make it so that you can breathe a bit out of your mouth. I'm not trying to torture you here. Not really." When Karras nodded, Rich grabbed the knife and carefully cut a small hole around Karras' mouth. As the other man started to gasp for breath, Rich held the taser in front of his eyes and said, "don't make me use this on you again. You make me use it too many times and you will have that heart attack."

Karras began to breathe more easily. Rich took the knife and the taser and placed them back on the coffee table and wrenched Karras and the chair back to an upright position. He turned it so it was once again facing the couch. The two men spent the next half hour or so discussing Rich's plans. Karras did most of the listening, but occasionally grunted out a question or two in a vain effort to get Rich to change his mind. Rich glanced at his watch. It was just past ten. He leaned forward, clasped both palms on his knees and said, "well, that's that. Time to go."

Karras struggled some more at his bindings. "No," he said. "Wait, what about ..." But Rich had already cut off a strip of duct tape and placed it back over Karras' mouth. As he started to head up the stairs, Rich paused and looked back at Karras, whose back was to him. "Now, remember, don't struggle too much. It's hard to breathe with that tape over your mouth."

Rich put the cap back on as he climbed the steps to the helm. Having already taken the keys to the boat out of Karras' pocket, he inserted them in the slot, turned the key and the engine roared to life. There was still a little activity on the pier, but not too much, just an occasional boat coming and going and people enjoying themselves at the dock. Rich kept the cap pulled down low as he carefully maneuvered the boat out of the slip. It had been years since he had done so, but it all came back to him in an instant. He did not find piloting the craft to be at all challenging.

That was good since the last thing he wanted was a fender-bender while trying to pull out of the dock.

Before long, he was clear of the buoys and out into open water. He went out further, another couple of miles. Then he anchored, the boat listing gently in the relatively calm seas. He looked back toward the shore and could see a few twinkling lights along the pier. Scanning 360 degrees around him from the deck of the *Scales of Justice*, Rich could see that he was alone out on the water. He could not see another craft anywhere around him. He took a deep breath and savored the sea air. He missed his boat and wondered how much his ex had gotten for it. He could see why Karras loved this lifestyle. He could see coming out here with a hot young thing and spending a couple of hours rocking the boat. No more of that for Karras. He sighed and went back downstairs.

Karras saw him and the taser in his right hand and his eyes went wide again. "I'm afraid I'm going to have to do this again," Rich said. Then he moved in closer and fired. The two jets hit Karras in the upper left chest, just above the duct tape. There was a slight crackle and he was out once again, his head slumping forward and to one side. The chair rocked with the weight of Karras' body before righting itself. Rich noticed that Karras had wet himself and shook his head. Then he took the knife and cut the other man free from the chair before pulling him up the steps to the deck. It took quite a bit of effort, for Karras, like Rich himself, was not a small man. Ultimately though, Rich get the job done and he dragged Karras across the deck to the back of the boat.

Rich retreated back to the salon and returned with the knife, the cord and the gun. He went back downstairs again and emerged carrying the basket. He placed it on the deck next to Karras' body, his hands and feet still bound by the duct tape. Rich pulled a pair of black leather gloves from the basket and put them on over the latex gloves he had been uncomfortably wearing for many hours now. He wrapped the cord around Karras' neck, pulled up a chair and waited. He looked around and saw no other craft in the vicinity that could see or hear what

298

was happening on the *Scales of Justice*. Tonight was pleasantly cool, with a hint of fog rolling in from the open waters. So much the better. Rich savored the moment. Just as Karras started to come around, Rich wrapped each end of the cord around his hands and said, "time to go, Nick. It's been great while it lasted. Say hello to Jimmy Moran, won't you?" Then he placed his foot in the center of Karras' back and pulled hard, the other man thrashing wildly. Rich strained at the exertion and Karras fought hard for a moment, before ultimately succumbing and growing still. Rich continued to pull with all his might until he knew without a shadow of a doubt that it was done. He hoisted Karras' body over the knee-high wall at the back of the boat and onto a small platform where you could mount a jet ski. Then he carefully stepped over the same wall and kicked Karras' body into the sea, the cord still wrapped around his neck.

Out of breath and perspiring heavily, Rich stood at the back of the boat and watched as Karras briefly floated along the water, before slowly sinking below the surface. Rich had made no real effort to weigh down the body, for he wanted it to reappear sooner rather than later, thereby making it crystal clear to the world that he wasn't done yet. He dumped the dishes and the remnants of the Chinese food over the side, then he returned everything else to the basket and went back downstairs and did a careful inventory. Everything that could possibly incriminate him, was carefully placed on the coffee table in the salon before he went back up to the helm to lift the anchor and navigate back to shore.

It was shortly after one o'clock when he finished maneuvering the boat back into its slip, the procedure having gone even more smoothly than it had when he had left. There was very little activity at the dock, but Rich went below and waited for almost another hour before he decided to leave. He wanted to make sure that anyone who had seen him arrive would simply assume that Karras had gone out for a cruise before returning for the night. His neighbors undoubtedly knew that he was more or less living on the boat, so it wouldn't be unusual to see the boat return and have no one leave until the morning. Rich, however, wasn't going to wait that long.

Finally satisfied that he could leave without much notice, he gathered everything in the basket and made his way up the stairs to the deck. All the lights were off and the door locked. He left the keys on the coffee table. He looked around and saw no one. Karras' end of the dock was quiet. Rich climbed out on the dock and headed for the parking lot. He walked purposefully, his head down. He saw another man off in the distance and heading in the opposite direction when he got to the steps that led to his car. Within minutes, he was gone. Another job well done.

48

Ben returned to work on Wednesday morning a bit tired, but determined to see things through. He spent most of the day considering how he could accomplish this feat, getting little actual law work done in the process. After lunch, he adjourned to the garage with a handful of files, ostensibly to catch up on his work. Shortly after two, he called Scott Nelson and told him about his decision. "Are you sure you want to do that?" Nelson said.

"Yeah, I'm sure. I've got no other choice really. It's the right thing to do."

"I suppose, but be careful. There are ways of doing it that are more careful than others. Don't be reckless."

After he hung up with Nelson, Ben called Lonergan and left a voicemail. The agent called back within minutes and was pleased to hear about his decision. Although he did not commit to a specific course of action, Ben indicated to Lonergan that he was willing to try to open up a dialogue with the killer. He said that he wasn't sure how exactly he was going to do that yet, but told the agent that he was committed to trying his best to bring the killer to justice. They signed off and Ben spent the rest of the afternoon trying to figure out how he could accomplish exactly that. In the meantime, he went through the motions of getting some of his forest preserve district work completed, with little success.

By six, essentially finding himself in the same position he was in when he had gotten to the office that morning, he decided

301

enough was enough and prepared to head home for the evening. He wouldn't be on television again until the following evening and he took some solace in the fact that he would at least have another day or so to think about it.

The extra time didn't help much and there was little opportunity in his next television appearance to insert much of anything of a provocative nature into the broadcast, something that Lonergan reminded him of when they spoke on Monday morning. "I'm trying the best I can," Ben said. "It's not as easy as it looks. I don't want to just come out and say that I have already spoken with him." Lonergan agreed with that. "It doesn't seem like this story is going to go away, so I'm sure the opportunity will come up soon enough."

"I certainly hope so," Lonergan said. "I don't think this guy's finished yet and I don't think that you think so either."

This statement was proven true just two days later when Nicholas Karras' body washed ashore on a beach near Santa Barbara and was stumbled upon by a college professor out for an early morning jog. Karras had not been declared missing since he had purportedly been on vacation through the end of the week, something Rich had discovered in his planning process. Therefore, no one was out looking for him, and given his divorce, no one had particularly missed him either. The model had tried to contact him a couple of times by phone, but finally gave up assuming that he had simply blown her off and moved onto some other fresh meat. She would do the same.

The media coverage, which had lost some of its intensity due to the holiday and the lack of new information to report, exploded. While not as famous as some of the others, Karras was well known enough to set the coverage ablaze once more. In his subsequent cable appearances, Ben grew decidedly less circumspect in his opinions, without going too far over the top. He suggested on one occasion that the killer might be on the verge of losing control and in another that it would be beneficial if the public could just understand the motives behind the slayings.

The shift in tone was not blatant, but it was noticeable if you paid attention, which Rich had been doing. Generally a fan of Lohmeier's commentary, Rich watched with interest as the other man subtly called him out. Though it would not appear obvious to others, the fact that the two of them had already communicated with each other made it obvious enough to Rich. He initially chose not to respond. He had other things on his plate and wasn't about to be drawn out of his carefully laid plans by a cable television commentator. Nevertheless, he made a particular point of trying to catch all of Lohmeier's television appearances, which had now been posted in advance on the law firm's website, something that had not been done previously.

Weeks passed, and Ben heard nothing from the voice. The silence was particularly frustrating because he was trying to do what he could to draw the voice out without drawing too much attention to it. Lonergan, undoubtedly under pressure because the investigation appeared stalled, continued to pressure Ben into going even further, something that Ben continued to resist.

Meanwhile, engrossed in the attempts to lure the voice into some sort of dialogue, Ben's work continued to suffer. He sensed the rumblings in the office and gradually withdrew from the usual interactions with friends and colleagues, skipping lunch with the guys on almost a daily basis and spending more and more time alone in the garage, where he wouldn't be easily observed by others. At home, he grew increasingly surly and nonresponsive, something that Libby was unwilling to tolerate. Her attempts to get him to engage in life with the family, often attempted with the sarcastic wit that served as the hallmark of their relationship, resulted in frequent arguments, mostly about nothing important and caused even more bad feelings.

The kids noticed too. Ben even had to force himself to put Natalie to bed, something that never happened before, and he found himself snapping at the children with alarming frequency. He came home from work late and went to bed early and his attempts to avoid interactions with family members were obvious to everyone.

Ben regretted his behavior, although he was unable to force himself to do much about it. He took to being alone as a way to minimize the confrontations with Libby and the yelling at the kids, but that was a Band-Aid fix at best. On numerous occasions, Libby had tried to get him to talk about it. During her quieter entreaties, Ben even seriously considered taking her up on it, but ultimately decided that he did not want to burden her with all the things going on inside his head.

One night in early September, still stinging from a conversation with Lonergan earlier that afternoon, Ben had gone for a long walk that took him around downtown Clarendon Hills before he eventually wound up sitting on a swing at the park behind the neighborhood school. It was late, well after ten o'clock, and the kids were already in bed. Libby would be going up herself before too long. Ben rocked slowly back and forth on the swing. The park was empty. The oppressive heat of summer had been broken and the night was cool. There would be more hot days ahead, but they would be fewer and fewer in number as fall arrived.

As he slowly swung to and fro, Ben considered the situation in which he found himself. His whole life was a disaster, his obsession and moods poisoning the atmosphere within his family. Work was even worse. Phil was no doubt already receiving telephone calls from frustrated clients wondering whether Ben was too busy appearing on television to properly handle their files. Ben had already been visited out in the garage a couple of days earlier by Casey Gardner, his close friend of more than a decade and now Phil's right-hand man in managing the office during those many occasions when Phil was out doing whatever it was that Phil did when he wasn't in the building. No doubt dispatched by his boss, Casey sought to give Ben something of a pep talk, while trying to figure out exactly what was bothering Ben, even though he undoubtedly knew already. Although the tone was unquestionably one of concern, Ben could feel the steel behind the words. He knew that this was the next step in putting him on notice that his performance had better improve.

304

Casey got up and headed toward the door and paused to say, "if you need any help, just ask." Ben simply nodded, having taken it as a warning shot across the bow. He didn't like it, but he understood. Truth be told, he was surprised it hadn't come earlier.

A couple of weeks later, Ben received a telephone call from Karen Tilley, the land acquisition manager at the forest preserve district. He trusted her and was confident that she would never do anything behind his back like go to Phil and complain about him. She didn't. She did, however, confide that she was growing frustrated with the fact that some of the district's cases seemed to be languishing. "I know it," Ben said conceding the obvious. "I'll try to get my head out of my ass and get things back on track as soon as I can."

"Can't you just get Brad Funk to help you out with some of this stuff?" Funk also worked on some of the district's files.

Ben laughed. "Do you really want to spend more time dealing with Funk?"

"Aw, come on, Brad's a good guy. He's not you, of course, but he's a good guy. He saved your life, after all."

She had him there. "That's certainly true enough. Even though you have to promise never to mention it, I agree that he's a good guy. I just so enjoy giving him a kick now and then."

"Why is that anyway?"

"No idea. Just how it works."

Ben was grateful for the fact that she never mentioned the deaths of the lawyers, although both of them knew that it was the source of the difficulties he was having in getting the district's work completed properly. They promised to get together for a drink sometime soon to catch up on things and Ben felt better when they signed off. She had managed to make her point while still doing so in a way that had made him feel at least marginally better afterward.

Ben thought about the voice and the man at the under other end of it. There had been no more bodies, at least no more famous lawyers, discovered since Nick Karras had washed ashore more than two months earlier. Not for the first time, Ben wondered why that was. Were there more bodies out there that had not been discovered? Certainly no famous ones, because he was not aware of any famous lawyers having gone missing. Everyone was on the lookout for that certainly. Why was it? Was he finished? Had he done all the killings that he planned to do? That question gnawed at him. Ben certainly did not want to see more lawyers killed, but he also knew that little progress was being made in the investigation. If the killer stopped now, he would likely get away with each of these murders. That was a sobering thought and Ben pushed it aside.

With the lack of additional information over the past couple of months, the story was simmering at somewhat less than a full boil. Obviously, this was due in part to the lack of information, but that wasn't the only reason. The truth was that the TV public was growing somewhat tired of the story. It had grown repetitive. Nothing was happening. No bodies were turning up. Occasionally, some of the coverage would point fingers at investigators for not catching the killer, but that didn't supply enough oxygen to keep the fires burning brightly.

The dirty little secret was that the cable television shows were also running out of talking heads to put on the air. More than a few of the lawyers who frequented the nightly talk shows were cutting back on their appearances, or eliminating them altogether. No one was talking about it, but Ben figured that these lawyers wanted to lower their own profiles in case they could be on the target list.

Ben thought back to the voice. Why just the one telephone call? It seemed innocuous enough now so long after the fact. What was the purpose of it in the first place? And where was the killer now? What was he up to? Ben pushed off the swing and walked slowly through the park and headed for home. Once inside, he sat in the dark and thought about it some more.

49

The next two months offered more of the same, with Ben struggling to keep his head above water and to keep Phil and his clients off of his back. The pressure of several pending deadlines brought about a surge in Ben's production in October and everyone breathed a sigh of relief. Things were even a bit better at home and the slight easing of pressures at the office brought about an improvement in Ben's mood. Halloween with the kids had also helped and as the month of November began, things seem to be looking up a bit. Still, Ben could never quite drive the killings from his mind and his regular television appearances did nothing to help. Libby and others had urged him to stay off of television for a while, but Ben found that impossible to do.

Things came crashing down on Veteran's Day, when Ben appeared on Loretta Bergen's show. It was supposed to be a short segment on updating Loretta's audience on the status of the various murder investigations. Ben was joined in the segment by Stan Feldman, with whom he had not spoken in quite a while. The segment had started innocuously enough, with Ben and Feldman alternating with updates from the various jurisdictions where the murders had occurred. Nearing the end of the segment, with less than a minute remaining it, Loretta started musing about the motives for the killings. In response to one of Ben's comments, she said, "don't you sometimes wish you could just talk to him, assuming it's a man, and find out what's going on inside his head?"

Without thinking, Ben blurted out, "I have talked to him and it didn't help."

From that moment on, all hell broke loose. Ever the good listener, Loretta went right through the commercial break and kept Ben and Feldman on for the last half an hour of the telecast. When they finally went to commercial, Ben heard Feldman's voice in his ear. "What the fuck," Feldman said. "You asked for it now."

Loretta grilled Ben about the telephone conversation from every angle. Ben's description of the telephone conversation, together with her questioning, took far longer than the conversation. When the show mercifully ended, Ben knew that he had to get home and explain this to Libby as soon as possible. They had taped the segment from the garage, and the two technicians knew that they had just been a part of a big news event. "Holy shit, man" one of them said. "They are going to be all over you like white on rice."

Ben nodded. He knew that was right. Hopefully, Libby missed the broadcast and he could get to her before she found out about it. That was not to be. Although she had not been watching, having gotten involved in homework with the kids, she nevertheless received three telephone calls before the show was even over and two more before Ben had pulled into the driveway. She was angry and scared and she unloaded on him as soon as he walked in the door. He knew that he had it coming, so he more or less stood there and took it, not knowing what else he could really do. Besides, he couldn't think of anything that would do him any good in the heat of the moment.

He tried apologizing, justifying his failure to tell her about the phone call with the notion that he was trying to protect her and didn't want her worry about it the way he had been over the last couple of months. It didn't do any good. He thought for a while that he might wind up sleeping on the couch, but he slipped into bed almost an hour after she had gone upstairs hoping to find her already asleep. While she wasn't asleep, she didn't say a word to him and he could feel the anger and resentment radiating off of her. Neither of them slept well.

308

Rich himself had been watching the broadcast with ever-decreasing levels of interest until Ben had dropped the bomb. He had been in the middle of eating spaghetti for dinner and paused with the fork halfway to his mouth when Ben told the world that he had spoken with the killer. Ben's description of their conversation was relatively accurate from Rich's recollection and he almost sensed relief on the lawyer's face when he finally got the matter off his chest. While Rich had considered calling him again in the preceding weeks, he'd been busy with more pressing matters and had never quite gotten around to it.

What particularly galled him was the apparent confidence Lohmeier had ultimately showed in the ability of the investigators to eventually bring Rich to justice. In response to one of Loretta's questions about how intelligent the voice on the phone seemed to be, Ben replied, "I'm sure that he thinks he's smarter than everyone else. Obviously, the more we learn about him, the better chance we have that he will ultimately be caught and have to pay for his crimes. That's probably why I haven't heard from him since."

"Bullshit," Rich said to the screen when Ben had said that. By the end of the broadcast, Rich was fuming and any chance that this story would be relegated to the back burners was now history.

The following day, the media descended upon Ben's office like the plague. Ben had been in court in the morning, and when he returned to the office, he was swarmed as he got out of his car. "I've really got nothing to add to what I said last night," Ben said as he pushed through the crowd on his way to the back door of the building. They shouted questions at his back as he hurried away. At the top of the steps, he turned and paused on the back porch. "I'm going to be on again tonight," he said. "The authorities have asked me to limit my communications to the media so my hands are tied. Sorry." That was a lie, of course, Ben having thought it up on the drive back from court, but he thought it made enough sense that he would try it out. The response was not positive. More screaming reporters.

Ben ran into Dan Conlan in the copy room. "Just when I thought you couldn't step in it anymore, you went ahead and stepped into it more," Conlan said with a laugh.

Ben shrugged. "Well, you know how it goes. Shit happens."

"Phil's upstairs."

"Great."

Ben found Phil in his office looking out the bay window behind his desk down at the reporters crawling all over the parking lot. "Hey," Ben said.

Phil continued to look down at the reporters. "Let me ask you this, was that planned last night or did it just kind of happen?"

Ben considered the question, wondering which answer would serve him best, then decided to simply tell the truth. "It just kind of happened."

Phil nodded. "That's what I figured." He finally turned and looked at Ben, who was standing in front of his desk still wearing his overcoat. "I suppose it had to happen eventually. I'm kind of surprised it took this long. I know they've been pressuring you."

"Yeah, there never seemed to be a good opportunity before last night and I really just answered the question without really thinking about it first. Probably not the best plan."

"So, how did the feds take it? It seems to be what they wanted after all."

Ben had finally spoken to Agent Lonergan on his way back from court. "I think they were hoping for a more elegant disclosure, and perhaps a heads-up, but I don't think they're too displeased, to tell you the truth. He kind of gave me shit about it. His heart didn't seem to be in it though. I think they just hope that somehow it moves the case forward."

Phil looked back out the window. "Yeah, it moved right into my parking lot."

Not unexpectedly, the phones rang off the hook all day. Somewhere around noon, Scott Nelson called. "I was just wondering how you are holding up," Nelson said.

"Not too bad," Ben said. "Lots of telephone calls, obviously, and reporters all over the place."

"I hear you."

"We even had to call the Itasca police a little while ago to have them get the riffraff off our property."

"Bet that went over well."

"About as well as you'd expect. It just means they're all standing out on the sidewalk, either in front of the bar next door or over by the train station. Didn't do much but piss them off really. The bar probably got some business out of it."

"I got a call from Lonergan earlier today," Nelson said. "He didn't seem terribly upset by any of this."

"I talked to him too," Ben said. "I think he's just looking for some juice to get the investigation moving. He must be getting plenty of heat."

"Him and me both. Next time you decide to go out and step on your dick, though, let me know ahead of time so I could set the DVR."

"I'll do that. By the way, I'm on again tonight."

"I figured you would be."

Loretta Bergen's show was based in Washington DC and her producers were all over Ben throughout the afternoon to get him to fly out and do the show live in the studio with Loretta. He had declined, politely at first, then growing increasingly impatient with the process before they finally backed off. It was now Tuesday and Ben did two segments from out in the garage as usual, reporters peering in through the windows during the taping. Fortunately, it had gotten colder overnight and the temperatures in the twenties had driven some of them away.

The broadcast itself was largely uneventful, mostly a rehash of the bombshell dropped the evening before. At the break for the bottom of the hour, which came after Ben's final segment, Loretta herself had implored him to come out to Washington DC. He politely declined once again. "Okay, then, they told me you were going to say that. So here's what I'm going to do. I'm going to fly out there tomorrow and we can do Thursday and/or Friday from that conference room, garage, whatever it is you call that place you're in now. If that's okay with you."

311

Ben was somewhat shocked. The mountain was coming to Mohammed. "Well," he said completely off-guard, "I guess that would be okay. It's your show."

"Okay, good. We'll touch base again tomorrow when I get into town. We could go through how you were hunted the first time, that sort of thing. Establish some context. Not everybody saw that interview we did six months ago. I also want to stop by the Hilton Hotel to get the lay of the land with respect to Jimmy Moran. Maybe even head out to that river or wherever it was, where they dumped his body."

In the end, she did the Thursday show from the Fox studio in downtown Chicago, having taped segments at both the Cal-Sag Channel and the downtown Hilton. Ben did not appear on the Thursday show since he was going to be more or less the entire focus the following evening. Ben watched the broadcast from his family room. He was by himself, Libby having insisted that she wasn't interested. She had stormed off and gone upstairs.

Ben was tempted to sneak upstairs himself to find out what she was watching, since he believed that she was probably watching the broadcast herself and just didn't want to do so with him. Although the fireworks between them had largely subsided, Ben almost preferred that to the silent treatment he was now receiving. She would walk by him, her chin raised and jaw clenched, saying nothing. Ben referred to this as giving him "The Jaw". She was never amused by the characterization. That didn't stop him.

The following day, the media swarm had been heightened by news of Loretta's Bergen's arrival. While one media outlet didn't necessarily want to promote the coverage of another, they nevertheless wanted to see her in action. On Phil's orders, the staff had been sprucing up the place most of the afternoon in anticipation of national television's arrival. If there was going to be a dog and pony show at the office, Phil at least wanted to put their best foot forward. The rest of the firm seemed to feel the same way and Ben didn't sense any resentment from anyone over the extra attention and cleaning duties. For her part, Loretta was gracious throughout. "I could see working in a place like this,"

312

she said after receiving the nickel tour of the place. They were in the lobby now and she had taken a seat on the church pew opposite the reception desk. "It's very casual, almost homey. I like that."

"I do too." Ben said.

"It kind of reminds of a place you would find in Wisconsin."

"I can see that. You know, there is a bar not too far down the road from here that would remind you of home too."

"Friday fish fry?"

"Yep, perch or cod. Good burgers too."

"How far from here?"

"Maybe five or ten minutes," Ben said.

"After the show?"

"Deal."

Eventually, they actually got to the broadcast, Loretta once again walking her audience with Ben's help through the facts of the Law School Murder case, which had culminated with a shootout in that very room, before moving on to the deaths of the six lawyers and the telephone conversation between Ben and the voice. Although relatively little new ground was broken, near the end of the telecast, she asked Ben how sure he was that he was speaking to the real killer. Ben thought about it for a second, then said, "he seemed like the real thing to me. Of course, it's entirely possible that he was just some crackpot."

Rich was not watching the broadcast live when Ben uttered those words. He had been off completing a separate project and had recorded the show. By the time he had returned, the show was already over long since over and he fired up the DVR to take a look. He had known, of course, that Loretta Bergen was going to be doing her show from Lohmeier's office since they had been promoting it for a couple of days now. He didn't even bother to watch the rest of the show. He simply clicked it off and went for his computer.

50

The renewed energy that had come from Ben's disclosure of the telephone call and the week or so of attention relating to it began to ebb when nothing of consequence with the investigation seemed to result. It hadn't worked. The killer had not responded. At least not with another telephone call. Every time the phone rang, particularly at the office, part of Ben hoped that it was the killer and part of him was relieved when it turned out not to be. Ben was clearly back in the doldrums and the week before Thanksgiving, he'd actually missed a court appearance in one of his files, something that never happened. Although it had basically been a routine status call and nothing bad had occurred as a result of Ben's failure to go, Phil nonetheless felt the need to call Ben into his office that Friday before he headed off to Florida himself for the week of Thanksgiving.

Phil Luckenbill did not like confrontation. In fact, he loathed it. He wanted little more than to be left alone. He would've preferred it had things at the office going on smoothly like an easy flowing river with as little intervention from him as possible. He did not want to micromanage, he did not want to interfere unless necessary. He wanted everyone to do their jobs and do them well so that all he ever heard was good news about things well done and successes well-earned. That's why he had Casey Gardner to do a lot of his dirty work for him.

Today, unfortunately, he had finally found it necessary to intervene. Although he undoubtedly recognized Ben's circumstances, he also knew that something had to be done and if that meant that Ben had to get a kick in the ass, then so be it. Ben came in and sat down on the couch in Phil's office as Phil went about packing up his stuff for his week in Florida. It was early afternoon, and the secretaries were out to lunch and Phil and Ben were the only people upstairs in the old part of the building. Phil was extremely tall, about six foot five, with dark brooding features. He was a man of many moods, ranging from dark to darker, as his subordinates in the office often joked. Yet Phil himself was aware of these moods as well and tried not to inflict them upon others unless he absolutely had to. He spoke in a low voice. "Look, I know you're under a lot of pressure," Phil said as he towered over Ben. "But let's face it, something's got to fucking give here."

Phil also had a gift. His skill in stringing together streams of profanity was virtually unrivaled. He dropped a few F-bombs now as Ben listened quietly. He went on like that for a minute or two before he sat back on the end of his desk and looked Ben straight in the face. "I think you need to take some time off and get yourself straightened out. Go somewhere and clear your head. Thanksgiving is next week and it's the perfect time for it. Take the whole week off." Ben started to respond and Phil waved him silent. "No, you have to get away and get this right in your head. Take next week off or take the next two weeks off, I don't care. Whatever you have to do to get back on track, you've got to do it and do it now. If we need to get a couple of the guys to pick up the slack for a while, that's fine. But if I come back from Thanksgiving and you're here, I'm going to assume that everything is back to normal and I can count on you again. If not, the next conversation we have is not going to be nearly as much fun as this one." They looked at each other for a moment. "That's it. Now have a good Thanksgiving and get the hell out of here."

Ben nodded. "You too."

*****

As Phil concluded his conversation with Ben in Itasca, Rich steered a white panel van through downtown Clarendon Hills. He had gotten into town the day before and was finally getting the lay of the land. Soon, he pulled the van to a slow stop in front of the elementary school across the street from Benjamin Lohmeier's home. It was after lunch now and the kiddies were back in class. The van itself was almost invisible, the kind of work van people see every day without giving it a second thought. Coupled with the jeans, work boots and jacket he had picked up at the Goodwill store the previous afternoon, Rich looked like just another hard-working guy trying to earn a living the best he could.

He sat there for a few minutes watching the house. It seemed empty. He knew that both Lohmeier and his wife worked during the day and their kids were in school. Rich knew from the previous day that the moms started lining up outside at least a half hour or so before school let out and that meant he didn't have all that much time. Besides, cars parked in front of a school drew attention that he didn't want.

He donned a Nike cap, took leather work gloves out of his jacket pockets and pulled them on as he got out of the van. He slid the side door open and took out a backpack and a toolbox. A moment later, he was walking down the driveway toward the Lohmeier's garage. He circled around the back of the garage, where he found a door leading inside. He paused and looked around. A large wooden play set sat less than fifteen feet directly in front of him and trees and shrubs lined the back yard. From where he stood, he could not be seen by any of the Lohmeier's neighbors and the garage blocked the view from Lohmeier's house.

He took another look around and feeling satisfied, zipped open the backpack and pulled out a set of tools, which he used to jimmy the lock on the door. Within seconds, the lock clicked open and he was inside. He closed the door behind him, waited a moment for his eyes to adjust to the darkness, then got to work. Ten minutes later, Rich was back in the van and was gone.

*****

Ben had taken Phil's advice to heart, at least as best as he could. He took a pad of paper and went out to the garage. He went to work on making a list of things that needed to be done over the next two or three weeks, things that Brad Funk or Dan Conlan could help out with if he indeed took a week or so off. The more he thought about it, the more he thought it was a good idea. It would give him some time to try and figure things out, even if he wasn't clearing his head on some beach somewhere as Phil had probably hoped.

He worked steadily for the better part of an hour. When he finished, he went back upstairs and dropped the list off with Nancy to be typed. He looked at his watch. It was shortly after three.

"I think I'm out of here," he said. "No TV tonight so I am getting home early for a change."

Nancy turned to face him. "Any plans? Supposed to be a nice weekend. Probably the last one we'll get this year."

"I saw that somewhere," Ben said. "I've got to finish up the leaves. I'll probably do that tomorrow."

"Sounds like a plan. Are you going to be in next week? I heard you might be taking some time off." Ben looked at her. Figures, he thought, there are no secrets in this office. He shrugged. "Not sure yet. I'll talk to Libby over the weekend and see. I may be in on Monday just for a little while."

"Take the time off," Nancy said. "It will do you some good."

51

Ben made it home early, picked the kids up from day care and had already started in on dinner by the time Libby got home. He was a little over-the-top with his cheerfulness as she walked in the door, something she undoubtedly recognized, but it seemed as though she was appreciating the effort. They watched a movie on Friday night, put a moratorium on cable news shows, and even got to bed early, together. Good progress.

Saturday was devoted to getting things done around the house, from finishing the leaves to putting the hoses away to getting the snow blower out for the Chicago winter that would inevitably arrive. It was a nice fall day – sunny with blue skies and temperatures inching into the low-fifties. Nancy was right. It would probably be the last really nice weekend until spring. Ben stood in the doorway of his garage for a minute and looked at the state of mild disorganization inside. He had just completed his tasks for the day and was about to go inside and take a shower. It was half past three and he could get a couple of loads of laundry in before they went out for pizza and a movie with the kids. Then he groaned. If he didn't straighten up the garage now, he wouldn't get to it until spring break or later. He groaned again and decided to bite the bullet and do it now.

It took him forty-five minutes to pull the big items out of the garage and reorganize the tools and yard implements and sweep out the entire space before turning his attention to the work bench and the shelves in the back. Like most families, they weren't always good about putting things away after they had used them and the work bench was piled with tools, paint cans and miscellaneous summer items. Ben removed these things one by one and put them back where they belonged. In the back corner of the work bench, under a blue tarp, sat a worn bankers box. Ben picked it up and discovered it was very light, with a couple of items rattling around inside. He set it down in front of him on the bench and took off the lid. Whatever was inside was hidden beneath a few sheets of crumpled up newspaper, which Ben pulled out without really thinking. Then he stared down into the box and gasped. There were three things inside – a hotel key card, a water bottle and a ceramic knife covered in a dark substance that looked like blood.

Ben turned quickly around to see if anyone was watching. There was no one there. He walked out to the garage entrance and looked down the driveway, then up at his house, and toward his neighbors to the left and the right. Not a soul around. His heart was pounding as he thought about what to do next. He went back inside and peered once again into the box, hoping for a different result. He didn't get one. The three items lay there as before. He took a deep breath, let it out, and took another before forcing himself to look more closely at the three things. The key card was embossed with the Hilton logo and the name of the downtown hotel and the water bottle carried a sticker with the same information. The knife was similar to ones he had in his own kitchen. He studied it. The blade was black and a dark substance covered much of the blade and a portion of the handle as well. It had to be blood. There also appeared to be tissue stuck to the blade. Ben swore under his breath.

He turned and leaned against the work bench as he fumbled his cell phone off the holster at his belt. His knees felt weak as he scrolled through the recent calls until he found Scott Nelson's cell phone number. He dialed and Nelson picked up on the second ring.

"It's a beautiful Saturday and I hope you're not calling to ruin it," Nelson said.

"I'm afraid I have a problem," Ben said.

"What's that?"

"I was cleaning out my garage and I found a box in the back on my work bench. It was hidden behind some paint cans and stuff. Anyway, I pulled it out and took off the top and looked inside."

"What did you find?"

"You won't believe it. There's a room key card, a water bottle and a bloody knife. The key and the bottle are from the Hilton. The knife probably is too."

"Holy fuck." Nelson paused before continuing. "You're sure?"

"Yeah, unfortunately. Not much doubt about it. I'm looking right at it. Don't know whose blood, but we can probably guess."

"Did you touch anything?"

"No, just the box."

"Okay, put the lid back on and wait for me to call back. I've got to get a hold of Lonergan. Don't do anything until you hear from me."

"Okay."

"And Ben?"

"Yeah."

"Tell me you didn't do it."

"Of course I didn't do it. Do you think I would have left this in my garage if I had done it?"

"No, but a simple denial was enough."

"Right."

Ben stood with his back against the work bench as if guarding the box while waiting for Nelson to call back. It seemed to take forever, but took less than five minutes. Nelson also had Agent Lonergan on the line. "Nelson told me what happened, but I want to hear it from you. I should probably read you your rights."

"Fuck you."

"Okay, I probably deserve that. I'll take that as a denial that you know anything about how this stuff got into your garage."

"Good idea. The first I ever saw any of it was ten minutes ago. If I hadn't decided to clean out my garage, I wouldn't have seen it until spring."

"Or until someone called the cops and suggested they look in your garage."

"Or then."

Ben walked them through it again, just as he had for Nelson a few minutes earlier. When he had finished, Nelson asked Lonergan if he was going to send a crime scene crew out to look at it. "I'm not sure," Lonergan said. "Let's think about that for a minute."

"What's there to think about?" Nelson said.

"Well, what was the purpose of stashing the evidence in Ben's garage? I can only think of two reasons – first, the killer may be trying to implicate Ben in one or more of the murders, probably Moran's. Or second, he may not care whether Ben found it or not. If Ben finds the box, then Ben has to decide what to do about it. Call us, don't call us, get rid of it. Regardless, Ben now knows that the killer has been to his house, been inside his garage, maybe inside his house too, and has Ben in his sights. If Ben doesn't find the box, then the killer has the stuff there and can drop the dime on Ben whenever the moment suits him. He could also be trying to intimidate you to back off on your commentary."

"You know I didn't do anything. I didn't kill anyone."

"No," Lonergan said, "I wouldn't think so. This does serve to put pressure on you one way or the other though. You must have gotten under his skin more than we thought."

"But what are we going to do about it?" Ben said. "I've got a family here to protect."

They talked about that for a while and considered the various options. "I'm inclined to leave the box where it is for now and see what happens," Lonergan said. "I think he'll probably drop the dime on you sooner or later and put the heat on you. He tends to plan this stuff very carefully. I don't see him warning you and then coming after you at home with everyone around.

321

We could be there waiting for him. No, I think he's trying to spook you."

"It's working. What am I supposed to do in the meantime? What do I tell my wife?"

They hashed that out too before Lonergan asked if there were any vacant houses on the block. Ben confirmed that there was an empty rental about four houses down. "And you've got the school across the street," Lonergan said. "I'll see if I can get some people in both places to keep an eye on things. Once the kids are out of school on Wednesday, I can have people right across the street for the long Thanksgiving weekend. I doubt he'll wait long. If he hasn't reported you by next Sunday, we can rethink things. That's eight days. In the meantime, I'll get a couple of people out there to keep an eye on things."

"We could alert the locals," Nelson said. "They could patrol the area or sit in the school parking lot."

"I'm not sure we want to bring them in on it yet. Can you get a couple of off-duty guys to do some surveillance of the area, Scott?"

"Probably, but why exclude the local cops?"

"Yeah, it makes it sound like you want them to think I did it," Ben said.

"Maybe we do, at least until he reports you," Lonergan said. "We may want to let this play out a bit and see how he does it. Scott, you don't need to tell your guys about the box. Just make it sound like you want to keep an eye on the counselor here without telling them exactly why. Let them jump to conclusions."

"What do you have in mind?" Ben said. "What happens after he drops the dime on me?"

"Does your family have someplace to go?" Lonergan said. "Don't your in-laws live in the area?"

Ben wondered how he knew that. "About five minutes away."

"Can your family go there for a few days if need be?"

"I suppose so. We were also talking about going to Disney World for a week or so."

322

"Okay," Lonergan said, "that would work. When were you planning to go?"

"Not sure yet. Maybe the day after Thanksgiving."

"Hope he waits that long. He may not. Is there a security system at your in-laws?"

"Yes, but I don't know how good it is."

"What about you, do you have someplace to go?"

"You mean, if I don't go to my in-laws?"

"Yeah, if you go on the lam, so to speak."

Ben thought about it. "Maybe. What are you thinking?"

"Well," Lonergan said, "let's assume he calls in a tip and tells us to look in your garage or somehow points in your direction. You could deal with it, deny it, whatever. Maybe you could go on TV and create quite a storm." He paused. "Or maybe you could do something different. Maybe you could just disappear. That would create a different kind of storm. I doubt he would expect that. It could shake him up and work to our advantage."

"Jeez, I don't know," Ben said.

Nelson finally spoke up. "What do you really have in mind?"

Lonergan told them. When he was done, both Ben and Nelson had questions, which Lonergan calmly answered.

"I'm going to have to tell my wife about this," Ben said.

"She's going to have to be in on it," Nelson said.

"Of course," Lonergan said.

They talked it through for five more minutes before Ben signed off. Nelson called back immediately. "I wanted to talk to you without Lonergan."

"Okay."

"I don't think you should tell him where you're going, if it comes to that, I mean."

"Why not?"

"I don't necessarily trust him, not completely."

"Because he's a fed?"

"Partially, but it's more than that. It's hard to keep a secret with the feds. Stuff always seems to get out. If you do have to go away for a while, it may be better for you to keep where you are to yourself. Take precautions. It's a big country. Get lost. If we're playing up the angle that you may be a suspect or even a victim, we can keep an eye on your family because we're trying to get information or because you may contact them. Something like that."

"Do you think he may try to pin this on me? I mean, come on, I was here in Illinois when all this stuff happened. That should be pretty easy to prove."

"No, I don't think he would do that unless he thought you did it and I don't think he believes that. It's just, I really think you may be safer on your own. It's not like he's going to put you up in a safe house with armed guards. Anyway, think about it."

"Okay, will do."

"In the meantime, I'll see about getting a couple of guys out there to monitor things."

"Thanks."

They hung up just as Libby came outside to check on him. "I don't see a lot of progress out here," she said.

"Speak for yourself," Ben said as he shoved the box back into the corner of the workbench. "I would have been done a long time ago if I had a little help."

They finished up in the garage and headed inside so Ben could take a shower. He decided not to tell Libby about the discovery in the garage just yet because he didn't want to ruin the evening. When they got home from the movie, Ben caught up on a couple of his favorite television shows while Libby surfed the web for possible deals on trips to Disney World. Though Ben had not committed to taking a second week off, and Libby wasn't sure if she wanted to skip Thanksgiving with her family, she nevertheless was excited enough about the prospects to at least look into it. Ben wondered if they would even get to go.

He broke the news to her after they got in bed and she was understandably freaked-out and scared to death. Ben tried to reassure her the best he could, emphasizing the fact that Nelson and Lonergan both would have people keeping an eye on them, but it did little good. "Ben, he's after you too. I told you to back off. What are we going to do?" she said.

324

"I don't think he's really after me like the others," Ben said. He wasn't really any more convinced than she was, but nevertheless tried to put the best face on it that he could. "There's no evidence that he warned any of the other lawyers in advance. I think he's just trying to shake me up, assuming the stuff in the garage is legitimate in the first place."

She gave him a disbelieving look. "What about Disney World? Maybe we should just go as soon as possible."

He thought about that. "Okay. See if you can get any flights for Monday night or Tuesday. I really can't go any sooner than that."

They talked about the plan he had discussed with Nelson and Lonergan as they lay in bed. She didn't seem at all on board, but they didn't have many options. They decided that they couldn't let anyone else in on the situation, including her parents, even if it came to moving in with them for a few days. Hopefully it wouldn't. Eventually, the conversation ceased and they tried to get some sleep, both of them mostly tossing and turning in the darkness.

Ben spent Sunday afternoon watching football in an effort to get his mind off of everything. He didn't entirely succeed. Libby got them on a Tuesday afternoon flight to Florida, using all of their available mileage bonuses in the process. She didn't like missing Thanksgiving, but it seemed the best alternative. The kids were thrilled. The adults hoped that nothing happened before they got there, although Ben thought it might turn out to be worse if the killer dropped the dime on him while they were out of town. He would somewhat lose control of the situation if he was out of town when it occurred. He would have to rely on Nelson and Lonergan to keep him out from under the bus. The situation was fluid.

52

Ben made it into the office on Monday morning by nine and Nancy met him in the kitchen as he glanced at the daily newspapers. "I thought you were taking time off," she said.

He turned and smiled his best phony smile. "I am. I'm going to be out of here by lunchtime. You may not see me again for a couple of weeks." Or longer, he thought.

He was indeed gone by lunchtime, if one-thirty counted. He dropped a book off at the library, then crossed the tracks that ran through downtown Clarendon Hills. Ben's house was located a couple of blocks south and west of downtown and he drove slowly through the downtown business district, turning right at the Starbucks. His street was two blocks down on the left. As he waited for an oncoming car to clear the intersection so he could make his left turn, he glanced toward his house, which was eight houses or so down the block. The car passed by and he started to turn, then stopped. Near his house, several police cars were parked, their lights flashing. He stared transfixed until the sound of a horn from a car behind him snapped him out of it. He changed his mind and continued straight and curved around to the next block more than a quarter mile away, where he took a left turn.

He drove a couple of blocks, the road curving in a big loop before taking another left. He had now circled the area where his home and the elementary school were located and had come around on the other side. But much closer. He crawled toward the intersection and stopped about thirty yards short of the stop sign. From this vantage point, he could now see the police cars. They were not at the school. They were at his house – two in the driveway and two more in the street. His garage door was open and he could see three officers inside. This was it. The killer hadn't waited after all.

It was broad daylight, the sun was bright, and he did not want to be seen. He made a three point turn and went back in the opposite direction, came to the next intersection and turned left. Then he pulled over and pulled out his cell phone to text Libby. "It's on. Cops at home. Hitting the road. You ok?"

The response came a minute later. "No, not ok but will follow plan. Stay safe."

"You too. Love you," he replied.

After a little maneuvering, he came back out onto a street that intersected with 55th Street. Ben waited for traffic to clear and took a left. He took the first ramp onto southbound Route 83, his head spinning.

He hadn't thought it would happen this quickly and he wished that he had packed a bag and left it in the trunk, but it was too late now. He thought about what Nelson had said about Lonergan and considered his options. He checked his gas gauge, saw that he had about half a tank and decided to fill up. He sure as hell didn't want to run out of gas. He got to a gas station and pulled into one of the forward spots and got out. He found $32 in his wallet and put $20 of that into his gas tank, cursing himself for not getting more cash on his way through town. He thought of Nelson again and decided that he didn't want to use his debit card now. That would point south and he didn't want that. After pulling his cell phone off his belt, he removed the battery and SIM card, then tossed both back on the front seat of the car.

He thought about where he was heading as he looked out at the traffic moving quickly down Route 83. A couple of minutes later, Ben turned right out of the gas station and continued south on Route 83. He looked at the clock on the dashboard – it was three o'clock. A couple of miles down the road, he took the interchange for Interstate 55-North toward Chicago. He quickly took the ramp for the southbound Tri-State Tollway. Ben knew that it was approximately twenty-five miles to the Indiana border, which he reached by three-thirty.

As always, traffic filled in between the Indiana border and I-65 heading toward Indianapolis. Ben made it through Gary okay and inched through the I-65 interchange before the pace picked up near the Indiana Dunes. He spent the entire time checking his rearview mirror, waiting for the police cars that would never come, at least not for him. At one point, he was prepared to pull over when he saw the lights of an Indiana State trooper flashing a quarter-mile behind him. Whoever the officer was looking for, he found him before ever reaching Ben.

Ben reached the Michigan border just before four-thirty, five-thirty Michigan time. He got off at Exit 1 for New Buffalo and pulled into the McDonald's just north of the interchange. It being mid-November, the sun was setting, but it was not yet fully dark. Ben really wanted it to be dark as soon as possible. He was hungry and anticipated a long night. Spending $3 of his remaining $12 in cash, together with change from his pocket, he bought a hamburger, small fries and large drink. He tried to appear nonchalant as he waited for his food, head down and the battery-less cell phone pressed to his ear. After what seemed to be an eternity, his burger, fries and plastic cup were handed over. His hands shook as he filled the cup with Coke and he fumbled with the plastic lid before eventually getting it on correctly. He could never be a spy, he thought to himself, as he headed outside.

Back in the car, he took Whittaker Road into downtown New Buffalo, eating as he drove. The light was red when he reached the intersection of Whittaker and Red Arrow Highway, a four lane road near the Michigan border. He was the third car in line. When the light turned green, he inched through the intersection toward the New Buffalo harbor and Lake Michigan. He looked at the clock on the dash. It was still too early. Two blocks short of Lake Michigan, he took a right and drove another two blocks and pulled into a space at the curb. He was outside the New Buffalo Public Library, which gratefully was open on this Monday evening. He browsed the library selections in a way that kept him largely out of view of the library's other patrons and staff members. He found a recent John Sandford novel in the fiction section and a table in the back corner, arranging his chair so that he was facing away from anyone who might approach.

Ben stayed at the library for about two hours, fighting the urge the entire time to look over his shoulder. Dressed in jeans, a black sweater and a leather jacket, he tried to assume the look of a casual library patron. All the while, he thought of the GPS on his SUV and the disassembled cell phone sitting on the front seat and imagined Lonergan tracking him.

He left the library at about seven-thirty. Heading back the way he had come, he turned toward the lake until he found Marquette Drive, then turned right. Marquette Drive eventually turned into Shoreline Road, the Gold Coast for the New Buffalo area. Ben was not in any hurry and drove only as quickly as traffic behind him dictated. He paused at the hidden entrance to the Dunes Club, one of the best nine-hole golf courses in the United States, a course Ben had played several years earlier.

He continued down Shoreline Road, past familiar landmarks hidden by the changes of the season and the cloak of darkness. It was taking longer than expected. Then, navigating along the contours of the lake, he eventually reached the spot he was looking for. He stopped at a Y-intersection. To the right, the road led a brief distance back out to Red Arrow Highway. Shoreline Road continued to the left. Ben went left. He slowly cruised the property in question. He turned around in a bed and breakfast past the next curve and cruised it again. He took the right at the Y and drove all the way back to the Dunes Club, turning around in the driveway, before heading back from where he had come. He followed this procedure three more times before his patience ran out and he stopped at a private drive and killed his lights.

Ben looked ahead and then behind him in the rearview mirror. There were no cars. He slowly made a right turn onto the private road and inched down about fifty feet. The road was approximately one hundred yards in length. To Ben's left, deep dark woods loomed the entire length of the narrow road. The fenced-in property of Albert and Mary Sandford extended off to his right. Their property was also heavily landscaped and from his current position he could not be seen from either the coach house or the big house beyond.

Ben put the engine in park and waited. He would only be seen by someone looked directly down the private road where he now sat. Even then, with the lights out and the car in park, it would be difficult to see him unless you knew he was there. There was very little chance of a car coming at him from the opposite direction, since the elderly couple off to the left at the end of the drive was either not home or in for the night. The Finney property in the center was empty and the Sandfords were off in the big house.

The southern end of the big house facing Ben was taken up in its entirety by a two-story great room, where the Sandfords spent very little time, particularly in the evening. Ben put the car in gear and inched a few yards down the road until he could see the big house through the trees. The lights in the great room were out, as expected. He kept going until he reached the end of the road, whereupon he continued around a set of bushes and on to the Finney property. He pulled the car around the art studio and parked between the studio and the garage. He was now completely hidden from the road. Fortunately, there was no snow on the ground and the area between the structures was a combination of scrub dirt and gravel and he would not leave any significant tracks.

Ben got out of the car leaving the engine running. He walked over to the garage, said a little prayer, then turned the handle and pulled hard. The door opened. He backed the SUV out from between the two buildings and stopped at the threshold of the garage before turning on his lights. The two-car garage was mostly empty, with an odd assortment of beach items and rarely used yard equipment piled on the right hand side. There was plenty of room for his car and he pulled it into the vacant space and turned off the engine. The lights went off casting the space into an eerie darkness. He grabbed his gloves off the seat, went outside and closed the garage door behind him.

Now he hoped for equally good luck with the house. He tried the front door first and found it locked. Swearing under his breath, he moved around the house to his left and came upon a door with glass paneled windows and stopped, placed his forehead against the glass and peered inside, his hands cupped on either side of his eyes. The door appeared to lead into a small mud room of sorts and then into the kitchen. He tried the handle. It too was locked.

Continuing around the back of the house, Ben found two more doors, a second door leading into the kitchen and a glass slider into a family room. These were also locked. He considered his options, and searched all the possible locations he could think of where the Finneys may have stashed a key. He figured that they might have a key hidden somewhere about the premises since it was unlikely that they would mail a new key to whatever friend of theirs might be using the place for a weekend getaway. He looked inside drain pipes, in bushes and under rocks. Nothing. By now, the wind off the lake whipped through the trees and bit into him. Although he was wearing a leather bomber jacket and gloves, his head was unprotected and his ears burned with the cold. Soon, his nose was running.

He continued to search for a while, but eventually gave up. He could probably try again in daylight, although he did not want to wait until morning or break in. While he doubted that the Finneys had any meaningful security at the place, it wasn't a risk he necessarily wanted to take. He would do it if he had too, but probably not until the following night.

He walked over to the bluff and looked down through the trees in the direction of the beach. He could see glimpses of the roiling surf through the branches, the low clouds providing just enough ambient light to make it visible. He came around from the back of the house and eyed the garage and the art studio. He knew he could return to the garage and spend the night in his car, but decided to give the art studio a try first.

The lone door out front was locked. Ben cursed again. Then he spotted a copper box attached to the wall next to the door, green from the lack of upkeep. It was about half the size of a normal mailbox and had a lid which folded up. Ben opened it and looked inside. He found a gold key attached to a small carabiner and hanging on a hook. "Eureka," he said and snatched the key off the hook. He tried it in the lock and it worked.

Then he turned and jogged back over to the main house, hoping that perhaps the key would fit those locks as well, because in Ben's mind, the house was a better spot to camp out in than the art studio. No such luck. He returned to the art studio and went inside. The studio was two stories and largely glass on three sides. A winding staircase rose up from the middle of the building leading to the second floor.

He went upstairs first, finding an open loft space devoid of any furniture, save for a battered wooden table about six by four feet in size. He tried a closet against the far wall and found it empty. He looked around the upstairs for the controls for the heat, realizing it was barely warmer inside than it had been outside. Apparently the windows were not insulated and did nothing to keep out the cold. At least it blocked the wind, he thought. Ben walked over to the window that faced out toward the lake and thought about his family. He figured that they were at his in-laws by now.

After a time, he went back downstairs and found the thermostat and attempted to turn on the heat. Nothing. He went over to a light switch on the wall and gave it a brief flick on and off. Still nothing. He found a bathroom behind the stairs, went inside and closed the door behind him. He fumbled around for the light switch, found it, then flicked it on. Nothing. He tried the cold water on the dated vanity. There was a rumbling sound of air releasing from the pipes, but no water. The utilities were off. "Damn it," he said.

He circled the entire first floor, which was largely open and contained no furniture. Adjacent to the stairwell, there was a small kitchenette complete with a refrigerator. The only things in the fridge were a box of baking soda and a can of diet cream soda. A musty aroma wafted out at him. The baking soda wasn't doing its job. Ben sat down on the steps, the only real place to sit other than the floor. He had been hoping for a couch and hadn't expected the place to be completely empty like it was.

He wondered what time it was. Although he felt exhausted from the events of the afternoon and evening, he recognized it probably wasn't any later than nine o'clock or so Michigan time. He was too tired to go back outside and check the clock in the car, nor did he want to risk turning his phone on. He wished now that he had been wearing his watch, something he rarely did any more. Not that it would make that much difference anyhow.

After a few minutes, he got up and stretched and realized that he had to go to the bathroom. Since the toilet wasn't working, he went outside and peed into some bushes behind the garage. As he unzipped his fly, he wondered whether there were any animals lurking in the woods. That would be a way to go, found out behind the garage with your zipper down. Back inside, he found a dark spot in the corner farthest away from the lake. He sat down and propped himself up against the wall and tried to get some sleep.

His attempts were largely unsuccessful, for thoughts of Libby and the kids dominated. He wondered what exactly happened at his house. They must be terrified, he thought. He wondered if they would still go to Florida. He doubted it. Then he thought about contacting Nelson and decided to hold off for now. He wished he had been given enough time to plan this better.

At one point, he had apparently drifted off, only to be startled awake by a noise outside in the darkness. He dragged himself to his feet, hunched over, his back killing him. He felt like a human question mark. He tried to get the kinks out. That was not going to work, however. Still wearing his gloves, his nose still running, he thought of the coach house. He was confident that he could spend a couple of days in the coach house without being noticed. There probably was even some food there from previous visits. Albert and Mary rarely went over there. They didn't have any reason to. It would be warm there, with actual beds.

He couldn't just walk over and open the gate, that caused a chime to sound in the big house, which would undoubtedly alert the Sandfords, nor could he squeeze through the fence. He could probably hop over it if he found exactly the right spot. He thought of the security arrangements at the Sandfords' estate. He knew they had cameras surrounding both houses, but he was pretty sure that they did not have motion detectors. He decided to at least check it out.

Ben went back outside and walked out to the private road. From the corner of the Sandfords' lot, he could peer through the bushes and see the back of the big house in the distance. There seemed to be a light burning in the family room, but he could see no other lights either on the main floor or upstairs. He slowly started down the length of the south edge of the property. He carefully looked for cameras or hidden sensors that would alert the Sandfords to any possible intrusion.

About halfway down the drive, he heard a noise and looked up to see two large deer poking through the trees about twenty yards in front of him. He stopped and stared, standing completely still. A 10-point buck pushed into the clearing and stood in the middle of the road facing directly at him. Ben slowly took two steps forward and stopped again. The buck did not move, though the second deer backed off into the trees. Ben took two more steps forward and stopped. The buck continued to eye him. Ben tried to appear as unthreatening as possible, keeping his hands at his sides and making no sudden movements. The thought of being impaled on one of those large antlers was not very appealing. If the buck charged, Ben had no place to go. The buck watched as Ben moved forward again. They eyed each other for a long moment, before the buck responded to a rustling in the woods by turning quickly and heading off into the darkness. Ben stood silently and watched him disappear. Then he continued his march down the fence line, always aware of the woods.

He reached the front of the property having seen no evidence of any additional security measures. Stepping out onto the Shoreline Road, he looked in both directions and saw a car turn in off of Red Arrow Highway. He slid back into the woods and waited for it to pass. The car took the fork to the left and went off in the opposite direction. Ben stepped back across the private road and through the bushes to the front gate.

A stone wall stood on either side of the front gate and Ben recalled a couple of years earlier that he had sent his son over the wall when the keypad that operated the sliding gate was not working properly. He took one last look around, and seeing nothing, pushed himself up onto the brick wall, his back screaming. Feeling exposed on top of the wall, he quickly hopped over into the Sandford's property. His feet slid out from under him and he landed on his ass. The ground was hard and he wiped off his pants as he stood. No alarms went off.

He looked across the way at the big house. There were no lights on anywhere on the side facing the street. Staying along the tree line next to the fence, Ben made his way around the back of the coach house and positioned himself opposite the near garage door. The garage was recessed somewhat from the rest of the building. There was an overhang and the walk was blocked from the view of the big house. The back entrance was straight ahead. He dashed across the drive and into the darkness under the eaves.

Ben walked quickly to the back door, pulled the screen door open and yanked the handle on the inner door. It was unlocked. He was pretty sure that there were no alarms on the coach house, this being rural Michigan after all, and he stepped inside. He moved through a short hallway and into the family room, which faced the great room of the big house across the way, and continued right through it and into the kitchen. He rummaged through the cupboard and found various leftovers from previous visits, such as pancake mix and a jar of salsa, together with a box of wheat thins and a roll of Ritz crackers.

He took four crackers out of the roll and put it back where he had found it, grabbed a glass off the shelf to the left of the sink and filled it with water. He wolfed down the crackers and drank the water as he looked out the window in the front door and across the yard toward the road, seeing no activity at all. He feared that he might be visible from the road. Stepping around the corner out of view of the windows, he leaned his back against the door leading into the garage. He finished the water, and went back to the sink in the kitchen for another half a glass, swallowed it down and then rinsed out the glass and put it back in the cupboard. No dishes in the sink. Then he quickly went back through the family room and headed upstairs.

The upstairs was dark, which was good, and Ben considered his room options for a moment. He glanced at the thermostat, which was set at sixty-four degrees. Plenty warm enough and much better than the art studio. The coach house was laid out like a long fat tube. At the top of the stairs, the three bedrooms were set on the left in a long line, each with its own bathroom. The hallway extended the full length of the building with stairs at the far end leading down to the last garage bay. The right side consisted of windows overlooking the gravel drive in the back corner of the Sandfords' property, fenced in and heavily wooded.

Ben initially walked down to the far bedroom, known as the kids room, because it contained two twin beds. Then he changed his mind, concluding that the back bedroom was too far away from the back door and that he might not be able to hear anyone come inside from there. He certainly wouldn't be able to hear anyone come in the front door, maybe not even from the front bedroom. In the end, he chose the front bedroom, his usual room when they visited. He kicked off his shoes, picked them up and headed into the large bathroom. He shed his jacket and gloves and dumped them in the shower stall with his shoes, before coming back out and pulling the big comforter back and preparing for bed. He was exhausted. He crawled into the bed and pulled the covers up trying to get warm. His back still ached and he struggled to make himself comfortable. Then he reached over and grabbed the clock, pressing the button on top to illuminate the dial and reveal that it was only a few minutes after midnight. Ben laughed. He assumed it was at least two or three hours later, maybe more. Mary Sandford, a notorious night owl, was probably still up. He thought of his family and the chaos of the past ten hours. Within a few minutes, even with that on his mind, he was out.

53

Albert Sandford punched in the code and the garage door started up. Upstairs, the sound of the door and the vibrations made Ben open his eyes. Ben was confused and disoriented for a moment, and when he realized where he was and what was happening, he knew he was in trouble. He jumped out of bed and glanced at the clock as he hurried to put the bed back together the way he had found it. It was after nine o'clock already, not what he planned. He ran to the bathroom and retrieved his clothes. He needed to pee, but he knew he couldn't flush the toilet and decided to wait. He got dressed, everything but the shoes, which he carried in his hand, and tiptoed to the door. He could barely hear Albert working in the garage stall below.

He considered his options and listened closely to see if Mary or anyone else was downstairs inside the house. Hearing nothing, he crept down the hallway to his left, taking great pains to stay away from the windows. About halfway down the hall, he heard an engine firing up below. Albert was starting his tractor. Must be doing the leaves, Ben thought.

Ben looked across the hallway and out the window. He couldn't be seen from the ground, though he could tell that it was a bright and sunny morning. That was good because it kept anyone in the bright sunlight outside from easily seeing inside the dark windows. He quickly moved across the hallway and against the wall between two of the windows. He inched up to the corner of one window and peered down below to see the tractor pulling out of the fourth garage stall. It was a large piece of equipment, about the size of the lawnmowers used when cutting the grass on golf courses, and it had an attachment to help pick up leaves.

Albert sat in the enclosed cab, wearing a brown barn coat, leather work gloves, a knit hat and orange soundproof earmuffs covered his ears from the deafening noise. It took him a minute, but Albert eventually maneuvered the tractor around the corner and up the drive toward the front of the coach house. Ben scurried down the hall and ducked into the back bedroom to look out the window overlooking the front yard. He stood about four feet back from the window, which was covered with sheer drapes. He watched Albert move away toward the front gate. He would undoubtedly be going back and forth in long sweeps while collecting the leaves. He would periodically have to empty the large container in the back, which he did by taking the tractor to the backyard and dumping the leaves over the bluff and into the bushes and trees down below.

Ben watched him for ten to fifteen minutes, going back and forth, back and forth, until he had to go out back and dump the basket. That took another ten minutes or so, but eventually Albert was back picking up where he had left off. Ben knew this entire process would take most of the day, even with the tractor. The good news was that Ben would always know where Albert was for most of the day. He was like a dog with a bell around his neck. The bad news is that he was out and about and Ben would be taking a chance if he decided to leave the house.

Ben went to the bathroom and peed. He waited until Albert was near the coach house before he flushed the toilet, confident that it couldn't be heard. He returned to the first bedroom to make sure that he hadn't left anything out of place, still holding onto his shoes. Satisfied that no one would notice that he'd been there, he went back out into the hallway and stood at the top of the stairs. He was hungry and he wanted to go back downstairs and raid the pantry. He probably didn't need to worry about Mary, at least not for the next couple of hours, as she was undoubtedly still asleep, and since he could tell where Albert was by the noise, he knew he could get something to eat without being noticed.

Downstairs, he hit the Ritz crackers again and peaked in the fridge to find an orange and a bottle of water. The problem with the first floor of the coach house was that there were a lot of windows. Even though Albert was fully occupied, Ben did not want to take a chance and get discovered by an odd glance.

He took his breakfast upstairs and ate in the middle bedroom. He figured that no one going upstairs would go to the middle bedroom first. He took frequent glances out the window to keep track of Albert as he ate. When he was finished, he put all of his trash into a small garbage bag he found under the sink in the bathroom and took it downstairs. Albert was now going back and forth in an area out in front of the space between the two houses and probably couldn't see Ben even if he had been looking in his direction.

Ben went back upstairs and laid down on the king-sized bed in the first bedroom, his feet crossed and his hands clasped behind his head. He had to come up with a long-term plan for his current situation. Just hiding out here wouldn't work. He would soon run out of what little food he had and certainly wasn't accomplishing anything either. He needed a shower, not to mention fresh clothes and a computer. Most importantly, he needed to make sure that his family was okay.

Sometime around noon, Ben heard the engine of the big tractor turn off. He had gotten so used to it that the silence was jarring. Albert must be taking a break for lunch. Since Mary was no doubt up and around by now, Ben had to keep his wits about him and stay out of sight. He looked at the small television sitting on the built-in dresser across the way. He needed to know what was happening. He got up and walked over to the TV, turned in on and lowered the volume so he could barely hear it. He found a news station and saw his own face staring back at him. Where had they gotten that photo? The anchor described him as missing following a search of his home by the authorities. Although the anchor emphasized that he had not been described as a suspect or person of interest, the undeniable implication was that the words "not yet" should be attached to that statement. Ben cursed and shut the TV off. He didn't need to see anymore. He pretty well knew the rest.

Albert finally finished the leaves in mid-afternoon and returned the tractor to the coach house garage, blissfully unaware that Benjamin Lohmeier stood upstairs, his eyes and ears peeled to prevent discovery. Ben listened to the distant sounds of Albert tinkering in the garage and made a snap decision, figuring he wasn't getting anywhere, and simply went downstairs and through the family room, into the kitchen and out through the door connecting to the garage. Albert was three garage bays over, his back to Ben when the door opened. Startled by the noise, he turned and saw Ben standing there, his hand still on the handle of the door. His eyes grew wide. "Hey," Ben said, "funny meeting you here."

Albert quickly regained his bearings and smiled. "Mary and I were worried. Glad to know you're someplace safe. This was probably a good choice. I'm glad you're here." Albert met Ben in the middle of the second garage bay. The two men shook hands. "What happened?" Albert said.

Ben gave him a sheepish smile and scratched his head. "It's a long story."

"When did you get here?"

"Last night, just after dark. I hung out at the library for a couple of hours before I came here. I hope you don't mind. I don't really want to drag you into this."

Albert was shaking his head before Ben had finished. "Don't worry about that," he said with a wave of his arms. "The important thing is that you're safe. Now we need to get to the bottom of this." He looked around. "Where's your car anyway?"

"It's in the garage next door," Ben said pointing. "I tried to get into the house over there, but couldn't and didn't want to break in. I eventually found a key for the art studio, but it's empty and the heat is turned off. I finally hopped the fence by the front gate at about midnight and came over here. I was lucky the door was unlocked."

Albert nodded. "We usually keep it open. No reason to lock it really. You're lucky Mary didn't see you. She was still up."

"I thought it was a lot later than that. Hanging out with no heat and no bed makes an hour seem like a week."

"Let me run over and get Mary. We can't hide this from her. You should probably stay out of sight until it gets dark. I doubt anyone would see you, but you don't want to take a chance."

"I agree."

Albert returned with Mary in less than five minutes. Ben saw Mary storm out of the big house, her coat unzipped, Albert trailing behind her. Ben waited for her in the kitchen, leaning up against the sink. She barged in the door, stood there and stared at him. Albert stood behind her on the steps. She pointed at Ben. "Did you do it?" she said.

Ben laughed. "What? Are you nuts? Of course I didn't do it."

She nodded. "Okay, I had to ask. I just wanted to hear you say it." Albert nudged her from behind and she stepped all the way into the room, Albert following and closing the door behind him. "So, tell me what happened." Ben did just that. When he was finished, Mary looked him right in the eye. "Now, tell me what you need."

Ben scratched his head. "The first thing I need is a shower and some food. And clean clothes. Or I could toss what I have into the washing machine and hang out in a bath towel or robe or something until they dry. I should have planned better, but this all happened pretty fast."

She waved him away. "That's the easy stuff. What do you really need?"

"I need a computer and Internet access, for starters. Then I need a couple of burner cell phones, those disposable ones you can get at the store, one for me and one for Libby so we can communicate without anyone knowing."

"Where's your phone?" Albert said.

"It's next door in the garage on the front seat of my car with the battery and SIM card taken out."

"Okay," Albert said. "The Internet and the computer are no problem. We have a couple of extra laptops next door. Internet access extends to the coach house here. You know that already. So that's no problem. The phones aren't a big deal either. Just make a list and we'll go out and take care of it."

"I'll pay you back when this is sorted out."

Albert waved away the thought. "Forget about it."

Ben found some paper and a pen in a drawer and made a list. They talked things through for a while, agreeing that it would make more sense for Ben to stay over at the big house since it was easier to avoid being seen. "I assume you're still going over to your sister's for Thanksgiving?" Ben said.

"Yes," Mary said, "we'll be leaving Thursday afternoon and coming back late Thursday night."

"Good, you can take a phone with you and give it to Libby and tell her that you've seen me and I'm alright. Then maybe you can send her back to my house to pick up some clothes and some of this other stuff, assuming she's not being watched. If she is, she's going to have to hide it somehow. She can figure that out. Then you can bring the stuff back here when you come home."

"That ought to work," Albert said.

Ben thought about it for a second. "I also think that you should talk to Libby privately, just the two of you or three of you. Don't tell anybody else I'm here. The less they know, the better. Don't even tell them that you heard from me. The less people that know, the better."

"I agree," Mary said. "We don't want anybody shooting their mouths off. Come to think of it, how long is this going to take? I mean, how long do you think you'll be here?"

"I don't know. No longer than necessary. I've put you guys in a bad enough spot already."

"Don't worry about that," Albert said shaking his head. "Stay as long as you need to. There's plenty of room and you need to get to the bottom of this."

They worked out a plan and Albert and Mary started out the door, before Mary turned and said, "stay here until it's dark. If you leave, go in through the back. It's usually pretty deserted around here this time of year, so I doubt anyone will see you. I think the people on the other side of us are gone, although they sometimes come out for the holidays. You better keep an eye out."

"Good enough. I'll throw my stuff in the washing machine and take a shower while you're gone. See you when you get back."

Ben watched them scurry back to the big house, grateful that they were here and he could count on them. He went upstairs, got undressed, threw his clothes into the washing machine and started it. As he made it back into the bathroom to take a shower, he saw out the window that the Sandfords were heading out the front gate, which closed slowly behind them. Ben figured that they would be gone for at least two hours, probably going all the way to the outlet mall in Michigan City, since they didn't have any real shopping options close by. It took them closer to three hours, but when they returned Albert was carrying three pizzas from the local Pizza Hut. After his clothes dried, Ben had gotten dressed and gone back over to the big house to wait for them to return. It was already dark outside. He was in the kitchen of the big house when they came in from the door to the garage. Mary had four shopping bags. Albert placed the pizzas on the island in the kitchen with a thump.

"We were going to get pizza anyway and you've got to be starving, so we picked it up on the way. I couldn't remember what you liked, so I got a veggie pizza, a cheese and a pepperoni. I seem to remember that you like pepperoni."

The pizzas looked and smelled great to Ben. "This is perfect. I'm starving."

Mary scurried about, closing blinds and curtains so people couldn't see in from the road. Meanwhile, Albert got out the plates and some silverware and Ben grabbed a slice of pepperoni and started chowing down. Mary came back an instant later and stood there, her hand on her hip, obviously with something on her mind.

"What is it?" Ben said.

She looked and saw that Albert had grabbed a slice of the veggie pizza for himself. "I see you couldn't keep the pig from feeding his face," she said. Both Albert and Ben laughed, their mouths full. "Not that I should be surprised. Anyway, here's what I think. I've closed all the drapes that face out toward the road. We can do the ones upstairs too. We should be pretty good from the beach side since the only way for anyone to see in would be to walk across the backyard. The gate and the fence should keep that from happening. If you stay over here, we shouldn't have any problem with anyone on the beach side of the property. As long as you don't go outside, even if the people on this side are around, they shouldn't see you either, not that I think they would necessarily know you if they saw you from a distance."

"Better safe than sorry," Albert said after he swallowed.

"I agree," Ben said. "No need to tempt fate."

"I think you should stay upstairs in the room on the beach side. No one should notice anything." She looked at him. "I see you did some laundry. I bought you a few things anyway in case Libby has some problems getting your stuff together at Thanksgiving."

They went out to the table in the front screened-in-porch to eat. The house had porches on each end, that were really just family rooms since they were fully heated and Mary rarely opened the windows. The blinds were down and they had all the privacy they needed. As they ate, Mary started pulling stuff out of the shopping bags. In addition to four burner phones and a couple of other electronic items, she had bought another pair of jeans, some T-shirts, underwear and socks, two long sleeved shirts and a sweater. Ben was now good to go. They talked about things for a while as they ate.

"This really hit the spot," Ben said as he finished yet another slice of pizza. "I was really getting hungry over there." He looked around. Mary had already begun the task of putting up Christmas decorations. The house was so large that all the decorating she did took many, many hours. They talked about her decorations, something she was always willing to discuss.

"We still need to go out and get a tree," she said. She usually kept a 14-foot artificial tree up in the great room year-round, but often liked to get a live tree as well during the Christmas season. "You guys always go to one of those do-it-yourself places, don't you? Those places where you cut down your own tree? You always have such a nice tree."

"Yeah, we do," Ben said. "We've been going to the same place for a few years now. It's not all that expensive, all things considered, and you get a really good, fresh tree when you cut down your own. If I had a house, one like this, with the big tall ceilings, I shudder to think the size tree Libby would be insisting on."

They talked about Christmas and Christmas decorations for a while, before eventually coming back around to Thanksgiving. Thanksgiving was always a big event in Libby's family and it was hosted by her parents virtually every year. More than twenty people typically attended and they had as many as four or five full turkeys and a couple of turkey breasts, oven roasted ones, deep-fried ones and even a couple on the grill, together with all the fixings. The desserts frequently included as many as eight to ten pies and, all in all, it was quite a feast. Libby would typically make two or three apple pies, a cherry pie and maybe a blueberry pie or a custard pie as well. Mary also brought a couple of pies, including a pumpkin pie, which Ben always enjoyed. "You know," Ben said, "I'm really going to miss all the food this year."

"There's always leftovers," Albert said. That was true. The large amount of food was planned to provide enough leftovers.

"There'll be enough food there to feed an army," Mary said. "We'll bring you back whatever you want. I'll make sure you see some of my pumpkin pie. What kind of turkey do you want?"

"I like it all," Ben said. "Oven roasted, deep-fried, grilled, whatever. As long as it's white meat, I'm good. You can bring some stuffing and mashed potatoes too, but let's face it, turkey is the star of the show. That and some of the pies."

Albert laughed. "You know, you talking about cutting down your own Christmas tree kind of got me thinking. They could do that with turkeys." Mary looked at him sideways. "No, really,

345

think about it. You could go to a farm and pick out your own turkey, kind of like you can do with your lobster at an expensive restaurant. You pick out your own turkey and they could kill it for you." She gave him the evil eye once again.

"I like that," Ben said. "But you can make it better than that. Sure, you could have somebody there to take it and kill it and cut the head off and all the other stuff. That would be one thing. You could also make it so that they put you in the pen and give you a hatchet and tell you to have at it. You pick it out, you catch it, you cut the head off, you take care of the guts and feathers. Maybe they've got a machine or something there that you can run it through to get rid of the feathers. It can be a real family event."

Albert chimed in. "You've got headless turkeys running around, blood and guts flying everywhere."

The two men were laughing now. They tried to flesh out their idea of the do-it-yourself turkey farm. Mary got up from the table, dishes in hand and looked from one to the other. "You two are sick, you know that? You two are effing sick." Then she left the room. The laughter continued behind her.

54

They got to work after dinner. Ben and Albert went upstairs to find the extra laptop and get Ben back online. Albert had a computer station/desk with multiple monitors set up in his large office upstairs. The room contained separate spots for Albert and Mary, together with a long conference room-style table and seating area in front of a rustic fireplace. A powerful telescope looked out the window to the west, toward the lake and downtown Chicago miles and miles away in the distance. Ben set up the laptop on the conference table and fired it up. Albert gave him the login and he was good to go.

He was clearly all over the Internet, as well as the television, and some of the information was not very flattering. Some outlets were speculating that Ben was indeed the killer, while others thought he was more likely the latest victim of the killing spree. Fox seemed to hold out some hope that Ben was neither guilty nor a victim, which he appreciated. He was certain, however, that they were simply keeping their powder dry, thus enabling themselves to move in either direction should facts on the ground prove difficult. Ben cursed under his breath.

Albert turned. "What?"

"Just reading about myself."

"That must be hard to get used to."

"Yeah."

Then Ben and Albert went at it separately in relative silence for a long time, before Mary yelled up the stairs. "Turn on the

TV," she said. "It looks like they just picked up Ray Fisher." Albert was closer to the TV and turned it to CNN. Fisher had indeed been spotted going into a Los Angeles police station. He did not appear to be in handcuffs, so perhaps he had gone in voluntarily for some reason or another. They watched for a few minutes and Mary came up and joined them. "What do you make of that?" she said. Ben didn't know what to think and said so. "Do you think he could behind all this?"

"All I know about Fisher is pretty much what I've seen on television," Ben said. "I've always had sympathy for the guy, but he does make it difficult sometimes. He just never lets up. I don't know what to make of this though. It would seem like Fisher would kill Owens, if anybody, not a bunch of lawyers."

"Maybe Owens would be the last one to go."

"Maybe," Ben said, "but he's got to be on the lookout now. He certainly is rich enough to afford security."

They watched for a while until the story started repeating itself and then turned the TV off and got back to work. Although they didn't really get much accomplished, Ben felt better being able to talk through some of it with Albert. The Sandfords went to bed at about eleven, with Ben staying in the home office and plodding along until after one o'clock, when he could barely keep his eyes open. He reluctantly headed off himself.

Wednesday brought more of the same. With his face plastered all over the television and the Internet, he now knew that he couldn't go anywhere without risking being recognized. He decided he needed to change his appearance. As he hadn't shaved since Monday, he now had a two- day growth of stubble, though that wasn't too significant since Ben did not have a particularly heavy beard. Yet, it would eventually grow into a completely different look if he let it go long enough. His dark blonde hair, never worn particularly long, was now inching over his ears and he was in need of a haircut. He thought about that. He could either die his hair, or cut it all off. Coupled with the beard, he expected that it would radically change his appearance.

He discussed the idea with the Sandfords on Thanksgiving morning and they knocked around the various possibilities. Ben had a clippers at home that he used to cut his son's hair and he added it to the list of things for Albert and Mary to have Libby pick up from the house, including his electric razor as well. Mary also decided to stop by the store and buy a couple of boxes of hair dye to try out. Like most men, Ben had never thought about dying his hair and was somewhat mortified by the prospects. Nevertheless, it could make him virtually unrecognizable, thus giving him at least some semblance of freedom of movement.

The Sandfords left for Illinois at about one o'clock. That meant that Ben would be alone in the big house for at least the next ten hours or so. He decided to take full advantage of it by putting together his plan of action now that they were gone. During the next couple of hours, he put together a plan that he hoped would lead to some progress in figuring out who was responsible for the deaths of the lawyers.

By the time the Sandfords got home, it was close to midnight and Ben had been chomping at the bit. Ben was in the kitchen grabbing a snack when he heard the chime that indicated that the front gate was opening. He peeked through the blinds to see the headlights of the Sandfords' car dancing off the trees. Soon, he could hear the garage door go up and a moment later Mary Sandford was coming in from the garage carrying Ben's leftovers. "Albert's out in the garage with a couple of boxes of stuff for you."

Ben hurried out and met Albert coming up the steps carrying a large plastic tote box filled with clothes and miscellaneous items. Ben started to reach for it and Albert said, "I've got this one. There's a second one in the trunk." Ben stepped aside and let Albert by, then retrieved the second tote box from the trunk of the car and headed back inside himself, hitting the button for the garage door on his way by.

"Any problems?" Ben said as he joined Albert in grabbing a small piece of turkey from a foil container on the kitchen island.

"We sent Libby back over with the list," Mary said, "and she came back with all the stuff. You should be good for a while. I have your electric razor and the clippers in there somewhere. I'll run out tomorrow to get the hair dye."

349

Ben was just finishing his slice of cold turkey. "How was she?"

Mary was taking off her coat. She put her hand on his arm and peered at him over the top of her glasses. "That poor girl was scared to death. She's not sure about all this, but she'll go along with it. I think they'll head over to her parents' house tomorrow. She wanted to tell everyone since they were already talking about it, but we told her that that wasn't the best idea and she eventually agreed. We gave her the phones. I'm sure the kids are in bed already so you should go upstairs and give her a call. Remember, this has been hard on her too."

Ben took one of the tote boxes upstairs to his room, then came back down right away and picked up the second one. Mary was scolding Albert for eating like a pig as she herself stuffed a bite of turkey into her mouth. "We're heading up to bed in a minute," she said. "I'm tired. Now go and call your wife."

Ben wanted to talk to Libby in the worst way. He sat on the edge of the bed for a moment before finally dialing the phone. She picked up on the fourth ring, probably to make him wait. It was great to hear her voice, even though he could tell that he had put her through a lot and that her emotions were a jumbled combination of worry, anger and fear. Since the phones only had a limited number of minutes, Ben told her that they needed to keep the conversation short. The Sandfords had given her two phones and Ben promised to call her at least every few days or so. By the time they were through talking, she was crying and Ben also had tears in his eyes.

"I love you," she said in a choked voice as they were about to hang up.

"Me too, more than anything. Tell the kids I love them and give them a kiss for me. I'll be home as soon as possible."

Mary Sandford came back with the hair dye at about noon on Friday. She had two packages, one black and the other an auburn red. "Jeez," Ben said when he looked at them. "I can't see myself with black hair, or red hair either, for that matter. Maybe I should just shave my head and be done with it."

350

"You can always do that," Mary said, "if this doesn't look right." She held up the box with the auburn color next to Ben's head. "I would try this first. You've got kind of a pasty complexion already so this color might work best."

"Thanks a lot," Ben said with a grimace. He glanced over at Albert, who was laughing. She reached into the bag and pulled out a set of rubber gloves. Ben groaned. "Are we sure about this?"

She snapped the gloves on like a surgeon preparing to operate. "Yep, we are. Let's get started."

They did it in the kitchen sink, with Mary in charge and Albert observing, always appearing amused. Ben balked when she got to his beard, which still hadn't really grown in enough to dye yet. "Wait a minute," he said. "You're just going to wind up dying my face with that." By the time they were done and Ben's hair had dried, he had to admit that he looked completely different. Once the beard grew in, he would not be easily recognized. Still, he wasn't sure he could stomach the hair color. They stood in the kitchen, under the bright lights turned all the way up, and Mary and Albert eyed him carefully. "What do you think?" Ben said.

"I kind of like it," Albert said. He rubbed his face. "When the beard comes in better, maybe you could do a goatee or something. I would probably recognize you if I looked carefully because I know you. I don't think it would be really easy for anybody else though."

Mary continued to study him. "I'm not sure," she finally said. "I agree that this color probably looks better than the black. The black would've looked too fakey. I just wish your hair grew faster. That might make a bigger difference."

Ben went into the bathroom to look at himself in the mirror. He came back unimpressed. "I hate it," he said. "I get it, but I hate it."

"Give it a couple of days," Mary said. "If it's not better by then, then you can always go with a buzz cut."

Albert was nodding. "You know what they say, the difference between a good haircut and a bad haircut is two weeks. If you

351

went with the buzz cut and the goatee, you would look like a neo-Nazi or something. I don't think people would recognize you then."

Ben gave it until Monday morning, still hated it, then took out the clippers, put on the guard for 3/8 of an inch, then took to his own head. He was in the bathroom down the hall from the kitchen and Mary came in when she heard the sound of the clippers. "Let me have that," she said. "You'll wind up cutting your ear off." She took the clippers from his hand and turned him around. Albert came in a moment later with a broom and within five minutes, Ben had yet another new look. His beard was now a week old, and while it came in darker than his hair color, it didn't at all match the reddish buzz cut he was now sporting.

Mary looked at him with her arms folded and her hand on her chin. "You're going to have to do something about the beard," she said.

A week later, Ben and Albert were up in the office eating leftover Chinese food for lunch. The hair color had toned down a bit after ten days of washing so that it didn't look that much different from the beard, but different enough from his normal color to probably hide his identity. Ben had shaved the beard into a goatee with long sideburns and Mary insisted that he looked like a cross between a truck driver and a convict. "You look a little like that guy on *Breaking Bad*," she had said the night before. Ben wasn't sure that was a compliment. He knew that he could also wear his glasses if he went out anywhere, rather than the contact lenses he typically wore. In fact, he had never appeared on television in his glasses, and between the hair, the beard and the glasses, he felt like he could now go out without being recognized.

They sat and ate in relative silence, both men frustrated over their lack of progress. "We must be missing something," Ben finally said.

"Maybe we're just looking at it the wrong way," Albert said. "Maybe you've already eliminated possibilities that you shouldn't have eliminated. Look, we've pretty much agreed that it has to somehow involve the Owens case, one way or another. We've eliminated certain people, some because they're dead, and others because it doesn't seem to make sense. Maybe our assumptions are off."

Ben stuffed a pot sticker into his mouth and thought about that. After a minute, he said, "okay, let's think about that a little. Maybe we have eliminated people or theories that we shouldn't have. We're not getting anywhere the way things are." They spent the rest of the afternoon going through some ideas based on that theory.

Within a couple of hours, Ben had hit on a rather far-fetched idea, one they decided they were going to pursue until they proved it wrong. By the end of the day, they had not proven it wrong. By the end of the following day, the seed that had been planted in Albert's offhand remark had now grown into a glimmer of hope.

They did most of their research on the Internet, although Ben also used the burner phones fairly extensively. Albert had bought another half-dozen of them at Best Buy and they were literally burning through them between the research and his conversations with Libby, who was growing increasingly frustrated over his failure to return home. Over Albert's objection, they had eliminated Stan Feldman as a suspect and Ben had been talking to him fairly regularly and using his friend in California as another research assistant. Although Ben kept in touch with Nelson too, he didn't tell Nelson what they were working on right away.

When Ben had told Feldman about the theory they were considering, Feldman originally told him that they were nuts, but the more they talked, even Feldman agreed that it was an idea at least worth eliminating. Feldman volunteered to help out any way he could and Ben had given him a list of things to follow up on, each of which required somewhat tedious work at the courthouse, various county buildings and elsewhere. Ben signed off and then went back to work on his own part of the puzzle. An hour later, Ben called Feldman back and told him to hold off. "I need you to talk to some people instead," Ben said.

"Who do you have in mind?" When Ben told him, Feldman said, "I know her already. I met her a few times over the years at various functions. A nice woman. Have you got any numbers?"

"No."

"That's okay, I can get them."

"That would be good. I'll do some of the property research. I think I need a pass code to get into the system though. Obviously, I don't want to give anyone my real name."

"No problem, I'll give you mine."

They talked again the following afternoon. "You know, I have actual work I'm supposed to be doing," Feldman said. "This took me all afternoon yesterday and into the evening. I even had to go over to her house. Then I was back at it again this morning."

"But did you make any progress?"

"Actually, I did. A lot. Nothing that disproves your theory, which is interesting. And a little unexpected."

"Good."

"I felt like an ass the whole time."

"Sorry about that. It goes with the territory. Did you get any addresses?" Ben said. Feldman gave him the addresses and property numbers for three parcels. "We already had two of those, but not the third. The two we had already have been bought and sold a bunch of times over the years. Especially the last five years or so. I can't tell if there was any actual consideration paid, or how much, maybe I'm looking in the wrong place, but the whole thing kind of smells. Lots of corporations and stuff involved, but I did come up with a name I would like you to check out."

"Okay, what is it?"

"Richard Burton."

"You mean like the actor? Liz Taylor's husband?"

"Yeah, like the actor. I came across his name a couple of times in corporate or property records. I'm not sure if he's a lawyer or maybe even an alias."

"Now that you mention it," Feldman said, "that name rings a bell for me too and not just because he was Liz Taylor's husband. I think I stumbled across him somewhere too."

"Well, that makes sense. So, run his name, if you could, and let me know if you come up with anything."

"Will do."

"You know how this looks, don't you?"

"I know how it looks all right, but we still have a long way to go. We're not even to midfield yet. Don't think about spiking the ball yet."

"I agree, but when I came up with this idea, I was back inside my own 5 yard line and now I'm up to midfield. That's a lot of progress in a short amount of time."

Ben told Albert, who had been listening, what he had learned. "Hmmm," Albert said. "We may not be so crazy after all."

They were knocking it around some more when Mary came up the stairs in a hurry. "Turn on the TV, guys," she said. "Another dead lawyer."

"Shit," Ben said as Albert turned on the TV. They watched as the Fox anchor reported in excruciating detail about the death of Thomas Franchetti, a prominent LA criminal defense lawyer who had previously represented a famous pop star in a sexual abuse case. Franchetti had also been a TV talking head on and off for quite a few years, although he was probably less prominent than some of the others. His battered and naked body had been found in an alley outside of a seedy bar in South Central LA.

The three of them watched the TV in silence, Ben leaning forward with his elbows on his knees, Mary biting her nails, and Albert, his hands folded across his chest and occasionally looking away. What had apparently been done to Franchetti was pretty wretched, beaten to death and all. "Did you know him?" Mary finally asked.

Ben looked down and rubbed his head. "No, only through TV."

"Brutal," Albert said shaking his head.

Ben stood up and paced around the room as the details of Franchetti's death were broadcast to millions. He walked around some more and finally sat down at the big table and looked back at his wife's aunt and uncle. "We've made a lot of progress and I think there's a reasonable chance that we know who did it, but we can't prove anything. Obviously, if we can't prove what we think we know, at least we can get me off the hook for good and give the authorities someone to focus on. That might at least put him back in his box and keep more dead lawyers from turning up."

"How are you going to do that?" Albert said.

"I don't know yet."

"Do you really think he did it?" Mary asked.

"I do. It feels right," he said. "It feels right."

55

Ben made significant progress over the next several days. With each passing hour, he became more and more convinced that he was on the right track. While he still knew that it was possible that he was wrong, he nevertheless felt that feeling in his gut that told him that he was right. Christmas was approaching fast and Ben was getting antsy. He missed his family and he wanted to drive this thing to a conclusion. A couple of days later, things were even more firmed up when he got a telephone call from Stan Feldman. "What have you got?" Ben said.

"A lot of nothing," Feldman said. When Ben groaned, Feldman said, "no, that's not bad. It's good. I've had my source run Richard Burton, our Richard Burton, against the known databases. The government may have a database or two that we can't get into, but the ones we got into should cover it unless he's an undercover CIA operative or something, which I doubt. Anyway, the records for our Richard Burton only go back about five years or so. Before that, he doesn't exist."

"Really?"

"Yeah, he doesn't exist. The driver's license is legitimate and the Social Security number is legitimate, although that number apparently belonged to a separate Richard Burton from Venice, California, who died in 1997. Our Richard Burton apparently just took his identity and Social Security number and moved on."

"Tax records?"

"None."

"No income?"

"Apparently not."

"Got a picture from his driver's license?"

"Yep, I do. He's a little older and wearing a hairpiece and beard, but I'm pretty sure it's our guy. No, I know it's our guy. I knew him, er, know him. I've got a stack of stuff I can send you, but that's the upshot."

"Bingo."

"I hate to admit, but I have to say that I think you're right. I think we can confirm that he's using the name Richard Burton. I couldn't get all his bank and credit card records, obviously, but the feds should be able to do that and when they do, that should help too. But remember, none of this proves that he killed anybody. We think he did and logically it makes sense, but it doesn't prove it."

Ben thought about that. "You're right, it doesn't prove it, but maybe once they get to some of these properties he owns, that might lead to other evidence that could implicate him in one or more of the killings."

"I agree. What are you going to do now?" Feldman said.

"I've been thinking about that. I've been trying to think of a way to push him out into the open without exposing myself or my family."

"But how do you do that?"

"Well, I was thinking of contacting Loretta Bergen."

Feldman thought about it for second. "How soon?"

"Tonight, maybe tomorrow. I think maybe I'll sleep on it and then decide."

"Okay," Feldman said. "It may just work. If we're right."

Ben talked about it with Albert and Mary over dinner. They ate in the dining room and each of them knew that they had reached a turning point.

"Well, something's got to give," Mary said.

They finished dinner, cleaned up the few dishes, before Albert and Mary decided to go downstairs to the movie room to watch *Game of Thrones*.

358

Ben stretched his back. "I think I'm going for a walk down to the beach." He had frequently been taking walks down to the beach in the evening after it got dark. Mostly, he stayed on the deck that overlooks the beach, enjoying the fresh air and thinking things through.

"Take my black jacket and waterproof gloves," Albert said. "You can take those boots out by the back door too, if you like."

"Okay, thanks. I saw that it's supposed to snow tomorrow and I might not get back down there for a while. It'll help me clear my head and make up my mind about what to do."

"If you're going to take the tram, remember you have to flick it on with the switch by the back door," Mary said.

"I'll probably just walk down then call the tram and ride back up when I'm done. It's more than a hundred steps. Down is easy. Up is the pain in the ass."

"A guy like you could use the workout," Mary said.

Ben pulled on Albert's black squall coat, took a knit hat off of a hook in the mud room and went on out into the hallway and flicked the switch for the tram, before stepping into the boots and heading outside.

He stepped out into the cold night air and paused to put on the hat and gloves and zip up the jacket. He walked down the stone steps and out across the back yard toward the tram. The night was clear and cold, probably about 30°, he thought, and the light from a full moon peeked through the trees casting dark shadows that looked like giant arms waving in the stiff breeze off the lake. He got to the tram, thought about it for a second, then took the steps. A hundred or so steps later, he reached the end of the line for the tram, and took the remaining steps down to the deck level. He looked back up the steps. A light on a pole at the top of the steps shone down at him.

He considered going all the way down to the beach and looked out at the rolling surf crashing on the shore. The wind was blowing directly in off the water and he could see the reflection of the spray dancing in the bright moonlight. He decided to head over to the deck instead, and stood on top of the bench that circled the deck and gazed out at the water, his gloved hands in his pockets, the hat pulled tightly down over his ears. The waves pounded the shore and he watched the rhythmic rolling of the surf for a long time before finally turning, hopping down and heading over to one of the two cabana chairs, flipping up the cover, and taking a seat. He found the deafening roar of the wind and surf relaxing and peaceful.

He leaned back in the chair, made himself comfortable, and closed his eyes. He thought of Richard Burton and the demons that drove him. He thought of the jealousy, hatred and resentment that compelled him to kill Marty Kessler, Spencer Laughlin, Jimmy Moran, Bobby Joe Gibbons, Nicholas Karras, Thomas Franchetti and probably Patrick Lindsay as well. Where was Richard Burton now? Was he out there hunting another victim? Ben felt safe enough now, hiding here at the beach, but for how long? The man had undoubtedly been in Ben's garage and had planted evidence implicating him in one or more of the murders. The anger welled up inside him.

Ben had done a good job of hiding it in recent days, but he knew in his own heart that much of his activity had been fueled by a fury over the fact that he too had been targeted. While the killer had not tried to kill Ben too, at least not yet, Ben had undoubtedly been targeted in another way by trying to make him look responsible for the killer's own crimes. And by doing so, he'd also put Ben's family in jeopardy. He looked out at the waves. It would all be over soon. One way or another, it would all be coming to a head very soon. He closed his eyes and thought about what to do.

After a while, Ben had to pee. He took off the hat and laid it on the chair as he got up. His head was sweating. He walked over to the back corner of the deck, stuffed his gloves into his pockets, then unzipped the jacket and his fly and peed into the brush at the back corner of the deck. When he was done, he zipped up his pants, turned and stretched his back again. It stiffened up any time he sat in one place for too long. As he started back toward his seat, he saw a shadow flash across the steps heading down from the tram to the deck level. Startled, he assumed for a moment that Albert had come down to join him, something he had done a couple of other times over the past week or two. But Ben had not expected him this evening. He stepped behind the cabana chairs and into the shadows to see who was coming. The rolling surf was too loud to hear footfalls and the shed blocked the view of the bottom of the steps where the tram let off.

He moved to the back of the cabana chairs where the deck ended and looked back toward the steps. The light from the top of the track, combined with the brightness of the moon lit some areas of the deck, while other parts were cast in dark shadow. Ben hid in the darkness, while the area at the top of the steps to the beach opposite the path to the deck was fairly well-lit.

Ben looked down the line formed by the back of the deck behind the cabana chairs and through the bushes and out toward the steps coming down from the tram. He saw the shadow move first, then a dark figure passed by about fifty or so feet away. It certainly wasn't Albert Sandford. The figure was taller and leaner than Albert, and dressed all in black, from head to foot.

Ben froze. He didn't know what to do. If the figure moved toward the deck, Ben would be trapped with nowhere to go. If he stepped out from behind the cabana chairs, he would be easily seen, even in the shadows. He listened carefully. All he could hear was the roar of the surf and the howling wind. He looked out toward the beach. Nothing there to help him. He looked back down the line for the steps. Nothing there. The beam of a flashlight slashed across the deck behind him. He made a decision, took a deep breath, removed the gloves from his pockets, put them on, and hopped off the deck into the brush and started climbing up the hill.

Ben reached up for his hat before remembering that he had left it on the cabana chair. He cursed under his breath. Then he pulled the hood up tight around his head and kept moving. He was grateful for the gloves. The boots were loose, as he had never tied them, and he struggled to keep them on his feet. The wild undergrowth twisted in front of him in all manners and directions, and the branches tore at Ben's arms, legs and body through his clothes. His face was scratched and he could taste blood in his mouth. Still he kept moving.

He tried to stay directly above the cabana chairs until he saw a denser thicket of bushes about twenty feet up the hillside and a little to his left. He moved in that direction, crab-like, at first trying to be as quiet as possible, but ultimately realizing that the sound of the wind and the lake would likely drown out anyone's ability to hear him thrashing through the brush.

He reached the thicket in fits and starts, now about forty feet or so above the surface of the deck and crouched in the center of the branches. A few of the leaves remained on the bushes and he huddled among them. He was beginning to get to the area now where some of Albert's leaves had filtered down the side of the bluff and Ben scooped at them in an effort to pull a pile over himself to use as cover.

He glanced down toward the deck. Ben could not see the figure in black, but he could see the flashlight beam bouncing over the deck and out toward the beach. He hunkered down and waited. He once again pulled the black hood down to cover as much of his face as possible. He took off the gloves and tied one boot, then the other. Then the flashlight beam turned and swung up toward the bluff. Ben didn't want to look, but could not help himself. The figure, tall and dark, his face in the shadows, appeared and looked into the brush below where Ben was hiding. He held the flashlight in one hand and what appeared to be Ben's hat in the other.

The beam from the flashlight moved back and forth in long arcs and slowly rose up the bluff. There was another thicket, a bigger one, about fifteen feet above Ben's position and another fifteen feet over toward the tram. He certainly couldn't go for it now and thought it might bring him much too close to the tram and the steps alongside it. The arc of the flashlight moved closer and closer. It was now about twenty feet below him. He knew he was dressed all in black, which helped, and he pulled the hood down as far as he could and tucked his chin into his chest. He wondered if the coat had any reflective patches. He hoped not. All he could do was hope that he would be hidden enough to avoid detection. The seconds passed slowly, the arc of the flashlight getting closer and closer. It swung back and forth further up the slope. Finally, the beam of the light passed over him, once, twice, three times, four, and blissfully without hesitation as it moved on up the bluff. From the center of the thicket, petrified and completely still, Ben waited. The flashlight arcs moved on. Above him, the arcs moved in a wider and wider swaths as they traveled up the bluff and eventually the figure in black pivoted and turned away. Ben sighed in relief.

He looked down at the figure, now in profile. He could not see the man's face, but this was no random event. He thought about Richard Burton, the killer's alter ego. Ben had never seen him in person, only on television, and that was largely from the chest up. He had no real feel for the size of the man. The man down below was a large man, at least six foot two or three, but Ben did not have a feel for his age and could not get a good look at his face. The man turned suddenly and moved away from the back of the deck.

Ben scrambled further up the bluff. He looked out to try and get a feel for where he was on the slope. He certainly could not see the top, but sensed that he was far closer to the bottom than to the top. He moved up and to the right, figuring that he needed to get further away from the steps and the tram. He assumed that the flashlight beam would be coming from the steps next. He pushed up the bluff through the trees, bushes and the tangled, overgrown brush until he moved deeper and deeper into the bank. He could taste the rotting leaves and feel them in his hair and in his clothes. On top, they were damp and stank. Underneath, they were drier and less slimy and offensive.

He continued to climb, his hands and feet thrashing through the dense foliage. The branches clawed at him. He angled away from the tram, which he now could not even see. He entered a more open area where the moonlight had managed to squeeze through the trees. He felt exposed and vulnerable. He dug onward, though he was growing very tired, and climbed further up the hill. The dry remnants of a dead branch tore at his cheek. He suddenly found himself back in the dark at the base of a small group of trees. He curled in and covered himself with a large pile of mostly dry leaves.

Then the flashlight beam swept toward him from the steps next to the tram. The light from the flashlight was searching below him and to his left. The beam moved up the bluff as the figure holding the flashlight climbed the steps. Ben figured he would now get a better sense for his position on the side of the hill. The light moved further and further away from him until they were out of view behind a small group of bushes. After a few moments, Ben saw the arcs of the flashlight coming down from the top of the bluff. He dug in, held his breath and remained still once again. He estimated that he was in a position roughly in the middle of the bluff and between sixty and eighty feet from the steps.

A few minutes later, the flashlight beam drifted away and disappeared entirely. Ben could breathe again. He still didn't know where the figure was, where he was going, or how long he would remain there. He paused, thought of Albert and Mary up at the big house with the killer out in the yard, then moved further on up the bluff. He was all-in now, in the middle the bluff, he could either go up or go back down, or head toward the steps. He decided to go up, exhausted though he was.

He climbed through the leaves, the brush and the bushes, in short bursts, with brief pauses to rest and regain his strength, before continuing to clamber up the hill again, occasionally slipping back down. Eventually, he could not tell how long had passed, Ben looked up and appeared to see the crest of the slope above him. He paused one last time, then pushed onward toward the top of the bluff. He reached the crest and carefully peered over toward the big house in the distance. He scanned from left to right, then back again several times, looking for the figure in black and not seeing him.

He crawled over the hill into one of Mary Sandford's flowerbeds. He lay flat on his stomach and waited, straining to hear the sounds of anyone coming. All he could hear was the wind and the surf howling down on the beach below him. He searched the grounds again, back and forth, back and forth, looking for the intruder. Finally, as satisfied as he could be that the man had gone, Ben pulled himself to his feet and crossed the backyard as quickly as possible, rounded the big brick wall to the steps leading up to the back door of the big house. He tumbled through the back door, and thoroughly exhausted, collapsed on the floor of the back hallway.

A moment later, Albert Sandford strolled in from the kitchen and saw him lying on the floor, cut, bruised and a dirty mess, his clothes and face covered with the debris and detritus of the bluff. Albert scrambled over to him and got down on his knees. "What happened? Are you okay?"

Ben rolled over onto his side, his voice a rasp. "Close the door. Hurry. And shut out all the lights."

Albert got to his feet. "Why? What happened?"

Ben coughed and looked up at him. "I saw him. He's here."

56

"What do you mean? What happened?" Albert's eyes were wide.

Ben rolled over onto his stomach and tried to push himself up. He coughed again. Mary hurried in seeing Ben lying there in a heap on the floor. "What the hell happened? We were about to send out for a search party."

Ben struggled up to his knees. "He's here. It had to be him. I saw him. He's here."

In her bathrobe and slippers, Mary was now down on her knees, her hands on Ben's shoulders. She looked into his face. "Jesus, what happened to you?"

Ben breathed in and out, trying to gather himself. "I was down at the beach, on the deck, when I saw shadows off to my right, coming down the steps. I thought maybe it was Albert." He looked over at the man, who knew, of course, that it wasn't him. "Then I stepped back behind the chairs and saw a figure pass by. It wasn't Albert. It was him, had to be."

"Who?"

Ben stared into her eyes. "I think you know who. Who else could it have been?"

Mary cursed. "Tell us what happened. No, wait a second. Let me get something for your face, help clean you up. Your mouth is bleeding."

She hurried off to the bathroom to get a first aid kit and Ben struggled to his feet as Albert helped him out of his filthy coat. Mary quickly returned.

"We've got to get away from these windows," Ben said. "We're sitting ducks standing here." They moved off into the kitchen. Ben had regained his breath and his senses, but his whole body burned from the exertion it took to climb the bluff. Albert got him a glass of water and he told them what had happened. When he was finished, Ben could see a mixture of shock and fear etched in their faces.

"You mean you climbed up the bluff?" Albert said. "I didn't think that was even possible."

Ben shook his head. "It is. Properly motivated."

Mary dabbed his face with a warm wash rag. "You're looking a little better," she said. "I hope you won't need stitches on your lip."

"I'll be fine. That's the least of our worries."

"Are you sure it was him?" Albert said.

Ben made eye contact with his wife's uncle. "Who else could it be?"

Albert got an idea.

"What?" Ben said.

"The security cameras. I can pull up the security cameras on my computer and see if they caught anything. Let's go."

They hurried upstairs and Albert fired up his desktop computer. Not quickly enough for Mary, who was almost frantic. "Where are the cameras located?" Ben asked as the computer came to life.

Albert punched in his password and swiveled his chair to face his wife and Ben, who were standing behind him and looking over his shoulder. "All around this house, around the perimeter, and the coach house as well." He gestured with his hands as he spoke. "Some of the cameras point out toward the yard, while others point straight down at the side of the building. There's also a camera near the front gate and another where the steps lead down to the beach, next to the tram."

Ben was excited. "He has to be on that one. That's how we came down to the beach, both of us."

Albert swiveled back and found the security program and called it up. After a couple of minutes of working through the menus, he got to the right place for the live footage for the cameras. They looked at the live footage first, set up on four split screen shots of six cameras each. The live feed was in black and white and the resolution was pretty decent. They scrolled through the four screens, totaling twenty-four camera angles, several times, seeing no discernible activity.

"Find the earlier footage," Mary said impatiently.

"That's in another part of the program," Albert said as he moved through the menus trying to find the right one. Eventually, he found it and they went to the camera by the tram first, backing up in much the same manner as you would on a DVR. "How long ago was it, can you remember?" Albert said.

Ben thought about it. "Probably at least twenty minutes or half an hour since he came back up the steps. I'm pretty sure he came back up the steps because I saw the flashlight coming from the top of the bluff later on. Maybe an hour or so from when he first went down, something like that. If you go back an hour or so, maybe a little more, we should be able to scroll through and find him."

Albert rewound the video feed in five minute increments. He went back ninety minutes, and then moved forward at double speed. At 49 minutes, a dark figure moved into the screen from the left, in three-quarter profile from behind. The camera was looking down on him from above. "There he is," Mary said.

Just as Ben had thought, the figure appeared tall and fairly lean, dressed all in black, and carrying a flashlight in his right gloved hand. "That almost looks like a scuba outfit or something," Albert said. The figure turned and was more or less in full view now, the camera looking down at him from above. He was obviously looking to see if anyone else was in the yard before deciding to proceed down the steps. "Can you print that shot?" Ben said.

"I think so." Albert fiddled with the controls until the print screen flashed. He hit send and a moment later, the printer at the end of his desk started to whirr and the screen shot spit out.

Mary pulled it off the printer and handed it to Ben, who studied it. "It sure looks like him."

He handed the photo to Albert. "Yeah, I think it does too." Albert handed the photo back.

"Keep going," Ben said.

Albert hit play and the figure jerked into motion. He looked over his shoulder, then briefly up in the direction of the light and the camera and Albert paused the screen just as Ben and Mary cried out simultaneously for him to do so. He quickly scrolled through the menu and printed a second photograph. Then he continued. The figure appeared to be considering what to do about the light, then looked over the wall at the top of the steps and down toward the bottom. He looked quickly back at the light, then back again, apparently having made his decision, then moved around the corner to the steps. The camera trailed him for about a third of the way down the steps and then eventually lost him off in the distance.

Albert hit the play button and fast forwarded in double, then triple and quadruple speed until the figure moved back into view thirteen minutes later. He hit play just as the figure, small in the distance at the bottom of the screen, appeared to shine the flashlight out over the bluff from the steps. He did that a few more times and moved closer to the camera before emerging with his head down and disappearing off the screen to the left. Albert fast-forwarded again for a few minutes of screen time, but the figure did not return.

"Can you save that"? Ben said.

Albert hit the pause button and then swiveled around in his seat and smiled. "No need to. It gets archived in the cloud somewhere. I can call it up by the date in 24-hour increments."

"About time one of your effing toys paid some dividends," Mary said.

They spent the next forty-five minutes scrolling through the camera footage outside both the big house and the coach house.

The footage from the big house didn't help much, only really getting a shadowy figure moving toward the tram out by the top of the bluff, then returning and pausing at the top of the bluff again to shine the flashlight down into the dense foliage below, before retreating off-screen to the left and in the direction of the coach house. He never got close to the house.

They had a somewhat better view of him picking through the bushes and trees at the back of the coach house, before crossing the gravel drive near the back gate and rounding the corner and heading up the fence line, just as Ben had done in reverse when he had first arrived several weeks earlier. They picked him up again as he hopped over the gate at the stone wall and disappeared into the night. "That's just what I did," Ben said with a point at the screen. They went back to the live feed and scanned the various cameras, finding nothing.

Ben and Mary sat down in front of the fireplace and Albert joined them. "How did he find you?" Mary said. There was no longer any doubt in any of their minds as to the intruder's identity.

Ben shook his head and scratched at his itchy beard. "I'm not sure," he said. He thought about it for a minute and shrugged. "It must've been the car. I can't think of any other way. He must either have hacked my GPS in the car or put a tracker on it somehow. Probably when he was in town planting that stuff at my house. He must have been there more than once. Or been to the office too."

"That doesn't mean he knows you're here exactly," Albert said. Ben looked at him quizzically. "I mean, your car's next door in an empty garage on a vacant property. He's probably looking up and down the beach to see where you might be. There's no reason to know for sure that you'd be here."

Ben nodded. "That's probably true, but it's unlikely that I would've gone far. I wouldn't leave my car a mile or two away. Wouldn't make sense. And how would I know that the house was vacant unless I knew someone that lived nearby. He might be over there right now sitting on the car, waiting for me to show. Maybe he's been in the house or the art studio." Ben

370

thought about it some more. "I doubt that he actually saw me. I left your hat on the cabana chair, but he may not have seen it or think it was done tonight."

"Or it may not have been yours," Mary said finishing the thought.

"I'm glad we left the car next door," Ben said. The others nodded. Ben looked from Albert to Mary. "I'm sorry I dragged you into this. I shouldn't have." Albert waved the thought away with his hand. "No, really. I've got to get out of here right away."

"Where are you going to go? You can't leave now. Like you said, he may be over there waiting for you to come and get your car," Mary said.

"Maybe, but I doubt he'll be over there in broad daylight. We can go over there and check the car in the morning and then I can hit the road."

Mary stood. She was clearly upset. "I'll be right back. Nervous bladder."

Ben looked over his shoulder and watched her leave the room. Albert eyed her as well. Ben looked back at Albert and asked, "do you have any guns in the house?" They had never discussed this before.

Albert stared back at him. "Mary doesn't like guns. I don't either, really."

"I didn't ask you whether you liked them. I asked you whether you had one. Or two."

Albert took a deep breath. "I've got two shotguns locked up in the basement. For hunting and skeet shooting. Not that I hunt."

"Any hand guns?"

"No. I got rid of them years ago. Mary didn't want them in the house."

"Nobody does, unless they really need them and they're not there. Any shells?"

Albert nodded.

Mary came back into the room and sensed immediately that they had been discussing something. "What?" she said.

371

The two men stood and faced her. "We're going downstairs to get the shotguns," Albert said in a soft voice. She nodded and said nothing.

Ben followed Albert down to the basement. Mary stayed up in the office. They went through the unfinished part of the basement, where the laundry and mechanicals were located and to a back cabinet behind the hot water heater that had a combination lock. It was a gun safe. Ben had been down there before, yet had never noticed it. Albert yanked on a pull-chain and a light over the adjacent workbench clicked on. He fumbled at the combination of the lock, not getting it right the first time, before finally getting it and opening the safe. Two shotguns stood vertically up against the back wall of the safe. There were two shelves at the top which contained various boxes of ammunition.

Albert took out the first gun and handed it over. It was a Remington, fairly old, but it appeared to be in good working condition. He would've expected nothing less from Albert Sandford. "That one only shoots birdshot." Ben didn't know much about guns, unfortunately, just what he learned as a prosecutor. He had been skeet shooting once and had been lucky to hit a moving target. Other than that, it had just been a few occasions during his Boy Scout days. He certainly wasn't an expert marksman.

Albert took out the second gun. It had a beautiful brown carved handle, on which the name *Albert Sandford* had been stenciled in gold script. It appeared to be a fine piece of equipment and looked very expensive. "This is a beauty," Ben said.

Albert nodded. "I had it made when I used to do a little skeet shooting over at the club. Haven't done that in years though. It's a 12 gauge. More stopping power, they said." Albert reached into the safe and pulled out six boxes of ammo, four for the Winchester and two for the Remington. Then he closed the door to the safe and locked it. He turned and looked at Ben. "She's doesn't like this," he said.

Ben nodded. "She'll like it a lot less if that lunatic breaks into this house and these guns are still locked in that safe."

They met Mary back in the office. She was sitting on one of the leather sofas in front of the cold fireplace. Albert held the Remington, while Ben had the Winchester. "Okay," Ben said, "I think we need to try and get some sleep." He looked at Albert. "Since you're the early riser, come and wake me when you get up. We can go over and check on my car when it's light out." He held up the gun. "We can take these with us. Then, I'll pack up and head out."

Mary turned and faced him. "Where will you go?"

Ben looked down at her. "Don't worry, I've got some ideas."

"What are you going to do?"

"I'm going to draw him away from here where we can catch him. Or kill him. Either works for me."

She stared into his eyes. She had often heard about the glare coming back at her, but had never witnessed it for herself. It gave her chills. "The asshole deserves it," she said.

"Yes. In the meantime, let's make sure all the doors are locked up tight, set the alarm and get to bed." He looked at the clock. "It's almost one in the morning. I need to get some sleep. Tomorrow's going to be a big day and I need to make a call."

57

Albert knocked softly on Ben's door about ten minutes after six. Ben was already up and getting ready to get into the shower after tossing and turning most of the night. "I'll meet you downstairs in a few minutes," he said through the door.

"Good enough."

Ben quickly showered and got dressed. He pulled on long underwear, jeans and a sweatshirt over a long-sleeved shirt. He knew he would be spending some time out in the elements later and he wanted to be prepared for it. He picked through his essential gear and left it on the bed. Then he went downstairs to find Albert on his first cup of coffee. He was wearing jeans and a flannel shirt. Mary stood next to him in her robe and slippers, drinking a glass of orange juice. Ben gave her the eye. She scowled. "I couldn't sleep."

Albert looked at him. "So what's the plan?"

Ben told them. Then they went upstairs to the office. Ben looked through the telescope, which was pointed out toward the lake. Although the sun was up, it was not visible. It was a cloudy, dreary day and bad weather would soon be moving in. Several inches of snow were expected throughout the day and into the evening. That would make traveling difficult, Ben thought.

They moved over to the sitting area in front of the fireplace and Ben told them what he needed. They had gathered up all of their research materials and stacked them on the large table to

Ben's left. Ben gestured at it. "Albert, I need you to take all of that and scan it, then send it to Stan Feldman. All of it. He has some stuff of his own, I'm sure. Anything you have on your computer, I want you to save it to a single file or one big file with subfiles, then email that to Feldman too. Put all of the electronic stuff onto a flash drive. You have a safe?" Albert nodded. "Take the flash drive and all of the paperwork we've accumulated and put it in the safe. Then delete everything off of your computer and shred any duplicates, notes or other paperwork that we don't need."

"Aren't you going to need that stuff later?"

"You'll have the stuff in your safe and what's on the flash drive, plus you will have already sent what you have to Feldman. You might want to delete the emails as well. Don't forget to empty your trash bin. When you've done all that, get the hell out of here for a couple of days. You won't need to be gone any longer than that. It should be over soon, hopefully by Christmas. Go anywhere. Grab a hotel room somewhere out here. Drive into the city, whatever. Just get out of the house. And don't come back until you hear from me or on the news that something good has happened. Got it?"

Ben looked from one to the other. They clearly didn't like it, but both nodded. "What about Libby?" Mary said.

Ben leaned forward. "Don't contact her or anyone else other than Feldman. Take your cell phones with you. I'll call you if I have to, but I shouldn't have to." Ben stood. "Are you ready to go next door and check on the car?" he said to Albert. The older man nodded and stood. They each grabbed a shotgun off of the table and headed back downstairs. Mary followed silently behind them.

Downstairs, Ben pulled on his leather jacket and Albert his barn coat. "I'm going to need those boots again," Ben said.

"No problem," Albert said. "I've got a couple of other pairs in the mud room."

A couple of minutes later, they were making their way across the backyard and toward the gate behind the coach house. Ben didn't really think that anyone would be waiting for them next door now that it was daylight, but they held their shotguns in the ready position as Albert punched in the code and the gate slid open. They worked their way around the back of the art studio and over to the rear of the garage, where Ben had previously left the door unlocked. There was no snow on the ground yet, which meant no tracks to see.

They entered the garage quickly with guns up and ready. It was empty. Ben circled the car. It appeared just as he had left it. His cell phone lay in pieces on the front passenger seat. Ben had considered the manner of the previous deaths, especially Bobby Joe Gibbons, and was concerned that perhaps Richard Burton had installed some sort of bomb in his car.

They turned on the interior light and Ben got down and looked underneath the car. Albert faced the back door with his shotgun ready. Though he did not find a bomb, Ben did find a magnetized GPS tracker affixed to the frame near one of the back wheels. "God dammit," he said. "here it is."

Albert moved around the side of the car. "What did you find?"

"Just like we thought, a tracker. That's how he found me." Ben got to his feet. "Let's go back to the big house."

Albert looked at him. "Are you just going to leave it there?"

Ben nodded. "Yep. That way I'll know exactly where he is, or least where he's going."

Ben started to walk past the older man, who reached out his hand and gripped Ben's arm. "It also puts a target on your back," Albert said.

Ben looked at him and smiled. "There's a target on my back whether I leave it there or not. This way, I've got some control over the situation. Don't worry," he said and patted Albert on the arm. "I've got it covered. I'm going to call in the cavalry."

They turned off the light and left the garage the way they came in, carefully looking in both directions, as they moved out from behind the art studio.

Mary came down a few minutes later, now dressed, and found Ben eating leftover chicken fried rice out of the container with a spoon. She shook her head. "I don't know how you can eat at a time like this. My stomach is churning, I'm so upset."

Ben swallowed. Then he gestured at her with the spoon. "I've got to keep up my strength somehow. It's going to be a long day and I have a lot of driving to do."

"I still think you're crazy," she said.

Ben shrugged and took another bite of the fried rice. "Maybe, but it is what it is."

He was ready to leave shortly before ten. He and Albert took his stuff over to the coach house and dumped it under the eaves outside the last garage stall. They went back over to the Finney property the same way they had before. Albert then went back around the front and opened the garage door as Ben started his car and backed out of the garage. He left the Finney property and backed through the gate at the coach house, stopping opposite his gear, and was loading the back of the SUV when Albert returned from next door. Ben looked at the Winchester and placed it carefully on the passenger seat. "You'll be getting that back soon enough," he said. "I hope I don't have to use it."

"You and me both," Albert said.

The two men shook hands and Albert slapped Ben on the shoulder. Then he smiled. "What?" Ben said.

"Your face. It looks even worse than last night."

Ben had thought the same thing when he looked at himself in the mirror while brushing his teeth earlier. "At least the bleeding stopped," he said. "I don't think I'll be needing any stitches. I look at it this way, it just makes me look more ruggedly handsome."

Albert laughed. "Be careful."

"Always," Ben said as he glanced over Albert's shoulder to see Mary standing across the way watching them through the window of the great room. When Ben noticed her, she turned and walked away. Ben got in the car, closed the door and gave Albert a thumbs-up sign before putting the car in gear and moving slowly through the gate, turning left on the private road. Within five minutes, he was on Interstate 94 heading back toward Chicago.

377

58

Ben put the pieces of his cell phone back together and plugged it into the car charger. He didn't care who knew where he was now. As he crossed back into Indiana, he noticed that snow flurries had begun to fall. Although traffic was light in the middle of the day, Ben recognized that the weather had the potential to make his day on the road a lot longer than he had planned.

Ben kept the SUV to the posted speed, not wanting to get pulled over with a loaded shotgun beside him on the front seat. He frequently checked his rearview mirror, aware that the man hunting him was back there somewhere, maybe on the road, maybe not. Just prior to the cut off for South Bend, he picked up the cell phone and dialed Stan Feldman in California."

"Not hiding anymore?"

"No need to now."

"I just got a bunch of stuff from your uncle. Is that all of it?"

"I don't know, maybe. But keep checking just in case he sends more."

"What do you want me to do with it? I've also got stuff of my own."

"I figured. I want you take all of the stuff you've got, print it out, and put it in a safe place. I haven't talked to Loretta yet. When I do, I may have her call you to confirm some of the stuff I tell her. If you want to send her some stuff so that she knows I'm not nuts, go ahead and use your best judgment. But make sure to put your stuff in a safe place and save it electronically too so that if anything happens, we can still get the information to the right people."

Then Ben told Feldman about his adventure on the bluff the previous evening. "Are you sure it was him?" Feldman said. "Never mind. It had to be. What's your plan?" Ben told him. "Are you already out on the road?"

"Yeah, I left about half an hour ago." They talked for a few more minutes and Ben signed off and called Marcia Roberts.

"Holy shit, Lohmeier! Is that really you?"

"Yeah, it's me. I need to talk to Loretta Bergen as soon as possible."

"Okay, but where are you? Where have you been hiding? We were afraid that you might be dead."

"I'm not dead. You were also no doubt afraid that I might be the killer, admit it."

"No, not exactly that, although they did take a bunch of stuff out of your house, you know that, right? I figured it was a setup, or least hoped it was a setup."

"It was a setup. Marcia, I really need to talk to Loretta now."

"Okay, I'll try and find her and have her call you. Is this number okay?"

"Yeah, this number is fine. Have her call me as soon as possible. It's important."

Ben stuck the phone into one of the cupholders. Then he waited. And waited. He was already in Illinois when his phone buzzed again. He picked it up and looked at the screen. He didn't recognize the number. He hit the green button and said, "hello?"

"Ben, is that you? It's Loretta."

"It's me. Thanks for calling me back."

"You created quite a stir, do you know that? Now, what do you need? I would ask you where you are and what you have been doing, but I have a sneaking suspicion that you wouldn't tell me anyway. So, why not just cut to the chase."

"Sounds good. I don't have the time to tell you everything, but I think I figured out who the killer is."

379

"It's not you?"

"Did you really think it was me?"

"Probably not, but I've been wrong before. Once or twice."

"It wasn't me. I guarantee you that it wasn't me. And I'm not going to be the next victim either."

"Then who is it?"

"William Delvecchio."

There was a long silence on the other end. "Ben, William Delvecchio is dead. He's been dead for years."

"No, he's not. And I can prove that. He's now going under the name Richard Burton, of all things. He found a guy named Richard Burton, and Delvecchio has assumed his identity. He's using Burton's name, Social Security number, everything. I can prove it. Maybe Delvecchio had Burton as his client, I don't know, but he's using Burton's identity. Burton has been dead for more than ten years."

"Okay, let's assume you're right. What's your proof?"

"I have lots of proof – driver's license records, corporate records, property records. We've talked to his wife, his kids and his alleged doctor. He's not dead and was never sick. Now, I don't know whether Jimmy Moran was the primary target, or whether he always planned on killing all of them. I just know there's no other reasonable explanation. We've got the proof that he's alive and none of it makes sense unless he's also the killer."

"You say we, who else is involved?"

"I talked to Stan Feldman a few minutes ago and I sent him some information with a lot of my research. The proof is there. Call Stan and he should be able to get you what you need."

"What else you want me to do?" Loretta said.

Ben took the next several minutes and told her. When he was finished, he could sense the wheels turning in her head. "I don't know, Ben, I don't have a lot to go on, at least until I see what Feldman can give me. You're asking a lot without a lot of proof."

Ben knew this argument was coming. "Don't worry, you won't get sued. You're a journalist. You can say anything and get away with it. Pass it off on what you were told by me, one of the most wanted men in the country right now. Pass it all off onto me. You won't get sued and I won't get sued either. That I can guarantee. And if I do get sued? I'm not worried about it. I know the proof I have and I know what the proof means."

"Okay, assuming Delvecchio is alive, why did he do it?"

"Isn't that obvious? Here he was, Chase Owens' lawyer, about to embark on the biggest case of his career, as the lead counsel in the trial of the century. And what happens? He gets pulled. But not fired. No, he gets demoted, so he's still on board, but gets none of the plum work and none of the glory when Jimmy Moran pulls a rabbit out of the hat and winds up with a not guilty he should never have gotten. What happened after that? Jimmy Moran became a bigger star. Marty Kessler became a big name in his field, a lot bigger than he was. Patrick Lindsay had a brief run at a renaissance."

"What about the others?"

"The others were making names for themselves as talking heads on cable TV. Remember Geraldo and all the others. Gibbons was on there almost every night, Laughlin too. Karras was on there and Franchetti too. They shot their mouths off on national TV, improved their profiles, generated more business, and made a lot of money. The other lawyers on the team basked in the glory of the victory. But what about Delvecchio? He was just the guy who got replaced. Sent to the showers, benched. He didn't even get to examine any of the key witnesses. He was like a glorified paralegal. That had to stick in his craw. All that glory, all that money going to all those other people, and not to him. I checked it out. His career didn't really go anywhere after the Owens trial. He didn't step up into the upper echelons of law practice in America, or even LA, his own backyard. No, he went right back where he was and had to watch everyone else benefit except him. Eventually, his marriage fell apart and I can only assume that's when he decided to die and come back as Richard Burton, the avenging angel."

"All of that is speculation," Loretta said.

"Informed speculation based on fact. Why else does he go off by himself, leave his family and friends behind, and fake an illness

381

and even his own death? Then he comes back unknown as a new man, Richard Burton, stealing the identity of a man who'd been dead already for years. Explain that to me."

"I can't. I can't explain it. It doesn't make any sense, but none of that means he killed anyone."

"He was out looking for me just last night. Hunting me. Explain that, if you can, outside of the comments I made about him on television. Outside of the telephone call I got from him a couple of months ago. I saw him with my own two eyes, not closely enough to identify, but ultimately I'll be able to get you a video of him, from a surveillance feed, live in the flesh."

"Give me that now and we've got something."

"I have already given you something, more than something. I certainly have given you enough to do what I ask. Out him. Right away."

She paused. Finally she said, "okay, I'll tell you what, I'll talk to my legal team and see what I can do."

"Bullshit, you're one of the best lawyers I know. You don't need to talk to anybody. Just do what I ask. You can trust me. You know you can. I've got a lot on my plate right now and a lot is going to happen in the next twenty-four to forty-eight hours, particularly if you help."

"What else is going to happen? Talk to me here. What have you have planned?"

"I can't tell you everything right now. It's a work in progress. But if you do your part, I think we can bring William Delvecchio to justice sooner rather than later."

"Don't put that on me."

"Loretta?"

"Yes?"

"Off the record?"

"Sure."

"If I were you," Ben said, "I would think about heading back home."

"To Wisconsin?"

"Maybe think about doing some snowmobiling. Gotta go."

59

It was ten-thirty Chicago time by the time Ben finally curved north on 294 and the snow was coming down like giant, floating cotton balls. Traffic was moving slowly, about ten to fifteen miles per hour below the posted speed due to the worsening road conditions. Ben moved through the Southwest suburbs bisected by the expressway. He gave a rueful smile as he passed over the Cal-Sag Channel, not far from where the body of Jimmy Moran had been found. He continued to drive.

Ben called Scott Nelson and filled him in on the past twenty-four hours and on what he had planned. When he was done, Nelson said, "You do have a way of attracting attention. I agree it was probably the killer. Whether it was Delvecchio, we'll find out soon enough. You could have picked an easier spot to get to, but I'll get in touch with Lonergan and mobilize as best as we can."

"Also call Stan Feldman and get the information from him. You might be able to get some search warrants. Tell Lonergan to use the Patriot Act if he has to."

"Don't worry, the feds can always get a warrant when they want one."

At Ogden Avenue, one of the exits that would have taken him home, he got off the expressway to get gas. Five minutes later, he was back on the expressway heading north. He knew where he was going, but wanted to make sure he would be alone when he got there. He grabbed the cell phone out of the cup holder and dialed a number he knew from memory.

"Ben, that can't possibly be you, can it?" Jeff Wyatt said from the other end of the line.

"It's me. I need you to answer a question for me," Ben said.

"Jeez, Ben, what's been going on with you? You've been all over the news for weeks."

"Have you heard anything new yet today?"

"No, nothing, but I'm at work. I haven't seen the television." Jeff and his wife ran several day care centers.

"Okay, good enough. I need to know if anyone is going to be at the cottage over the next few days."

"Up north? Are you up there? Is that where you've been all this time?"

"No, I haven't been up there. No comment on where I'm heading. I just need to know when someone is going to be up there next."

"Not for a few days," Jeff said. "A few of us are going up there after Christmas. We may stay through New Year's and do some snowmobiling. Why?"

"You don't want to know. When are you planning to head up?"

"Probably not before the 26th or the 27th. It should be empty until at least mid-afternoon on the 26th, if not the 27th."

"Great, that'll work out just fine."

"Ben?"

"Like I said, you don't want to know. I'll be gone long before then, I hope. Everything will be fine. Trust me."

"I do. Whatever is going on, be careful."

"And Jeff? Whatever happens, we didn't have this conversation."

"Sounds good to me."

It was now the 22nd of December. Ben had at least four days to put his plan into action and bring this to a conclusion. His eyes narrowed. More than enough time. It took him almost two more hours to reach the Six Flags Great America amusement park outside of Gurnee. The snow was coming down so hard now he couldn't even see the roller coasters that soared off to his right near the highway.

It was past two by the time he reached the Wisconsin border and close to three when he reached the snarled traffic south of Milwaukee. He had stopped looking with panic in the rearview mirror, since traffic was so heavy and moving so slowly, he was fairly confident that William Delvecchio could not be right behind him. His phone buzzed. It was Stan Feldman.

"I hope you've got good news for me."

"I talked to Loretta Bergen. I think she's on board. I sent her some stuff, she called me back and we hashed it out for little while, then she said she had to go to work things out. I think she's on board though."

"Okay, good. Call me when something breaks."

"Will do."

He escaped the interstate and took Highway 41 north of Milwaukee as it angled toward the northwest. At first, it was as crowded as the interstate, the roads thick with snow, but eventually, traffic thinned out the further he got away from the city and he was able to move consistently at about forty. He made his way past Menomonee Falls and through Fond du Lac, curving around Lake Winnebago, before coming to Highway 45 at Oshkosh. He still probably had close to three hours to go in this weather. He hoped that Delvecchio was on the road, growing increasingly frustrated by unfamiliar roads and unfamiliar weather.

Highway 45 finally turned north for good at Wittenberg, where Ben began feeling an increased sense of unease. About thirty minutes earlier, he had noticed distant headlights in his rearview mirror peeking through the pelting snow. Visibility was so poor that Ben could not tell how far the car actually was behind him, but it seemed to maintain a steady pace. When Ben slowed, it slowed, and when Ben picked up his pace, the headlights did so as well.

Ben hoped that the junction at Wittenberg would cause the trailing car to go off in another direction, but it didn't. It took another hour or so to go thirty miles north, the trailing car still back there, neither gaining nor losing ground. Ben decided to force the issue. He eased off the road at a McDonald's and parked parallel to the road, his hand on the Winchester and ready for anything. A minute later, the car cruised by, the driver never giving him a second look. He gave a slight sigh of relief before heading inside to pick up a quarter pounder meal for the road.

He ate his food as he moved slowly north on Highway 45, constantly checking his rearview mirror again for company. It was now past sunset, although the heavy snowfall and cloud cover made it appear very bright outside notwithstanding the actual time of day. Absent the continuing heavy snowfall, visibility would have been extensive even long after nightfall.

Another hour passed before Ben hit the speed trap at Elcho. He was getting closer now and pulled off the road again to get gas at a minimart. He recalled stopping at the same gas station back in February, when it was 10° below zero outside and he had to get back in the car to keep from freezing as he filled the tank. Tonight, with the temperature probably 40° warmer, he felt a different chill inside him. He was now in the home stretch, almost ten hours since he had gotten into the car back in Michigan.

His phone buzzed again just as he was turning back out onto Route 45 and he stopped at the exit of the gas station. It was Feldman again. "Yes?"

"She just dropped the bomb. It's all out there now, at least most of it. She did right by you. I don't know if Delvecchio has seen it, obviously, but it'll be everywhere before you can bat an eye."

"Good. How much deal detail did she go into?"

"She pretty much put most of the big stuff out there. She mentioned talking with you, ran through the whole Delvecchio and Burton thing, and even showed pictures. It was pretty good. My phone has been ringing off the hook. I would think he'll shit a brick when he sees it."

"All right then. He's now flushed out into the open. Let's see what he does. Did you manage to get the surveillance camera footage to her?"

"No, not yet. We're still working on that. It keeps timing out on the download since it's such a big file, but I'll keep trying. Where are you? Are you up there yet?"

"No, not yet. It's been slow going with the weather. I probably have an hour or so to go, maybe a little more."

A snow plow passed in front of him, clearing the northbound lane of the two lane road. Ben coasted out and settled in behind the truck, following it out of town. Half an hour later, he passed Pelican Lake and reached Monaco, the last hamlet of any size before his destination of Three Lakes. Another twenty or so minutes later, Ben got off of Highway 45 at Highway X and inched his way through snow-covered roads between a series of vacation lakes – Spirit Lake, Big Stone Lake, Medicine Lake and finally across the bridge between Island Lake and Little Fork Lake before turning onto Reed Road for the final stretch of his journey.

Reed Road had not been plowed, and Ben carefully navigated through curve after curve as the road cut through the old pine forests of northern Wisconsin. His headlights reached the apex of one curve and several deer, more specifically their eyes, reflected in his headlights and scurried off into the trees. He slowed to a crawl and continued around one curve, then another. He remembered that it had always been further then he thought and he wanted to make sure he neither drove off the road, missed the driveway or hit a roaming deer. He was close now. He rounded one final curve, his headlights leading the way, and coasted down a slope. Up ahead to his right, he saw the mailbox he was looking for with "Wyatt" across the top and gradually slowed the car to a stop.

He'd seen no cars behind him since leaving Highway X. He looked out the passenger window at the drive, which curved down a steep slope to the cottage on the left. Checking his rearview mirror one last time and finding nothing, he inched off the road to his right and crept down the driveway, his engine in low gear, his foot on the brake. The four-wheel drive cut through the heavy snow. Probably close to a foot of fresh snow had already fallen, and Ben parked in front of the two-car garage.

He got out of the car, found the key and unlocked the door into the kitchen. He cut through the kitchen to an interior door that led into the garage, hit the light, then opened the garage door. Wishing he had brought the Winchester in with him, he glanced back up the driveway as he went out into the falling snow, got back in the car and pulled it into the garage. Shotgun in hand, he brought the garage door back down and locked it.

60

When Rich had dropped the dime on Lohmeier, he was fully expecting good news when he sat down in front of the television. He had deliberately avoided any chance to get news updates for most of the day, preferring to savor his little victory at home in front of his television, a cold Heineken in his hand. What he got was a surprise. Lohmeier had not been picked up by the police, as expected. He had simply disappeared. Rich watched with amusement as the competing cable networks fell all over themselves trying to decide whether Lohmeier was simply another victim, or actually the killer himself. Where had he gone? When would he be found? Would he be alive when they found him? Did he do it? All of these questions and more replayed across the screen night after night in the immediate aftermath of Benjamin Lohmeier's disappearance.

Rich, of course, knew exactly where Lohmeier was, or at least where his car was. It was a few miles across the Indiana border into Michigan. Why it was there, Rich had no idea, but he was determined to find out. The GPS tracker had done its job extraordinarily well. It had pinpointed the car's location to within a few feet. Rich used the tracking program to identify a satellite image of the location, a nice property overlooking the beach and right on Lake Michigan. But why there?

He checked the tracker daily, and had confirmed that the vehicle had never moved. Days passed, turning in two weeks, and still Lohmeier's car never moved. Rich considered the possibilities. Either Lohmeier's car was indeed holed up somewhere in what the lawyer considered to be a safe place, or he had dumped the tracker, or perhaps he'd even dumped the car and had gone off somewhere in another vehicle of some kind. The fact that the tracker was still functioning properly and not moving, however, led Rich to believe that Lohmeier had found a hiding place and was staying put.

Although he didn't want to risk taking another flight and navigating through airport security, Rich nevertheless felt comfortable enough in his identity and cover story that he knew it wouldn't present much difficulty. He thought about flying into Detroit, but no one likes Detroit, so he flew back into Chicago's O'Hare Airport, rented a mid-sized sedan and began the hunt. He'd made a reservation at a Best Western hotel in New Buffalo, Michigan, then had sent himself a package at the hotel via Federal Express that was waiting for him when he arrived.

The package consisted of fresh fish, packed in dry ice, together with the various components of Rich's 9 mm Beretta, in special foam packaging that resisted x-rays and made the gun parts look like food accessories. Rich had shipped gun parts to various aliases on several occasions over the years as a test to see if it could be done when he really needed it. It had succeeded every time, either the x-ray scanners had been fooled, or because there were too many packages to scan, and those containing fresh fish packed in dry ice from the West Coast were less likely to attract much scrutiny.

The package was waiting for him just as he expected it would be. The twink at the front desk simply handed over the box with a smile, along with his plastic key card and map of the premises. Once in his room, Rich opened the package, removed the gun parts from their containers and assembled the weapon. Although it did have a slight aroma of fish, he removed a jar of gun oil from its foam compartment and cleaned and oiled the Beretta to ensure that it was in proper working order. He installed the clip and was ready to go. Firing up his computer, he was pleased to see that Lohmeier's car was still in place.

Rich went to the McDonald's up the road for a quick bite to eat, preferring to hunt later in the evening when it was full dark. People were less likely to be out and about, particularly in the winter months, he knew, and he was nothing if not careful. After dinner, he returned to the hotel and lay on the bed watching television for a while, adjusting to the time change. At about nine, he got up and changed into the wetsuit, covering his lower body with a huge pair of snap-off warm-up pants. He wore a black waterproof jacket and pushed the hood of the scuba top back under the jacket, and stuffed his hat and gloves into the pockets. The Beretta had already been placed into a black waterproof pouch that Rich wore around his waist. A hunting knife was in a sheath strapped to one ankle.

He picked up the box of fish, double-checked everything, and left his room, exiting the hotel unseen out of a side door. He would later dump the fish in a yard not far from the beach, a gift for the local wildlife, before disposing of the box in a dumpster in the back of a restaurant. Although he knew where he was going, or least thought he did, having confirmed the route on his computer before he left, Rich nevertheless wanted to get a good feel for the place. He hadn't planned on doing anything tonight other than conducting his due diligence.

He followed the main drag, Whittaker Road, into downtown New Buffalo. It was nice, he thought, for Michigan. Nothing compared to his home on the West Coast, but you take what you can get when you live in the Midwest. He circled the downtown area once, then again, before backtracking out to Red Arrow Highway and turning left. He turned off after a couple of miles and then headed toward the lake until he found Shoreline Road and turned right. He moved carefully through the darkness, rarely even seeing another person or vehicle. He drove for a few minutes before he realized that he had probably missed his street. He turned around in the driveway of a dark house and retraced his steps. He missed it again.

On the third time around, he recognized that it was next to the gate of a much larger property. It's a private road, he thought. He hadn't realized that from the satellite photo. He didn't know who or what he would find at the end of the private road, so he maneuvered back out to Red Arrow, where he parked his car in the back of a small store that sold knickknacks to wealthy weekenders from Chicago. He got out of the car and pulled off the warm-up pants. He decided to leave the jacket on for the time being and headed out on foot. He pulled the hat on, just another guy out for a walk on a chilly evening. *How can anybody live here? It's miserable and cold. Even the lake was a pale imitation of a real body of water like the Pacific Ocean.*

Rich paused briefly when he reached the private drive, then continued on past the gated estate. Still just a guy out for a walk. He turned when he reached a bed-and-breakfast down the block and calmly strolled back from whence he came. He admired the gated estate as he went by the second time, mostly to see if anyone was out and about or watching from any of the countless windows facing the road. He paused again at the private road, then turned down it and moved over to the left-hand side, creeping down the entire length of the road inside the tree line.

He reached the end of the drive and surveyed his surroundings. Directly across from him was the back gate to the large estate. There were two houses, an oval structure on the other side of the gate, and a massive, white frame mansion in the distance. To his left, a driveway curved around and out of sight. He recalled from the satellite photo that there was a modest-sized home on that property. He would check that out next. But now, he quickly crossed onto the property directly ahead at the end of the road. He moved around the bushes and the full property came into view. He saw three buildings – a large, white frame house in the back of the property, then two structures, a garage and an odd-looking glass box near the front of the property.

The house and glass building were both entirely dark. The whole place felt empty. Rich moved around the back of the glass building, fully aware that he might easily be seen by anyone hiding inside. He felt much better when he turned around to the back and found only two small windows on the second floor. He went to the garage, where he found the back door unlocked. Pulling the Beretta from its hiding place, Rich turned the handle and pushed open the door to see Lohmeier's SUV sitting inside. He pulled the door closed.

He walked around the back of the garage and peered out at the main house. He had no need to look at Lohmeier's car, because it was exactly where the tracking device had said it would be. Everything was in working order. The main house still looked vacant. Although, he reasoned, if Lohmeier were hiding inside, that's undoubtedly the way he would want it to look. It wasn't late enough to go peeking in windows, so Rich retraced his steps back out to the private road, turning into the property on the left side.

It was another modern-looking rectangular structure, with a small detached garage. It too looked vacant, with no lights shining anywhere. Rich stood there and thought about it. He turned back and returned to the road. He looked through the back gate at the large house across the way. The smaller house closer to him was dark like the others, but there were still lights on in the bigger house. The gate would keep the average busybody away, but unless it also came with cameras, sensors or the like, it would not keep out a determined trespasser. Satisfied that he had accomplished all that he needed to, he walked back out to Shoreline Road, got in his car, and headed back to the hotel.

61

Back at the hotel, Rich recalled the moment when he discovered Lohmeier's car sitting in the garage, exactly where he knew it would be. He thought of the cold breeze, the smell of the pine trees, the thrill of the hunt. It gave him chills. As he always did, he had made his plans carefully and completely. Around lunchtime the following day, after confirming that Lohmeier's car hadn't moved, he cruised the neighborhood a couple of times in the daylight, trying to get a feel for where Lohmeier could be hiding. Rich figured he was still around. Later that evening, he would cruise the neighborhood again and try to get into the house where Lohmeier's car was located. Of course, he would be taking the Beretta along.

His search proved fruitless. He tried the usual places in an effort to find the key, but proved unsuccessful. He did find a key to the glass building at the front of the property, which was vacant and empty. There was no sign that Lohmeier or anyone else had been living inside. After all, he had to eat and go to the bathroom and since the utilities were off, that made living there extremely difficult.

He tried the smaller property to the south next, coming to a similar conclusion. Although the house was not vacant in the sense that someone did appear to visit regularly, no one appeared to be there now. That left him with the big estate to the north. He had checked property records and could not link Lohmeier to that property. With the five-car garage, Rich figured that if

Lohmeier were staying there, his car would simply be stored in one of those garage stalls. During the course of his search of the middle property, Rich had discovered a set of steps that led down to the beach. He took them down to the shore, moved to the north and came across a set of winding steps that led to the south end of the large estate. A second set of steps, accompanied by a motorized tram of some kind, entered the estate on the north end of the property. He retraced his steps and went back out to the private drive, and took up a spot a few feet back into the woods, from which he would have a vantage point to see if Lohmeier entered or left any of the three properties. An hour passed with no movement of any kind. Rich was cold and frustrated. He made his way through the woods back to Shoreline Road and eventually to his car, and returned to the hotel.

The following day was more of the same. No movement from Lohmeier's car. He cruised the neighborhood again during the day and went back again in the evening. He was becoming more and more intrigued by the estate property. Repeating his movements of the night before, Rich came up at the back of the estate. He made his way over in the direction of the tram. He reached the tram, turned, not happy with the light at the top, then having decided it was too big a risk to take the light out, he proceeded down the steps that ran next to the tracks.

Reaching the bottom of the steps, the hair on the back of his neck was standing up, and he gazed out over the beach. The waves pounded the shore. He thought he sensed something to his left and turned to face the large deck. Something didn't seem quite right. He unzipped the pack around his waist so he could get at the Beretta if need be. He moved over to the deck, just the flashlight in hand. There were two Adirondack chairs and two more cabana chairs, the kind you might see at a resort in Florida. One had the cover down, but the other had the cover flipped up. He tried to remember whether the chair was like that when he had come by the night before, but he hadn't walked all the way out onto the deck then and couldn't be sure.

He found a black knit cap sitting on the chair, picked it up and examined it. He took off one glove and felt around the inside and the outside. It was damp, but that could be from the elements. He smelled it. It seemed to smell faintly of sweat. How long could this have been there? The adrenaline flowed. He turned the flashlight on and searched the area around the deck, then out toward the beach. Nothing. He turned back behind the deck and looked into the darkness and up the steep overgrown slope that ultimately led up to the backyard of the estate. He shone the flashlight in wide sweeping arcs across the slope, searching for evidence of his quarry. Back and forth, back and forth, he went, for several minutes, seeing nothing.

If he'd been on the deck himself, and someone unexpected had come along, where would he have gone? He looked around. Out on the beach, he would've been exposed, but up the bluff, he might be able to find cover, at least for a while. He went back and studied the wooded slope, searching for movement. He carried the hat in one hand and the flashlight in the other and went back to the steps leading up the side of the hill. About a third of the way up, he stopped and shone the flashlight out into the densely wooded area. Nothing. He moved further up the steps and did it again, still coming up empty. Finally, he went all the way up to the top of the steps, moved out to a small bench sitting at an overlook and shined the flashlight over the side of the bluff. He went back and forth throughout the area, but saw no one.

Cognizant of the fact that there were people living in the large house behind him, and not wanting to be discovered, he moved off toward the smaller house, down the fence line parallel to the private drive and left the property by hopping up and over the stone wall. He was angry and frustrated, in full hunting mode now. He wanted Lohmeier. Having the police capture him would not be enough. He wanted him in the same way that he had wanted the others. He wanted him and he needed him. And he would get him.

Rich tried to break up the monotony the following day. Although he knew it was likely that Lohmeier was somewhere in the area, and something told Rich he couldn't be far from the car, he hadn't yet been successful in locating him. In fact, he hadn't seen much of anyone. It was apparent that this part of Michigan was more of a summertime destination and that people cleared out once the weather turned. Since he didn't want to be seen cruising the neighborhood in the daytime too often, he had breakfast at a diner in downtown New Buffalo, then he headed out to the local Indian casino for some action. Although he knew that casinos had cameras covering every square inch of the premises, Rich was not concerned because he knew no one was looking for him. He had $500 in cash burning a hole in his pocket and he was determined to have some fun with it.

He spent some time at the roulette table, then moved on to craps, before settling in at his favorite, blackjack. He just about broke even at roulette, lost about $75 at craps, but managed to lose most of his cash at blackjack despite having been up over $400 at one point. He grabbed a burger at one of the restaurants in the casino on his way out. Rich had enjoyed the last two or three hours, which was interesting given that casinos are inherently depressing places, populated by desperate people and lonely blue hairs spending their life's savings trying to hit the big score. He made his way through the blue hairs and out the front door to find it snowing heavily. His rental car was fully covered in snow. He swept it off with a brush he found in the trunk.

Not used to driving under such conditions, he took his time getting back to the hotel. Then he surfed the web looking for new information on Lohmeier, finding nothing. It was almost two before he checked on Lohmeier's car, only to discover that his adversary was on the move. Lohmeier was now nearing the Illinois-Wisconsin border heading north.

"God dammit," he said. In this weather, Lohmeier probably had at least a three or four hour head start. He quickly checked his gear and prepared to leave the hotel. He took a deep breath. This isn't so bad, he thought to himself. No matter where he goes, you will be able to find him. It's just a matter of time.

62

Ben tried to think quickly. He was not successful. He didn't know how much time he had, didn't know how far behind him Delvecchio was, or in fact, whether he was on his way or not. Ben figured he probably was, given that he had shown up in Michigan and that certainly wasn't done in order to wish him a Merry Christmas. When was the million dollar question. Given the weather, and the fact that Ben knew where he was going and Delvecchio didn't, even with a GPS tracker, Ben figured that he'd bought himself some time. How much was the key. Ben assumed that his adversary was not used to Wisconsin winters. From what Ben could tell, Delvecchio had spent his entire life living in California. People who never drove in the snow, didn't know how to do it properly, and were rightfully intimidated when the experience was thrust upon them. Ben, on the other hand, had lived his whole life in the Midwest and he still found driving in bad weather like this to be both challenging and stressful.

He walked over to the picture window in the living room that faced out across the frozen landscape of Big Fork Lake. It was a decent-sized lake as Wisconsin cottage lakes go, about a half to a three-quarter of a mile wide where this particular cottage was situated, and maybe twice that in length. Of course, in this part of northern Wisconsin, several lakes were strung together to form what might be known as one reasonably large lake, perfect for fishing, water skiing and snowmobiling.

Despite the fact that it was well after sundown, the low cloud cover and heavy snowfall on the ground made for perfect visibility. Ben could easily see all the way across to the other side of the water. He tried to decide as he stood there whether this was good or bad. It was good because it was almost like being in broad daylight. It was bad, because he couldn't hide easily either. Under normal circumstances, he would have relished the view. Not tonight.

The cottage was built on two levels, with a basement. There were a couple of bedrooms upstairs, another on the main floor, along with a living room and dining room combination, plus the kitchen. There was a dormitory-style bedroom in the basement, along with a family room area, storage and the mechanicals. The place had three entrances, plus the garage. The first was the front door on the side of the house off of the garage. It led into the kitchen. The second, on the opposite side of the house, consisted of a sliding door off of a small balcony. The third entrance was a basement walkout that faced the lake.

Ben did a quick tour of the house turning on lights as he went. There was no point in hiding for the moment. He was trying to get Delvecchio to come, not convince him that he wasn't here. He looked for anything that might help his efforts. There was nothing much on the second floor, and he quickly concluded that he wouldn't be spending any time there. He found two sharp hunting knives in the garage, which he brought in and placed on the kitchen counter, before heading downstairs.

The basement contained exactly what he was looking for. Propped up in a corner next to the furnace, he saw an old Remington 12 gauge shotgun. He had seen it before. One of Jeff's brothers liked to hunt. He found shells for the gun on a dusty shelf next to some old paint cans. He grabbed them as well. He placed them at the bottom of the stairs and then he went back into the laundry room, where cold-weather gear hung on pegs across one wall, together with boots, gloves, hats, snowmobile suits and an odd assortment of snowmobile helmets.

He rummaged around for the best fits and brought those over to the stairs as well. Then he gathered all the stuff up in his arms and took it back up to the lone bedroom on the first floor, which did not have any outside windows. He placed the Winchester on the bed next to the Remington. He now had two shotguns and two hunting knives, and as he looked at them, an idea began to form. He went back downstairs and searched the utility room for tools and other materials. He found a length of rope, electrical wire and part of an old pulley, used for the garage door in an earlier year era. He gathered these things up, along with a toolbox, and took them all upstairs. He was no engineer and wasn't sure exactly how to design and construct what was in his head. He tried his best to think about how it had to fit together in order to work. The cottage did not have Internet access, which didn't much matter since Ben did not have a computer.

It was now close to ten, and Ben was getting tired, all the driving having taken it out of him. He took chairs from the kitchen and placed them on an angle at every entrance, together with glasses balanced on each chair that would fall, break and hopefully make noise in the event someone tried to get into the house. He also placed empty pop cans around from a recycling bin he'd found in the kitchen. All of this was intended to make enough noise to alert him in the case Delvecchio tried to get in.

Ben decided to go downstairs and get some sleep. He would sleep near the entrance of the dormitory-style room in the basement, near enough to hear if anyone came through the basement door and hopeful that the booby-traps he had set upstairs would provide him with enough warning to defend himself. Not surprisingly, he slept poorly, circumstances not conducive to restful slumber. He woke up once, the Winchester wedged beneath him, next to the snowmobile suit, hat, gloves and helmet. Every noise jerked him awake. A cottage built in the 1950s had its own set of peculiar sounds, from the clicking of the wood-burning furnace to the rattling of the pipes to the whistle of the wind whipping through joints and windows. Too soon, he saw that it was beginning to get light outside and felt relieved that he had survived the night. He closed his eyes for a moment before willing himself to his feet to begin the real work of the day.

Rich packed up his stuff, checked out of the hotel, and was soon out on the road, heading west on Interstate 94, following the path Benjamin Lohmeier had taken hours before. He'd been cursing himself for the better part of an hour since he had discovered that Lohmeier was on the move. Why did he have to go to that God damned casino? He just couldn't believe it. Weeks passed and Lohmeier's car hadn't moved a single time. And now, the one time he doesn't pay attention, that fucking Lohmeier gets the jump on him. The laptop sat on the front passenger seat, closed for the moment, with the Internet drive sticking out on the right side. The only way to track Lohmeier was via the computer, but Rich did not have the ability to charge it in the car. Either he would have to find an adapter somewhere, or just use it sparingly, pulling over periodically to check on Lohmeier's position.

Only he wasn't worried about Lohmeier's whereabouts right now. With the heavy snow and the miserable conditions of the roads, he had to focus his entire attention on keeping the rental car out of the ditch. His hands held the steering wheel in a death grip and he'd actually worked up a bit of a sweat while he stayed in the right lane, thinking about the four-wheel drive offered by the woman at the rental counter, which Rich had declined in favor of the sedan.

As he slid his way through northwest Indiana, he considered the possibility that Lohmeier had sent a decoy off in the SUV. No, that can't be. Who would he send? But whatever he thought of Lohmeier's escape, it did seem to confirm that it had been Lohmeier down on the beach the previous night. The timing otherwise would be simply too coincidental. He must've been there. It had to have been his hat on the cabana chair. How did I miss him? He considered the possibilities as he drove.

After an hour, he thought about pulling off the road to check the laptop, then decided not to. Regardless of where Lohmeier had gone, he was likely still heading in the right direction. Then, nearing Gary, Rich thought about calling it quits for a while, pulling off the road someplace until the snow stopped and the

401

roads got properly plowed. The way he was going now, he was literally spinning his wheels. He looked out the window at the industrial smokestacks of Gary. He wouldn't be stopping here.

He made it into Illinois a while later and kept his eyes out for a decent hotel. He crawled all the way up to the western suburbs of Chicago, where he got off and found a room in an extended stay hotel in Oak Brook, not ten minutes from Lohmeier's home. Rich brought the laptop into the room and plugged in the charger. Lohmeier's car had stopped, way up in northern Wisconsin, not far from a place called Eagle River. What in the fuck was he doing there? Rich had never been able to identify any second homes belonging to the Lohmeiers. He must either be squatting, like in Michigan, or someone was helping him.

Rich traveled a mile or so up the road to a shopping mall, where he stopped to have a chicken sandwich and fries at a sports bar. The room was fairly dark and anonymous, with most of the attention focused on the myriad of televisions lining virtually every wall. After he finished eating, he disappeared into the droves of Christmas shoppers clogging the serpentine paths of the upscale outdoor mall. He stepped into the Apple store to check out the latest iPhone, then watched the yuppies pouring into the Pottery Barn store to furnish their little yuppie mansions. Tired of wandering through suburban excess, he cut through Macy's to get to the parking lot where he had left his car. On his way through the electronics department, he eyed a bank of televisions for sale on the far wall and casually strolled over to take a look. He wasn't within thirty feet when he was stopped cold in his tracks.

There, staring back at him on two columns of televisions on the far right-hand side of the display, was his own face, at least his face from a decade earlier. He felt like his heart had stopped and he could feel his face flush. He inched a few feet closer to read the scroll at the bottom of the screen.

LOHMEIER NAMES WILLIAM DELVECCHIO AS KILLER OF SIX LAWYERS...SAYS DELVECCHIO FAKED OWN DEATH TO SEEK REVENGE.

63

Rich's eyes widened and he looked down at his shoes. He felt as though everyone's eyes were upon him. He willed himself to avoid looking at the televisions as he finally made it out of electronics department in a cold sweat, then passed through the lawn and garden and hardware departments, with their snowblowers and power tools, before finally reaching the door, his head down. He fumbled around in the parking lot for several minutes trying to remember what the God damned rental car looked like.

It took forever to get out of the parking lot, driveways clogged with holiday shoppers, the roads curving, Rich not knowing what street he would come out on and where it would lead. He screamed, taking out his frustrations at every transgression of every driver who happened into his path. It took a while for him to make it back to the hotel. He went in the side door to avoid questioning eyes and once he finally made it to his room, scrambled for the remote and the right channel even before removing his coat. He circled through all the channels once, then twice, then a third time without finding it. Then he grabbed the little cardboard tent with the channels on it that was sitting next to the television and punched in the number. Commercial. He cursed again. Then Loretta Bergen returned with the bell sounding a breaking news story. He was the breaking news. How had this happened? How had Lohmeier done it? He had clearly underestimated the little bastard.

He took deep breaths trying to calm his nerves as he impatiently listened to her tell the tale. She had spoken to Lohmeier on the telephone, who had laid out how and why William Delvecchio had faked his own death and was now going around the country killing the lawyers under the name of Richard Burton. She talked about driver's licenses and stolen identities. The room disappeared. He had planned so well. He'd been so careful. Now everything was unraveling. What made them think of him? He needed to know.

He pulled back to the here and now as Loretta continued, her clipped note of condescension cutting into him. She mentioned doctors and family members and property records. And hiding in plain sight. He thought of his ex-wife, that bitch, and his kids. This hadn't been about some perverse sense of abandonment, not at all. This was about revenge, pure and simple. Proving that he was smarter than the others, those people who never listened to him, who thought they could go on television and act like they were smarter than him.

The rage was beginning to blind him. All he could see was Lohmeier. He had to get Lohmeier. If he just got Lohmeier, then he would win in the end. He clicked off the TV and tossed the remote on the floor. Then he grabbed the laptop, opened it and checked on Lohmeier's position. No change. But there'd been no change for weeks before and then look what happened. He would have to stay on this. He got on MapQuest and did a search for directions. While he didn't have the exact street address, he could get close enough. The detailed blow-by-blow of the directions appeared on the screen. He looked at the bottom of the list. He was still six hours and eighteen minutes away from Lohmeier, however they calculated that number. In this weather, it was probably a lot longer, particularly since Rich was not used to driving in the snow and didn't exactly know where he was going.

He felt like a lab rat in a cage. He had to get out of there, but didn't know quite where he was going. If he left now, he wouldn't get there until well after midnight. No, he would have to calm down, stick it out for the evening and hope that the idiot who had checked him in at the front desk hadn't noticed anything. She surely didn't watch cable news. Then he thought of the credit card he'd used. It was a company card, but Burton's name was on it. If they somehow traced that, assuming they knew where to trace, the FBI knew everything didn't they? He shut the laptop and thought through his options. Fortunately, he had left most of his things in the car, so he grabbed everything, checked the room quickly, and then left.

He picked his way through the holiday traffic and made it back to the expressway heading north on Lohmeier's trail. The traffic had thinned and the roads were better, with snow plows here and there. He drove carefully, still not confident in his bad weather driving skills, but his anger urged him to push it harder than he probably should. By the time he made it to Wisconsin, the roads were actually pretty clear. You had to hand it to the cheeseheads, he thought, at least the morons plowed the roads. He stopped at a McDonald's on the north side of Milwaukee to check on Lohmeier's location. Still unchanged. He brought up MapQuest again. He scribbled directions onto a pad of paper he'd stuffed into one of the pockets of the laptop's carrying case as he sipped a blisteringly hot cup of coffee he'd gotten from the drive-through. Running on adrenaline, Rich knew that he soon would not be at his best. Within the next couple of hours or so, he would have to find a place to stop for the night, be it a truck stop somewhere or a cheap motel that took cash. He had about $250 in his pocket. Cash wasn't a problem.

Just past Oshkosh, he found exactly what he wanted, a sign for a Mom-and-Pop motel a half mile off the highway. He found it easily enough and pulled into the parking lot. The place looked old, but relatively presentable as the entrance and parking lot were well cleared of snow. The place consisted of a one-story office up front, trailed by a long row of rooms heading straight back off of the road, probably fifteen or so in all. Rich kept his head down low and went inside. A teenaged kid, maybe a son or grandson of the owners, sat behind the counter watching a video of some kind on his cell phone. He glanced up when Rich came in, looking bored, just putting in his time. The place smelled like musty, old furniture and tomato soup. He put up the briefest of fusses when Rich told him that he wanted to pay cash, but went along easily enough when Rich slid a $100 bill across the counter and told him to keep the change, which meant that almost half of the bill would wind up in the kid's pocket. The kid looked pleased with himself when he handed Rich a metal key attached to a blue diamond-shaped plastic tag with the number 7 on it.

The room was clean but dated, the carpet threadbare and the furnishings long since past their prime. Still, it would do for the night. It had a clean shower and a bathroom that smelled faintly of pine cleaner. Good enough. He didn't bother checking the TV. He didn't want to know.

64

Ben spent most of the day getting prepared for what he expected to happen after dark. Although the cottage did not have cable television, he managed to get a weather forecast around lunchtime by adjusting the rabbit ears on the decrepit old television set and finding a channel from God knows where. The sun had actually come out, the skies were blue, the reflection off of the fresh snow almost blindingly bright. More snow was expected overnight, perhaps as much as four to six inches worth before morning. The tracks of the SUV had already been obliterated, which didn't matter much since Ben was expecting company one way or the other. Based on what he had planned for later, he hoped that it would start snowing by nightfall.

He worked on his other project for most of the day, putting his limited engineering skills to the ultimate test, and stopping only to pop a frozen pizza into the oven and eat it accompanied by a can of Budweiser he found in the fridge. Taking the shells for the Remington, Ben pulled them apart and replaced the pellets with rock salt from a bag in the garage. After all, he didn't want to kill Delvecchio unless he had to. Killing him, Ben decided, might be too good for him and Ben did not want to let him off easy. Ben preferred to make him pay publicly for his crimes, but would kill him if he had no choice. He completed his engineering project around four, curious to see if it would actually work, though he had no real means of testing it. He walked around the cottage carrying the Winchester over his shoulder, feeling a bit like a family under siege in one of those old cowboy movies.

Later, he stood in the living room picture window, holding a glass of water in one hand and the scatter gun in the other, gazing out the window at the frozen lake, as an occasional snowmobiler sped by. The sun began to set. It had clouded up significantly and now gave off the look of snow. Ben smiled, unquestionably afraid, yet at peace with what was to come. His cell phone didn't work up here in the middle of nowhere and he had to resort to making the series of necessary phone calls on the cottage landline. That completed, he gathered all his gear and readied himself for the night's activities.

About six, he began getting dressed. He took off his jeans and slipped into a pair of old sweatpants he'd found in the laundry room, together with a cotton sweater, and stepped into one of the snowmobile suits. He emptied two boxes of shells for the Winchester and stuffed them into the pockets of the suit. He'd found a box of hand warmers, little pouches of something or another that got hot when shaken together. They lasted several hours and would help to keep his hands and feet warm. He slid one into each of his boots and put the boots on, tying them tight. He found a good pair of glove liners, and waterproof ski gloves. He put on the liners, inserted a hand warmer in each glove and pulled them on as well. Then he donned a knit cap. He took a snowmobile helmet off of one of the pegs, grabbed a hunting knife and the Winchester and headed outside through the basement door.

Although the sun was long gone, the ambient light reflecting off the fresh snow made it very easy to see. Like the night before, he could see all the way across the lake to the pines on the other side. It had just started to snow and the temperature hovered somewhere just below freezing according to the large round thermometer nailed to the side of the outside wall of the cabin near the kitchen window. It was perfect weather for snow.

Ben took a deep breath and grinned. It was time. About fifty feet away from the front door to the cottage, on the other side of the drive, stood a small wooden shed. It opened with two small doors that swung out and met in the middle, kind of like a closet. Ben pulled the doors open and went inside. Earlier in the afternoon, he'd taken a round plastic bucket and lid, half-full of salt for the walkways and brought it into the shed. He had propped it near the door and now sat down to wait, the two doors not quite closed, with just enough space to offer a clear view of the front door. He put on the helmet. Although it would restrict his visibility and hearing significantly, it would help keep him much warmer. He thought about the cavalry and hoped it would arrive in time. He had his doubts.

*****

Rich awoke shortly after seven, checked his watch, then tried to go back to sleep for a while. As he struggled to get back to sleep, he thought about everything he had accomplished and what he needed to accomplish today to finish this off right. If he didn't get Lohmeier, all would be for naught. All his hard work would be wasted. He would not let that happen. Whatever happened after he got Lohmeier, would happen in due course and he was okay with that, but everything in his mind hinged on getting Lohmeier.

He had studied the map. Lohmeier's location was relatively close to the Canadian border. Once he had finished with Lohmeier, he would make his way across the border into Canada and take it from there. He planned to eventually move west, perhaps settling in Vancouver. He visited there once, years ago, and it was indeed a beautiful place. He could also think about returning to California at some point. He had money squirreled away, he doubted that even Lohmeier and his friends in the media could have found that. Whether he had a place he could go to anymore was unclear. It seemed as though the condo and the farm had been compromised, but Rich wondered about the other place he had and rarely visited, a small house in the hills north of LA.

He was showered and out of the motel by nine. He hadn't shaved in several days and his beard had come in thick and dark, filling in the area previously uncovered by the goatee he'd been sporting for more than a year. He wasn't too concerned about being recognized now, people were undoubtedly not expecting him in northern Wisconsin, and context was everything. He crossed back to the other side of the highway where he had seen a Hardee's the previous evening. He went inside and had breakfast – an egg and sausage biscuit with gravy. Not his first choice, but it would keep him going for a while. All he needed now was a flannel shirt, an orange vest and some cheese and he would feel like a local.

He made slow and steady progress, finally stopping in a place called Elcho to get gas. He put forty dollars in the tank and paid with cash, before moving on up the road. He was out of town in less than a minute, the sun glinting off the barren fields, forcing him to wear sunglasses. He moved steadily northward, always keeping at or below the posted speed limits. The roads were now relatively clean and clear, although Rich had heard from the radio in the restaurant that more snow was coming later on that night. He looked out the window at the desolate landscape covered with snow and somehow thought of the moon. Eventually, in mid-afternoon, he reached a place called Three Lakes, not far from where Lohmeier's car was located. He stopped at a fork, downtown Three Lakes to the left, Lohmeier's location to the right. He went left and cruised the small town, past the grocery store and the Dairy Queen, the hardware store and the farm equipment dealer, snowmobiles and snowblowers lined up outside the front door in a row.

This town wasn't very big either, and he traversed the main drag in a couple of minutes. At the other end, he circled the block and headed back through town, this time taking the fork toward Lohmeier. He drove into a forest, bisected by the narrow two-lane road. He came around a curve, then another and another. He passed a bar, then a small clearing to his right with a natural gazebo. There was probably less than an hour or so of sunlight left and much of it was blocked out by the woods. There were properties set off the road in each direction, carved into the trees on the left and appearing to head down to water on the right. He moved around one final corner and saw that he was almost there.

He stopped the car and looked down the curving drive, which descended rather steeply to a small cottage. Rich could not see any tracks, but the fresh snow had probably covered them. He had found Lohmeier again, or least his car. He continued further up the road, driving carefully on the slippery road.

About half a mile up the road, Rich turned around in a driveway and headed back toward Lohmeier. He paused again at the drive and looked down the slope. He hoped that most of the neighboring properties were vacant due to Christmas coming in a couple of days. He decided to return to town and come back after dark.

65

Time dragged on as Ben sat inside the shed peering out through the gap in the doors. It was cold, and doubtless getting colder, but the hand warmers had helped a lot and at least he was shielded from the wind. His footsteps had almost been completely covered by fresh snow. In another hour or so, Delvecchio would not be able to tell that he was in there. He removed the snowmobile helmet and set it on the floor next to him. It got a little stifling and hard to breathe with the protective shield down. His nose was running and he wiped it on one of his gloved fingers, then stood to stretch his legs. His knees and hamstrings were barking at him and his back ached from sitting in the same spot for so long.

The problem with the shed was that it limited his visibility and his capacity for hearing the sounds around him. A couple of times, he thought he had heard a rustling from off in the trees behind him. Sensing this, he had prepared for an assault, only to find that nothing materialized within his relatively narrow field of vision. He thought about members of the US military, on a ridge somewhere in Afghanistan or Iraq, always on alert, never knowing when ten hours of boredom would be punctuated by ten minutes of activity and sheer terror. He didn't know how they did it and was grateful that he had found another way to make a living, albeit maybe not with the best results at the moment.

He tried not to let his mind wander, but he couldn't help himself. He thought of Libby and the kids and the anger welled up again inside him. Delvecchio had targeted him and by extension, his family, and now he was going to pay for it, one way or another. He wondered again about Nelson and Lonergan. Would they ultimately do him some good? And would he need them?

*****

Rich cruised Reed Road once again, rounding curve after curve until he finally reached the target, about three curves later than he thought it should be. It was still early enough that he should be able to tell from lights in the neighboring cabins which ones were occupied and which ones were not. He drove up to the target driveway, paused briefly, noting that there were no additional tracks in the falling snow, then continued on down the road and around a couple of more curves, until he turned around in the driveway of a dark cottage. He faced back toward Lohmeier's position. There had been more signs of life on the far side of the cottage, than on the near side. He would come in from this side.

He decided on a place just around the final corner and went slightly passed it, before backing the car into the driveway about twenty feet off of the road between two large trees and right before the driveway began to slope away toward the lake. He got out of the car, checked his pockets, and slowly pressed the door back into place as noiselessly as he could. He wore the scuba suit, with a jacket over the top, the Beretta in the pouch at his waist, a hunting knife and two boxes of ammo in his pockets.

He pulled the hood up over his head, topped it with the knit hat, and looked around the area, surprised at how bright it was. Light reflected off of the white snow, but at least visibility was hampered somewhat by the continually falling snow. Rich moved down the driveway, satisfied that this cottage was indeed empty. The snow hadn't been plowed in some time. As he came around a stand of trees near the end of the driveway, he looked toward the neighboring cottage, which was also dark. The cottage where Lohmeier was hopefully staying was two down and

413

mostly invisible through the trees. Rich cut through a small outcropping and came out near the back of the neighboring cottage, the snow up to his knees.

He pushed through a set of scrub bushes and the target cottage peeked through the far trees. He could see a small deck or balcony on the near side, with steps leading down to the ground, sloping down to Rich's left in the direction of the lake. He moved off to his right, where the woods were a bit deeper and darker and inched his way closer to the target. The place also looked dark. Had Rich not known that Lohmeier's car was in the garage of this cottage, he would've expected that it was empty too.

In the back, on the right-hand side of the building, there was a window which seemed to look into a garage, a small back door to the right of the window covered with logs and assorted firewood. Rich moved closer to the window, and took a large flat log about two and a half feet high and eighteen inches in diameter and placed it firmly on the ground under the window. He stepped up first on one foot, and confident he wasn't going to fall, stepped up with the second foot so he could see into the window. He saw several snowmobiles, some miscellaneous boating items and Lohmeier's SUV in the two-car garage. This was the place.

He hopped down and crept through deep snow around the right side of the garage and saw the sloping driveway coming down from the road, from his right to his left. He pulled the Beretta from its pouch and moved carefully toward the front of the garage. Leading with the Beretta, he peered around the corner and could see all the way down to the frozen lake and beyond. Up ahead of him and off to his right stood an old work shed, probably used to house tools and gasoline for the snowmobiles and boats in the summertime. To the left of the shed was a circular open area amidst the trees that may have formed a small patio. Steps were carved into the slope leading down in the direction of the water.

Rich saw no evidence of Lohmeier, nor any tracks in the snow. He lowered the gun and backed his way behind the side of the garage and around to the back. He climbed through the snow

414

until he came to the back of the steps that led to the balcony and the door leading into the house. The floor of the balcony was just about even with Rich's head and he studied the door looking for signs of life. There were none and he slowly moved around the balcony supports until he was at the base of the stairs, never taking his eyes or the Beretta off of the doorway.

He reached the front of the house, the part that faced out toward the water. He thought about Patrick Lindsay, who started it all a year ago, as well as the others. It would be over soon. A noise off in the woods brought him back to the moment and he turned in the direction of the sound, the barrel of the Beretta following his eyes. He held his breath and waited. A minute passed, then another. Nothing. Probably an animal. They had to be somewhere, even in weather like this. He stuck his head out again and examined the front façade of the cottage, a large picture window in the center, flanked by smaller windows on either side. Steps rose from a walkout basement. A second floor, no doubt with bedrooms, rose to a peak in the middle of the structure. Rich moved back around the corner, past the balcony to the back of the garage. He leaned up against the garage, his back flat against it to the left of the window.

He figured that Lohmeier would likely be either upstairs, or downstairs in the basement, figuring he could always make an escape out the door leading directly out to the yard. He didn't like the idea of going in at the small balcony, as he didn't know what was on the other side of that door. He thought about the front door, the one off of the driveway. Next to the garage was probably a kitchen, maybe with an eating area. Next to that would be a living room or great room of some kind, hence the picture window. Any bedrooms would be on the near side and upstairs. There may be even be a bedroom or two in the basement, this being a vacation home.

He thought about it. If he were Lohmeier, he would be in the basement, having established some sort of fortress that he could defend from the stairs up to the first level, or through the outside entrance. The more he thought about it, the more he was convinced that the door off of the driveway was the one to take.

Ideally, he would've liked to have planned this better, but now that the news was out there, he had very little choice but to make some sort of assault on the cottage, take Lohmeier out, then get back to the car and head across the border into Canada if he could. He moved across to the side of the garage and waited.

66

Cold and stiff, his joints aching and his nose running, Ben began to feel himself growing tired as well. Fighting to stay alert, he reminded himself yet again of those Army Rangers on some far-off hillside as he took in deep gulps of the cold air. He suddenly felt very alone, as if everything was now riding on his shoulders. He put the helmet back on, raising the visor. He thought about opening the crack between the doors a little wider, but was afraid it would leave him unduly exposed. As it was, while he could see all the way past the front of the house to the right, he could only see to the middle of the garage door to his left. He stood again and stretched, leaning the Winchester against a rusted oil drum to his right. Then a figure came into view, from the left, moving slowly. Ben almost jumped out of his skin. This was it.

He reached for the Winchester, missing it, not wanting to take his eyes off of the figure that crept in past the garage door, a gun in his right hand. Ben looked away, only for an instant, located the gun, and carefully retrieved it with his right hand. He wanted to slide the bucket of salt back with his foot, but was afraid it would make too much noise. Instead, he straddled it. He was close to the doors, too close to aim properly without the barrel of the long gun extending far out through the opening. He backed up a foot, then another six inches, a standing toolbox poking him in the back.

His heart was pounding now and he felt like the whole world could hear it. Delvecchio, it had to be Delvecchio, crouched low to ease under the window at the kitchen sink. Had he wanted to shoot now, Ben probably had a clean shot at him. He couldn't remember whether he had already cocked the rifle. He didn't want to do it now, the noise would be unmistakable.

Ben had never shot at another human being and had spent the last several hours wondering on and off whether he could pull the trigger if the time came. Ben had thought all along that under the right circumstances, he could pull the trigger. Now, staring face-to-face at the moment of truth, he thought of his family – his wife and his kids. He knew that he would do it if he had to. He waited, and watched Delvecchio move closer to the kitchen door.

Delvecchio reached the stoop and stepped up with his left foot, his left hand reaching for the handle of the door. Ben tensed as the other man paused and looked around, his eyes not quite reaching the shed in which Ben was hidden. Delvecchio grabbed the handle and pulled slightly, it appeared to catch, then he pulled harder and his left foot slid and he lost his balance. Ben inched behind the right side door of the shed.

*****

The time had come, there was no sense in waiting any longer. Rich took a deep breath, and let the anger and resentment course through his veins. He thought of the hours of planning, the meticulous attention to detail, every attempt taken to ensure a perfect plan, well thought-out, and fully implemented. His crowning achievement. He moved around to the side of the garage and quickly to the front. He glanced to his left, then to his right, up the driveway toward the road. The night was still, even the wind appeared to have stopped. He felt a moment of complete clarity, all his senses focused on this one moment and he moved off to his left toward the front door. A tall man, he had to crouch down to make it under the kitchen window.

He moved forward, stepped up onto the stoop and reached for the handle. He took a brief look around and tried to pull on it as quietly as possible. He was afraid it would be one of these old rusted doors that screeched when opened, thus alerting

Lohmeier to his presence. He pulled a little harder, the door still appeared to be stuck. He pulled once more, putting some strength into it, and it caught again and released just as his left foot slid out, and he lost his balance, one foot on the stoop, the other off.

67

The kitchen door exploded in a crash of metal, wood and glass. The blast pockmarked the outside of the shed, the noise echoed in the still night. Ben pushed open the door and stepped out. He saw Delvecchio laying on the ground, remarkably intact, and his mind raced. He looked from Delvecchio to the door. It had worked, the spring gun had worked. It had fired through the door when Delvecchio tried to open it, just as planned, although it appeared to have drifted off to the killer's right and had largely gone through the door jam and adjoining wall. It had not exited directly through the glass as intended. It must have been pulled off kilter when Delvecchio had yanked on the door and then started to fall.

He looked back down at Delvecchio, who was lying on his back, but had now begun to turn, attempting to roll over in Ben's direction, the gun still in his right hand. Ben cocked the Winchester, discovered it was already locked and loaded, and brought the gun up. But Delvecchio was faster. He rolled over and fired in one motion, not bothering to aim. The slug slammed into the shed as Delvecchio rolled over onto his hands and knees and as Ben slid back behind the shed, Delvecchio fired again. This one missed wide left.

Ben pulled around the corner of the shed, aimed the Winchester, and fired in Delvecchio's direction. He heard Delvecchio scream and he ducked back behind the shed, expecting another shot. When he looked back, Delvecchio had gone. Ben moved around the side of the shed and he saw what was left of the door and door jam. As soon as the Winchester had poked around the corner of the shed, another shot rang out from Delvecchio's gun. That was three, Ben thought. He didn't know how many rounds Delvecchio had in the magazine of the gun. He peeked around the corner and fired another round from the Winchester. Delvecchio moved off the driveway and into the woods to the left.

Ben paused, ejected the shells, fumbled around in his pockets and reloaded. He moved around the front of the shed and up the driveway, following Delvecchio's path. He looked down and saw drops of dark blood in the white snow. Good, he thought, Delvecchio had been hit. Now he would be leaving breadcrumbs in the woods.

Ben crept up the drive and ducked into the tree line as another shot rang out from Delvecchio's gun. He jumped up against a large tree and waited. He could hear the other man thrashing through the woods and then looked out from behind the tree, saw a flash of movement, and fired at it. He picked through the overgrown brush and mature trees, and fought through heavy snow, trying to keep an eye out for the man out in front of him, while still glancing down at the snow for more telltale droplets of blood.

Ben moved up and to the right, hoping to hem Delvecchio in and keep him off the road. He probably had a car stashed somewhere and Ben needed to get to him before he got to the car and managed to escape. The further they went in this direction, the further they got from Ben's own car and his ability to keep up if Delvecchio got to his car first.

The minutes passed like hours as Ben pushed through the woods and snow. The cottages were all down to the left now, and he was fairly near to the curving stretch of Reed Road. At one point, he saw Delvecchio about forty yards up and to his left as the other man entered a small clearing. Ben stopped and readied the rifle to fire, but decided that he had to get closer. He wasn't that good a shot and would just be wasting ammo.

Delvecchio must have heard something and fired wildly, almost 90° to the left of where Ben was stalking him. A few minutes later, Ben crossed through the same clearing, feeling exposed. This was the Cathedral in the Pines, he thought, having driven by the place numerous times without ever stopping. He moved through it as quickly as possible, another shot ringing out in his general direction, closer this time, but not close. He reached a large tree, surrounded on one side by a row of hedge bushes and paused to catch his breath as he was beginning to get a stitch in his side. His adrenaline pumping, coupled with the anger he was feeling, made his heart pound frantically.

Ben caught a glimpse of Delvecchio, who dove out of sight. An instant later, another shot flew by overhead. Ben stopped and knelt down. He peered between two trees and in the direction of the last shot. About ten feet in front of him, he saw footprints and more blood drops. He scrambled through some low hanging pines and continued to move forward, the snow now around his knees. Delvecchio had fired at least five shots, maybe more. He probably carried an extra magazine with him. Ben could not count on him running out of bullets.

Ben sensed that he was getting closer. He saw lights up ahead through the trees and heard the faint sound of music floating on the wind. It must be the bar, he thought. If Delvecchio got to the bar, he could take hostages. On the other hand, this being Wisconsin, he might get more than he bargained for if he went inside, even with the gun. Ben quickened his pace and the lights of the Pine Isle poked through the trees up ahead and to his left. He saw a flash of movement and thought about firing, but didn't want to risk collateral damage. He moved quickly forward, hoping to flank Delvecchio and keep him trapped up against the lake.

His legs heavy, Ben came out of the woods not far from the road and ran up the drive to the Pine Isle just as Delvecchio hobbled around the corner, gun in hand. Ben could hear snowmobiles coming from the far side of the bar, out near where the land met the frozen lake. As he reached the end of the drive at the back side of the restaurant, he heard another shot, followed by screams. He rounded the corner to see Delvecchio shove a wounded man off of a snowmobile, two other snowmobilers diving for cover. Ben took a stance and aimed the Winchester at Delvecchio, just as Delvecchio put the machine into gear and swerved in Ben's direction, bringing him directly in line with the two others, and Ben paused.

Delvecchio saw him, stopped and fired off another shot just as Ben jumped back behind the corner of the building. Ben readied the Winchester as the snowmobile engine roared, then appeared to die away slightly. He stuck his head around the corner to see Delvecchio bumping down the snowy slope and out onto the lake. Ben fired again and missed. Still wearing the helmet, his visor up, Ben turned the corner and ran down the slope in the direction of the two men, who had now come to the aid of their fallen friend.

"Let me have one of those," he said gesturing toward the snowmobiles. He ran with the Winchester at his side. The men saw him and raised their hands in surrender. "No, you don't understand, I'm chasing him. I'm not with him." Their hands remained raised. Ben shook his head, frantic and desperate. "No, you don't understand. He's the guy who's killed all the lawyers. His name is William Delvecchio. Go inside and get a hold of the police. Tell them it's William Delvecchio and he's being chased by Benjamin Lohmeier."

Their hands came down to their sides, yet they still looked puzzled. "You're Lohmeier?" the nearer man said.

"Yeah," Ben yelled, "that's me. Go inside and call the cops. Tell them what I told you."

The man motioned toward the far machine. "Take that one. It's fast."

Ben nodded and climbed on, tucking the Winchester under his legs. He flipped the visor down, got himself quickly acclimated, and then sped on down the slope and up and over the rough shoreline. He looked out into the distance. Delvecchio was probably two hundred yards ahead of him already, maybe more, and pulling away.

68

Rich pulled harder, felt something click as his foot gave away and then hit the ground as the shotgun blast ripped through the door. He landed on his back, hit, somewhere near his hip and rib cage. He rolled over to see Lohmeier coming out of the shed. Lohmeier's shotgun raised just as Rich rolled onto his left side and fired. Lohmeier took cover behind the shed. Rich scrambled to his feet and fired again, before hobbling away. Lohmeier peeked out from behind the shed and fired a blast of his own, but Rich had already gone. His insides were on fire as he made his way up the driveway. He fired back at Lohmeier, without looking. A fucking spring gun. He couldn't believe it.

Rich knew he couldn't get back to the car, he would be wide open and exposed to Lohmeier's follow-up volley, so he cut into the woods on the left and moved as quickly as his legs would go. His side, just above his hip, was on fire and he looked down to see drops of blood dotting the snow as he escaped. He cut through the trees not bothering to look behind him. He knew Lohmeier was coming, he didn't have to look. Lohmeier was younger and undoubtedly in better shape, although Rich was in better shape than he had once been, and Lohmeier had to worry about getting shot.

Rich thought about making a stand, trying to ambush Lohmeier, but the other man had a shotgun and Rich only had the Beretta. He kept moving, cutting through the trees, the brush and the snow as quickly as he could. Visibility was worse in the woods and he tried to avoid coming out into the open. Another shotgun volley came from behind and hit the trees ten yards to his left. He turned and fired back wildly, not really knowing, nor caring, where Lohmeier was located. He kept pushing through the woods until he came to the clearing that he had seen earlier from the road. Trying to make it through as quickly as possible, he paused only long enough to fire again at Lohmeier over his shoulder.

He kept pushing through the woods, the pain in his side turning into more of a dull ache. Adrenaline kicking in maybe. Still, he was tiring fast. He needed to find a vehicle, some means of making a quick escape. He knew he wasn't going to get anywhere on foot, particularly when he was already hurt and did not know where he was going. He figured that Lohmeier must've had some sort of connection to this part of northern Wisconsin and would certainly know the surrounding countryside better than Rich did. He came into a clearing, turned and fired again. Then he raced onward. Up ahead, he saw lights filtering through the trees and heard the sounds of music. He turned and squeezed off another shot at Lohmeier, trying to slow him down. The bar must be up ahead. There must be vehicle there. He could force keys out of someone and get back out on the road someplace. He could even take a hostage.

Rich plowed through the woods and into the parking lot. The lot had about ten to twelve cars, but he saw no one around. He heard the noise of snowmobiles pulling up on the other side of the building, followed by voices laughing over the din. He hurried around the building, the Beretta raised, looking for someone on a snowmobile or on his way to the parking lot.

Three men had just pulled up on snowmobiles and Rich pointed the Beretta at the small group. Two of them had already climbed down, while the third still straddled his machine. They stopped when they saw Rich. He reached for the man on the snowmobile, who pulled away. Rich shot him in the stomach and shoved him hard, the man toppling to the ground like a ten pin spare. He climbed aboard.

Just then, he saw Lohmeier come around the side of the building. Rich swung the snowmobile around and fired a shot in Lohmeier's direction, clipping the side of the building. He swerved toward the lake and scrambled down the bumpy crest of the shoreline and bounced his way out onto the frozen lake. It took him a few seconds to figure out the controls, for he had never ridden a snowmobile before. He stuttered and stopped a couple of times before getting the hang of it, hitting the gas and roaring off away from the shore as a shotgun blast echoed behind him.

69

Ben quickly got himself acclimated, stabilizing the Winchester so he wouldn't lose it, before putting the hammer down and skidding out into the darkness after the vanishing headlights of Delvecchio's machine. Having driven a snowmobile faster than he had even driven a car, not to mention doing so on this very lake several times previously, he felt confident that he could run Delvecchio down. Within seconds, he had the machine up to seventy, then eighty, then ninety.

Delvecchio swerved around the corner of the first lake, Ben following and gaining ground with each passing second. Ben took a wider path, trying to force Delvecchio away from the middle of the lake and toward the shoreline. Now Ben was the hunter and Delvecchio the hunted. They were in a long straightaway, the end of the second stretch of lakes coming fast, Ben further out to the right, but gaining rapidly.

Delvecchio was staying closer to the shore, perhaps in an effort to find a place to bump back up onto dry land and make his escape that way. Ben thought quickly, wondering where Delvecchio had stashed his car. He was less than one hundred and fifty yards back now and closing quickly. Soon, he had narrowed the distance to one hundred yards and still he continued to close. Ben looked down at the speedometer. He was now going over one hundred miles per hour and he continued to reel in his prey.

Suddenly, he saw the headlights in front of him veer to the right and correct to the left. And he saw the flash of a gunshot before hearing the echo of the blast cross the frozen water. Ben did not hesitate or back off the throttle a single bit. He tried to calculate where Delvecchio could be heading. Obviously, the other man did not know these lakes. Delvecchio rounded the second corner, out of one lake and into another, Ben still behind him, to his right and closing fast. Now he was less than seventy yards away. The Wyatt's cottage was another lake or two away. Ben recognized that he needed to stay wide to the right going around the curves, something Rich obviously did not know.

Ben felt the weight of the Winchester under his leg and wondered whether he could maneuver to get a shot off while still staying on the machine. Not at one hundred miles an hour, he knew. He also knew that Delvecchio was running himself into a dead-end. Two or three lakes down, there would only be one escape route, a small path in the back left corner, a narrow serpentine slalom route that snaked up and down through the woods until it came out on the road. If the road was plowed, Rich would be done, trapped with no place to go and forced to make a stand or proceed on foot. His only other alternative prior to reaching the path would be to turn around and try and outflank Ben and head back toward the Pine Isle. There were escape routes in that direction, something Delvecchio could not have known.

Ben continued to barrel down on Delvecchio from behind, less than fifty yards behind, then forty, then thirty. He knew what was ahead and he moved further out to the right to force the other man to take the next curve as tightly as possible. Ben could see the end of Delvecchio's headlights shining on a small finger of trees sticking out at the next corner. Ben continued to fly across the frozen lake. He was within twenty yards now. The trees up ahead were closing fast and Ben continued to push the killer toward the corner. He was within ten yards and angled briefly toward the left, his headlights cutting across the killer's snowmobile, before veering back out to his right just as Delvecchio reached the corner.

Delvecchio tried to take it tightly. Suddenly his headlights went haywire, as he hit the soft patch of ice and open water a quarter-mile or so from the Wyatt's cottage. His machine did not clear the open water. It nosedived into the lake and augured into the bank, three-quarters over on its back, the tail end of the machine sticking out of the water like the stump of a fallen tree, its rider trapped beneath it.

Ben sped past, then slowed and swiveled around in a wide arc until he lined his headlights up on the partially submerged snowmobile. He slowly brought his machine closer, still illuminating the grisly scene. He stopped and got down, the Winchester in hand, and looked closer. He was fifty feet away and slowly moved in. Delvecchio's snowmobile continued to roar, its lights illuminating the area beneath the surface of the water. Ben saw the gun sitting benignly on the ice, ten feet from the edge of where the ice started to soften, turn slushy and then become water.

Delvecchio was trapped underneath the weight of the machine, the upper part of his body submerged, his head bent at a grotesque angle, his neck clearly broken. Ben paused, realizing that he had aimed the Winchester at his fallen adversary. He would not need to fire it. He lowered the gun. Then he saw the red and blue lights, first reflecting across the ice, police snowmobiles, then squad cars up ahead at the Wyatt's, coming down the driveway.

The snowmobiles driven by the police officers came first, two together, followed fifty yards or so back by two more. Ben stood still and waited for them. Up ahead at the cottage, he saw a group of officers with large flashlights make their way down the slope to the shore. The police snowmobiles took the curve in a wide arc, their headlights shining on Ben, who had placed the Winchester down on the ice. He raised his hands to make it abundantly clear that they were empty. He slowly removed his helmet and placed it on the ice next to the Winchester.

He looked at both officers, who were now off their snowmobiles and advancing slowly toward him. Twenty yards

429

out, the larger of the two said, "keep your hands right where I can see them."

Ben nodded. "No problem. My name is Benjamin Lohmeier." He gestured down toward the hole in the ice. "That's William Delvecchio, also known as Richard Burton. He's the killer of all those lawyers we've been hearing about for months."

The officer nodded. "We know." The officer moved a little closer and they both looked down into the water where Delvecchio lay. The second officer looked at Ben, whose hands were still in the air. "Did you fire at him?"

Ben thought about his answer. "Not here, no. He crashed when he hit the open water."

The officer shook his head. "He must not have known about it. Everybody around here knows about that spot. You?"

Ben nodded. "I've been out here a few times with the Wyatts."

The first officer looked at the body, then back at Ben. "Lucky you."

430

70

Ben coasted to a stop at the frozen shoreline. Lonergan and Nelson picked their way down the frozen bank of the lake to greet him. "About time you guys showed up," Ben said.

Lonergan, dressed in a black FBI squall jacket with FBI stenciled in large yellow letters on the back looked sheepish. "We had some weather issues. Couldn't get the plane or the chopper up in this weather, so we had to drive. Then when we got here, we had a couple of problems finding the place."

Ben shook his head and laughed. "But you're the fucking FBI, for crying out loud. You get more gadgets than eBay and a bigger budget than God. Look at you, you're probably wearing FBI underwear."

Lonergan cracked a smile. "No comment."

"That's a pretty good look for you too, Scott," Ben said gesturing at the Chicago police detective, who was wearing a heavy green parka with fake fur fringe around the hood, big clunky boots and a black mad bomber hat.

"Hey, it's cold up here in the Great White North," Nelson said.

Ben turned and they all looked out where cops and assorted personnel had gathered in the area of Delvecchio's body. "This would be a beautiful night, but for that," Lonergan said pointing a gloved finger. "I take it he's dead?"

Ben looked back to him and nodded. "Yeah, he's dead."

Just then, a cop in a snowmobile suit with a badge pinned to the outside showed up with Ben's helmet and the Winchester. "I think these belong to you?"

Ben took them and handed the shotgun over to Nelson, who examined it carefully. "Albert Sandford?"

"My wife's uncle."

"It's been fired?"

"Yeah, it's been fired," Ben said. "I don't think I hit anything, at least not with that."

Nelson laughed and looked back at the cottage, where some FBI techs were examining the area in and around the kitchen door. "We saw your handiwork up there. Spring gun? I think there might be laws against that sort of thing."

"Not in Wisconsin. Besides, he was trying to get in the house with a gun in his hand. There was certainly a threat of great bodily injury or imminent death."

"Spoken like a lawyer," Lonergan said. When Ben started to protest, Lonergan held up his hand. "Take a breath and relax. Nobody's disagreeing with you. If you did take him out, that would've been a public service. No one would've blamed you. It didn't quite work exactly right though, did it?"

Ben scratched his head. "Not exactly. I didn't really know what I was doing. I think when he pulled on the door, it somehow lurched off line and went sideways a bit. It was supposed to go through the glass and blow his head off. All I did was wing him a bit. Besides, the shells in the spring gun were loaded with rock salt. I didn't want to kill him unless I had to."

"That explains the look of the door and the debris on the stoop. I would have expected a bigger bang out of a 12 gauge," Lonergan said.

"I got the idea from a case I heard about in Indiana where the jury let a guy off because his spring gun was loaded with rock salt."

Lonergan laughed. "Always looking for an angle."

"We saw blood in the snow. We were afraid it might be yours," Nelson said.

432

"No, I was hiding out in the shed over there." He pointed at the shed and the others turned and looked in that direction. "I had a chance to get him when he was on the stoop, but I couldn't remember whether I had cocked the gun. He surprised me. Plus, I think I kind of wanted to see if the spring gun was going to work. At first, I came out and thought he was done for, but then he rolled over and got off a shot at me and I had to duck back behind the shed. He scrambled up to his feet and took off."

Ben proceeded to tell them the story of the chase, through the woods, culminating at the Pine Isle, where Delvecchio a/k/a Burton had shot a snowmobiler and took his machine. "I hope the guy's going to be okay," Ben said. "We've had enough innocent people killed."

"They said he was gut shot over the radio," Lonergan said. "That usually isn't fatal if he gets medical attention soon enough. Hopefully, he'll be fine." Lonergan nodded back out toward Delvecchio. "What happened there exactly?"

"There's a small area of open water right near where that finger of trees comes out. There is underground drainage or something and the ice right there never freezes. When you go around that point you have to take a wide berth or cut through the trees. Otherwise, you run the risk of that happening," Ben said gesturing. "He had a lead on me when he left the bar, but I don't know that he'd ever been on a snowmobile before. I gained on him pretty steadily and tried to force him to the shore. I wasn't sure where he was going to go, because even though I don't think he realized it, there was no real escape out in this direction. I figured maybe his car was up here somewhere."

"We're looking for it," Lonergan said.

"I would assume it's got to be around here somewhere pretty close. Anyway, I was pulling up on him from behind and he tried to cut the corner and he hit the open water and that was it. He sort of nose-dived into the ice. His neck was broken. You could tell right away."

Still holding the gun, Nelson looked back at Ben and said, "would you have shot him?"

"You mean out there on the ice?" Ben said. Nelson nodded. Ben did too. "Sure. I was looking at him, trying to figure out whether he was still moving, alive or dead, when I realized I had the gun up and I was pointing it at him. I would've had no problem shooting him."

"Good for you," Lonergan said.

Lonergan looked at the gun. "This is some scattergun," he said. "I wish I had one like this."

Ben and Nelson made eye contact and both shook their heads at the same time. "You're the God damned FBI," Ben said. "You can get whatever you want."

They climbed up the hill to the driveway. "Have you found out anything else about him?" Ben said.

"As a matter fact, we have. We had a team raid a ranch or farm or whatever it was outside of San Francisco and we found some evidence relating to Gibbons. There were radioactive traces in a barn. We figure it will match the radioactive fingerprint of the stuff in Wyoming. There were also plans for the suicide machine, the thanatron. There were also a couple of other things, cord that looked similar to the stuff they found on Karras, that sort of thing. Enough to put him away for at least some of the killings."

"It only takes one," Nelson said. Ben nodded.

They looked at the remnants of the front door. "I think you're going to have to get that fixed. Your cousins aren't going to be happy." Lonergan said.

"I can use some of that reward money on it. What was it? $100,000?"

Lonergan laughed now. "I've got no problem with that. You've earned it. You and Stan Feldman and maybe your wife's aunt and uncle. Besides, it ain't my money. I think it was only $50,000, by the way."

One of the local cops overheard them and said, "I can probably get Bob Strauss from the hardware store out here to take care of it and get it buttoned up for you. He and the Wyatts go way back. He'd be happy to do it."

"Sounds good," Ben said.

"Once the scene is free, I'll get him on the phone."

"Thanks," Ben said.

Ben noticed that Nelson was looking at him funny. "What?"

"That's some look. You look like Larry the Cable Guy."

Ben scratched his beard. "I'll take that as a compliment. By the way, what time is it anyway?"

Lonergan looked at his watch. "Two-fifteen. Christmas Eve. Or Christmas Eve morning, whatever you call it."

Ben began whistling *I'll be Home for Christmas*. Nelson slapped him on the shoulder, "you and me both," he said.

"Hopefully all three of us," Lonergan said.

Ben looked over at the cottage. "I've got to go call my wife. I really want to get home bad."

71

Ben did make it home to spend Christmas Eve with his family, everyone thrilled to see him and happy to have him back. He had shaved the beard, trimmed the sideburns, and attempted to get the reddish hue out of his hair with something that Libby had brought home from the grocery store. It didn't work very well and he still looked a little off, but no one cared. They'd gone over to Libby's parents' house on Christmas Eve. Albert and Mary Sandford had come too, and greeted Ben with warm embraces and moist eyes. Ben made sure that everyone understood the vital role the two of them had played in keeping him safe and in cracking the puzzle of William Delvecchio.

In a quiet moment, while others were off singing Christmas carols at the piano in the living room, Ben took Albert aside and thanked him once again for all of his help. The older man shrugged it off as Ben knew he would. "I should be getting your gun back from the FBI in a few days," Ben said.

"No hurry," Albert said with a smile.

The day after Christmas, Ben was downstairs in the basement doing laundry, happy to be grumbling under his breath over the way it had piled up over the holidays. It was mid-afternoon and Libby was upstairs baking one thing or another and Ben could hear activity throughout the main level as he sorted laundry and tossed things into the washing machine, and then into the dryer. The TV across the way on the shelf was blissfully off, Ben profoundly uninterested in the latest news. He'd seen enough news to last him for quite a while.

He heard Libby's footsteps on the stairs. She was covered in flour, from her turtleneck to her apron to her jeans. "I made a little mess," she said sheepishly. "I know that you'll be happy to make sure everything gets washed properly. She kicked off her shoes first, then removed the apron and tossed it on a pile at Ben's feet. She peeled off the turtleneck and followed with the jeans and handed them to her husband. "Here, take care of these for me, will you?"

She stood before him in her bra and panties. She smiled. He did too. "Where are the kids?" he said.

"Friends' houses."

"When will they be back?"

"Not for a couple of hours at least."

"Hmmm."

She looked at him for a moment, then turned to head upstairs. "I'm going upstairs to change," she said. She paused and looked over her shoulder. "But maybe not right away." She took a couple of steps around the corner and soon he was watching her disappear from view, still holding her clothes in his hand. "Are you coming?" she called down the stairs.

He dropped her clothes on the floor and hurried after her.

72

Two days later, Ben was back in Three Lakes, having agreed to do an exclusive interview with Loretta Bergen from the scene of the crime, so to speak. Loretta had twisted his arm and Ben had gone along with it. She really wanted an exclusive interview, loved going back to her home state of Wisconsin, and hoped it would be a huge ratings boost as well. Besides, Ben felt like he owed her. She had come through and had gotten most of the key information out there to push Delvecchio out into the open and force his hand.

They toured the area of the cottage, the front door fixed, now bustling with people from the Wyatt family up to snowmobile and enjoy the time between Christmas and New Year's. They also hit the Pine Isle, where they sat down in the back of the bar over some cold ones to go through it all. It was a beautiful day with bright sunshine, clear blue skies and mild temperatures for northern Wisconsin. As they stood on the bank of the lake at the bottom of the Wyatt's property, Loretta looked out across the shimmering frozen surface, snowmobiles flying by in each direction. She was beaming. "I love this place," she said. "I miss this more than I can tell you living out east."

"I know how you feel. It is something."

Back on camera, framed by their beautiful surroundings, Loretta looked up at him and said, "this is becoming kind of habit for us."

Ben smiled. "I know. I think I'm going to have to take it easy for a while, kick back and relax."

"Stay out of trouble?"

"Stay out of trouble."

She gesturing out over the lake. "So, I've got to ask you, where do you go from here?"

Ben laughed. This had been all set up in advance, of course. He looked at Loretta and smiled, then gave the $50,000 answer that would be seen all over television over the next several weeks. "I'm going to Disney World."

www.ingramcontent.com/pod-product-compliance
Lightning Source LLC
Chambersburg PA
CBHW031413240626
47154CB00001B/19